Spring
at
Blueberry
Bay

ALSO BY HOLLY MARTIN

TOWN CALLED CHRISTMAS SERIES
Christmas Under a Cranberry Sky
Christmas Under a Starlit Sky

WHITE CLIFF BAY SERIES
Christmas at Lilac Cottage
Snowflakes on Silver Cove
Summer at Rose Island

The Guestbook
One Hundred Proposals
One Hundred Christmas Proposals
Fairytale Beginnings

HOLLY WRITING AS AMELIA THORNE
Tied Up with Love
Beneath the Moon and the Stars

FOR YOUNG ADULTS
The Sentinel
The Prophecies
The Revenge

Spring at Blueberry Bay

HOLLY MARTIN

Bookouture

Published by Bookouture
An imprint of StoryFire Ltd.
23 Sussex Road, Ickenham, UB10 8PN
United Kingdom
www.bookouture.com

ISBN: 978-1-78681-185-1
eBook ISBN: 978-1-78681-184-4

To all the wonderful bloggers for your tweets, retweets, Facebook posts, tireless promotions, support, encouragement and endless enthusiasm. You guys are amazing and I couldn't do this journey without you.

CHAPTER 1

Bella Roussel looked up at the tangerine sky as the sun set into the sea over Hope Island. She could look at that view a thousand times and never get bored. It never failed to make her smile either. Growing up on the tiny island she knew plenty of people that were immune to the beauty of the place – many of her school friends had grown up and moved away – but she was sure she would always love it. The Isles of Scilly were absolutely among her favourite places in the world. Even the fact that she was going home to a bowl of porridge for her dinner for the tenth meal in a row couldn't dampen her spirits.

She turned into her road. Blossom Grove was a horseshoe of cottages in every colour of the rainbow facing out onto a little green. All the cottages were named after their house colours and with names like Sapphire, Emerald and Ruby Cottage she felt like she was living in a treasure trove. She loved this part of the island. Lots of new houses had popped up on the far side over the last few years, all uniform, red-brick identical houses with no soul, but here on her street were all the old houses that had been there for hundreds of years. They had lumps and bumps, uneven roofs, large windows and cobbled paths, some were thatched, some had slate tile roofs, but all of them were cute and characterful.

Blossom Grove was the most expensive part of the island, mainly because of the panoramic views from the top of the hill of the harbour, the long beautiful Buttercup Beach and the sea beyond. The only way she could afford the rent was because her uncle was the landlord. Even though Finn had assured her the rent was a fair amount, she knew in truth it should be double or even triple what she was paying. She hated the thought that he was losing money because he was renting to her. She knew he didn't need the money. But the fact that he was family and she had just missed her rent payment for the first time made it worse.

It was a temporary measure, a little setback. And as of Monday she was going to get a fantastic new job working for the Umbrella Foundation. Yes, she had a panel interview to get through, and yes, the company was notoriously picky when it came to employing new staff, but she was absolutely the best person for the job and she would just have to prove it to them. Then she could pay back her uncle, hopefully before he noticed, pay off any other debts too and she might even be able to get some decent food in for once.

Mr Kemble from Jade Cottage waved at her as she walked past and she somehow knew there'd be some kind of cake from him sitting on her doorstep when she got there. Although no one, not even her family, knew of her dire financial situation, the cakes had started appearing a lot more regularly lately, as if somehow he knew that she didn't have a penny to her name.

Dorothy from Indigo Cottage came running out of her gate as Bella passed, no doubt rushing off to play bingo at the local town hall or some other pressing social engagement.

'Hello Bella, how are you doing? I haven't seen you in a few days.'

'That's because you're always so busy,' Bella laughed. 'You have a better social life than most of the people on this island.'

'It's good to keep busy, you can't just stay in your house every night with your books.'

'I like my books, they take me on adventures, introduce me to dashing heroes, fly me to foreign lands.' Books also didn't judge her or pick on her for being different. They were loyal, steadfast and always made her feel happy.

'You need to be having adventures of your own; meet a nice young man.'

Bella smiled. Most of the people on the island wanted to see her married off. As far as they were concerned she needed a nice man to look after her, but Bella was more than happy on her own. She'd had a few boyfriends over the years but nothing serious. Relationships were just another way for Bella to get hurt and she would prefer to keep her heart intact.

'Anyway, must dash,' Dorothy said. 'I have a salsa lesson starting in ten minutes. If I don't see you before, good luck with the job interview on Monday.'

Bella stared at her in surprise. The only people she had told about her job interview were her family but somehow Dorothy had found out. Despite growing up on Hope Island, she'd never get used to how much everyone knew about everyone else's business. There were around one and a half thousand people who lived on the island but many of them had changed over the years; a lot of the younger crowd had grown up and left, new people had moved there and, though she knew most of the people of the town by name, she'd never had any interest in who was dating who or what people were up to. Clearly the same couldn't be said about the islanders and her business.

Dorothy bustled off down the hill before she suddenly turned back. 'I hear the boss is a bit of a dish so maybe you could wear that pretty green dress to the interview. You never know, he might just sweep you off your feet.'

Bella shook her head affectionately. Dorothy wouldn't be happy until she had a ring on her finger and probably five kids running around her feet.

She turned back towards her home. The little cul-de-sac looked idyllic and peaceful in the setting sun. The neighbours all took great pride over their gardens and everything was in its place, from the rows of terracotta pots brimming over with daffodils and tulips, to the hanging baskets that were a tumble of red daisy-type flowers. The blossom trees were just starting to bud and the box hedges were pristinely shaped. Bella felt almost untidy walking into her road in the clothes she had worn volunteering at the dog home that day. With her dirty jeans, tatty Converse and stained red hoodie, she stuck out like a sore thumb, but the neighbours fortunately loved her so she knew she got a pass.

As she walked up the hill, it took her a moment to realise there was something out of place in her little haven, as her eyes fell on the man huddled in a blanket outside her Strawberry Cottage.

She walked closer, noticing he looked even tattier than she did. His stubble was clearly three or four days old, his jumper had more holes in it than Swiss cheese and the blanket was filthy. He had a woolly hat pulled down over his head, shielding his face from hers, but she could see he was young, maybe around her age, and the hands that were clutching the blanket were large and strong. He had a sleeping bag with him and a rucksack and he clearly intended to spend the night there.

Bella frowned in confusion. Hope Island didn't have a homeless problem and that wasn't a naïve opinion; in all her twenty-seven years living on the island she had never seen a homeless person on the island before. And if he had somehow managed to get stranded on the island and had nowhere to stay for the night, why wasn't he down in the little town where there were shops and cafés that were open until quite late? Rosa's café was open throughout the night because of the fishermen who returned home in the very early hours of the morning. Rosa certainly wouldn't turn anyone away who needed a free meal or a place to hang out until the next ferry left to go back to the main island of St Mary's at five in the morning.

He looked up at her as she approached and she was struck by his deep indigo eyes. There was something about him, something so familiar, though she knew they had never met.

'Do you have any spare change?' he said as she stopped by her gate.

'No I don't,' Bella said, honestly.

'Right.' He turned his attention back to the floor, clearly not believing her. If only he knew.

'No I really don't,' Bella said, hating that he thought she was a liar. She never lied. She grabbed her purse from her bag, opened it up and tipped it upside down. Nothing came out. She gave it a good shake for extra proof and a smile twitched on his lips.

'OK, OK, I believe you.'

He looked so forlorn and dejected and her heart went out to him.

'Are you OK, do you not have anywhere to stay tonight?'

'I don't have anywhere to stay any night, tonight is no different,' he said, simply.

'Oh no, I'm sorry.' She looked around. Hope Island was such an unusual place to pick to spend the night. The cost of the ferry from the main island of St Mary's was not cheap. Why would a homeless person pay that just to sleep on the streets here? 'What are you doing here on Hope Island, how did you get here?'

'I came over to try to get work. They were looking for staff at the docks. I didn't get the job. Now I'm stuck here until I can raise enough money to get the ferry back to St Mary's.'

'Well, you can't stay here tonight,' Bella said, gesturing to her gate.

He sighed and then got to his feet, grabbing his bag, and she realised how tall he was, towering nearly two feet above her tiny five-foot frame. 'Of course, sorry, you don't want trash outside your door.'

He made to leave but she grabbed his arm, her fingers making contact with solid muscle underneath all the layers.

'I meant that the wind rips over this hill like a hurricane and with the cold night temperatures, you'd freeze to death. Why don't you come in, you can sleep on my sofa tonight and then tomorrow I'm sure if you explain the situation to the ferry captain he would let you travel back for free. Bob is lovely; he'd never leave you stranded out here.'

He stared at her incredulously. 'You're inviting me in? To stay?'

'Of course. I don't have much food to give you, but there's probably some cake on my doorstep and I have a log burner which gets very cosy; you'd be very warm.'

She walked up her path to the front door and, as she fumbled in her bag for her key, she knew he was still watching her from the gate.

❦

Isaac watched her root around in her bag and a jumble of tissues, old receipts, hair clips, a tattered old book, a ferry pass, a scarf, a hat, sweet wrappers, and a broken umbrella all appeared as she tried to find her keys.

Her long red hair was tied back in a ponytail, she had a large smudge of dirt across her cheek that she either didn't know or didn't care about and the baggy clothes she was wearing were shapeless, but there was something very pretty about her. Her eyes were huge and an unusual shade of clover green and she had a sweetness about her that made him smile.

He had been doing this for over three years and not once had he ever been invited in to stay at someone's house. He had been told to get lost, had the police called on him, had stuff thrown at him, occasionally some people had given him food, but never this.

The girl clearly had no regard for her own safety and that alarmed him. Maybe growing up on a small island had made her naïve to the dangers of the world. Part of him wanted to refuse her kind offer just because he didn't like the idea of her putting herself in danger like that, but here was the perfect opportunity to get to know her better and that had been the whole point of camping outside her door in the first place.

He stepped up behind her and she flashed him a bright smile. 'I'm Bella by the way,' she said, though he already knew that.

'Isaac,' he said instinctively just as a motorbike zoomed past at the end of the road, piercing the quiet of the island with an ear-splitting roar. He cursed himself; he always gave a fake name if anyone asked and his real name had just fallen from his lips.

'Sorry, did you say Zach?'

He grabbed the opportunity with both hands. 'Yes, I'm Zach,' he lied.

Bella accepted this and let him into her home, scooping up a small Tupperware container as she stepped inside. She closed the door behind him and he felt like he was crowding her in the tiny hallway; she was almost half his size and for the first time he saw a glimmer of fear at having him so close. He tried to back up but was met with a solid wall behind him.

'You could have a shower if you want,' Bella said, discreetly taking a step away from him. He knew he didn't smell, having had a shower in his own home that morning, and he cursed that their close proximity would probably lead her to smell his body wash and deodorant. He really hadn't thought this through. 'I have some clothes upstairs you could change into. An old boyfriend left some things here; I never did get rid of them. They might be too small for you as you're so big. . .' she trailed off, embarrassed, and he had to suppress the smirk when her cheeks flamed red. 'But they're clean and dry and don't have holes in.'

'That would be great,' he said. He needed a few minutes to decide how he was going to play this and what he could say to her safely without giving the game away. Normally, people who were kind enough to give him food didn't hang around to chat with him for too long. Now he had a whole evening ahead of him probably filled with probing questions and he needed to work out how he was going to answer them.

'Top of the stairs and the bathroom is the first door on the left. Clean towels are in the cupboard. I'll be up shortly to dig the clothes out for you.'

'Thank you.'

She smiled again, her whole face lighting up, and he stepped past her and went upstairs. He closed the bathroom door and leaned against it with his hands. This was a mistake.

As CEO of the Umbrella Foundation, one of the leading homeless charities in Britain, he wanted to make sure that everyone who applied for a job with the foundation had compassion for the homeless and held that at the heart of every decision they made at work. Being the CEO of two other big technology companies meant that lots of people used the Umbrella Foundation as a stepping stone to get into the other two companies or to get to him. He wanted to make sure he had the right people working for the foundation so he always tested them like this to see what their reaction was to having a homeless person right outside their door. A lot of his colleagues thought it was madness, but it was important to him. It also helped to remind him what the homeless population went through on a daily basis, the judgemental attitude, the abuse and how hard it was for them. It was very easy to forget that sometimes when he was living in his large house overlooking the sea or in his old penthouse apartment in London.

He had read Bella's application and liked what he saw. He had expected that she would be one of the few to give him money or even food. He hadn't expected this.

He would talk to her; this was the best chance to get to the bottom of what happened at her old job because, having met her, he somehow knew she would be the last person in the world that would embezzle thousands of pounds' worth of money.

Bella poured the last of the porridge oats into two bowls and sighed. She had worked out she had enough to last her until Sunday for breakfast and she could always invite herself round to her sister's house for dinner. Eden wouldn't mind and then she had the interview on Monday. Quite what she would do once the interview was over she didn't know. Even if she got the job she wouldn't be starting straight away and then she would have to wait a month until her first pay cheque arrived. But at least if she knew she had guaranteed money coming in she would feel better about getting a loan off Eden or Rome.

She hadn't liked to ask before; their family had already given her so much. But things were starting to get a bit desperate. Right now she couldn't even face them. She had avoided the Friday family dinner the night before with some lame excuse because she knew the conversation would inevitably turn to work and her finances and she couldn't bear to see the looks of sympathy and offers of help. Her sister Eden would come up with a hundred different plans to help her out, every one as flighty and ridiculous as the next, while her brother Rome would be more practical and throw money at her, telling her that she never needed to worry about paying him back. Her aunt and uncle would probably insist she move back in with them, 'just until you sort yourself out dear, then you don't need to worry about money', and then they'd proceed to fatten her up with home-cooked meals, cakes and delicious puddings. And while that sounded wonderful and a huge part of her needed that unconditional love right now, she valued her independence above anything else. She was already humiliated enough over her last job ending so spectacularly badly – not being able to get another job and being destitute was something she would prefer her family not to know about.

She heard the shower start upstairs and the noise of the pipes made her jump. She wasn't used to having someone in her space. She liked being on her own and now suddenly she had invited a complete stranger into her home to stay the night. What was she thinking? Rome would have a fit if he knew. He was so protective over her, they all were, and this would not sit well with him.

Right on cue there was a knock on the door. Somehow she knew it would be Rome. He had texted her earlier and she hadn't replied. She had been going to come up with a suitable response later that night, but clearly he wasn't going to wait. How on earth would she explain the strange man that was currently probably stark naked just a few feet from where they stood? Rome had most likely come round to see why she had missed dinner the night before. She could make some excuse. She only hoped he didn't know that she had missed her rent because she had no excuse for that. Another knock came on the door; clearly Rome wasn't going to just go away. Bella stared at the bowls of porridge and was quickly shoving them inside a cupboard when he knocked again.

She went to the door, plastering a smile on her face before she answered. She could pretend everything was normal.

'Rome,' she said, her cheeks aching from the huge smile as she subtly blockaded his entrance into the house. 'What a lovely surprise.'

There. That was normal and not at all obvious that she had been hiding in the kitchen hoping he would go away.

Though Rome didn't look convinced.

He stepped forward, all six foot five of him, towering over her as he moved to give her a hug.

'Hey Bella,' he kissed her on the cheek. 'We missed you yesterday, is everything OK?'

'Of course.' She leaned into him, glad of the comfort for a moment and as she wrapped her arms round him, he used that moment of weakness to slip past her into the house.

Damn him.

She watched him as he took his coat off. Rome Lancaster was tall, muscular, athletic and could easily have walked straight off the catwalk. All the Lancasters were ridiculously good looking with their dark hair and blue eyes. As a Roussel, she had somehow missed that gene.

She heard a clonk upstairs and Rome looked up, following the noise.

'I was just going out actually,' Bella said, loudly, trying to distract him. He turned back to look at her, his eyes casting down to her bare feet. 'Well, in a few minutes.'

'That's alright, I won't stay long. I just wanted to make sure you were OK.'

'Of course I am,' she said, breezily. 'What makes you think I'm not OK?'

He cocked his head slightly in that way he had when he was studying someone. He had that way of commanding honesty from people. Fortunately for her, she was immune to his powers.

'Well, let me see, you look like you've lost a ton of weight, you cancelled dinner plans last night because you were supposedly out but I stopped by on my way home and you were fast asleep on the sofa. Your voice has that note of desperation and bravado to it as if you are pretending everything is just fine and you missed the rent on this place yesterday for the first time in… well, forever. So *are* you OK?'

She felt herself deflate, the smile fading from her face. He knew her too well.

'I'll get Uncle Finn his money; you don't need to worry about that. I'm just having a tiny setback.'

He stared at her. 'Do you honestly think I'm here because of the money? I'm worried about you, we all are.'

'You don't need to be. I'm fine,' Bella said. All her family fussed over her and though she knew it was out of love for her she did find it a bit suffocating sometimes.

He strode into the kitchen and opened the fridge, which was completely devoid of any food. He started opening cupboards and they told the same story.

'I haven't had a chance to go grocery shopping for a while.'

He turned to face her, his arms folded across his chest. He looked furious. 'What's going on, Bella?'

She sighed. 'I may have lied when I said that I was still working for Magic Wishes. The company went under after Clara's embezzlement went public. No one was willing to donate money to the charity any more and I don't blame them.'

'That was three months ago,' he said, his voice getting louder as he clearly got more angry. 'What have you been doing for money since then?'

'I've struggled to get work ever since. I think a lot of people think that I had something to do with stealing the charity's money; that somehow I knew what Clara was doing.'

'That's bollocks. Everyone on this island knows what kind of person you are and would never think you are capable of doing something like that. You are one of the most honest, genuine people I've ever met.'

Her heart filled with love for him. He never doubted her for a second. Tears filled her eyes at his unwavering love and loyalty.

'So are you telling me you've not had any money coming in for three months?' Rome almost shouted.

'I've had savings, I've been OK.'

He spotted the packet of porridge. 'You're having porridge for dinner.'

'I like porridge,' Bella lied. She would be glad if she never had to see another bowl again.

He looked around her lounge. 'You've sold your TV and your stereo?'

'Admittedly things have been a little bit tight lately.'

'Why didn't you come to us?' Rome shouted. 'You should have come to me. I would always give you money, you know that.'

'I don't want your money Rome, you work bloody hard for that money,' Bella shouted back.

'And it's mine to do with what I want and I would much rather spend it on my family than buy material things that hold no value. I think you should come and stay with me for a few days. I can help you, at least until you get back on your feet. And I'll make damn sure you eat something better than bloody porridge.'

God, that was the last thing she wanted.

'I'm not moving in with you. I'm fine here.' Bella dashed angry tears out of her eyes.

'The hell you are.'

A cough at the door of the lounge drew both their attention. There was Zach, completely wet and naked apart from a towel wrapped round his waist. Without his hat, she noticed the blond curly hair that was swept back from his face.

Good god, he was glorious. He was so big and toned. His stomach was sculpted and he had that delicious V-shape that disappeared just below the towel. His chest was smooth and he had a tattoo that curled from his chest and over his shoulder, a black curly pattern that looked like it might be Celtic in origin.

He was literally dripping and Bella suddenly had an overwhelming desire to lick him dry. Any coherent thought had been wiped clean from her mind.

CHAPTER 2

'Bella, are you OK? I heard shouting,' Isaac said. He'd had no intention of getting involved when the row broke out, but although he couldn't hear the words, as the shouting sounded pretty heated, he knew he couldn't just stand by and do nothing.

Isaac glanced at the man Bella had been shouting at and the man glared straight back at him. The man was big but not as big as he was. He was pretty sure it wouldn't come to a fight but, if it did, Isaac knew he could take care of himself.

He turned his attention back to Bella but she seemed frozen to the spot, her eyes transfixed on him but seemingly not seeing him. She certainly wasn't looking at his face.

The other man cleared his throat. 'Bella, I didn't realise you had company. Will you come to my house for lunch tomorrow and we can talk about this some more?'

Bella still wasn't moving or talking but she managed to nod her head absently.

The man stepped forward and kissed Bella on the cheek and Isaac experienced an unexpected jolt of jealousy. Then he walked out, flashing Isaac a glare as he walked past.

Isaac waited for the man to leave before he turned his attention back to Bella who still looked like she had seen a ghost.

'Are you OK?'

She nodded.

'I'm sorry to interfere. I heard shouting, I was concerned.'

'No, it's fine. Rome is just a little protective of me sometimes.'

'Boyfriend?'

She smiled. 'Brother.'

He frowned slightly. The two of them didn't look anything alike. He had dark hair, she had a flame of gorgeous red. She was tiny, her brother was tall.

'Well, cousin technically. I was raised by my mum's older sister. Aunt Lucy and Uncle Finn are Rome's parents, so I always think of him and Eden as my brother and sister even though they're really my cousins.' Her eyes cast down his body again. 'Let me get you some clothes.'

She walked past him, trying to avert her gaze, and he followed her up the stairs.

'Why was your brother shouting at you?' Isaac asked. Whilst in the shower, he had decided that he would direct the conversation onto her, find out more about her and that way avoid questions about him at the same time.

'Because I'm one step away from being in your position.'

He watched her open the wardrobe and root around inside. 'You owe him money and he wants you to pay him back?'

Bella laughed. 'No, he's angry that I'm in this situation and never told him. He's my knight in shining armour, he would come in, pay all my food and bills if I'd let him, and then buy me some new shoes to cheer me up and never once ask for the money back. I'm just a little tired of playing the damsel in distress. His family have already done so much for me; I refuse to go to them for help again. I got myself into this mess, so it's up to me to get myself out of it.'

He thought about this for a moment. 'Sometimes bad things happen and it's nobody's fault. We all need a little help sometimes and it's OK to ask for it.'

'What about you, do you not have anyone who could help you out?'

Crap. He didn't want to lie to her but he could hardly tell her the truth either. 'My dad died when I was seven and I'm an

only child. I'm very close to my mum, speak to her every day...
well I used to,' he quickly amended. Bella didn't need to know
he'd had an hour-long chat to his mum just that morning. 'She
lives in Australia.'

'And she wouldn't be able to lend you some money?'

'She doesn't know about my situation.'

She smiled at him sympathetically as she laid some clothes on
the bed. 'Sometimes, it's nice to bask in the rose-tinted view they
have of us, isn't it, rather than have them know the truth and
feel let down by us. When was the last time you spoke to her?'

He hesitated. 'It's been a while.'

'She'll be worried about you. You can call her from here.'

'You've just told me you're one step away from being homeless.
I'm not going to rack up a huge phone bill for you too. There's
accepting help and then there's taking the piss.'

'I want to help you.'

'Why?'

She shrugged.

He stepped closer. 'Why do you trust me in your home? How
do you know I won't steal anything?'

She laughed again. 'I have nothing to steal. I've sold everything of value; I have no expensive jewels or technology. I have
no money stashed away in shoe boxes under the bed. My most
precious things are my books but I don't think anyone will want
them. If you can find something of value here and you're really
that desperate that you need to steal it, then go ahead.'

This complete trust in him was disarming. This attitude of
putting his needs before her own was something he had never
come across before. Almost everyone he had ever met had a
hidden agenda. Apart from his mum, his friend, Dougie, and
his PA, Claudia, he trusted no one. Everyone wanted something
from him, money, a job, an endorsement, expensive jewellery or
clothes. She had nothing and wanted to give him what she did

have. Why did she trust him so much? In his world, trust had to be earned but she had given it so willingly.

'What if I hurt you?'

The smile fell from her face. He didn't want to scare her; he just wanted her to think twice about inviting a stranger into her home. 'Why would you hurt me when I'm trying to help you?'

'I'm not going to hurt you Bella, I promise you that, but other people might. You just need to be a little bit careful about who you trust and who you invite into your home.'

'You sound like my brother. Although I've always been accepting of what people tell me. I'm a very honest person and I always see that virtue in others even when it isn't there. Trusting my boss was what got me into this mess in the first place. Maybe I am too naïve for my own good.'

Her trusting nature was part of her charm; he didn't want her to lose that.

'I never said naïve. Just... be careful.'

She nodded. 'I'll leave you to get changed.'

He watched her leave and quickly threw on some clothes. He was going to get to the bottom of what happened with her old job. He pulled a hoodie on over a t-shirt and glanced at himself in the mirror. Without his disguise of a holey jumper and dirty blanket he looked more like his normal self. He hadn't shaved when he'd had a shower so he still had a bit of stubble to hide behind but he wondered if she would recognise him.

Being so successful in his line of work meant that everyone knew who he was and everyone wanted a piece of him. Well, that was how it was in London. Bella seemed to have no clue who he was. Unless... she knew exactly who he was and this was all a ploy to get in his good books for the interview. No. He refused to believe she was that deceitful. He'd only known her for a few minutes but she was clearly an open book. What you saw was what you got with Bella Roussel.

He went downstairs and found her on all fours, lighting a fire in the log burner. He looked away, not wanting to stare at her inappropriately. The tiny lounge was strewn with books, the three bookcases were overflowing and there were multiple piles on the floor. Most looked like they had been read numerous times. There was a real mixture too, crime, fantasy, sci-fi, books set in foreign countries and a few romances as well.

She stood up and looked over at him. 'You look good.'

He looked down at himself. The tracksuit bottoms she had given him were about six inches too short and it felt like the hoodie belonged to a man half his size. She stifled a giggle and he looked back at her in surprise.

'Well... you look clean.'

He smiled.

She disappeared into the kitchen and came back with two bowls of porridge. She passed one to him and then curled herself up in the corner of the sofa to eat her own.

Isaac looked at the porridge and sat down next to her. The night before he'd enjoyed steak in a gorgeous red wine sauce at one of his favourite restaurants and now he was eating a very small bowl of watery porridge. Bella was tucking into it like it was her favourite meal, though he knew it was probably more due to hunger than actually enjoying it.

'I have to say this is not what I expected when I came up to the richest part of the island.'

Bella laughed. 'Is that why you came up here?'

'I was begging down in the town and someone said I should try Blossom Grove as they were all rich up here.'

'You chose the wrong door to sit outside, I'm afraid. Sorry to disappoint you.'

'I'm not disappointed. Not at all. I get to spend the night with a beautiful woman and that was a lot more than I had hoped for when I came up here.'

She paused with a spoonful of porridge halfway to her mouth as she stared at him. Then she returned her attention to her porridge and didn't look at him after that. He knew he had embarrassed her and he had no idea why he'd said it.

He took a few spoonfuls of his own porridge.

'So tell me your story. Why are you living on porridge?'

She carried on eating for a few moments and it was clear she was toying with whether to tell him or not. She finally finished her porridge and put the bowl on the coffee table before curling back up into the corner of the sofa.

'I had a job, a fantastic job as events manager for a local charity – well, it was based locally over on St Mary's, but they did charity work all over the UK. Magic Wishes, have you heard of them?'

Isaac hesitated because of course he had heard of them. They had been all over the news a few months before. But was it only of interest to him because he was a CEO of a charity himself? Would the average Joe know the story? 'It rings a bell,' he said, vaguely.

She nodded. 'Yeah, probably for all the wrong reasons. We were a very small charity, but we did wonderful things, giving special days out to children with cancer and their families. Clara was my boss, and the owner and founder of the company. Her husband did the accounts. I arranged all the fundraising events and Clara helped to co-ordinate all the days out for the families. There was an admin girl who worked part time a few mornings a week too. It was a great team to work for and Clara was lovely. I say that because I literally had no idea that between her and her husband they had been embezzling thousands of pounds of the charity's money over the last five years.'

He knew all this of course. He knew that Bella herself had been investigated and cleared of all charges and even Clara and her husband Phil had been adamant that Bella and Sally, the admin girl, had nothing to do with it.

'You didn't even have an inkling?'

'No, god no. Clara lost her own son twenty years ago to cancer and she met so many families during that time that were all going through the same hell that she and Phil went through and she wanted to do something to help them. She was passionate about the charity and the work we did and I always thought she was such an inspiring person to work for. I was so naïve. She had a big house, a nice car, she went on expensive luxury holidays and I didn't think twice about it. I knew her husband was a success-ful, high-paid accountant, not just for the charity but for other companies too, and I just assumed a lot of their money came from him. She got paid a salary, I knew that; I just didn't realise how much and that her salary was over ten times as much at the end as it was in the beginning. All these events that I arranged to raise funds, I was working my arse off for them, thinking I was doing something good and worthwhile, and they were taking almost all of it for themselves. I was horrified when I found out. All those people that had donated money and it was going to line Clara's pockets.'

Bella sighed, playing with a hole in the knee of her jeans.

'I think the worst thing was people's reactions and attitudes towards me. Of course I was investigated but the police could clearly see that beyond my tiny salary I hadn't got a penny from the company. But despite everyone knowing I was cleared of any wrongdoings, many people, like you, still think that I had something to do with it or that I must have known something was going on.'

'I don't think you had anything to do with it.'

Bella looked at him in surprise. 'You don't?'

He shook his head. 'I think anyone who really knows you would know you couldn't have done it. I've spent five minutes with you and I can see how genuine you are.'

'Well, you see more than most people. A lot of them have been supportive. But some people over on St Mary's don't want anything to do with me. I've been asked to leave some restaurants and shops and consequently getting another job has been harder than I thought.'

'Have you tried the other islands? They might not be so judgemental.'

'I have, but to no avail. And work here on Hope Island is almost impossible to come by.' She turned to face him excitedly. 'But there's a job going at the Umbrella Foundation, a fundraising events manager, so it's perfect for me. They are the most fantastic company to work for too. I've checked out how much of their funds goes directly to the charity and they have one of the biggest percentages of all the charities in the country. The CEO doesn't even get a salary from the charity, he owns some other big companies and obviously gets paid a load from them so he takes nothing from the charity and a lot of the charity staff get paid from his other companies too. So almost all the money that is raised by the charity goes directly to help the homeless. And they don't just provide meals and clothes and somewhere to sleep for the homeless, they actively help to get them off the streets. They help them to start their own small businesses, funding them in the first few years. They help to get them jobs too. It sounds like such a wonderful company to work for and it's right here on Hope Island, albeit on the completely opposite side from here.'

Isaac watched her getting excited about his company. Though he had plenty of committed staff members, he had never seen someone with so much enthusiasm or passion for the charity before.

'You should contact them,' Bella said. 'They might be able to help you. There's a restaurant in St Mary's that is owned by a former homeless person. All of the staff there are or were homeless. They are trained up as waiters, chefs, bar managers and many of the staff then go on to be leading chefs or managers in other restaurants. It's a great stepping stone and the Umbrella

Foundation works closely with the restaurant. I bet they would give you a job – even if it's only a few hours a week to start with, it's something. You should come with me on Monday to the interview and at least speak to them.'

God, this was getting more and more complicated.

'Maybe I will.'

'Monday could be a good day for us both,' Bella said excitedly.

He smiled. It could be a good day for her if he could persuade the rest of the panel to take her on. He wanted her for this job; someone with passion and enthusiasm for the role. However, it wouldn't be a good day for him when she found out he had been lying to her. From the way she'd handled herself in the row with her brother, something told him there would be hell to pay once she found out the truth.

CHAPTER 3

Bella plonked herself down on the sofa next to Zach and passed him a glass of water and a small chocolate brownie, courtesy of Mr Kemble. 'So tell me your story, how did you end up on the streets?'

She watched as the smile faded from his face. 'It's not something I want to talk about.'

'Oh.' She felt the rebuke like a slap in the face.

'I know you trusted me with your story and it's not that I don't trust you with mine. It's just that if I told you the truth, I don't think you would be happy to be sitting here with me now. I love that you have no judgements of me, that we can sit here and talk like this, but I rather wish that... the path that led me to here had never happened because it's something I can't undo.'

'I would never judge you. We have all made mistakes in our past and it would never be fair to judge you on them now. But I understand if you're not comfortable talking about it. Let's talk about something else instead. Where were you born, where did you grow up?'

Zach smiled, obviously relieved to move on to a subject that he was comfortable talking about. He took a bite of his brownie and chewed slowly, almost as if he was considering his answer.

'Born on St Mary's but I lived here for the first eight years of my life.'

'You lived here on Hope Island? We might have played together as kids. How old are you?'

'Thirty-three.'

'Oh I'm twenty-seven, we probably didn't mix in the same circles. Rome is thirty-one and Eden is thirty, so you might have known them.'

Zach shrugged. 'The names don't ring a bell. They would have been a few years below me at school.'

'How funny that we probably used to play on the same beach, go cycling through the same woods. It's a small world. Do you remember the funfairs we used to have here every spring?'

He grinned. 'Yes, they were amazing. The bumper cars, the haunted house, the ghost train—'

'And the big wheel! I used to love and hate going on that in equal measure. It was always a thrill to see the whole of the island and everyone there below us like tiny ants and feeling like I was king of the world as the wheel went up in the air but then we'd get to the top and I always felt like we were going to fall. I remember feeling so scared but as soon as we got back down we'd queue back up to ride it again. The tourists would come over just to see the fair and they'd always tell us local kids that we were so lucky to live here all the time. I never really appreciated that until I was older. I loved the smells, the candyfloss and the toffee apples and Uncle Finn would always try to win us the biggest, fattest teddy to take home on all the little games.'

'And the fireworks at the end of the night,' Zach went on. 'All that colour exploding over the sea, it looked magical. We came back to Hope Island every year just for the funfair, until they stopped doing it.'

'I know, it was such a shame. It was Dougie's parents that used to organise it.'

'Dougie?' Something in Zach's eyes registered recognition and she wondered if he remembered him from his time on the island.

'He's a friend of ours, me, Eden and Rome. We used to hang around together as kids. Do you know him?'

He hesitated before he shook his head.

'His parents emigrated to New York when Dougie was eighteen and Dougie went with them. After that no one wanted the hassle of organising the fair again and it stopped. There was talk of starting it again but it never happened. Do you remember the ice cream shop at the end of the pier?'

'Yes,' Zach laughed. 'Maddy used to give us free samples of any new flavours. Whenever a sign went up advertising there was a new flavour, the kids used to queue up all the way back to the start of the pier to try it out.'

'I remember that too. Quite clever marketing really, because we would all use our pocket money to pay for an extra scoop or for toppings. Do you remember those little white chocolate bears she used to sell, with caramel in the middle? They were my favourite toppings. I used to go in there sometimes and just have a bag of those and Maddy never minded that I wasn't buying ice cream.'

'She was wonderful, what happened to her? The shop was still there when I left.'

Bella shrugged. 'I think she moved to Australia or somewhere. I remember being more gutted about the shop closing than Take That breaking up and I loved Take That. There's a new ice cream shop in town now. It's nice, I suppose, but nothing will ever beat Maddy's ice cream.'

'I know. When I moved to St Mary's when I was eight, I missed her shop so much. I missed a lot about Hope Island actually. I still had the beaches but it wasn't the same as here. There's something magical about the beaches here. There's something about the people on Hope Island too, they look out for everyone else. I ended up moving to London when I was fifteen and lived there for many years with university and work but I wanted to come back to the Isles of Scilly. I just missed the place too much. I sold my house, made some changes at work and...' he trailed off.

'Is that when it all went wrong? Coming back here?' Bella said but she could see Zach didn't want to talk about that. 'I'm not prying. I just wonder if you had all your hopes pinned on here and now you feel let down.'

Zach didn't say anything and she took his hand. 'I know it feels hopeless but my nan has a saying. "What's meant for you won't go by you." Something bigger and better is just around the corner for you. And I'll do whatever I can to help you.'

It was good to remember that although she had nothing, there were people who were in a far worse situation. She had a roof over her head and a loving family who wanted to look after her. Zach didn't even have that.

'If you wanted to stay here for a bit longer, until you sorted yourself out, I'd be happy to have you here. You could be my lodger.'

He laughed. 'I can't pay you any rent.'

'You don't have to. There's odd jobs you could help me with. There's a bulb that needs changing at the top of the stairs and I can't reach it even with a step ladder. I normally get Rome to do it for me whenever he comes round. I have a door that won't close and a shelf that needs putting up. You could do those jobs for me in return for the use of my sofa and as much porridge as you want if I can get another box next week.'

'Did I eat the last of your porridge?' Zach said, horrified.

'It doesn't matter. I'll be able to get some food from somewhere. And now that Rome knows my situation, he won't let me live on porridge for any longer. I guarantee lunch with him tomorrow will result in me leaving his house with several bags of groceries. We could eat like kings tomorrow night. And as much as I hate relying on him like that, I need the help. And it's a temporary measure. When I get this job for the Umbrella Foundation at least that will be a guaranteed income at the end of the month and then I can pay him back. So do you fancy some steak tomorrow night?'

'Thank you, that's really kind, but I really need to try to get back to St Mary's tomorrow. There's more chance of me getting a job there than there is here.'

'Oh, of course.'

She got up to throw another piece of wood into the log burner. She couldn't help but feel disappointed about that fact. She was offering him a warm place to stay, some decent food and some company and he would much rather face a night on the streets of St Mary's than stay with her.

She talked too much, she knew that. Asked too many questions. 'Sorry, I'm used to being on my own. When I have company I start talking and just don't stop. Look, I'll leave you to some peace and quiet; I have a good book upstairs with my name on it.'

He caught her hand as she walked past.

'Don't go, I'm enjoying our chat. Sometimes living on the streets can be so lonely. Days go past and I don't speak to anyone. It's been lovely chatting to you tonight.'

'Really? You don't find me too much?'

'Too much of what? Too much kindness and generosity? Too much giving your time to help those in need? Too much chatting to me like I'm a normal human being and not someone to be avoided or treated with disgust? I don't think there can ever be too much of that. I've never met anyone like you before, Bella, and believe me when I say that that's a good thing.'

'OK, but if you get sick of listening to me talk, just tell me to shut up, I promise I won't be offended.'

'I don't think I could ever get sick of listening to you talk,'

She smiled and sat back down. 'I know I talk too much. I don't have many friends; I like to keep to myself. Some evenings I spend with Eden and Rome and our friend Freya, every Friday I have dinner with my family but most nights I'm here alone. And it suits me. I can read a book without being disturbed, go to bed when I want, watch what I want on TV – when I had a TV – but it means when I suddenly do have company I could talk for England.'

'Why don't you have many friends?'

She shrugged but in reality she knew that there must be something wrong with her. She knew lots of people on the island but none of them were really her friend. Eden was her best friend but she was also her sister, which didn't say much. Freya was her only real friend outside of the family, and Dougie of course, but he lived in America. She kept people at arm's length, she knew that, and over the years she'd let so very few people in. Zach was still waiting for an answer so she gave him one which was at least partly true.

'No one stays on Hope Island. The youngsters don't anyway. The older people will never leave and many retire to here, but there is always a mass exodus of young folk leaving every year. The island is too small and there's so much world out there for people to explore. Every single person in my class at school went away for university and no one came back.'

'But you never wanted to leave?'

'I went away to university but I couldn't wait to get back here. This place just feels safe. I'd love to travel one day, see the world, but I think Hope Island will always be my home.'

'I understand that. I've always missed Hope Island. I've wanted to come back for a long time. Do you not get lonely though, sitting here every night on your own?'

'I do enjoy being alone and reading a book. Some people on the island have not been kind about the embezzlement and I was bullied as a child. Books are not mean or unkind. I can dive into a book and not fear that I'm going to get hurt. But sometimes, I do get a bit lonely. I was going to get a dog for company, someone to talk to in the evenings even if he couldn't talk back. I went to the dog home here on Hope Island and I met the most beautiful husky-labrador cross called Alfie. Six years old and he was abandoned by his owner. I had all the house visits and I'd been to the dog shelter to take him out for walks and we just clicked. But I am struggling to find the money to feed myself, so I couldn't realistically take him when I wouldn't be able to feed him. Jenny at the dog home has promised to keep him as long as possible for me but I don't want to stand in the way of him getting his forever home; someone who can love him and look after him when I can't. That's where I was today, visiting him. I help out there too now and again in return for them keeping Alfie for me.'

Zach smiled. 'Well, maybe when you get this job you can go and get him, bring him home where he belongs.'

'That's the plan. *If* I get the job.'

'You're perfect for it. Look at you helping the homeless tonight. If you can stop and help me, think of all the other people you could help too.'

She laughed. 'I never even thought of that. I should use you as a reference. Look at this homeless person I helped. Give me the job.'

Zach laughed too.

'If only it were that simple. This job is perfect for me and I think I am perfect for this role but I think the embezzlement and my past history is going to be a hard obstacle to get past, at least as far as they are concerned.'

'You just need to show them the other parts to you, show them why you would be perfect for the job. OK, I'll be the interviewer. Why do you want this job, aside from the money issue?'

She smiled and turned to face him, crossing her legs under her. 'Because, Mr Umbrella, I—'

'Wait, Mr Umbrella?' he laughed. 'You don't know the name of the person interviewing you, this CEO that you were talking about? You don't know his name?'

'Of course I do, but Isaac Scott isn't going to be interviewing me. He has underlings for that sort of thing. I have no idea which underling will be picked for the job. I had a letter from an Amanda Jackson and I know she will be on a panel of four people who will be grilling me but it didn't say who else will be on the panel.'

'Don't you think that this Mr Scott bloke, who as you say puts a lot of time and effort into the charity, has a vested interest in who he employs?'

'Nah. He probably does this charity for tax purposes or something. Offsets a lot of the company expenses from his other companies against the charity and then he won't have to pay so much tax. I'm not sure how it works. I'm sure he is a very clever and very generous man but he is probably way too busy to get involved in the inner workings of the charity. And from what I gather, he lives in London. It's a bit far for him to travel all the way down to the Scilly Isles just for an interview. I probably need to do some more research on him. I know he owns BlazeStar which makes computer programs for big companies and I know two years ago he created SparkStar which makes phone apps for companies but his photo isn't on the websites. I probably need to find that so I recognise him if he pops his head round the door. I'm sure I can find it online somewhere, but I imagine him to be quite a portly gentleman who wears braces with his suit and probably a bowler hat. He'll have a curly moustache and a little goatee which he styles into a point.'

Zach burst out laughing. 'That's quite an image. Anyway you were telling me why you want this job.'

'Well, Mr Umbrella,' Bella said and continued despite Zach's smile. 'I want this job because I want to make a difference and I know this company has made great strides in reducing the home-less population and really helping to get them off the streets and into jobs and homes and I want to be a part of that.'

'That's a corporate line, they'll hear that from everyone they interview. What's the real reason?'

Bella frowned, her heart sinking. 'That is the real reason. I love working for a charity. I want to help people.'

Zach studied her for a moment. 'You really are one of a kind, Bella. OK, forget the interview with Mr Umbrella for a second. Why is it you want to help people?'

Bella thought about this, or more specifically what she could tell him. But there was something about Zach that made her want to spill her deepest secrets.

'Life dealt me a crappy hand from a very early age but fortunately for me I had my aunt and uncle to look after me. I had someone to help me out and not everyone has that. If it hadn't been for them, my life would have turned out very differently and I guess I want to be that person, maybe in some small way, for someone else.'

'That's why you want to take Alfie on?'

He understood.

'He was abandoned by his owners just like I was abandoned by my parents.'

She looked down at her knees, so she wouldn't have to see the pity in his eyes. She quickly moved on before he could ask her any questions or make any comments about that.

'Working for a charity means I can help someone just like I was helped and whether that is Magic Wishes, helping people to create some special memories with a loved one before they died, or the Umbrella Foundation, helping people not as lucky as me to find a way back into work and off the streets, I want to do something to help people.

'I'd be great at this job; I have experience as a fundraising events manager. I've done it for five years and I love it. A lot of people think that if they have experience in events management then the skills are transferable and I suppose they are, but events management for a hotel or other corporate events organisation is a different ball game to a fundraising events manager. Corporate or banqueting events is about giving the customer exactly what they want; the flowers, the food, the seating plans. Fundraising events management is about creating events that people want to be a part of. It's about inspiring people to join in. It has to be imaginative and fun and uniquely different and I love stuff like that. Honestly, this job was written for me.'

Zach was smiling by the time she finished speaking, his grin growing as she explained her passion for the job. 'You need to say all this in the interview. Your passion is what is going to stand you apart from the rest of the interviewees. Tell them where your desire to help people comes from. They need to see that it comes from the heart.'

'You want me to tell my prospective employers that my parents abandoned me? That my dad walked out on me when I was five and then my mum ditched me with my aunt and uncle for the weekend when I was six years old and never came back for me. I don't think that showing my new employers how unwanted I was is going to help them to want me. They might think that something is wrong with me if both my parents walked out and left me. I know I do.'

Good lord, the secrets were spilling forth tonight. Next she'd be telling him what age she was when she started her first period and how she had cried for a week when her pet goldfish had died. He didn't say anything for a moment, just watched her. She felt her cheeks flame, probably going as red as her hair.

She decided to change the subject quickly. 'So Mr Umbrella, the question is not what I can do for you. I've already told you why I am absolutely the best person for this job.'

'That's true, you have.'

'The question is, why should I work for you? What would you be offering me if, *if* I decided to work for your company?'

Zach burst out laughing. 'You're not going to ask that in the interview?'

'I might,' she smirked. 'It has to be an equal partnership.'

Zach nodded seriously, a smile tugging on his lips. 'Yes you're right. Well, Miss…?'

'Roussel.'

'Oooh nice, French?'

'I have no idea. It's my dad's. The only thing he left me with.'

Zach hesitated for a moment but clearly decided not to pursue it. 'Well Miss Roussel. I'd offer you a company car, maybe something like a Ferrari or a Porsche.'

'I'm listening; this sounds like a very fair offer to go alongside my million-pound-a-year salary.'

'Plus bonuses,' Zach clarified.

'Oh yes, I'd forgotten about the very generous bonus, private healthcare, and one of the best pensions around. What else are you offering me?'

'You want more than a million pounds a year and a Ferrari?'

'Porsche. Chauffeur-driven. Yes, I think I'm worth it.'

'A beach house in Florida?'

'Generous. Anything else?'

'You name it, it's yours.'

'I want…' She thought about it for a moment. 'A housekeeper and cook and maybe a hot butler, to, you know, answer the door for me if I get too tired to do it myself.'

'OK, deal.'

'Wait. I'm not finished.'

'You have more demands?'

Bella nodded. 'My own boat.'

'A hundred-foot yacht with a crew of fifty to cater to your every whim?'

'Well, no, that sounds a bit greedy.'

'And a salary of a million pounds and a beach house in Florida isn't?'

'No, that's just practical. Just a small boat with an engine, something simple to operate by myself so I can visit the other islands whenever I wanted. I'd like it to be purple and have her name written in silver down the side.'

'I feel I'm going to regret asking, what's her name?'

'Boaty McBoatface.'

Zach laughed loudly. 'You got yourself a deal, Miss Roussel.'

He held out his hand and she reached out and shook it, enjoying the warmth of it, the softness of his skin. There was something special about Zach, the ease with which she could talk to him. It was a pity she only had tonight with him, she would have enjoyed getting to know him more.

✾✲✿☙

Oh this girl was going to be trouble. Isaac watched her as she moved to the fire to add more logs. She was smart and funny and cute as hell. He really liked her.

He frowned. But if she came and worked for the Umbrella Foundation, he would be her boss and he knew he could never let anything happen between them. That could be unbelievably tricky and messy at work. Never mix business and pleasure; that was something he always stuck to.

Unless of course he didn't hire her. Although talk about cutting your nose off to spite your face.

She turned back to him with a smile and he found himself frowning slightly, which had her smile fading away.

'I think I might head to bed, it's getting late. Let me get you some blankets and pillows.'

She disappeared out of the room. She had been completely honest with him that night and in return he had lied to her. How was she going to react when she found out the truth? Would it be better for him to tell her the truth now? Apologise profusely and offer to make it up to her by buying her a decent meal out? Something that wasn't porridge. Sure she'd be pissed but at least they could start the interview back on honest ground and she'd have a day to get over her anger with him.

He stood up as she came back in and she immediately set about making up a bed for him on the sofa.

She stood back up when she'd finished. 'Will you still be here when I get up or do you intend to get the five o'clock ferry?'

Isaac didn't say anything for a moment, the truth getting stuck in his throat. 'I think I'll get the early ferry. I might be able to get a few hours' work down at the harbour in St Mary's; they pay cash in hand and don't ask for references.'

Bella nodded and he saw the look of disappointment flash across her face. 'I understand. And the offer still stands. If you change your mind and want to sleep here tomorrow, I'd be happy to have you back again.'

He nodded. He knew he had to tell her, but he liked the easy relationship they had right now and he couldn't bring himself to break the spell.

She seemed to hesitate, maybe hoping he would change his mind. A lock of hair fell across her face and she absently pulled out her ponytail, letting her red curls tumble over her shoulders. It was so long and all he could suddenly think about was what it would look like when it cascaded over her naked body as he made love to her. Crap, where the hell did that come from?

'It was lovely meeting you tonight,' Bella said, scooping her hair back up into a ponytail again, though this did nothing to diminish her effect on him. 'It was really nice chatting and getting to know you. If I don't see you again, then I wish you all the success for the future.'

He wanted to kiss her. He wanted to step forward, take her in his arms and kiss her and he didn't know what to do with that feeling, because he sure as hell couldn't act on it.

'You'll see me again,' Isaac finally said. 'I promise.'

Her face brightened at that and she gave him a little wave and left the room.

He sighed as he took off his hoodie. He certainly wasn't going to get any sleep tonight knowing she was sleeping just a few feet above him.

❦

Bella stood outside the door to the lounge for a second. There had been chemistry between them and she was pretty sure he felt it too. She wanted to go back in there and kiss him but she'd never been brave enough to make the first move in a relationship. He could easily have kissed her if he'd really wanted to and he hadn't, so maybe he didn't feel the same. She sighed. He would be going back to St Mary's tomorrow and she'd probably never see him again. Just because she had enjoyed talking to him that night didn't mean they had any kind of future together.

She sighed and had started to head upstairs when she remembered about the spare logs for the log burner. There was a huge pile in the kitchen but he wouldn't think to look for them in the cupboard.

She quickly went back into the lounge to find Zach completely and gloriously stark naked.

CHAPTER 4

She yelped. He swore and grabbed a cushion to hide his manhood. Bella quickly clamped a hand over her eyes and turned to get out the room, bouncing head-first off the doorframe and landing on her back on the floor.

'Ow!' Bella said, her hand still over her eyes.

'Crap, Bella, are you OK?' came Zach's voice from somewhere just above her. She didn't dare look.

'I'm so sorry, I just wanted to tell you there were spare logs for the log burner in the cupboard under the microwave. I should have knocked. I didn't realise you'd be naked and, erm…' All she could think about how delicious he looked. 'Why are you naked anyway? Where are your boxers?'

'I normally sleep naked. Well, I used to before I ended up on the streets. Force of habit, getting undressed for bed,' Zach said.

'You sleep naked?' There was something so sexy about that thought. 'God, that's hot.' She peered through her fingers at him. He was standing over her, thankfully still holding a cushion with one hand. He smiled at her comment. She flushed, clamping a hand over her mouth. She'd just told him he was hot. Was there no filter on her mouth at all? 'I can't believe I just told you I think you're hot. I must have banged my head harder than I thought.'

He offered a hand to help her up, she took it and he pulled her to her feet. He gently swept her hair off her forehead to look at her bruise, his eyes clouding with concern. 'I think you'll live.'

'Not if I die of embarrassment first.'

'There's nothing to be embarrassed about. If I told you I think you're incredibly sexy would that make you feel better?'

She stared at him, finding it impossible to believe that they were standing there having this conversation when he was stark naked.

'You're attracted to me?'

'Of course I am; you're smart, funny, passionate, incredibly beautiful.'

She literally felt her mouth fall open though there were no words to fill the silence. No one had ever said those things to her.

'I'm attracted to you too,' she said, quietly.

Neither of them said anything for a moment and she found her cheeks burning red again.

Eventually he took a step back away from her. 'Goodnight Bella.'

Feeling stung and confused she took a step away from him and then, when he didn't say anything else, she left the room, closing the door behind her.

Her day had started off so normally and now it had ended in a very bizarre way. But one thing was for sure, her life was suddenly a lot brighter now that Zach had crossed her path.

※℃℃Ⓠ

Bella woke the next day to a bright spring sun bursting through her curtains. She opened the window and smiled at the blackbird that was going into full song right outside her window. The sea glistened like gold as the little white boats in the harbour bobbed about in the gentle spring tide.

She stood up and stretched, guessing from the complete silence in the house that Zach had already gone but she couldn't help smiling when she thought of him.

Something had passed between them the night before and she somehow knew she would be seeing him again.

She padded downstairs into the lounge and sure enough there was no sign of him. The blankets were neatly folded on the sofa but the smell of him lingered in the air and it made her stomach clench with need.

On the coffee table there was a pink peony on top of a piece of paper. She scooped up the flower and sniffed it, relishing in the wonderful smell, then picked up the note and read it.

Thank you for letting me stay. Good luck tomorrow at the interview, go show that Mr Umbrella that Bella brilliance. They'll be very lucky to have you and even though I know you'll hate Isaac Scott when you see him, don't let that put you off the job. You'll be perfect at it. You're the most wonderful person I've ever met. My biggest regret is not grabbing you and kissing you last night and also not being brave enough to tell you why.
Xx

She smiled even though the message left her thoroughly confused. She focussed on the bit she did understand. He had wanted to kiss her. She wanted to leap up and let out a little whoop of joy at that fact. But what was the reason that held him back?

She looked at the big kiss and little kiss at the end of the note and thought that perhaps it was symbolic of Zach and her together. She shook her head at her silly romantic whimsical nature.

Bella read the note again. He had never mentioned that he knew Isaac Scott the night before when they had talked about him; why would Zach think that she would hate him? Had something happened between them in the past? Was Isaac Scott responsible for Zach being on the streets? She doubted Isaac would even be there at the interview so why would she even see him, let alone hate him?

She sighed as she fingered the soft petals of the flower for a moment, before walking into the kitchen and putting it in a bowl of water.

She guessed she would find out what the note meant soon enough, but for now she had lunch with Rome to deal with and she knew her brother wouldn't make it easy for her.

✿❧❀

Bella let herself in through the back door of Rome's thatched cottage and called out to him. He called to her from the dining room. There was a wonderful smell of lasagne and garlic bread in the air. Her favourite. She smiled that Rome had been thoughtful enough to make that for her but the smile faded from her face when she walked into the dining room and saw her aunt, uncle and her sister Eden sitting at the table too. She glared at Rome as she moved to greet her aunt and uncle though her brother remained unmoved by her stares.

'Hi Lucy, Finn. What a lovely surprise,' Bella said. 'I didn't know you'd both be here.'

Eden smirked at her and Bella returned her smile. Whereas Rome had always taken his job of protective older brother very seriously, she and Eden had become best friends very quickly. They had slept in the same room, shared their toys and clothes growing up. Bella adored her. And while she adored Rome too, it was a different kind of love.

Bella sat down at the table. In the middle, propped up against the hugging salt and pepper pots, was an envelope with her name on it. She didn't need to be psychic to know there was money inside it, quite a lot judging by the thickness of it. Rome took her hand, distracting her from deciding how best she could turn it down.

'I've filled these guys in,' Rome said.

'I thought you might have,' Bella said. 'Finn, I'm sorry about the rent.'

Her uncle's eyes widened and a flash of hurt crossed his face.

'We don't care about the rent. Why didn't you come to us?' Her aunt Lucy immediately went in for the kill.

'I was doing OK, I had savings to fall back on. It was only in the last week or so that things started getting a bit tight.'

'And that's when you should have come to us,' Finn said. 'We're your parents. We would have helped you.'

'This is a tiny little blip. I have a job interview on Monday and I'm going to get it. This is my problem to sort out not yours. I didn't want to burden you with it.'

'You're our daughter, and we love you so much. You are not a burden. You never have been,' Lucy said.

Bella smiled. The love she felt from her adoptive parents was unconditional, unwavering and more than she ever deserved. She often thought that she was showered with more affection than her older siblings and she knew it wasn't just because she was the youngest. Her real parents had never loved her and her aunt and uncle had spent the last twenty-one years trying to make up for that, as if they somehow felt guilty for the behaviour of Lucy's younger sister.

'If we were in the same situation and were struggling to pay our bills and pay for food, would you help us?'

'Of course I would,' Bella said. 'But it's different.'

'Why is it different?' Rome argued.

'Because… Because you've all supported me my whole life. I'm like the cuckoo chick, unwanted by my own parents and dumped in someone else's nest to be looked after. You took me on when I was six years old, gave me food and clothes and a roof over my head. Rome, you paid off all my student loans and debts after I came back from university and I know that wasn't cheap; Eden, you shared all your clothes and toys and never once raised any objection and – more important than that – you all gave me this endless love which my own parents never did. It was more than I ever deserved. You've all done enough.'

'You know all that money came from the accident,' Rome objected. 'What else was I going to do with it? Build a gold palace and live in luxury while the rest of my family struggled? I wanted to help you, you worked so hard at university and it didn't seem fair to start your working life with so much debt hanging over you. I was more than happy to give you the money. Paige would have been happy too.'

Bella cringed, knowing that the compensation money Rome had received after his fiancée's tragic death was always a sore point for him. He had never wanted that money and felt it was wrong to benefit from Paige's death, especially with such a huge sum. In the end he had given most of it away, paid off his parents' mortgage, paid for Eden's shop and paid off Bella's student debts, given some to his best friend, Dougie, and given over half of it away to charity. Rome had always been ridiculously generous and that's why she felt so reluctant to come to him for help again. He had done enough.

Eden leaned forward. 'You are my sister and my best friend and I love you with everything I have. Love is not given because you deserve it, it's given unconditionally. That love is not going to go away because we give you money or food. And that love means we care about you and will do whatever we can to help you. So you're going to accept the food we've bought for you and you're going to accept the money that's in that envelope and we're going to say no more about it.'

Bella looked around at the angry, defiant and upset faces around the table. She had hurt them by not asking for their help when she needed it the most and that was the very last thing she wanted to do. Her family were pushy, overprotective and interfering but she loved them with all her heart. This was important to them, she knew that. And so what if her pride was taking a battering? Even if she did get the job on Monday, she still needed money and food for the next month until she got her first pay cheque. She knew she had to take this.

She reached across the table and picked up the envelope. It was really thick and she winced inwardly.

'This is a loan and I'll pay every single penny back,' Bella said. No one moved or nodded their agreement. 'But thank you.'

She tucked the envelope into her jeans pocket and there was a small collective sigh of relief.

'Right, lunch time,' Eden declared, getting up from the table and heading to the kitchen.

'We can't stop,' Lucy said. 'We promised your aunt Cassie we would help out at the cake sale on the pier.'

Lucy got up from the table and Bella stood up too. Before Bella could say a word, Lucy had yanked her into a big bear hug. Bella felt tears smart her eyes at the love her family had for her.

'We'll see you for dinner, Friday night. No lame excuses this time. And give us a call tomorrow night and let us know how the interview goes.'

Lucy moved to give Rome a hug.

Finn gave Bella a hug goodbye. 'We love you. Before you came to live with us, we loved you. Our nest was half empty until you came along to fill it up and while I don't have many good things to say about your mum, there's not a day that goes by that I don't mentally thank her for giving us such a brilliant, warm and beautiful daughter. You have never been a burden, you never will be.'

Finn kissed her on the head and she felt the hot tears fall down her cheeks.

They both left and she could hear them saying goodbye to Eden in the kitchen.

Rome stared at her, clearly wondering if she was still angry at him for telling Lucy and Finn. 'Am I forgiven?'

She wiped the tears away. 'That depends. Is the garlic bread I can smell the stuff you make or is it shop-bought?'

'I'm offended, Bella, it's homemade of course.'

'Then you're forgiven.'

He stepped forward and hugged her, kissing her head. 'I love you, don't ever forget that.'

She hugged him back, smiling to herself.

Eden came back from the kitchen and plonked a large lasagne in the middle of the table and then rushed off back to the kitchen to grab the garlic bread. 'Get the plates, knives and forks, Bella. Rome, you can grab the water.'

There was a flurry of activity for a moment before they all finally sat down to eat.

Bella took a big bite of the lasagne then moaned her appreciation. It tasted so good and it wasn't just because she had lived on porridge for the last few weeks. Rome was a ridiculously good cook and she knew if he wasn't busy decorating the world with his wonderful stained glass pieces he would be a brilliant chef at some high-paid restaurant in London, he was that good.

She watched Eden and Rome tuck into their food and when she took a big bite of the wonderful fresh garlic bread Eden chose that moment to speak.

'So tell me about this gorgeous hot naked man that was at your house last night?'

Bella choked and Rome passed her a glass of water. 'I'd just like to say that I never said he was gorgeous or hot. He's not really my type.'

'Admittedly, he never said that, but he did say he was naked,' Eden said, giggling. 'And I presumed that he was gorgeous and hot because you have good taste when it comes to men.'

'Well I wouldn't agree with that, the last guy you dated was an ass,' Rome said.

Eden nodded to concede this. 'He was, sadly, though he was a hot piece of ass.'

'Hang on, is nothing private? Who I date is my business,' Bella protested. 'And I'm not dating Zach, he's just a friend.'

'A friend that was naked and wet in your house,' Eden said, waggling her eyebrows at her from across the table.

'He was just getting changed out of his dirty clothes,' Bella said.

'Where do you know this friend from?' Rome asked.

There was no way in the world she was telling him the truth about that. He would go mad that she had invited a stranger into her home. 'I don't know, just around,' Bella said, vaguely, and Rome narrowed his eyes.

'I'm sure I recognised him. What did you say his name was, Zach what?'

Bella grabbed the first name that came to mind.

'Umbrella.'

There was silence. She would make a terrible spy. Her cover story would be so flimsy everyone would guess straight away.

'Umbrella?' Eden laughed.

'No, Unbella,' Bella corrected, realising she was making the situation worse. 'OK I don't know his surname. I haven't known him long. And his surname never came up in conversation. He just got into a spot of bother yesterday and I was helping him out by letting him get washed and changed in my house. It's no big deal.'

'I've definitely met him before,' Rome said, chewing on a piece of garlic bread. 'Though it was a really long time ago. Is he from the island?'

'He was born here and lived here until he was eight. He lived in St Mary's and then London for a while after that but moved back this way recently,' Bella said, trying to skate over the fact that he wasn't living anywhere at the moment. She didn't care that Zach was homeless and she knew that Rome and Eden wouldn't care either, but it was the inviting a complete stranger to stay in her house that Rome would have issue with. And although she knew she wouldn't change what she'd done the night before, helping someone out when they were in trouble, she knew she had been silly to put herself at risk like that.

Rome was still watching her suspiciously so she decided to change the subject away from Zach.

'How's Freya doing with her apprenticeship?' Bella asked Rome.

His face lit up into a smile.

'Good, really good,' Rome said, proudly. 'Although to be honest she stopped being my apprentice a long time ago. She's such a fast learner, works hard and she's brilliant at making her own stained glass pieces. She's away for a few days at the moment and I really miss her at work. We make a really good team. I'm going to offer her a full partnership in my firm when she comes back.'

'I bet Freya will be over the moon with that offer,' Bella said, exchanging a quick smile with Eden. They both thought that Freya had a bit of a soft spot for Rome. Though Rome had no idea and was far too busy sleeping his way around the female population of Hope Island and the rest of the Isles of Scilly to notice his wonderful apprentice.

'Oh I spoke to Dougie last night; he said he's coming over for a week or so,' Rome said to Eden and Bella watched her as she studied her lasagne carefully and she nodded vaguely. 'I think he arrives Thursday.'

'I haven't seen Dougie for ages,' Bella said, still watching for any kind of reaction from Eden. There was none. 'I can't wait to see him again.'

Dougie Harrison had made up their foursome growing up. As Dougie was a red-head too, people often though that he and Bella were related. Dougie, Rome, Bella and Eden had been inseparable when they were kids, going everywhere together. That was until Dougie had emigrated to New York with his family at the age of eighteen and Bella suspected he'd broken Eden's heart at the same time. He'd come over at least twice a year and they all kept in touch with him. She knew that Rome especially had a lot of contact with him. Bella talked to him quite a lot on Facebook and she saw Eden comment too, but she wasn't sure if they stayed in contact more than that.

'How is he?' Bella asked when Eden continued to focus an extraordinary amount of attention on a piece of pasta on the edge of her plate.

'Fine, really good,' Rome said. 'Though he just split up with his girlfriend.'

Eden's head snapped up. 'With Kirsten?'

'Yep. He said he liked her a lot but it wasn't love and he didn't see the point in continuing with it.'

Eden returned her attention to her lunch. 'Poor Kirsten.'

Rome shrugged. 'He probably did the girl a favour. There was no point in stringing her along if it was never going to lead anywhere. That connection is important. Some people only find that once in a lifetime. Most people will never have that twice.'

'And even when you do find it, it's not reciprocated,' Eden said, quietly, grabbing another chunk of garlic bread

Bella looked at her brother and sister. They were both victims of a broken heart though for completely different reasons. Eden had fallen in love with her best friend, only to have him leave before she could tell him how she felt, and Rome had never got over the death of his fiancée six years before. She didn't know what she could do to help them. Bella had never had that, though she knew it was because she never let anyone get that close to her to be able to have her heart broken.

Eden got up to refill the jug of water and Bella turned her attention to Rome. He was the least likely person to look for that connection with someone. He seemed to be with a different girl each week but the way he spoke about Dougie looking for love made her think that Rome was ready to make that change.

'Are you looking for love again?' Bella said, gently.

He stared at her for a moment and then resumed eating. She didn't think he was going to answer her.

'I'm not sure what I'm looking for if I'm honest, Bella. We are so alike in many ways; you protect your heart, never taking a risk with it. I've seen that and I know I'm doing the same. It's easier not making attachments; just having fun with someone who means nothing to you. Then we can never get hurt. But I miss that companionship that comes from being in a real relationship. Those long, stay-up-late-into-the-night conversations, laughing so hard with someone, the intimacy of making love to someone who means the world to you, of being with someone you know inside and out.'

Eden sat down and refilled all their glasses. 'Don't you have that with Freya? I mean not the making love part but you get on so well; I've seen you together and how hard you two make each other laugh.'

Rome smiled as he thought of her. 'Freya is brilliant fun, but she's a friend, nothing more.'

'It could be something more,' Bella said.

Rome shook his head. 'We work together; it would get awkward and messy if we broke up. And let's face it, my attention span when it comes to women isn't a good one.'

'That's because you don't go for the right women. I don't think the type of women that you date are ever going to be your forever,' Eden said.

'Dating someone from work is tricky though,' Bella agreed. 'I would never date someone from work again.'

'God yes, Andrew was a tit,' Eden said, vehemently.

Bella flushed as she nodded her agreement. It had been several years since she had given Andrew any thought but it had made her wary of making that same mistake again.

Working in an open-plan office of fifty people, everyone wanted to know the details when word had got out about her and Andrew's romance. Andrew loved being the centre of attention and he was quite happy to share all the details of their sex life to anyone who asked, including how noisy she was in the bedroom.

Utterly mortified, she had left her job vowing that she would never date someone from the workplace again.

'Though you and Freya wouldn't have the same problem I had. There's only you two so no one to interfere and ask you inappropriate questions about how it's going. That's mine and Eden's job.'

Rome smiled. 'But if it did end between us, we would lose that camaraderie that we have now. Going to work every day is fun because I get to spend it with her. I wouldn't want to lose that.'

Eden rolled her eyes and Rome saw.

'Will you be seeing Dougie while he's here?' he asked pointedly and the smile fell off Eden's face.

She shrugged and returned her attention to her plate.

Rome opened his mouth to push it but Bella shook her head at him.

God they were a messed-up bunch.

She picked up her water glass and held it aloft. 'A toast.'

Rome quirked an eyebrow at her and Eden looked up, clearly hopeful for the distraction.

'Spring is here, the flowers are growing, baby animals are being born, it's a season of new beginnings here on Hope Island and yet between the three of us we have no hope for a happy romantic future. So here is a toast to our own new beginnings. A pact. This year we are going to take risks, we are not going to dwell on our pasts or fear getting hurt. We shall say what we mean, tell those who we love how we feel, we're going to believe in wishes and magic and dreams coming true again,' she said, staring pointedly at Eden. 'And we are going to grab any chance of love and happiness with both hands.'

Her brother and sister stared at her for a moment, neither of them raising their own glass to join her.

Rome finally shrugged and picked up his glass, holding it in the air. 'What the hell.'

They both looked across at Eden and she picked up her glass. 'Here's to happiness in whatever form that might come in.'

It wasn't quite the promise from Rome and Eden that Bella was hoping for but as she didn't exactly hold out much hope for herself, she couldn't really complain.

They chinked the water glasses together, sealing the very tentative pact, and as Bella took a big swig of her water, for the first time in a long time she was looking forward to the possibilities of what spring and the rest of the year would bring.

The interview would be a new beginning for her and she couldn't wait to see how that would change her life for the better.

CHAPTER 5

Isaac had spent the whole of Sunday telling himself he wasn't going to go back and see Bella again. He had done some decorating in his house, repainting the whole of the lounge in order to try to distract himself from her. He'd taken Rocket, his spaniel, for a long walk and he was quite looking forward to spending the evening with a glass of wine and a good book.

But somehow here he was, standing outside Bella's house again, waiting for her to come home.

He'd thought perhaps he would come to her and explain the truth but what he wanted more than anything was another night of chatting to her, of things being wonderful between them. He was drawn to Bella in ways he just could not explain. His experience of dating other women just didn't compare. In London everyone knew who he was and how much he was worth. He never knew whether women were only after his money or whether they were really interested in him. Conversation was always stilted, and whether that was because he held himself back or because he didn't have anything in common with these women he didn't know, but Bella was different. She made him laugh, he could listen to her talk for hours and, despite knowing that he was getting way above his head, despite knowing that if she got the job he would be her boss and that would be all kinds of wrong, he just couldn't stay away from her.

He'd been waiting outside her house for over an hour, a sure sign that fate was telling him this was a bad idea. He'd go before she got home and she'd never know he was there.

He'd grabbed his bag and was just about to leave when Bella walked into her street. He would tell her. As soon as she got close he would tell her the truth. Her red hair gleamed like fire in the setting sun as she walked. She had a bounce to her step that she hadn't had the day before and he liked seeing the smile on her face. Could he really be the one to take that smile away from her?

Coward.

When she saw him her whole face lit up into a huge smile and before he knew what was happening she ran towards him, throwing her arms around him and hugging him tight. It was so unexpected that for a second he just stood there frozen. This was all kinds of wrong but he found her just so damned endearing. Without his consent, his arms wrapped themselves around her tiny frame and he found himself leaning into her, with his head on top of hers.

He was going straight to hell.

※❧❀❦⅏

'I'm so pleased you're here, I've been thinking about you all day. I even spent an hour tonight down on the docks hoping that you might be hanging around there if you weren't able to get a boat to St Mary's and I tried in the main high street too. And all this time you were up here waiting for me.'

She pulled back to look at him and he stared at her in bemusement.

God, why had she hugged him? She barely knew him. She had just been so happy to see him again and she had forgotten that they were still in the very early stages of their friendship. It felt like she had known him for months, not just one day.

She tried to take a step back but his arms were still locked around her.

'Sorry. I, er—'

'Don't be sorry. That was the best greeting I've ever had.'

She noticed Barbara from Sapphire Cottage walking slowly past them, a lot slower than her normal speed as she took in Bella and Isaac standing there with their arms wrapped around each other. She gave Bella a huge smile and what she clearly thought was a discreet thumbs-up and a wink before scurrying off to her house. Bella knew half the town would probably know before Bella had even got inside her own house and, considering the population of Hope Island was around one and a half thousand people, that was no mean feat.

Isaac released her with that gorgeous smile. 'Have you had a good day?'

'I saw my family and they strong-armed me into taking some food. As predicted Rome has bought me some steak. Two pieces actually so we can eat like kings tonight. I need to have a quick bath so my hair has time to dry before the interview tomorrow, but then we can eat after.' She walked to the door and he followed her. She let them both in. 'Did you have a good day?'

He hesitated before he spoke and she cursed herself. Stupid question. Zach was homeless and good days were probably few and far between.

'I couldn't get off the island.'

'I'm sorry… Well actually I'm not. I had a lovely night last night and I was really hoping I would see you again. And tonight you can have a decent meal and a warm place to sleep and tomorrow you can come with me to the Umbrella Foundation to see if they can help you.'

He followed her into the lounge but he didn't say anything for a moment as she went to fill the kettle up in the adjoining kitchen. A cup of tea was definitely in order; she hadn't had tea in a long time and she'd missed that.

'I don't think that's a good idea,' Zach said, quietly.

She filled the kettle with water and put it on to boil before she turned back to him.

'You know Isaac Scott?'

He stared at her.

'Your note said that I would hate him as soon as I saw him, so I'm guessing you know him to make that statement.'

He didn't speak for the longest time but eventually he spoke. 'He's a nice bloke, I think. But he's very protective over his charity. Some of his methods for ensuring he has the right person for the job are a little unorthodox. I don't think you will like them or agree with them.'

Well this was just sounding weirder and weirder. What on earth did Isaac Scott do in his interviews that she wouldn't like? Zach said he was a nice bloke so surely whatever Isaac did couldn't be that bad.

'How do you know him?'

He rubbed the back of his neck, awkwardly, and stared at the floor. 'I've known him forever.'

'And does he know you're homeless? Because if a friend of mine was in your situation I would do everything I could to help him. This Isaac doesn't sound that nice if he would leave you on the streets.'

'He doesn't know…' Zach trailed off. He looked so miserable about this conversation and so uncomfortable talking about it. 'Look Bella, I need to tell you something—'

'No, don't. I'm sorry, it isn't my place to pry. This is clearly a difficult subject for you and you don't want to talk about him so let's just leave it. How do you like your steak?'

She went to the fridge and pulled out the steaks. There was a lot more to this Isaac Scott than Zach was letting on but hopefully, one day, he would trust her to talk about it.

'Why don't I cook dinner for us?' Zach said, coming up behind her he took the packet from her but she could feel his heat all down her back and it made her breath catch in her throat. 'I make a mean steak. Do we have potatoes and cream? I could do dauphinoise potatoes to go with it.'

She turned to face him and he was standing so close, staring straight into her eyes. His were the most beautiful shade of blue, with deep tones of purple, indigo and that midnight blue of damsons.

She swallowed and she saw his eyes go to her lips for a second. 'There's cream in the fridge and potatoes in the cupboard next to the microwave.'

He nodded and stepped back out of her space. 'Why don't you go and have a bath or something and I'll have it all ready for you by the time you come back down.'

'OK. Thanks.'

He shrugged. 'It's the least I can do.'

She left him to it and went upstairs. It was a very weird feeling to hear him clattering about in the kitchen when she was used to silence. Though he did seem to be clattering with extra force than was necessary. That conversation about Isaac Scott had upset him and she didn't know why. There was so much to Zach that he wasn't telling her and she wanted to know everything there was about him.

She quickly had a bath and washed her hair, then plaited it and wrapped the plait around itself into a bun.

Bella thought about what she should wear. Normally after a bath, she would just get into her pyjamas but there was nothing sexy about them and while she doubted anything would happen between them that night, she liked seeing that look of desire in his eyes when he looked at her. She pulled her black satin robe on but that felt way too forward.

She padded out into her bedroom in her robe, determined to find something sweet, sexy, but not overly dressy to wear, when there was a knock on the bedroom door.

Crap.

She opened it slightly to see Zach standing there.

'The steak is ready, you should come eat it while it's hot.'

'Oh, let me just get dressed.'

His eyes cast down her appreciatively. 'You look perfectly respectable. Come on. It's just me and you. I hardly think you need to wear a ball gown for dinner.'

Bella laughed as he offered out his hand and she placed hers inside his warm strong paw.

They walked downstairs and though she had wanted him to appreciate what she was wearing, she was glad that the robe came down to the knee and was fastened up quite high round the neck because when Zach had looked her up and down it was the same look a ravenous lion would give to a deer.

There was a solitary white candle burning in the middle of the dining table and she was touched that Zach had made an effort.

He held out her chair for her as she sat down and she smiled at his impeccable manners.

The steak looked delicious and that gorgeous scent of garlic hit her nose as he sat down opposite her.

'This all looks wonderful, thank you.'

'A celebratory meal for when you get the job tomorrow,' Zach said, offering out a glass of wine.

She picked hers up and chinked it against his with a smile. 'Thank you. But apparently I have some hoops to jump through first.'

Zach put his glass down. 'Please don't be worried about tomorrow. I already know you're going to get this job. You're one of the most incredible people I've ever met and they will snap you up.'

'I'm not worried.' Bella took a sip of wine and let the bubbles dance over her tongue. 'Isaac Scott, if he turns up, and the rest of the panel will have to take me as I am. I'm certainly not going to pretend to be someone I'm not just so I get the job. What will be will be. I'm honest, hardworking and passionate about making a difference and if that's not good enough for them, or they don't want me just because I'm not wearing the right shoes, then there's nothing I can do to change that.'

Zach laughed. 'I fear I've given you a terrible impression of the charity and that's not what they're like at all. They are looking for someone special and, believe me, you tick every box.' He took a bite of his steak and sighed. 'Isaac was homeless himself for a short time when he was in his teens. He was basically adopted by a couple of people who lived on the streets who helped him and made sure he was looked after. So the charity is really important to him. Just bear that in mind when you see him tomorrow; that his passion for the charity comes from the heart.'

She stared at him. 'I didn't know.'

'He's very private.'

'You really do know him.'

'Yeah, and I'm questioning his life choices right about now,' he said, shaking his head. 'Look I'm sorry, I really am. I shouldn't have come here last night and I certainly shouldn't have come here a second time. I shouldn't be sitting here with you now like we're best friends and giving you all this completely ambiguous information. Please know that coming back here tonight was nothing more than me wanting to see you again and spend time in your company. But I should go. This was a mistake.'

He stood up to leave and Bella felt a slice of panic rip through her. 'Wait. Please don't go. I have no idea what's going on between you and Isaac Scott but I promise not to say anything more about it.'

He hovered.

'I really enjoyed your company last night too and I was really looking forward to another night talking to you. You've made this delicious steak, you should at least get to finish it. If you still want to leave after that, I won't stop you. I'm really sorry if I've upset you.'

He sat back down. 'You haven't upset me. Not at all. I'm more concerned about my actions upsetting you because that's the very last thing I want.'

'Well, you leaving would upset me, so how about you eat your steak and we can talk about something else?'

He nodded, a smirk fighting on his lips at her bossiness, and as she tucked into her steak she cast around for a more suitable topic.

❦

Isaac watched as Bella plonked herself down on the sofa next to him and poured some wine into their glasses. The steak had been finished a long time before and they had polished off most of the bottle of wine between them. They had moved to the sofa and the log fire was burning away quite merrily, casting a cosy glow over the room. Things were good and easy between them and – apart from that little blip earlier when he had ended up talking about himself in the third person – she hadn't suspected a thing.

He hated deceiving her like this but he had made a very selfish decision not to tell her the truth. He strongly suspected that if he told her now, she wouldn't show up for the interview at all and he needed her for this job. His company needed her. He wasn't sure how he was going to play it tomorrow. He had intended on sitting in on the interviews with all the candidates but maybe it would be best if he left it to the rest of the panel to conduct them or at the very least not sit in on Bella's interview. Then she wouldn't have to see him and wouldn't know who he was until she had agreed to do the job and turned up at her first day of work.

It was messy and complicated and he knew he only had himself to blame but it was important that he got Bella on board, someone with real passion for his charity, someone who could tackle the job of events manager with a breath of fresh air. He would take any anger from her when she found out as long as he could get her to work for him.

'Tell me what you wanted to do when you were a kid, what was the dream?' Bella asked him as she passed him his glass of wine.

He put it down on the coffee table; he needed a clear head because right now, with her sitting so close, her intoxicating scent swirling round him and a glass or two of wine inside him, it was taking a lot of willpower not to lean over and kiss her.

'That's easy,' Isaac said. 'I wanted to create computer games. I was an avid video game player when I was a child. There was one called *Dizzy* which was basically the adventures of an egg trying to solve puzzles, collect treasure and save his friends. It was a platform game and a really fun one but even as a child I kept thinking of ways I would make it better. Later I loved all the *Crash Bandicoot* ones, they were brilliant and I knew I wanted to create something like that. I went to university and learned about coding and how to design basic programs. And then I learned how to make those programs better and more convoluted. I loved it. It's funny though how life takes you in a completely different direction than the one you envisaged.'

She smiled sadly, taking his hand. 'This is a little bump in the road for you; you'll get back on your feet again.'

He smiled.

'I didn't mean this. I just meant that after university I never ended up working for the gaming industry as I thought I would. My skills at computer programming led me down a very different path.' This was getting too close to home and he knew he had to change the subject. 'What about you? What did you want to be?'

'A vet,' Bella said.

He couldn't help but smile. Of course that's what she'd wanted. She would always be someone who wanted to help others.

'Nursing sick animals and making them better appealed to me.'

'And what happened to that dream?'

'Oh I'm terrible around blood, makes me ill. I used to pass out in science lessons in school when we used to have to dissect animals. It obviously wasn't going to be my calling. Shame really as I've never been great with people. Much better with animals.'

He frowned. 'You're doing pretty well with me.'

'Oh, I'm much better now but as a child I wasn't great. After what happened with my parents I had trust issues and was afraid of letting people in. Still do in many ways. I end up pushing people away.'

'I don't see that at all. You're warm, happy, funny, achingly endearing, so kind, easy to talk to, engaging…' he trailed off as she was watching him with surprise. He brushed a red curl off her face. 'And beautiful,' his mouth said, without any consent from him.

She stared at him for a moment and then without warning she leaned forward and kissed him.

CHAPTER 6

Desire slammed into his stomach as soon as he tasted her on his lips and he immediately kissed her back. God she tasted so good, the scent of her was too much, overpowering his senses. He cupped the back of her head as she slid her hands down his arms. He pulled her against him; feeling her body next to his was incredible, and when she slid her tongue inside his mouth every rational thought went clean out of his mind.

He rolled her backwards onto the sofa so she was under him and she let out a little giggle against his lips before she continued kissing him. It was a wonderful sound. He realised her robe had come slightly undone and he slid it open the rest of the way. He ran his hand over her body and she moaned against his lips. She felt so divine, so soft and smooth and warm.

Isaac ran his hand over her breast and a breathy gasp escaped her lips. He pulled back slightly to make sure she was OK and realised that under the robe she was completely naked. Her skin was pale and her hair looked like fire as it escaped the plait on her head and tumbled over her shoulders. She looked so beautiful and he could see from the desire in her eyes that she wanted this as much as he did.

He kissed her again and she wrapped her arms around him, kissing him with an urgency that he was feeling too. He ran his hand up her inner thigh, moving his mouth to her neck.

'Oh god, Zach,' she moaned and he froze.

Zach. That's who she was kissing. The homeless guy she had been kind enough to help, to offer a bed and food to. She certainly hadn't offered this and now with half a bottle of wine inside her he was clearly taking advantage. There was no way he could sleep with her or kiss her when she had no idea who he was – and there was no way he should be kissing her and groping her when in less than twenty-four hours he could be her boss.

He leapt off her so fast that he tumbled over the coffee table and hit the floor.

'I can't do this, I'm sorry.'

Rejection washed across her face and she quickly pulled her robe together. 'I'm sorry, I shouldn't have kissed you.'

He got up quickly. 'This isn't about you, please don't think it is. This is about me being a complete and utter arsehole. This is wrong for so many reasons I couldn't even begin to list them, but not one of them has anything to do with you. And it definitely isn't about me not wanting you, I can assure you that isn't the case.'

She stood up too. 'Then what's wrong?'

'You've been drinking,' he said, grasping at straws.

'So? I'm not drunk or half unconscious. I'm pretty sure I could still walk in a straight line.'

'You have no idea who I am,' Isaac said. He ran his hands through his hair. Christ, what a mess.

'I know enough.'

'I need to go, I'm sorry, I really am.'

He walked out into the hall and he heard her bare feet follow him. 'Zach, wait. Talk to me, please. Tell me what's wrong.'

He turned back so he could see her looking at him with affection one more time, rather than the anger and hate he'd no doubt see the next day, and then he grabbed his bag and walked out, closing the door behind him.

He walked out of her gate and then sank to the floor against her wall. What the hell was he doing? And what was he going to do now?

Bella stared at the front door feeling utterly confused. They had eaten and talked and laughed, and though he had got a bit uncomfortable talking about Isaac Scott, once they had moved on from that subject things had been good and wonderful and easy between them. And his kiss. It was like nothing she had ever felt before. It was quite obvious that he wanted to kiss her too. So why had he run off?

She peered out the window by the door and saw him sitting outside her garden wall with his head in his hands.

She needed to talk to him because if she let him walk away now she was scared she'd never see him again.

She ran upstairs to get changed, pulled some jeans on and, just as she was pulling a t-shirt over her head, she heard voices outside. She peered outside her bedroom window and saw there was a gang of boys hassling Zach.

She rolled her eyes. There was a little alleyway between two of the houses a few doors down that led to the fields and a lot of the kids from the island would hang out there after dark and some of them would use the alley as a cut through. Most of the time the kids never caused any trouble but sometimes they were a bit loud and if she bumped into them when they had been drinking they were sometimes a little lewd or lairy but they never touched her and she felt more annoyed by them than intimidated. They were only kids after all.

She pulled on her Converse and marched downstairs to tell them to clear off.

She opened the door and saw they were all huddled around Zach laughing and jeering at him. Zach could more than take care of himself but she wouldn't stand around while they hassled him like that. As one nudged Zach with his foot, she stormed out the gate.

'Hey, sod off, all of you.'

'Oooh, need your girlfriend to fight your battles, do you?' one tall, lanky boy said.

'Bella's so desperate for a shag that she'd pick a guy up off the streets.'

'Hey,' Bella said indignantly. That was too close to home.

'I told you she needed a good seeing to,' sniggered one of the boys that Bella recognised.

Zach stood up and he looked so angry that Bella suddenly feared for the boys' safety. Time to nip this in the bud now.

'And you'd be the one to give it to me, would you Frankie? I don't think so. Your mum would ground you for a year if she heard you speaking like that. Now clear off before I give her a call.'

Frankie flushed and the other boys jeered at him.

Another boy suddenly grabbed Zach's bag. 'What's in here?' the boy asked, clearly a little bit drunk.

Bella grabbed the strap and tried to snatch it back but the other boy tugged it towards him.

'Let it go now,' Zach said, towering over the boy, and as Bella gave it an almighty tug, the boy let it go and she tumbled sideways, her forehead slamming into the brick wall. She bounced off it and hit the floor and a sudden wooziness engulfed her.

The boys ran, disappearing up the alley within seconds as Zach knelt down by her side, putting his arm around her.

'Bella, are you OK? Christ you're bleeding.'

She felt sick and dizzy and she didn't know if she was going to pass out or throw up or both.

Zach scooped her up into his arms as if she weighed nothing and carried her back into the house. He laid her gently on the sofa and ran off to the kitchen and after that she wasn't really aware of anything else.

❦

Bella opened her eyes and realised she was in a hospital bed with Zach sitting next to her holding her hand.

He immediately sat forward when he saw she was awake. 'Are you OK?'

She blinked as she stared at him. She had vague recollections of what had happened since she banged her head, as she'd drifted in and out of consciousness. She remembered Zach carrying her into a taxi which whizzed them down to the harbour and she remembered Zach carrying her onto a boat. But not the ferry, a small power boat which Zach drove himself while she lay on a plush white leather seat at the back. She recalled that Zach had then carried her to a car which he had driven to the hospital and then it all got a bit grey again after that.

She tried to sit up but Zach pushed her back down. 'Don't try to get up, just rest.'

'My head hurts,' Bella muttered feebly.

'I'm not surprised, you face-planted a wall. What were you thinking? I didn't need you to run out and defend me. They were kids and have you seen the size of me?'

Bella closed her eyes, trying to make sense of everything that happened. She looked over at Zach again. 'You stole a boat? And a car?'

She watched his cheeks colour and she groaned. 'Oh no, Zach, you're going to get in so much trouble.'

'I didn't steal the boat or the car, they're mine.'

Bella stared at him. She still felt really woozy. 'I don't understand. You own a boat and car? But you're homeless? Are you the richest homeless person in the world?'

She let out a little giggle at the ridiculousness of the situation but that made her brain wobble inside her head.

'I'm not homeless.'

She tried to focus on him but she felt like she was drunk. 'You're not making any sense.'

'I know I'm not, I'm sorry,' Zach said. 'I've not been truthful with you.'

Bella closed her eyes again.

'Hey Bella, stay with me OK, just open your eyes.'

She forced her eyes open for a second or two to look at him. 'You lied?'

'Yes, about everything.'

She didn't understand but a wave of disappointment washed over her. 'The kiss was a lie?'

'God no, that was definitely not a lie.'

'When you said that you enjoyed spending time with me and came back to my house tonight just so you could see me. You lied about that?'

'No, that wasn't a lie either. I really did want to see you.'

'So what did you lie about?'

'Pretty much everything else. My name isn't even Zach.'

She felt her eyes widen in horror. When he'd said that she didn't know him, he'd been speaking the truth. She had no idea who he really was and yet she'd kissed him, let him undress her and touch her. She felt suddenly really ashamed.

She closed her eyes again and this time when unconsciousness crept up on her, she didn't even fight it.

CHAPTER 7

Isaac watched Bella as she dozed, the early morning sunshine flooding through the window. He had to get back for the interview but he didn't want to leave her. Though the doctors had reassured him that she was fine, he wanted to make sure of that for himself and more than anything he wanted to clear the air between them, explain to her why he'd done what he'd done.

They hadn't spoken since his half-hearted confession the night before and he strongly suspected she was only pretending to be asleep. She had seemed to come round again an hour or so later but she had closed her eyes again and rolled over away from him.

His phone vibrated in his pocket and he pulled it out to have a look. It was a text message from his PA to say that his assistant manager had called in sick. Amanda lived in Cornwall and it was a long way to come if she wasn't feeling well. If he stayed here and didn't go to the interview that would only leave Madge and Eric on the panel and he didn't trust either of them to choose the best person for the job.

Crap.

He'd have to go. And the worst thing was, the person he really wanted for the job would no longer be able to come to the interview. The only way round it would be not to appoint at the interview today and then re-advertise the position a few weeks down the line and hope she applied for it again. But if she found out who he was before then, there was no way she would apply. What a complete mess and it was totally of his making too.

A nurse he'd met several times already since their arrival at the hospital came into the room and fussed around Bella for a minute or two, checking her pulse and the monitors, but Bella didn't respond to her either.

'Are you sure she's OK?' Isaac asked.

'She's fine, she'll have a headache for a few days and some soreness and bruising but she just needs some rest. There's absolutely no reason for you to worry.'

Isaac nodded and looked at his watch. Damn it, he really needed to go. He stood up and leaned over Bella, placing a kiss on her cheek. 'I have to go,' he whispered. 'I'm sorry. About everything.'

She didn't move, though he did see her eyelashes flutter ever so slightly.

He hesitated for a moment but when there was still no response, he moved to go.

'Will you keep her in overnight tonight?'

The nurse shook her head. 'I imagine she'll be here for most of the day, but that the doctor will discharge her early evening.'

He looked at his watch. The interviews would probably take until lunch. 'Can you tell her that I'm really sorry that I had to go but that I'll be back this afternoon?'

The nurse nodded and he left.

What the hell was he going to do now?

❦

'He's gone,' the nurse said. 'You can stop pretending you're asleep now.'

Bella opened her eyes and surreptitiously checked the room then rolled onto her back and the nurse helped her to sit up. Her back ached and she felt stiff. Her head was sore but the wooziness was mostly gone. 'How did you know I was awake?'

'Honey, I've been doing this job for nearly thirty years. I'm pretty good at spotting the signs. Did you and your boyfriend have a row?'

'He's not my boyfriend.'

'Relative? Friend?'

'No. I have no idea who he is,' Bella said, sadly, realising that was the truth.

'Well he seemed to be very concerned about you for someone you don't know.'

Bella stared at a poster on the wall without really seeing it. They had talked so much over the last two nights. They had a connection that was so real, something that she'd never felt with any other man before, and she refused to believe that all of that was a lie.

Her memory from the night before was still groggy but she was pretty sure that he'd said that the car and the boat was his, that he wasn't homeless and that his name wasn't even Zach. Had she imagined all of that? Perhaps she should have talked to him instead of pretending that she was asleep. But if what he'd said was true then she felt so let down that he had lied to her and, even worse, disappointed in herself for trusting someone again.

Suddenly a thought struck her. 'What time is it?'

The nurse checked her watch. 'Quarter past nine.'

Bella gasped. She had to be at the Umbrella Foundation at ten. She was still in her clothes from the night before which were covered in dirt and blood. If she left the hospital now she might be able to get the nine thirty ferry which would get her into Hope Island around quarter to ten. The Umbrella Foundation was about a ten-minute walk from where the ferry came in so she could make it on time but there was no time to go home and get changed. Damn it. Though turning up in blood-covered clothes was at least better than not turning up at all or turning up late. Another idea came to her. Her aunt Cassie's charity shop was near the harbour. She might have something that was semi-respectable for an interview. Although, knowing her aunt's sense of fashion and what she liked to display in the shop, it was more likely to be something from the seventies than anything modern, but it would have to do.

She threw the sheets back and stood up. 'I need to go.'

'Oh no you don't, young lady, the doctor has to discharge you,' the nurse said, folding her arms in disapproval.

'I'll discharge myself. I take full responsibility for my actions. But as you already told...' she waved her hand at Zach's chair '... my friend, there's absolutely nothing to worry about, I think I'll be fine.'

The nurse glared at her but what was she going to do, manhandle her back into bed and tie her to it?

The woman shook her head with annoyance. 'I'll get you the form.'

Bella nodded and waited for her to leave the room. She looked around the room: no coat, no bag, she couldn't even clean her teeth. None of it mattered though, if she could just get to the Umbrella Foundation in time, then she at least would have tried her best.

Without waiting for the nurse to come back with the discharge form and her disapproving glares, she opened the door and peered out. When she could see the corridor was clear, she ran down it, down the stairs and outside, and then out onto the street.

She had fifteen minutes to get to the quay which she knew was about ten minutes away but how much time had she lost getting out of the hospital?

She ran as fast as she could and just hoped it would be enough.

Bella made it just as Bob was untying the ropes of the ferry and she waved and shouted like mad as she ran down the jetty. Bob smiled at her and held out a hand to help her aboard which she gladly took.

'I haven't got my pass or my purse or any money, I'm going to have to owe you,' Bella said, panting for breath.

Bob frowned. 'What happened to your face?'

'I fell, I'm fine. Can I pay you back tomorrow?'

Bob waved away her concerns as he went off to drive the boat. She sat down relieved and looked up at the clock. The boat was leaving two minutes late. This wasn't good at all.

She looked around. Although there were a few tourists on the boat heading over to enjoy the delights of Hope Island, most of the passengers were people she knew either from her time working on St Mary's or because they lived on Hope Island.

'Bella, dear, what happened?' Alexandra from the fish shop sat down next to her with concern.

Before Bella could answer, Molly who had worked in the shop opposite Magic Wishes on St Mary's, leaned forward to look at her. 'Someone probably punched her for stealing all their money.'

Alexandra clearly took great offence at that, pulling herself up to her full height. 'I don't think that's appropriate or at all accurate.'

'Should be ashamed of herself,' chimed in Nora, who Bella knew worked on St Mary's but lived on Hope Island.

Alexandra looked shocked. 'I'll have you know—'

Bella rested a hand on hers to stop Alexandra fighting her battles for her. She was used to this and, while it didn't happen that often on Hope Island, she knew a lot of people felt this way.

'It's OK, Alexandra. People will believe what they want to believe. And I'm not ashamed, not in the slightest, as I had nothing to do with the embezzlement at Magic Wishes. If people want to waste their energy being bitter and angry with me over something I didn't do, then let them get on with it.'

Molly and Nora fell silent though Bella knew she had done nothing to change their minds.

Alexandra nodded and then gestured to her injuries. 'Are you OK?'

'I just fell, I'm fine,' Bella reassured her.

Elizabeth, the lady sitting on the other side of Alexandra, leaned forward. 'Don't you have that interview at the Umbrella Foundation this morning?'

Bella blinked. Was there really nothing more exciting going on in Hope Island that meant that her applying for a new job wasn't a hot topic of conversation? It wasn't exactly a secret but she would prefer some of the islanders not to know in case it somehow prejudiced those in charge at the Umbrella Foundation before she'd even walked through the doors.

She cleared her throat. 'Yes, sadly in about twenty minutes.'

Elizabeth regarded Bella's clothing and then took off her scarf. 'Why don't you use this to cover up some of the blood?'

'Thank you, that's very kind, but I'm going to my aunt Cassie's shop to see if she can lend me something. I don't think your scarf will be enough to cover up my jeans and Converse trainers too.'

Elizabeth pulled a face. 'Child, there is nothing in that shop that is anywhere near suitable for an interview. Take the scarf, just in case.'

Bella took it, wondering if it was large enough to wrap around her whole body because she knew in her heart that Elizabeth was right. 'Thank you.'

They arrived at the dock and Bella jumped ashore before Bob had even tied the boat up, giving him a wave as he shook his head fondly at her.

She ran out of the harbour and burst into her aunt's charity shop. Everyone stopped to look at her, some of them tutting at her behaviour.

Her aunt Cassie came running towards her, clearly concerned. Cassie was Finn's sister and, never having had children of her own, she had taken to spoiling her nieces and nephew with great abundance. It was just a shame that a lot of her generosity was passing on some of the more ghastly donations that landed in the shop.

'Bella, what happened to your head, are you OK?'

'I'm fine Cassie, I fell. I've been at the hospital, they've stitched me back up, they said I was fine,' Bella lied. 'I need your help. I have an interview in ten minutes and I've just got back from St

Mary's. I haven't got time to go home and change, do you have anything smart that might fit me?'

Cassie looked her up and down and then bustled off to one of the rails. 'I don't really stock suits.'

Bella looked around the shop, which was full of a mishmash of old paintings, chipped and stained crockery, ugly vases, and even a dead stuffed squirrel, perched on a branch that was propped up against a metallic painting of Jesus. There were some clothes, but all of them were garish, hideous and probably had never been in fashion even when they were made.

'A dress maybe,' Bella said desperately. 'I just need anything that's smart and that fits me.'

'Well that's the problem, dear, you're so tiny. Oh, I have something that's just come in.'

'I'll take anything…' She looked down at her red Converse. 'And I'll need some shoes too.'

Cassie disappeared out into the stock room and Bella looked around the shop, hoping that a nice black suit would grab her attention. Even if it was a few sizes too big, it would have to do.

'I have this,' Cassie said, as she came out the store room, holding a bridesmaid dress with large puffy sleeves that was bright neon green in colour. It was so bright, it actually hurt Bella's eyes and could almost be classed as hi-vis. If she had been working as road maintenance she would have been visible from miles away wearing this. Cassie turned it round so Bella could see the back, which had the world's biggest bow over the bottom.

'Do you have anything else?' Bella said, looking down at her own clothes and wondering if the blood and mud would be better than the green monstrosity.

'I can check,' Cassie said, doubtfully.

Bella looked up at the clock over the till that was made entirely of knives and forks. She had five minutes to get there and she knew it would take her ten minutes to walk.

'I'll take it,' Bella said. 'I'll get changed here, if that's OK. And can I pay you back tomorrow?'

'Consider it a gift,' Cassie said smiling. Bella couldn't think of a more horrible gift but she hugged her aunt anyway as she went into the changing room and threw it on.

'What size shoe are you, Bella?' Cassie asked through the curtain.

'Four,' Bella called, as she tugged up the zip at the back.

She looked at herself in the mirror, realising that the dress was perhaps even more hideous now it was on than it had been on the hanger. But there was no time to find anything else.

She pulled back the curtains as her aunt offered her a pair of bright pink stilettos. 'Sorry, it was these or the walking boots.'

Bella forced on a smile and took the shoes, placing a kiss on Cassie's cheek.

'Thank you, I owe you.'

Leaving her Converse on for now, and with the shoes in one hand and the bottom of the dress in the other, Bella set off at a run for the Umbrella Foundation.

Isaac adjusted his tie in the mirror. He'd had enough time to throw on his spare suit that he kept in his office before he had to go out and address the people that had arrived for the interview. Quite a few of those waiting in the foyer would not be coming into the interview stage. He would always try to 'visit' potential candidates in his homeless disguise before they were invited in for an interview in order to whittle down the candidates, but occasionally he couldn't get round to them all before the interview letters were sent out. He'd had to visit five of them after they had been invited to interview, including Bella. Normally he would go through the motions of interviewing them anyway as he didn't want to be seen to be wasting anyone's time. But today he didn't want to waste his own time like that. He wanted to get back to the hospital, make sure that Bella was OK and explain everything to her.

He straightened his jacket and stepped outside where his PA, Claudia, was waiting. Ever efficient, she handed him the list, although he already knew the names of the people he wanted to interview in his head.

He took the lift down to the foyer and as soon as he stepped out the buzz and chatter of the candidates died down.

'Ladies and gentlemen, thank you for coming today. I'm—'

Just then the front door burst open and there stood Bella, dressed in a floor-length neon green dress that might have been a bridesmaid dress at one point or a really bad eighties ball gown. Her hair was a tangle of curls, she was sweaty and panting, but he'd never seen anything so beautiful and welcome in all his life. She looked around but didn't see him. Unfortunately, his gaze on her drew all the attention of the candidates on her as well and some of them stifled giggles at her outfit.

She bent down and removed her red Converse trainers and pulled on some Barbie pink heels, giving everyone in the room an eyeful of her ample breasts as she did so.

He cleared his throat to divert everyone's attention back on him and as he addressed the crowd he saw Bella look over in his direction too. He didn't dare look at her but here was his chance to explain to her.

'Thank you all for coming. I'm Isaac Scott, CEO of the Umbrella Foundation. The charity is very important to me and whenever a paid position comes up in the company I always like to make sure we have the absolute best person for the job.'

He saw Bella stepping closer and he glanced at her very briefly. Her eyes were wide and her mouth had fallen open as if she was in a cartoon. He looked away and carried on.

'Compassion for the homeless is integral to everything we do, so that is why I visited you all over the last few weeks, in disguise, to see how you would react to having a homeless person outside your own home.' There were a few gasps of shock from the candidates. 'Many of you here acted as I would hope, offering me money, food, blankets, even in one case a bed for the night.' He locked eyes with Bella but the shocked expression had now faded and in its place was pure anger. 'Some of you, sadly, did not pass this first test and as such I can't progress your application to the interview stage. I'm very sorry for wasting your time. If I do not call your name out now, you are free to go and I will of course reimburse you for your time and any expenses occurred coming here today. You just need to speak to my PA, Claudia, and she will make sure you are not out of pocket. If I call your name now, you can come with me to the waiting area where we have teas, coffees and pastries for you while you wait for your turn to be interviewed.'

He ran down his list of successful candidates, making sure that Bella's name was called out too. He looked over to her one more time, trying to convey in that single look how sorry he was before he walked over to the door that led to the waiting room. There was an angry buzz from the people that were not successful but he'd let Claudia deal with that. She was calm and polite and, once they were all reimbursed, he imagined they would all go away.

He held the door open for his candidates, greeting them politely, telling them all to make themselves comfortable, taking on the comments from them about how they had no idea they were being tested when he'd visited them, but all he could think about was what he would say to Bella when she walked into the room, or what she would say to him. However, as the last person walked into the room and helped themselves to a pastry, Bella was conspicuous by her absence. He briefly checked the room again but he knew that he wouldn't have missed her walking in, her or that dress. He looked back out into the foyer where the unsuccessful candidates were still gathered around Claudia but there was no sign of Bella anywhere. He moved back out fully into the foyer and cast around for her desperately but she was nowhere to be seen. She had gone.

CHAPTER 8

Bella stormed up the street, anger and hate boiling through her veins. He'd made a fool out of her. She had trusted him, she had let him into her home and she had opened her heart to him. She had told him everything, from her parents abandoning her to her childhood dreams, and in return he had lied to her. It had all been part of a test.

She'd seen him naked and – god – he had seen her naked too. Her cheeks were burning with shame.

As the kids who had hassled Zach… Isaac … the night before, had said, was she really that desperate for company and for love that she would let the first person who showed her any interest sleep with her?

No, there had been a connection there; that was what she had fallen for. She shook her head. No, she had absolutely not fallen for the asshole that was Isaac Scott.

'Bella, wait.'

His voice from behind her made the anger bubble over into a furious rage and she rounded on him, trying to hit everywhere she could reach but he captured her hands and held her close.

'I'm sorry, listen—'

'Get your hands off me. If you don't let me go in five seconds I will slap a sexual harassment lawsuit on you and your company so fast you won't know what hit you.'

'Bella, please—'

'Four.'

'Let me explain—'

'Three.'

He let her go and she stormed away from him again. He caught up with her, snagging her arm, but she flinched away from him.

'You can stick your job, I don't want it,' Bella said, angry that tears had filled her eyes. God her head was pounding, her feet were killing her in these stupid shoes and after all the running, she just wanted to sit down and have five minutes to catch her breath and now this. This job had been perfect for her in every way and now it was tainted by the cretin that she had let into her home.

'I'm sorry. I really am. This charity is so important to me and I've always tested the potential employees like this. I never saw anything wrong with doing it before. Until I met you.'

'I shared my last bit of porridge with you. You saw I had no food and you took my last meal.'

'I know, I felt bad about that.'

She stared at him in shock. He felt bad about it? Was that all he had to say?

She stepped closer to him and jabbed a finger into his chest.

'Less than twenty-four hours ago, you had your hands on my breasts, your fingers between my thighs,' she swallowed down the shame, tears burning the back of her throat. 'And I let you, I let you touch me because… because I thought that what we had was real, and genuine, and none of it was.'

'The kiss was real, Bella, I promise you that.'

'Is that how you test all your future employees, see if they will go to bed with you? I couldn't help but notice how many beautiful women were on your roll call of candidates in there. Is that how you operate? Employ people that you can sleep with any time you want? And then what? If I sleep with you I'll get promotions and bonuses? Well if that's part of the job offer you can stick the job where the sun don't shine.'

'I can assure you that nothing has ever happened between me and my employees.'

'Of course you'd say that. You've probably slept with most of them. Everyone speaks so highly of you but it's all a lie, isn't it? You sleazy, disgusting—'

'Why do you think people speak so highly of me and my companies? Why do you think so many people want to work for me? Why do you think I had over fifty people apply for this job on a tiny island on the furthest reaches of Cornwall? My companies have an excellent reputation because of the people that work there – and that includes me. If I was sleeping with all my staff, there would be rumours, allegations, complaints against me and you won't find a single one, either online or if you speak to any member of my team. Don't mix business and pleasure is the one rule I always stick to and I know with you it was definitely more about pleasure, but believe me when I say you are the only exception to that rule. If you were to take the job it would be strictly professional between us.'

'Oh I can assure you of that too because if you ever touch me again, you will lose your hand.' She shook her head and took a step away from him. 'After what happened with my last job, I swore to myself that I wouldn't trust people so easily. But yesterday afternoon, over lunch with my brother and sister, I promised myself that I wouldn't guard my heart so fiercely, that I would take risks and if there was a chance of love then I would take it. What a completely gullible idiot I am.'

He had the good grace to look embarrassed and she walked away.

'Bella, please.' Isaac caught up with her. 'I know what I did was wrong and I wanted to tell you the truth, but… Every woman I meet looks at me with pound signs in their eyes. For a while I got to be someone else, someone you talked to without any ulterior motive. It's been a long time since I've had such a genuine conversation with someone. You had no idea who I was and I enjoyed being Zach. We were getting on so well and I was really enjoying your company. I've never had that connection with anyone before. I didn't want to break that spell between us. Last night I honestly came over to tell you the truth but then I selfishly decided it would be best not to.'

'It would be best not to? You thought you'd just let me carry on pouring out my heart to you without once offering me an ounce of truth in return?'

'I want you for this job. You have so much passion for it. You are experienced and you really care. I have never met anyone as wonderful as you. This charity is close to my heart and it's so important for me that I get the right person for this job and I know that person is you. This job was made for you and I want you here working for me.'

She stopped and stared at him. If she took the job, how often would she see Isaac Scott anyway? His other companies were in London, he'd be away a lot. As fundraising events manager she'd probably have very little to do with the CEO of the charity. God she wanted this job. Not just for the money but because she *was* perfect for it. Isaac Scott was a complete and utter arsehole but she wasn't going to let him spoil this for her.

'Come on Bella, don't make me beg.'

She smiled triumphantly. Time for a little payback. 'No, I'm going to make you beg for it.'

His eyes widened and then he cleared his throat. 'Please Bella, I beg you—'

'No, on your knees.'

'You're kidding.'

Bella walked off, wondering just how badly he wanted her. He had humiliated her and now it was his turn.

'Bella, wait!'

She turned round to see Isaac getting down onto his knees. The floor was damp from the light rain they'd had the night before and she got some satisfaction from knowing when he got up he'd have damp patches on his knees. 'Bella, I'm begging you, please will you come in for the interview.'

She walked back towards him. 'You'll get me some water, some paracetamols, some mints and a hair tie.'

He stood back up, nodding at the conditions.

'And you'll explain to the rest of the panel why I'm dressed like an eighties reject and why I look like the bride of Frankenstein's monster.'

'Yes of course.'

His eyes went to the cut on her head and he reached out to sweep her hair away from it but she slapped his hand away. 'And you'll never touch me again.'

She saw the brief flash of disappointment cross his face before he nodded again.

'Then I'll come for the interview. Though I'm still not sure if I'll accept the job.' She stormed past him. 'And there better be some bloody pastries left by the time I get there.'

'I'll personally go and get some more if there isn't.'

Bella suppressed her smirk and walked back into the building.

❦

Isaac rested his head against the desk for a moment and banged it a few times as he groaned, 'They're all idiots.' They had interviewed seven applicants so far and none reached his high standards. He was trying to decide if that was because none was Bella or just because they really were all idiots.

He sat up and watched Madge toss another application form into the bin which for dramatic purposes worked, but he knew he'd have to fish the application forms out of the bin later to give to Claudia so she could contact the unlucky applicants and let them know they had been unsuccessful.

'They aren't all bad,' Eric said. 'That Charlotte seemed to have her wits about her.'

Isaac looked at Eric in surprise. The guy was a dick. As HR manager, he seemed to do a good job in dealing with any staff issues, training and staff development. People were happy working for the charity, not just in this office but in the other three offices around the UK, and he knew Eric had a huge part to play in that. But his recruitment abilities were shocking, which was why Isaac had resorted to testing new employees in his unorthodox way. Several people had secured jobs with the charity just so they could get to Isaac and his other companies and he also strongly suspected that several of the girls who had been employed by Eric in the past had got in on looks alone.

Charlotte was beautiful, there was no denying that. But she lacked any kind of real events management skills and the experience she had referred to in her application had turned out to mean she had arranged a sale of her knitted stuffed animals and a sponsored walk in her last job, but nothing on a bigger scale. She had failed to answer many of the questions coherently and, although she seemed very nice, she was clearly on another planet, one that probably had fluffy puppies gambolling through flowers on a daily basis.

'The girl had candyfloss for brains,' Madge said, succinctly.

'And when I've asked them what plans they have for fundraising events for the charity, every single one of them said cake sales,' Isaac said, with some annoyance.

'That's not true,' Madge said, dryly. 'Angela suggested a coffee morning where they would sell tea, coffee and cakes.'

Isaac smirked and nodded to concede that. He liked Madge. He had no idea how old she was as she always looked ultra-smart and glamorous but he suspected she should have retired a long time ago.

'And Matthew suggested a sponsored dog walk *and* a cake sale,' Madge said, throwing another application form in the bin.

While Eric would employ anyone pretty if it meant he could go to lunch early, Madge was at the complete opposite end of the spectrum, always finding fault in everyone. She did a lot of the admin for the charity but somehow she always seemed to be involved in the recruitment process. Isaac didn't dare say no to her but not a lot of people would meet her impossibly high standards.

'Who's next?' Madge said.

'Bella Roussel,' Isaac said.

Eric groaned. 'How on earth did she get selected for the interview process? I rejected her application myself.'

'And why was that?' Isaac said as he imagined picking up the thick pile of application forms, rolling them up into some kind of baton and smacking Eric round the face with them.

'All that business with her charity embezzling funds. That's not the kind of person we want working for us.'

'Firstly, Magic Wishes was not her charity, she merely worked for them. She was investigated and cleared of all charges. Secondly, we are a charity that believes in second chances, that's what we promote with the homeless people we work with. As you know, it's not just about giving them food and clothes but about giving them work and a second chance in life. We don't judge them on the life they led before but the people they are now, so we should have that same ethos with our own staff and not be judgemental about stuff that happened to her in the past. Her application was outstanding and I decided to judge her on that. Thirdly, having spent time with her when I was in disguise this weekend, I have absolutely no doubt that she is telling the truth when she says that she didn't know about or have anything to do with the embezzlement. She is a remarkable woman and I think she would be perfect for this job.'

'You've already made your mind up?' Madge sniffed her disapproval.

'No,' Isaac lied. 'I want to see her in this interview and compare her fairly to the other applicants and I will make my decision at the end of the day, but yes, from what I've seen so far, I'm impressed. Now last night while I was in disguise, there were some kids that started giving me a hard time and Bella came to my defence, which resulted in her head-butting a wall.'

Madge gasped. 'They attacked her?'

'No, she grabbed the bag they were trying to take from me and when they let it go she went flying. She was in hospital last night in St Mary's and she didn't have time to go home and change before the interview so I believe she ended up trying to get something smart from the charity shop near the harbour.'

'Oh no, not that animal charity shop? There's nothing in there from this century and probably not anything from the last century either. What on earth did she find that was suitable to wear in there?' Madge said.

'Well, I don't think suitable is the word I'd use to describe what she is wearing but don't judge her on it. Her face is a bit bruised and cut up too.'

'Well, go and get her then,' Madge said, looking through Bella's application form. 'Let's see how much your golden girl shines.'

From that tone of voice, Isaac didn't think she was going to be impressed by anyone today but he got up and went to the door.

Bella was sitting at one end of the waiting room and the other applicants were gathered at the other, as if they didn't want to be associated with her and her hideous green dress. She didn't seem that bothered though as she was curled up in an armchair, having kicked off her pink stilettos, reading a battered book that had obviously been abandoned in the room along with a few magazines.

'Miss Roussel,' he said and she looked up at him in confusion as he had clearly torn her from the world she had been immersed in. Her vivid clover green eyes blinked a few times before she remembered she was still mad at him and her face set into a furious scowl again. 'We're ready for you now.'

She stood up, grabbing a leaflet off the table to mark her place in the book, and then slipped her feet back into the stilettos and followed him into the office. He closed the door behind her. He saw Madge and Eric stare at her in shock as he introduced everyone.

He sat down and Bella sat in the chair opposite him but as she did so her dress slid down, exposing one of her breasts almost entirely. The dark areola around her left nipple was just poking out over the top of the dress. Thankfully the nipple was still hidden but it was only millimetres away from making an entrance too. As the puffy sleeves of the dress were fitted over the arms not the shoulders, he guessed she had been unable to wear a bra with it, although to be honest visible bra straps would have been the least offensive thing in this outfit. She crossed her legs and the dress slipped fractionally lower; clearly she had no idea.

He glanced over at Eric whose eyes were firmly on Bella's assets, willing the dress to continue on its southbound journey, and Madge, who was sucking her lips together so tightly with disapproval that they'd practically vanished. Madge was firmly of the belief that women should not use their bodies to advance their careers and this accidental sexual provocation on Bella's part was not going to go down well.

He tried to catch Bella's eye to tell her but she was resolutely not looking at him. He cleared his throat but she didn't even spare him a glance.

'Miss Roussel,' he said, hoping that at least would grab her attention, but she continued to focus on Madge and Eric. 'Why did you apply for this job?'

She would look at him, she'd have to if she was going to answer the question properly. Interview rules 101, always make eye contact with the interviewer.

She forced herself to look at him for a second before she went back to addressing the rest of the panel with her answer. 'I want to help people…'

He started making gestures with his hand, trying to attract her attention as subtly as he could, but she was still talking and what she was saying was the corporate line she had given him the other night about making a difference. Though he knew it was from the heart, he also knew that Eric and Madge would be less than impressed by it. He had to stop her but if he caught her attention for a few seconds should he tell her about her exposed breasts or try to get her to open up more with a personal answer? He knew he wouldn't have time for both before she looked away again.

He coughed loudly and she looked at him and he made a snap decision. 'From the heart,' he mouthed, pointing to his heart.

She paused mid-sentence as if she understood perfectly what he was trying to tell her. But before he could warn her of her impending exposure she looked away again. She shifted in her chair, obviously feeling uncomfortable about what she was going to say, and as she did so her nipple peeked out over the top of the dress.

Crap.

'I know what it's like to need help,' Bella said. 'I had a difficult childhood and I was lucky that I had a very supportive family growing up. My aunt and uncle raised me and I always knew they were there for me and they still are. Things could have gone very differently for me had they not been there to look after me and I want to help other people in the way that they helped me. Events management—'

'Miss Roussel,' interrupted Madge. 'In the spirit of helping people, let me give you a piece of advice. Put your breasts away. That is not acting in your favour at the moment.'

Bella looked down at herself and gasped with horror as she pulled her dress back up. Eric nearly groaned with disappointment and she flashed an accusatory glare at Isaac as if it was his fault.

'I'm so sorry, I didn't realise. This dress isn't mine.'

'We're aware of the dress's origins but you're not the first person today that thought that flashing their breasts at Mr Scott would be a good idea.'

Isaac looked at Madge in confusion. Had there been someone else who had come in wearing revealing clothes? He hadn't noticed and he knew that was because his mind had been on Bella all morning.

Bella blushed and sat up straighter. 'I can assure you that Mr Scott is the last person I would want to expose myself to. He's—'

'You were talking about why events management in particular holds your interest,' Isaac interrupted, not wanting to find out how she was going to finish her sentence about him.

Bella looked at him and then back towards Eric and Madge. 'Events management is what I've always done. It was a huge part of my degree and I've had years of experience at it. I'm very good at it too, but it's also something I love. The organisational side of events, pulling everything together to make something flawless, but more importantly it's about creating something that is fun that appeals to a wide range of people.'

'Isabella – may I call you that?' Eric said, patronisingly.

'No. That's not my name. If you want to call me Bella instead of Miss Roussel then that's fine but I wouldn't call you Ernie as that isn't your name either.'

Isaac nearly snorted.

'*Bella* then,' Eric said with some annoyance at being corrected. Clearly now the breasts were hidden away he was back to not approving of her again. 'We know that you worked for Magic Wishes, a charity well known for its embezzlement. We understand that Isaac *believes* you had nothing to do with it. That you didn't know what was going on. If that is the case—'

'It is,' Bella said, defiantly.

'If that is the case, why should we employ someone who is so spectacularly unobservant?'

Christ. He had no right to talk to her like that.

'Eric, that's not—' Isaac started but Bella just talked right over the top of him.

'Because you are not employing me for my observational skills, *Eric*. Nowhere in the job description does it mention that I would need to be observant, or that I would be required to spy on the accounts of your company to make sure the same thing didn't happen again – as that is what I would have had to have done at Magic Wishes to know that my boss was embezzling money. I did not see the money or how it was spent, that was not part of my job. As fundraising events manager, it was my job, as it will be here, to co-ordinate and organise fundraising events. If you are actually employing me to spy on the staff then you've got the wrong person.'

There was silence in the room then and Isaac had to suppress the big grin that threatened to emerge on his face. She really wasn't going to take any crap.

Bella turned to Madge. 'I'm honest and hardworking and I know you have no reason to believe me considering my past but if you give me a chance, then I'm not going to let you down.'

Madge looked down at her notes, clearly unmoved by Bella's plea. 'Do you have any experience leading a team of people?'

'No, Magic Wishes was quite a small charity and I was the only person working in fundraising events management. But events management involves co-ordinating with large amounts of different teams and people. To organise a concert for example, I had to liaise with the council to gain permission to hold the event in the park, staging companies to arrange for stages, lights and electrics, different agents and artists to secure the talent, catering companies and food trucks to provide refreshments, ice cream vans and local pubs to put on drinks tents, car park attendants, ticketing companies, even companies that would provide Portaloos. The events I've arranged have been big and small but all require liaising and co-ordinating with other people so I have experience of that. Being in charge of a team of people isn't that different.'

'I beg to differ,' Madge said. 'Working with people outside of your organisation and actually having employees under you who you have to organise and be in charge of are two very different things. We already have a great team in charge of fundraising. Why should we put you in charge of them when you have no management experience?'

'Well, I'm afraid I don't agree that you have a great team in charge of fundraising. I'm sure they work really hard and are passionate about helping the homeless but the advert for this job said you needed someone with enthusiasm who could inject imagination and creativity into the fundraising team. I know I can be that person. This is something I'm passionate about. I looked at your last five fundraising events. Two sponsored walks, a sponsored run, a cake sale and a car boot sale. These are hardly events that are going to stay in people's minds as a great day out. These kind of events are not going to put the Umbrella Foundation on the map when it comes to charities. I know the charity has only been running for a few years and I know that a lot of the funding for the brilliant initiatives to help the homeless has actually come from Mr Scott's other companies, which is fantastic, but we can do a lot better than that. We can raise our own money and not be reliant on funding and handouts from Mr Scott. The kind of events I'm used to organising have thousands of participants, and have raised huge sums for the charity—'

'Which was then embezzled,' Eric muttered.

'I can arrange the same kind of events for you here,' Bella said, completely ignoring Eric's barbed comment. 'Events that will have people talking about them and wanting to take part. You want people to go to social media with how much fun they had at an Umbrella event. You want people queueing up to take part, to be shouting about it to all their friends. I can do that. And I can inspire the people in your fundraising team to aim bigger and better too.'

'Give us an idea of what kind of events you would organise in order to raise money for our charity,' Isaac said.

'Well, we want something fun, something that people will want to join in with and not just to raise money for the charity but because it's something different, a fun day out. Zombie runs are very popular in America and are becoming increasingly popular over here too. We create a relatively easy obstacle course – there are many providers that offer these things to companies for corporate team building – and then we charge people to become zombies for the day. Most people will make or buy their own costumes but we can add another charge if they want us to provide them with costumes and make-up. Then other people will pay to enter the obstacle course and be chased by zombies. It's good fun. We then sell refreshments and we could even charge a small fee for spectators to come and watch. Something like fifty pence or a pound so they aren't put off paying for it but lots of small spectator fees would soon add up. We'd have to hold it somewhere central and easy to get to, maybe London or Bristol or some of the other bigger cities. That's important too. You don't want to put people off with the expense of travelling somewhere really far, so we can offer a zombie event in London for example, and then if it proves popular we distribute the same event in cities across the whole of the UK.'

Silence fell over the room again. Never in his wildest dreams had he ever expected her to come out with something like that.

'Zombie runs?' Madge finally said.

'Yes,' Bella said, confidently. 'People would love it.'

Silence again.

Eric cleared his throat. 'Well, if you have nothing else to suggest—'

'Oh believe me, I have a hundred more ideas where that came from,' Bella said, excitedly. 'Firstly…'

Isaac smiled as Bella rattled off her ideas, barely drawing breath as she explained how each event would raise money and how they would work and why people would want to take part. She asked to use his iPad at one stage and she then proceeded to show some examples of the things she was talking about on YouTube. She was so passionate, so inspired, and he was going to stop at nothing to get her to work for his company. If he had to pull rank as CEO to get her in, then he'd do it. Eric and Madge could shake their heads with disapproval as much as they wanted. Bella was going to work for their company whether they liked it or not.

CHAPTER 9

'Well thank you, Miss Roussel,' Madge said, an hour later. 'Maybe you can apologise to the remaining candidates on your way out for keeping them waiting. That interview was a lot longer than we anticipated.'

Isaac rolled his eyes. Madge really was a tough nut to crack. Bella had absolutely shone in the interview and Madge's expression of disapproval hadn't changed at all.

He stood up. 'I'll walk you out.'

Bella didn't say anything but he could see that she was less than happy with that.

He escorted her out of the building and as soon as they were outside she turned on him.

'You didn't think to tell me that my breasts were hanging out?'

'Believe me I tried, but you wouldn't even look at me. Besides, do you not think it might have been better to actually wear a bra with that dress?' he hissed back.

'I didn't put one on last night, there wasn't time when I came rushing out to save your ass.'

'My ass did not need saving,' Isaac said and then, knowing that she had every right to be angry with him, he decided to stop snapping back at her. 'I do appreciate what you did though. I'm sorry that you got hurt, that's the last thing I would want.'

She was clearly thrown by this as she had nothing to say in return.

'I am sorry,' he said, seizing the advantage. 'When I said to you last night that I was on the streets myself when I was a teenager, that wasn't a lie. It was only for a few weeks but the people I met who also lived on the streets were remarkable people and so many of them were willing to help me when they had nothing themselves. This charity is very important to me. Lots of people try to get into working for this charity in order to get into my other companies or to get to me and so I try to make sure that the people we have working here genuinely do care about the homeless. Asking them if they care for the homeless in the interview isn't good enough as most people will just trot out anything in an interview to make themselves sound good or to get the job. A lot of the stuff that comes out of a candidate's mouth in an interview is either completely exaggerated at best or completely made up. They tell you what you want to hear. I want to get an idea of the kind of people applying for the job before the interview and this method has worked very well for me in the past. I should have told you the truth, I know that. But I kept thinking that this was the perfect way to see the real Bella, chat to you over dinner, see how you tick. Before I knew it, several hours had passed and I was enjoying myself more than I have for a very long time. I didn't want to ruin that.'

'But you came back last night,' Bella said. 'Was all that part of the test too?'

'No, I wanted to see you again. That was the only reason I came back. I wanted to tell you the truth but… There didn't seem to be a right time.'

'You're a coward.'

'I was scared of losing what we had, yes. I've never felt that kind of connection with someone before. You felt it too. I know that.'

Bella stared at him.

'I felt a connection with a man called Zach who doesn't even exist. I have no idea what was real and what was a lie. Maybe you were just telling me what *I* wanted to hear,' she said, using his words against him.

'What we had was real, you know that. That kiss was real.'

Just then Claudia, his PA, popped her head out of the door. 'Mr Scott, Madge says she's waiting for you.'

Isaac nodded and he turned back to Bella.

'I think you did very well in the interview.'

'You're the only one,' Bella said. 'I'd like to say it was nice meeting you, but that would be a lie. Goodbye Isaac.'

She walked off and didn't look back.

He stared after her for a moment before he went back into the interview room where to his surprise Madge was sweeping all the application forms into the bin.

'What are you doing? We still have three more candidates to interview,' Isaac said.

'Well that would be completely redundant as we have quite clearly found the perfect person for the role.'

Isaac smiled. 'You liked Bella?'

'Isaac, she is marvellous. After talking to her for the last hour, I'd quite like to rename the charity the Bella Roussel Foundation instead.' Madge pulled her jacket back on and did up the buttons. She picked up her notepad and made for the door.

'Where are you going?'

'I'm going for lunch. If you want to waste your time interviewing the three other candidates, be my guest. I wasn't even supposed to be part of the panel today, but I can't say I trusted either of you to make the right decision on who to employ. But now we've found her, I've got a job to be getting on with.'

'Eric, do you feel the same?' Isaac said, not really caring if he did or not.

Eric flicked through his copies of the application forms, umming and erming as he killed for time.

'Eric, do you?' Madge snapped from the door, folding her arms across her chest.

Eric nodded, clearly fearing for his life. 'But we can't not interview the others. They could complain that they were not given a fair chance. We could already be risking some kind of complaint from those you got rid of before the interviews this morning.'

Isaac nodded his agreement. 'Fine, but let's make it quick.'

'Knock yourselves out,' Madge said, airily, waving her hand in the air as she walked out the office.

Isaac sighed as he walked out into the waiting area. It was going to be a long afternoon.

❦

Bella walked into Pots & Paints, the pottery painting café owned by Eden. She needed to let off steam to her sister. Eden would listen and make all the right noises and give her a big hug, which was exactly what she needed right now. She was equally delighted and disappointed to see Rome was having lunch in the café with Freya.

Rome would be sympathetic and supportive too but he would also get angry and protective and in addition it meant that Bella would have to edit her version of events slightly. She certainly couldn't tell Rome that twenty-four hours before she'd been lying half naked on her sofa kissing Isaac as he lay on top of her.

'Bella!' Eden came running towards her. 'Bob told Steve who told Alec who came in here for coffee earlier that he'd seen you on the St. Mary's ferry with bruises over your face. I've been calling you all morning. Are you OK?'

'I'm fine. It's a long story. Sorry, I didn't have my phone on me. I just went home now to get it and get changed.'

'Well sit down and I'll get you a cup of tea and a slice of cake,' Eden said.

'Do you have any of that delicious coconut cake?' Bella asked.

Eden smiled. 'Coming right up.'

Rome kicked out the chair at his table, indicating that she should sit down.

'Who do I need to beat up for that?' Rome said, pointing to her bruise.

Bella was very sorely tempted to say Isaac Scott but she didn't hate the man that much.

'No one, I'm OK. Let me have my cake and I promise I'll tell you everything. I'm starving.' She gave Freya a big hug. 'Lovely to see you back from your holiday. I know we all missed you. Did you have a good time?'

Freya grinned at her. 'It was brilliant, I saw the Colosseum, the Pantheon and the Trevi Fountain and, Bella, the ice cream is amazing.'

Bella watched her with a smile as she talked about her holiday. Freya had short pixie-cut hair that was streaked with hues of blues and green amongst the blonde. She had a tiny blue nose stud and had those gorgeous feline flicks on her eyes that Bella had never managed to pull off successfully with the liquid eyeliner Freya had bought her once as a Christmas present.

'Sounds great,' Bella said. 'I hope you took lots of photos.'

'Freya has been telling me all morning about the wonderful Roberto that she met,' Rome said, dryly. 'I'm sure she has lots of photos of him.'

'You met someone?' Bella said, her own troubles momentarily forgotten. Freya never dated anyone and Bella had long suspected that was because she held a torch for her brother, though she didn't know why. Bella loved Rome but Freya was so bubbly and fun and Rome was so serious and, quite frankly, him not realising how wonderful Freya was and sweeping her off her feet was a definite negative in Bella's book.

Freya blushed, the huge smile saying it all. 'He was just a holiday fling. A very sexy, holiday fling.'

Rome rolled his eyes and deliberately changed the subject. 'I want to know what happened to your face.'

'I want to know more about Roberto,' Bella said, obtrusively. Freya deserved to be happy and she clearly wasn't going to find that with Rome. After the death of his fiancée six years before, he'd never let anyone in since.

'Oh we met at the Trevi Fountain, while I was doing the whole throw-a-coin-over-your-shoulder-into-the-fountain thing, and we just clicked. Have you ever met someone where the chemistry is off the charts from the very first time you meet? Where you can talk for hours and hours and never get bored or run out of things to say. And when you kiss him, it's like nothing you've ever felt before.'

Bella nodded, hating that Isaac had been that person for her.

'It was ridiculous how easily we got on. It was as if we had known each other our whole lives.'

'It sounds magical,' Eden said, as she handed Bella her slice of cake and sat down at the table with them.

Bella looked around the shop. Eden's lovely assistant, Clare Crissell was behind the till today but even on the days that Clare didn't help, Eden always seemed to have time to have tea or cake with Bella and Rome whenever they popped in. As it was, there was one family in the corner happily painting their pig, owl and dragon moneyboxes while a young couple were painting a large cake plate together and giggling and whispering to each other while they did it. None of them needed Eden's attention.

'It was,' Freya said, dreamily.

'This is all great,' Rome said. 'But in all seriousness Bella, why are you covered in bruises? We were worried this morning when we heard. And then we couldn't get hold of you. What's going on?'

Bella sighed. Rome was not going to take kindly to her taking in a complete stranger but if she was going to tell the truth about Isaac Scott, and she knew she had to, there was no other way round it.

She took a bite of cake to help give her courage. 'Oh Eden, this is incredible.'

Rome arched an impatient eyebrow at her and she swallowed the cake and then spilled the whole story, telling them almost every detail, including that she and Isaac had kissed, but leaving out the fact that the kiss had turned to something a lot more heated very quickly. They didn't need to know every detail.

'Let me get this straight,' Rome said, once she'd finished. 'You let a complete stranger stay in your house?'

Bella rolled her eyes; of course he would focus on that part. 'Yes but—'

'That man that I saw, that was him?'

'Yes.'

'Bella, he was huge. He could have snapped you in half.'

'But he didn't.'

'But he could have. Where's your sense? You're a smart girl, went to university, got a first in Business Studies. You have a lot more brains than me and then you do something like this.'

'I trusted him.'

Rome shook his head angrily and Bella knew he was right. It had been a stupid thing to do. And the worst thing was that trust had been betrayed. Isaac had lied to her. And if he had lied to her about who he was, then he could have easily lied to her about not being a serial killer too, even if that was unlikely on Hope Island.

'I can't believe Isaac Scott did that to you,' Eden said, stealing a chunk of cake from Bella's plate. 'He's just moved his office here so I've only met him a few times but he seems really nice and I've heard only good things about him. He is well thought of by his staff, the company has a great reputation. Everyone that has met him says what a nice bloke he is. And then he does something like this.'

'Well I can kind of understand why,' Bella said, annoyed that she was defending him. 'He says people use the charity to get to him or his other companies and he wanted to make sure that the people who work for the charity genuinely do care for the homeless.'

'I get that. But he could have tested you to see what your reaction was to having a homeless person outside your front door but as soon as he stepped foot in your house, he should have told you the truth then. He definitely shouldn't have carried on the charade for the rest of the night, let alone two nights,' Eden said.

'I feel such a fool,' Bella said. 'I thought that what we had was really special.'

'If you felt that, then I imagine he felt that too,' Freya said, practically. 'By the sounds of it, the original goal was to get to know you. There was no need for him to pretend that he liked you or to kiss you. He could have just chatted to you and then left. But he came back because he couldn't stay away, not because he wanted to test you even more. Don't doubt what you had. He shouldn't have lied and he knows that, but once he told the lie about who he was, it was really hard to undo it without losing the connection that you had. And you shouldn't throw away what you had so easily either. That kind of connection is really hard to come by.'

'He'll be my boss. *If* I get the job. That could be painfully awkward.'

'So?' Freya shrugged. 'People meet their husbands and wives at work all the time. I would never be put off dating someone just because I worked with them.'

Rome choked on his coffee. 'You'd really date someone from work?'

Bella smirked at Eden and she shook her head with affection for her brother.

'Of course. The way I see it is it's only weird if you let it be. If I date someone from work, we'd both be mature adults not little children. There's no need for it to get silly.' Freya paused. 'Would you never date someone from work?'

Rome stared at her for a moment then down at his coffee mug. 'I don't really do dating at all. Relationships, falling in love. It's not for me.'

'You can't stop yourself falling in love, Rome,' Eden said. 'It just happens and there's nothing you can do about it. You can stop yourself from acting on it but then it just eats away at you until you can fall out of love with them and sometimes that never happens. No matter how much you want it to. If you're in love and you're lucky enough that the other person returns those feelings then you should never let anything get in the way, whether that's work, or a friendship or a silly little lie. You should grab it with both hands and never let it go.'

They all stared at her and Eden flushed.

Suddenly Bella's phone rang in the back pocket of her jeans. She fished it out and saw it was a local number she didn't recognise but something told her that Isaac was on the other end of the phone.

She answered it.

'Miss Roussel, it's Isaac Scott.'

God his voice was sexy and she hated that she thought that about him. She mouthed that it was Isaac to the rest of the table.

'We were very impressed with your interview and we've decided to offer you the job,' Isaac said, keeping it all professional.

Bella had nothing to say. She wanted this job but she still felt so conflicted over what had happened with Isaac over the weekend. And could they honestly work with each other when there was so much chemistry flying between them? What if something happened? Or, even worse, what if nothing happened? And there was still the fact that he had lied to her. Could she ever trust him again?

'We're keen for you to start work straight away. Would you be able to start tomorrow?' Isaac said.

She looked round the table at Rome, whose arms were folded angrily across his chest, and Eden and Freya, who were looking at her with hope.

'I'll think about it,' Bella said before she hung up.

Eden stared at her in surprise. 'Did you just hang up on Isaac Scott?'

Bella nodded, suddenly regretting that decision.

'From what I hear, he's a man who always gets what he wants,' Freya said. 'I'll give him half hour before he's banging down your door.'

'Well, he'll be out of luck then because I'm here,' Bella said, stubbornly.

'Look, if you really don't want the job or you can't face working for him, I get that,' Eden said. 'But at least have the decency to tell him. Other people applied for that job and if you don't want it he can offer it to someone else.'

Bella immediately felt guilty; Eden was right.

'Well I'd better get home so I can talk to him.'

She stood up and waved goodbye. She probably didn't have much time to make up her mind about the job and she had no idea what she should do.

❦

It had been over an hour since Isaac had called. Bella had checked the time of the call on her phone several times. He hadn't called back and he hadn't come banging on her door. But then he had offered her the job and she had said she'd think about it. Why would he call her again?

She had made her mind up and changed it again several times. What kind of man would Isaac Scott be like to work for? Would there be other tests and hoops to jump through? And how could she even look at him knowing that he had kissed her so intimately? She had never done that with a man before. She took ages to build up to a kiss, let alone making love to someone. But after that promise to Eden and Rome she had decided to grab the chance and now she was embarrassed by it. She had made a fool of herself in front of her future boss. There was also a part of her that wanted to pursue what they had and she knew she couldn't really do that if she worked for him. Would it be better to turn the job down so they could see each other without the complications of work? But then did she really have the luxury of refusing work? She needed the job, she needed the money and here was a job that was perfect for her offered on a plate. She would just have to get on with it. Be professional, do the job and see what happened.

Suddenly there was a knocking on the door and Bella wondered if Rome had come to give her another lecture.

She opened it and saw Isaac standing on her doorstep looking all sexy and annoyed. A jolt of desire slammed into her. It wasn't just that he was beautiful, it was the chemistry that had bubbled between them over the last two nights, how easy it had been to talk to him and that kiss they had started and never finished that lay between them. The air almost sparked as they stood staring at each other. Part of her wanted to grab him, drag him into the house and finish the kiss off properly before he officially became her boss.

She was distracted with a joyous bark and she tore her eyes away from him to see that Isaac wasn't alone. Alfie, her beloved husky-labrador cross that she was supposed to adopt a few weeks before, was standing next to Isaac wagging his tail.

'Alfie!' Bella said, sinking to her knees and wrapping her arms around the big dog. Alfie licked her face, giving her a thorough washing as his whole body shook with the ferocity of his tail wagging. What was he doing here with Isaac?

'Consider him an introductory bonus,' Isaac said.

Her head snapped up. 'What?'

'He's yours. I've bought enough food for a month and there's a bed, toys and food bowls in the car. I also bought pet insurance for a year.'

'You bought Alfie for me?' She stared at him in shock. How had he remembered what she'd said not just about wanting a dog but Alfie in particular?

'It took a lot of persuading for the dog home to give him to me. Apparently he was reserved.'

Oh god. This man. She hugged Alfie tight, tears clogging her throat. He was hers now. She wouldn't be alone any more. And Alfie had his forever home. He wouldn't be living the rest of his life in a cold cage at the dog home. He was here, he could sleep on the sofa and curl up in front of the fire and he would be loved so much.

'You have no idea what this means to me,' Bella said, pressing her face to the top of Alfie's head.

'I have some idea,' Isaac said.

He turned and walked back to the car and she watched as he lifted a huge dog bed and several bags out of the boot and came back to her. She shifted sideways so he could go into her house and he left them in her hall before coming back out again.

Alfie licked inside her ear and she let out a giggle as she stroked his velvety head. 'I love you too.'

'I think you'll be very happy in your new home,' Isaac said, patting Alfie's back.

She looked up at him and saw the affection in his eyes as he watched her with Alfie.

'Thank you.' She leapt up to hug Isaac but he stepped back out of her reach, holding his hands out to stop her.

'Let's keep this professional, Miss Roussel. Let's not forget that if you take this job then I will be your boss and, as we've both already said, nothing will happen between us.'

Bella nodded, taking a step back herself. She felt a bit hurt but what did she expect? She had enforced that rule herself. It was all so complicated but it seemed that Isaac didn't have any issues drawing the line between them.

'Will you accept the job?' Isaac asked.

Bella knew that he wouldn't ask again. She could see that she had pissed him off by making him come down to her house.

'Yes.'

Isaac nodded, seriously. It was so stilted between them and Bella hated that but despite this wonderful generous gesture she wasn't sure if she could forgive him yet.

He stuck his hand out and she looked at it for a second before she shook it, a spark leaping between them as soon as they touched. Her eyes shot up to look at him and she knew that he'd felt it too. 'Congratulations, Miss Roussel. I'll see you tomorrow at nine o'clock.'

He held her hand a fraction longer than he should have and then let her go. He hesitated for a second, looking as if he wanted to say something more, before he turned and walked down the path. He got in the car and drove off without giving her another glance.

Bella watched him go until he turned the corner and disappeared from sight.

Alfie gave another bark, distracting her from her new boss. She knelt down to stroke and fuss him again. She had a new job, she had Alfie but she couldn't stop the swirl of emotions flooding her body. Nerves, excitement, anger and disappointment twisted in her gut. The next day was going to be a strange one.

CHAPTER 10

'Well, did you take the job?' Eden asked Bella when she called her later that night.

Bella smiled as Alfie made himself comfortable on the sofa, stretching out the entire length of the three-seater with a huge grin on his face.

'Yes, he came round.'

'He came round,' Eden whispered to someone else. 'Hang on, I'm going to put you on speakerphone, Freya is here.'

The line suddenly went all echoey.

'He came round?' Freya asked. 'Did anything happen?'

'No. Well yes.'

Eden squealed and Bella laughed.

'No, nothing like that. He bought me Alfie. He went to the dog home and bought him for me. He turned up with a load of food, toys and other things for him and told me Alfie was an introductory bonus.'

Freya and Eden were silent and for a moment Bella wondered if the line had gone dead.

'He bought you a dog?' Eden said, softly.

'Yeah. I know. I told him all about Alfie when I thought he was Zach and he listened to me. I was so touched I nearly burst into tears.'

Bella heard Eden and Freya whispering and then Eden murmured, 'This is the one.'

Bella laughed at Eden's romantic rose-tinted view on life. 'He is not the one. He lied to me and now he is my boss. He made it very clear nothing was going to happen between us and I think that's for the best.'

'Eden's right. What you two have is something special. He could have just come round with a box of chocolates and a bunch of flowers, or even offered a cash incentive of say five hundred pounds as he knows you need the money, but instead of some worthless chocolate gesture or instead of offering you something you needed, he gave you something you wanted more than anything. He listened to you, really listened. I guarantee you the last two nights meant as much to him as they did to you.'

Bella knew Freya was right. Buying Alfie for her went above and beyond what he could have done to persuade her to take the job. It was the sweetest thing anyone had ever done for her. But that still didn't mean that she was going to let herself fall for him as a result. The lie still hurt and maybe it would be best to focus on that to ensure nothing would happen between them. Alfie rolled over onto his back and let out a big snore and she smiled with love for him. Being angry at Isaac was going to be a lot harder than she thought.

❦

Bella arrived at the Umbrella Foundation at half past eight the following morning, determined she would make a better impression on the management team than she had in the interview. She was under no illusions that she had got the job only because of Isaac Scott; the other two members of the panel had clearly decided she wasn't suitable as soon as they laid eyes on her. Well, Eric had probably decided that she wasn't suitable as soon as he'd seen her name and who she had worked for. She was going to prove them all wrong. She was going to be amazing at this job and a little power dressing didn't hurt to make a good second impression. She had dressed smartly in a black trouser suit with a white shirt buttoned up to the neck. She doubted she would see much of Isaac Scott now that he had employed her but just in case she did, she didn't want him to think she had dressed to encourage him. There was nothing sexy about this suit.

She checked in with the reception desk, happy to see at least one friendly face. Mary used to live in Ruby Cottage up on Blossom Grove before she'd moved down into the town the year before.

'Hi Mary.'

'Oh, Bella. I was so pleased to hear you got this job. I told my Jim that we were advertising for a fundraising manager and he said it was just the sort of thing you needed. And when the application forms came in, and I saw you'd applied, I made sure yours was on top of the pile. I'm not sure if that helped at all, but it couldn't hurt, right? And now you're here and by all accounts you're going to turn this company around. I know Isaac Scott is very impressed with you. I'm so happy for you,' Mary gabbled at a hundred miles an hour.

Bella smiled. 'Thank you. At least you're pleased to see me. I'm not sure how friendly the others will be once they know my history and I'm sure Eric will waste no time letting people know all about that.'

'Oh most of the people on this island know the truth about that awful embezzlement scandal. They know you and know you would never have anything to do with such a thing. And those who think otherwise are really not worth your time of day.'

Bella nodded. That was true. 'I'm not sure where I'm supposed to go, do you have any ideas?'

'I'm not sure. You'll be in the fundraising office I presume but I think you better check in with human resources first, they'll probably have some forms you'll need to fill in and someone will need to show you round and tell you what to do in the case of a fire. Go up to the second floor and have a word with Matilda, she'll know where you're supposed to be.'

Bella walked into the lift and pressed the button. As the doors were closing she heard a voice that made her heart leap.

'Hold the lift.'

A hand appeared through the crack in the closing door and as the doors opened again, Isaac walked in wearing a t-shirt and shorts. He was sweaty and out of breath, clearly having been for a run. His blond curly hair was dampened with sweat too. His face broke into a huge grin when he saw her, but he quickly straightened his facial features into a much more serious expression as he tried to cling onto his professionalism.

'Nice to see you're more suitably attired today, Miss Roussel,' Isaac said, pressing the button for the top floor.

'Wish I could say the same about you. Is it dress-down day at work today?' Bella said and had to suppress the smirk when she watched him chuckle softly to himself. 'Do you not have to rush off back to your big swanky office in London?' she went on. 'Surely you have better things to do with your time than keep stalking me?'

'I live here on Hope Island now. It is true that I will have to return to my *big swanky office* for several meetings from time to time, but I'm hopeful I can conduct more and more of my work from here.'

She stared at him. 'You live here?'

He nodded. 'Bought an old house on the far side of the island and spent the last few months doing it up.'

So much for never seeing him again. Even if she could avoid him in the office she'd see him around the town.

The doors closed and she was suddenly hyper-aware of being alone with him, of his proximity, his divine smell which was tangy like citrus fruit, of how he filled the tiny space with his size and presence. The air crackled between them. He looked up at her, the heat in his eyes telling her he felt it too. She was immediately dragged back to that kiss, his mouth against hers, the taste of him, the feel of his strong body on top of her own. She just couldn't believe none of that had been real.

He cleared his throat and when he spoke his voice was croaky. 'How's Alfie settling in?'

Bella forced herself to speak when her mind was a jumble of emotions. 'Fine. He—'

The doors pinged open on the second floor. She looked out at the reception desk and back at Isaac. 'Have a good day, Mr Scott.'

She walked out just in time to hear him say: 'Oh I intend to.'

Before she could ask him what he meant, the lift doors closed. She let out a sigh of relief. Things were going to be difficult between them but if she only saw him once a day for a few moments in the lift then she was sure she would cope.

She walked over to the reception desk and recognised Matilda who used to be a few years below her at school. She knew her from around the island but not that well.

'Hello, Bella, how can I help you?' Matilda said, breezily.

'Hi, I'm starting work today as fundraising events manager and I'm not sure where I'm meant to go or—'

'Oh that's right, Isaac has asked me to send you straight up to his office. He's going to take care of your induction today and show you around.'

Bella's heart dropped. 'I'm sure Mr Scott is very busy, if you just show me my desk and introduce me to the fundraising team then I'm sure I'll be able to pick up the job as I go along.'

Matilda's smile fell from her face as she looked around for an answer to the problem, as if it might be lying on her desk along with all the heart-shaped Post-it notes.

'I'm not really sure what to suggest. Isaac was quite adamant that he wanted to deal with your induction himself. There isn't really anyone else who can do it. I could give Eric a call...' she trailed off.

'No, that's OK,' Bella sighed. Out of the two, Isaac was the lesser of two evils. 'I'll go and see Mr Scott.'

Matilda smiled again. 'His office is on the top floor, I believe he is expecting you.'

Of course he was, though he had neglected to tell her that when they had been in the lift together. Bella marched back into the lift and jabbed the button for the top floor. What was he playing at? There were lots of people who could have shown her around, Isaac could have delegated the job to anyone. Why did it have to be him? They were supposed to be professional, but how could they maintain that when there was so much tension bubbling between them? Surely spending as much time as possible apart would be for the best. When the doors pinged open, she recognised Claudia, Isaac's assistant, from the day before. She was sitting behind the desk and she smiled at Bella.

'Go on in, he's expecting you,' Claudia said, waving her hands towards a closed door.

Bella marched in and closed the door behind her just as Isaac walked out of a small side room, presumably a bathroom, in nothing but a pair of black trousers. He had a white shirt in his hand and he stopped when he saw her.

God he looked divine. Bella blushed as she remembered how inappropriate it was for her to be thinking that about her new boss.

'Gah!' Bella turned away. 'What is it with you and nudity? Are you not capable of keeping your clothes on for longer than a few minutes?'

'I would have thought you would knock before coming into my office,' Isaac said.

She turned back briefly to see that the white shirt was now on and he was slowly doing up the buttons, his eyes on her the whole time. It was hot as hell.

'Claudia told me to go on in, that you were expecting me.'

'I was. But I figured HR would have you filling in loads of forms first. I thought I had time to get changed before you came.'

'Well they weren't the instructions you left with Matilda. She told me I was to report to you straight away. Though quite why you need to be the one who goes through my induction and shows me around I don't know. You could have asked anyone to do it.'

He sat down and gestured for her to do the same. 'If you're going to be working for me, it's important we are on friendly terms.'

'We've done friendly. In fact you kissing and touching me was definitely more than friendly.'

Isaac sighed. 'I miss the girl that I chatted to over the weekend, when everything was so easy between us. What happened to her?'

'She's still here, behind the wall I've built to protect myself.'

His eyes softened. 'I'm not going to hurt you, Bella.'

'You already have.'

Remorse crossed his face and Bella felt guilty for making him feel that way. Especially after what he had done with Alfie.

'Look, yesterday morning I hated you more than I've ever hated anyone. I was hurt, angry, humiliated and then, last night, you bringing Alfie to my house was the sweetest, kindest thing anyone has ever done for me. And that's left me in a bit of a quandary. I can't hate you any more, even though I'd like to. I'm not sure we can be friendly yet, but we can certainly put all that behind us and I can be professional and courteous.'

He nodded. 'I'll take that.'

As he stretched over to grab some paperwork off the edge of his desk, she noticed his shirt straining against his muscles. Either unintentionally or deliberately he had missed the top button of his shirt and she could see his smooth chest peeping out the top. She had a sudden overwhelming urge to stroke it.

Professional, she reminded herself, even if she did want to climb over the desk and lick his chest.

'What was that?' Isaac said, frowning with confusion as he turned back to face her.

Bella flushed. Surely she hadn't said that thought out loud? 'What was what?'

'You made a noise. It sounded like a whimper.'

Good lord. Had she really whimpered at the thought of licking him? That was almost as bad as saying it out loud.

'Just clearing my throat.'

Isaac nodded, though he didn't look convinced. 'Why don't you wheel your chair round here and I'll show you a few things.'

'I can see perfectly well from over here,' Bella said, not wanting to make the situation even worse.

He looked at her with exasperation and Bella wheeled her chair round so she was at the very edge of his desk. For the first time she noticed the incredible view behind his desk of the cliffs and the sea. How had she not noticed that when she came in? She flushed when she remembered she'd been rather taken with a completely different view. She glanced back at Isaac and he was pointedly looking at how far she was away from him. Suppressing a smirk, he reached out to grab the arm of her chair and slid her closer so she could see his computer screen.

'So when you turn on your computer every morning you'll see this login screen. You type in your username, which is just your name and then your password. I've taken the liberty of giving you one for now. The love of your life.'

Bella looked at him sharply and saw the smile playing on his lips. He gestured for her to enter her password. If he had put his own name as her password she was going to kill him. Obtrusively, she entered the word *Alfie*, pressed enter, and to her surprise the screen came to life.

He smiled. 'I'm hurt that you didn't try my name first.'

'You're a long way away from being the love of my life, *Mr Scott.*'

He laughed.

'You can change your password in here if you want to,' he said, hovering the cursor over a cog button. 'This is the internal messaging service. You can also message people who work in the London, Birmingham and Manchester offices too. The main thing you will need to access is the diary.'

He pressed a book icon and a calendar filled the screen that was almost entirely empty.

'This is the events diary. When you add an event you need to put what it is, time, location, any other details, and then you can tag in certain people or departments at the top if they need to attend.' He clicked on a menu button, selected his own name and a different layer appeared over the top of the calendar, this one filled with dates and meetings. Some were colour coded green, some were coded red. There was a whole band of red the following week and as she looked closer she could see all those meetings were in London. 'If you tag me using this button here, then it goes into my calendar as well and I'll get an email to tell me that my calendar has been updated with an event.'

'Anyone can tag you in an event? No wonder your diary is so full.'

'No, the only people who have access to my calendar are me, Claudia and now you.'

She frowned. 'Why me?'

He looked at her. 'Because I will need to attend every event that you create.'

'Why, to check I'm doing a good enough job?'

He looked at her in surprise. 'No, because this is my company, I need to be present at all events,' he said, simply.

'Oh.'

'My diary is colour coded. If something is in red there's no way I can move it, so you'll have to be careful not to arrange anything for those days. If it's green then there's some flexibility.'

'Most of the events I hold will be at weekends or evenings,' Bella said.

'That's fine. I'm free most weekends, so that shouldn't be a problem. This is your diary.' He clicked a button. 'There will be some events that you will need to attend with me.'

'With you? Like a date?' Her voice was suddenly high and tense.

'Definitely not like a date, Miss Roussel. I'm trying to gain sponsorship for our charity from some big companies and as fundraising manager you can talk to them about how their logo or name will appear at our events and how you can bring awareness to their companies through our events.'

'Oh, I see.' Bella flushed again.

'What I would like you to work on is creating a list of outside contacts that we can tap into for every event, if we need to: caterers, staging, crew, fireworks, things like that,' Isaac went on, smoothly ignoring her mistake. 'This will be a list that you will build every time you have an event and a list that hopefully you can make a start on today with your experience and people that you've used before. The hope is we will eventually have access to their diaries in the same way that you have access to mine so we can see if they are free without having to go through ringing them all individually. Eventually they will all appear on this system and you can tag them in an event so they are automatically informed about it and booked simultaneously.'

'That's impressive.'

'It's quite easy really, it's the same thing that couples or families have on their phones to sync their diaries. Once you've added them to the list I will contact them and ask them if they want to be a regular supplier with us and discuss with them about syncing their diaries. I can set all that up. But that's why it's important that the people you put on the list are not just people who can provide that particular service but people that are reliable and do a great job.'

'OK.' Bella watched him as he clicked through a few screens on the computer. This was a man who knew exactly what he wanted and she found herself quietly impressed with his skill and knowledge.

'Easter is coming up and although it's last-minute I would like some events scheduled for the bank holiday weekend and maybe for the school holidays which start at the end of next week. It doesn't have to be anything big. You can save the zombie run for later on in the year,' he grinned. 'Just please, promise me, no cake sales.'

Bella laughed.

Isaac stood up, towering over her. 'Come on, I'll show you around.'

He moved to the door, holding it open for her before he followed her out, placing his hand on her back for a second before he snatched it away. 'Sorry,' he murmured.

Bella didn't say anything as embarrassingly enough she had quite liked him touching her like that, it was sweet and protective.

They walked into the lift and the doors closed behind them.

'I'm going to introduce you to your team, Elsie and Roger...' He hesitated before he spoke and Bella knew he was trying to find the right words. 'I can't fault their enthusiasm but... You were right when you said our fundraising team could do better. They lack any kind of the imagination and creativity that we need. If I get one more suggestion of a cake sale I might actually scream. You really are going to be a breath of fresh air to our fundraising team. I'm not sure how susceptible they will be to change and being told what to do but I'm relying on your kindness and endearing charm to get them on your side. Elsie actually applied for your job and she wasn't at all happy about not even getting shortlisted for an interview.'

'My endearing charm?'

He grinned. 'You have that in abundance. Just be your natural, wonderful self and she'll be putty in your hand.'

She smiled at the compliment.

'You charmed Madge too. She never likes anyone we interview. After your interview, she actually walked out and said there was no point in interviewing anyone else.'

'Really?'

Isaac nodded.

'I thought she hated me.'

'She wears that disapproving look like a uniform.'

'And Eric, did he like me too?'

'Oh no, Eric thinks you're going to come in here and rob us all.'

Her heart sank. 'Seriously?'

'Yes,' Isaac shrugged.

'Don't sugar-coat it, will you?'

'Hey, I don't want to massage your ego too much. You impressed Madge, no one impresses her.'

The doors pinged open and Isaac waited for her to walk out. He led her down a corridor into a large office where two people were sitting at their desks. She knew Roger; he'd often gone fishing with her uncle Finn. The lady was presumably Elsie. She'd seen her around the island but didn't really know her to talk to. Roger stood up as they walked in and Bella couldn't help smile at his manners. Roger had a thick mane of silvery hair and she knew he was in his late sixties. Elsie was around the same age, with matching silvery hair styled in a tight perm. But whereas Roger was smiling at her, Elsie had the same disapproving look that Madge had worn during her interview.

'Elsie, Roger, I'd like for you to meet Bella, our new fundraising manager.'

'Hi, lovely to meet you,' Bella said, more for Elsie's benefit than Roger's. She smiled, hoping that would put them at ease.

'Hello, Bella.' Roger shook her hand warmly, despite having known her for several years. 'It's lovely to see you again. We've heard such good things about your experience. We're both looking forward to working with you.'

Bella glanced over at Elsie, who didn't seem to share his enthusiasm.

'Nice to meet you,' Elsie sniffed.

Bella looked at Isaac who was suppressing a smile. He obviously had expected this. 'Let me show you your office.'

Isaac directed her to a door in the corner of the room and when she opened it she saw only the incredible view of the rugged coastline, the sweeping cliffs and the emerald meadows set against the sparkling blue of the sea.

'Oh, it's beautiful.'

'Yes, well, it seemed fitting.'

She turned back to face him, wondering what he meant, noticing at the same time that there was of course a desk, computer, two chairs and a sofa in the room which she had missed before.

'Let me show you around the rest of the building.'

He took her round, showing her where the staff lounge and the canteen was and introducing her to several people. By her reckoning there were about fifty people that worked in the office, though Isaac explained that some of them worked part-time or from home a few days a week as most didn't live on the island. Bella easily recognised the ones that did live on the island. Although she didn't know them all to talk to, on an island as small as Hope Island she couldn't help but identify the locals. Isaac knew everyone by name, which put her to shame, but growing up with most of the kids bullying her because her parents had dumped her, she'd tended to keep to herself a bit more than was probably necessary. Isaac was charming and friendly to everyone; she enjoyed watching him as he interacted with different people. It was no wonder she had fallen under his spell over the weekend, he was just so damned likeable.

He escorted her back to the entrance to the main fundraising office, handing her the forms she needed to fill in.

'If you have any ideas you want to talk through or any questions you want to ask, just give me a call. You'll find my extension on a list in your office. Or you can use the internal messaging system.'

She nodded.

He hesitated a moment. 'And if it isn't too unprofessional, would it be OK to treat you to lunch in the staff canteen – nothing fancy, just a sandwich or a baked potato? I feel like I owe you a meal after I ate the last of your porridge.'

She paused but found it impossible to say no. As much as she was still angry over what he had done, she enjoyed spending time with him.

'Is it a date?'

That wonderful smile lit his face. 'Definitely not a date, Miss Roussel.'

'In that case I accept.'

She walked into the office and somehow knew from the goosebumps down her neck that he was watching her go.

✿❦⚭

Isaac walked back into his office with a huge smile on his face. There was something about Bella that just made him feel so happy. And although he knew they couldn't take it anywhere he was just enjoying being with her.

He logged back into his computer and immediately received notification that Bella had updated his diary with an event. That was fast work even by her standards.

He opened his diary and saw he had been added to a cake sale. He burst out laughing. As he wondered how to reply, another notification popped up. Lunch in the staff canteen at one o'clock with Bella. He clicked on the details and laughed.

Definitely not a date.

He carried on laughing when he realised that, like the cake sale, lunch was colour coded red so he couldn't change the booking.

Oh god they were flirting and he was loving every single second.

CHAPTER 11

Bella spent a while creating a list of reputable people that she had used on events before, adding their contact details and comments about the different services they offered. She finished the list and emailed it over to Isaac so he could make contact on behalf of the company. As she closed down the email program, she looked up at Roger and Elsie in the main office.

What was she supposed to do with them? Did they have jobs to do or was it her job to delegate to them? Madge was right, being in charge of a team of people was very different to working on her own or working with outside companies. When events were underway, there would be lots for them to do to help with the organisation and admin, but what were they doing now?

She noticed Elsie was searching for handbags on some website and when she glanced over at Roger she realised he was completing a crossword.

She stood up. It was time for her first team meeting. She picked up a pen and notepad and walked out into their office.

She grabbed a chair and wheeled it between their two desks.

'OK, Isaac would like us to come up with an event for Easter weekend, and I know that's only two and a half weeks away which doesn't leave us a lot of time but do we have any ideas?'

Elsie and Roger looked up from their very busy workloads and stared at her blankly as if they weren't used to being asked their opinion.

'No cake sales,' Bella said, hoping she wouldn't offend them if they were responsible for the cake sales in the past. 'Isaac is looking for something different.'

Roger wheeled himself closer to join the meeting, though it was quite clear he didn't have any inspiration.

'I thought you were the fundraising events manager, isn't it your job to come up with ideas for events? We're just the admin staff here to assist you,' Elsie said, making her disapproval very clear.

'We're the fundraising team, we're supposed to work together, bounce ideas off each other. You're both integral parts of the company; it'd be great to use your experience,' Bella said, smoothly. In truth, she had a ton of ideas but she couldn't just sit in her office and handle it all herself. Well she could, but they were her team now and she knew she'd need them.

Elsie hesitated for a few more moments before grabbing her notebook and pen and wheeling herself over to join the impromptu meeting.

'Isaac wants something for Easter weekend?' Elsie shrugged. 'What about an Easter egg hunt?'

Bella thought about this. It would attract a few hundred people maybe, if the weather was nice. It would raise a bit of money but it was hardly unique or different.

'That's a good idea, but it'd be good if we could offer something that could be done on a bigger scale, something that would attract more people, maybe around the UK.'

'We could co-ordinate with our different offices and arrange an Easter egg hunt in Manchester, Birmingham and London too.'

Bella sighed inwardly. Maybe Isaac was right, maybe they just needed something small and she shouldn't aim so big straight away. Easter was coming up in just over two weeks and anything big would never be organised in time. Even though she really wanted her first event to be an impressive one, an Easter egg hunt would be really easy to pull off too. She knew from past experience that little local events were as important as the bigger ones.

'Any other ideas?' Bella said. 'What would make you come along, what would capture your interest?'

'Geocaching,' Roger said excitedly, his eyes lighting up.

'What's that?' Elsie said.

'It's like a treasure hunt type thing,' Bella explained. 'People leave a little box in a hidden location with some kind of treasure in it and upload the co-ordinates and description of where to find it on a geocache website so other people can go looking for it. It's very popular in America, but it's becoming more popular over here.'

'With real treasure?' Elsie asked.

Roger shook his head. 'Normally people leave toys for kids, or perhaps some jewellery they might have made, like a bracelet, or football cards, old coins, poker chips… some people leave vouchers or coupons. Some people take it very seriously and have their own coins made, you know those squashed coins with some kind of stamp on them, but that stamp will be individual to the person. Then when other people find the cache they will trade something of equal value for whatever they find in the box. It's great fun, but generally the treasure isn't really anything of worth, people just enjoy finding them. Maybe we could do some kind of Easter egg geocache.'

Bella smiled. 'I really like the idea of that, but if we leave real chocolate eggs then they could get ruined in the weather and, once someone finds the cache and takes it, that would ruin it for any future children that find it.'

'Could we leave some kind of egg tokens that the kids could swap for real chocolate eggs once they find them?' Roger suggested.

Bella thought about this for a moment. People would love it – a whole new meaning to the world of Easter egg hunts. But it would require people all over the UK to commit to placing a cache with egg tokens that were somehow coded so they could be swapped for prizes. They could end up with lots of people volunteering in one area and nothing in several other areas. But this was definitely something she could work on.

'How about some kind of Easter egg decorating competition?' Elsie blurted out, keen not to be outdone.

'Maybe,' Bella said, not wanting to offend her by telling her it had been done a thousand times before. It was not hard to see who was responsible for all the cake sales. 'Maybe we could do it on a bigger scale.'

'Bigger eggs?' Elsie asked in confusion. 'Well, ostrich eggs are quite big but I'm not sure—'

'Bigger eggs! That's a great idea,' Bella said and saw the first smile from Elsie. 'We could get some large plastic moulded eggs for people to decorate. We could even do it on a bigger scale, get companies to join in and decorate their own eggs and place them in locations around the country,' she said, writing the ideas down on her notepad. 'Like the Cows on Parade in Chicago. But that would take a bit of organising so maybe we can put something like that in place for next year. But we could certainly do some kind of competition with large painted eggs. OK, let me think about this.'

'How about some kind of Easter or chocolate-themed ball?' Roger suggested, clearly getting into the swing of things. 'Everyone loves getting into their posh frocks and having a bit of a dance. We could have chocolate fountains or Easter egg table decorations.'

Bella nodded.

'Or some kind of funfair or theme park for the children,' Elsie said. 'They have that Winter Wonderland in London at Christmas, we could do our own Easter Wonderland. Have fairground rides, games, all with some kind of Easter or chocolatey kind of theme. We used to have a spring funfair here every year; we could do something like that again.'

'I love that idea too,' Bella said, genuinely, and Elsie's smile grew. 'I remember the funfair when I was a child. It would be good to bring it back to the island again.'

They talked through a few more ideas and how they could make them work before Bella went back into her office.

A fair and a ball would be fairly easy to organise, she'd done quite a few of those in the past and they were always good money makers. But there was something about the geocaching and the Easter egg hunt that spoke to her – but how to make it work?

Isaac's diary was still up on her screen after she had added him to the cake sale and lunch. He had a few meetings coming up for his technology-based companies, BlazeStar and SparkStar. She knew from her research that Isaac's companies made apps and other computer programs to help companies run their businesses more smoothly. She remembered what he'd said when she thought he was Zach: that he'd always wanted to go into computer gaming, designing and building his own games but that had somehow passed him by. Maybe he could create some kind of Easter egg hunt computer game.

Suddenly an idea came to her. She wrote down some notes and spent a few minutes researching on the internet. She smiled. Isaac would really like this. Bella picked up the phone to call him but then she changed her mind. He might be busy. She opened up the internal messaging system and sent him a message instead. That way, he could get back to her once he was free.

I have an idea I'd like to talk to you about, do you have a minute?

She pressed send and saw the icon next to the message change to show he had read it. She stared at the screen, willing him to answer or to pick up the phone and call her but after a few minutes it was quite clear he wasn't going to reply.

She checked her emails and saw he hadn't replied to her about the list she'd sent over earlier either. Nor had he made any comment about the cake sale or the lunch date she had put into his diary.

Maybe he really did want to keep things professional between them and he didn't appreciate her banter or her bothering him every few minutes with her silly ideas.

She opened up the internet and started researching large Easter decorations that she could use if they were to hold a fair or ball.

A knock on the door distracted her from the screen and she looked up to see Isaac standing in the doorway. She couldn't help the grin from spreading on her face when she saw him.

'You have an idea you wanted to discuss, Miss Roussel?'

'I didn't expect you to come running down here to talk to me, a phone call or a reply to my message would have sufficed.'

'I don't do things by half. Besides, we have our lunch meeting shortly and as it was in red on my diary I certainly didn't want to be late for it.'

Bella let out a little giggle.

He moved into the office. God he was so big. Her office was quite roomy but now he was in there, it felt very small. 'I also got a notification about a cake sale. I must say, I expected something more from you.'

She shrugged. 'Well I like to give you something unexpected. You weren't expecting a cake sale so I think I achieved that.'

'I guess you did. So this cake sale—'

'You can't get out of it, it's in red.'

'It's at your house.'

'Yes.'

'And I'm the only one invited.' The humour had gone from his eyes and in its place was something else she couldn't put her finger on. 'It's not exactly professional.'

She swallowed. That undeniable chemistry was back in the room again, sparking in the air between them.

'You're not the only one invited, Alfie will be there too. I'm sure he'll love cake.'

'Well as long as we have a chaperone; wouldn't want you throwing yourself at me again.'

He sat down and that spark of humour was back in his eye but, despite the fact that he was only teasing her, she couldn't stop her cheeks from flaming red.

'I didn't throw myself at you…' she trailed off, knowing she couldn't really call it anything else. 'Besides, you didn't exactly seem unwilling.'

He stared at her for a moment. 'I regret that more than anything.'

His words were like a slap round the face. He regretted the kiss. Had she completely misread the signs from him? She thought he had been flirting with her since she had started work that morning. Did he genuinely have no interest in her at all? But if he didn't then the whole weekend really had been a lie.

Well if he wanted professionalism, she would give it to him. She straightened in her chair.

'I discussed some ideas with my team; Elsie suggested an Easter egg hunt and Roger talked about incorporating that into a geocaching hunt. So I've had an idea that combines both ideas. I thought about creating an app similar to *Pokémon Go*. It'll be a location-based game where children and adults can use the GPS in their phones to locate virtual Easter eggs in real-world locations across the UK. We can even use augmented reality so that the eggs appear on the screen using the phone's camera as if they are really in front of the person using the app. It'll be free to play but there'll be in-app purchases to help find the eggs more easily or maybe different tools to smash the eggs once they've found them or something like that. And that's where we will make our money. The eggs they manage to collect will equal points and once they reach a certain point total they can swap those points for real chocolate eggs in the real world.'

He stared at her. 'And once again you've given me the unexpected. You sound like you know what you're talking about. Is that through research or because you play?'

'I did some research before I messaged you but I know a little about video games. Before I got so broke I couldn't afford to eat, I used to have a Wii and an Xbox. *Pokémon Go* was hugely popular last year, as I'm sure you're aware, and although *The Great British Egg Chase* wouldn't be as advanced, we could still attract a wide audience, especially as parents will be looking for something fun to do with their kids over the Easter holiday and this gets the whole family out of the house and exploring different areas. Coupled with the reward of real chocolate eggs it could be very popular and very profitable for us with very little outlay. We can get someone like Cadbury's or Nestlé to donate eggs; they love this kind of thing as their name would be all over it in terms of sponsorship.'

He nodded. 'I really like this idea and catchy title too. Are you thinking that someone from SparkStar would design it for us?'

That took the wind out of her sails. 'I was actually thinking that you would design it. Thought it would be something that you'd enjoy. Presuming that not everything you told me over the weekend was a lie, you said you always wanted to be a game designer. That's what you trained to do.'

'That was a long time ago.'

'So you can't do it?'

'I didn't say that. I could do it but it would take me over a week to do it and that's if I didn't work on anything else. You'd be better off outsourcing it to SparkStar, though that would come with a fee. I can't have my staff working for nothing.'

Bella felt disappointed. She had hoped he would want to do it and he had just palmed it off as if he had no interest in it. But in reality she knew how busy he was, she'd seen his diary. And in all her bright ideas, she hadn't accounted for it taking so long to make.

'Well it's nearly one o'clock, shall we continue this discussion at lunch?' Isaac said, standing up.

'I've got some work I need to do, maybe it's best if we leave it,' Bella said, turning to her computer under the pretext of work.

He watched her for a moment. 'Our lunch meeting was in red, Miss Roussel, it's not something I can rearrange.'

She stared at the screen for a moment but Isaac made no movement to leave so she got up and walked with him to the door.

Isaac escorted her to the lift and turned to her as the doors closed behind them.

'I've upset you about the Easter egg app, that wasn't my intention. I think it's a brilliant idea.'

'I'm not upset about that.'

'So you are upset about something.'

The fact that he regretted the kiss was the thing that was upsetting her the most but she couldn't tell him that.

I regret that more than anything. That's what he'd said.

He was still waiting for an answer, his indigo blue eyes filled with concern.

'I just thought you might enjoy making the app; that it would be fun for you.'

He smiled, sadly. 'There's not much time for fun in my working life, not much time for fun at all actually.'

'Well then you're doing something wrong. I appreciate that to be the CEO of three companies is a lot of hard work but you should have some time for yourself. You should delegate more. If you don't have people in your managerial team that you can trust to get on with the job in your absence then you have the wrong people working for you. Life is to be enjoyed and I imagine that you make a lot of money in your line of work, so you should be able to enjoy it now and again.'

'You make it sound so simple, when in reality it isn't.'

'Only if you insist on making it complicated. You say that you need to be present at every event that we have. And while I appreciate the support, you have hired me to be fundraising manager so I can also be the representative for our charity too. You have an assistant manager here; she can do some of that for you as well. You spent time showing me around today when you could have passed that responsibility to Eric or Madge or anyone else, it didn't need to be you. You could have used that time to do something you enjoy, even if it was only half an hour reading a book you've been meaning to read for some time or designing a computer game that's just for you, just for the pleasure of doing it, even if you never sell it. As fundraising manager, I can help you with a lot of things to do with the charity. You don't need to take it all on yourself.'

He didn't say anything, just stared at her as if she was some puzzle he was trying to work out, and she wondered if she had perhaps said too much. He was her boss after all and this was only her first day, she shouldn't be telling him how to live his life. It wasn't her place.

The doors pinged open.

'Sorry, it's none of my business,' Bella said. 'Let's have lunch and then you can get back to your very busy job.'

She walked out and after a few moments he followed her.

❦

Isaac didn't know if he was coming or going with this girl. Lunch felt stilted. He knew he had upset her with his actions over the weekend, but after buying her Alfie, she'd seemed to have forgiven him. It had even seemed as if they'd been flirting that morning. But now it felt like she was upset with him again and he knew it wasn't just that he didn't have time to develop the Easter egg app.

Although they had talked over lunch, it had been solely focussed on work. The friendliness had gone. It was still easy between them but it was quite obvious she was trying to be professional at all times. They talked more about the Easter egg hunt and how they would make it work, bouncing ideas off each other about the different in-app purchases they could use. They talked about Elsie's suggestion to bring the funfair back to the island and her plans for it and how next year Bella wanted to do some giant Easter egg statues dotted around the UK, painted and funded by different companies, which would bring awareness to the charity too.

She didn't talk about him doing something fun again or taking the time to enjoy himself. He hadn't dared tell her that the reason he had insisted on being the one to show her around that morning was because he had wanted to spend time with her, that he enjoyed her company. And although he didn't really have a lot of time for fun, he had made sure there was time to indulge in that.

Bella finished her lunch and stood up to go. 'I better be getting back, there's work to be done.'

'I'll walk you back,' Isaac said, standing up too.

She didn't object and they walked back into the lift together.

As soon as the lift doors closed and the lift started moving, she leaned over and pressed the emergency stop button, bringing the lift to a juddering halt.

She turned to him, her eyes flashing. 'Do you really regret the kiss?'

Oh. That was why she was upset with him. Crap, that had been really insensitive and she had taken it completely the wrong way. But what could he say? That in reality he wanted to power her back against the wall of the lift and kiss her until neither of them could remember their own names? He was her boss. He couldn't be that person who dated one of his employees. That opened himself up to a load of problems. What if it ended between them, then that would make it very difficult at work.

He swallowed. 'Don't you?'

She stared at him. 'No. Not at all. I mean I regret that I didn't really know the person that I was kissing. I regret letting it get as far as it did as I'm normally much more restrained and cautious when it comes to relationships and men. I normally take my time before I feel ready to progress to that level. And there's a huge part of me that regrets that we never finished that kiss properly because now there's all this sexual tension between us that is frustrating as hell. But I can't regret that kiss. Even if nothing ever happens between us again, that kiss was not like anything I've ever felt before. I'm not that experienced with men, there haven't been that many in my life, and maybe the kiss was just run of the mill for you, just another meaningless kiss in a whole line of meaningless women, but for me it was incredible. It showed me what a real kiss should feel like, what it means to be with someone you share a real connection with and I could never regret that. Did you not feel that too?'

Good lord. He had never met anyone so completely and utterly honest. She was someone who wore her heart on her sleeve and was proud to do so. She didn't hide her feelings and there was something so achingly endearing about that. But what could he say? He didn't want to do anything to encourage her.

He looked away from her when he spoke so she wouldn't see the lie in his eyes. 'It was just a kiss, Bella.'

He saw her watching him out the corner of his eye.

Eventually she stepped forward and released the emergency stop button.

'Right.'

The lift came to her floor and when the doors pinged open he let her go without saying a word.

Bella walked back in her office and closed the door behind her. She sank into her chair and let her head fall into her hands.

She was such an idiot. Why did she not have a filter on her mouth so she could run through what she was going to say before she said it?

Tears of humiliation and rejection smarted her eyes.

She had kissed him because she had never felt that kind of connection with anyone before and because she had sworn she was going to take a chance with her heart and not hide from the chance of love. He had kissed her simply because she had thrown herself at him and proved she was more than willing. He was trying now to get things back on professional ground and she had just told him how incredible the kiss was, making her sound like an inexperienced lovesick schoolgirl with a popstar crush.

But the kiss *had* been incredible. She'd had five semi-serious boyfriends before and several other dates that had ended in wonderful kisses but this had been something completely different and Isaac just hadn't felt what she had experienced. She had assumed he was holding back because he didn't want to get involved with someone at work, and she understood that, but the fact that he never felt that connection, that she meant nothing to him, really did mean that the whole weekend had been a lie.

The door burst open and when she looked up Isaac was standing there. She quickly wiped the tears from her cheeks.

'I don't want to see you right now.'

He slammed the door behind him. 'Tough.'

She stood up, defiantly. 'I don't think I've ever hated someone before, but for you I could make an exception.'

He stormed round to her side of the desk. 'I felt it too. The connection we shared, the kiss, it *was* something special. Every minute, of every damn day since I walked out of your house on Sunday night, I've been thinking of that kiss. And the only reason I stopped it was because it wasn't fair to you for me to continue kissing you, to make love to you when you didn't know who I was, but it took more strength than I knew I had to walk away from you that night. I didn't come back on Sunday night because I wanted to test you some more or find out more about you, I came back because Saturday had been one of the best nights of my life and I didn't want to let you go.'

She stared at him, no words in her head at all.

'I rather selfishly considered not hiring you for this job so then we could carry on exactly how we were and there would never be this professional conflict of interest, but this company needed you. I needed you. I wanted to do your induction this morning because I wanted to spend more time with you, which was completely stupid on my part as it was absolute torture. I sat there talking about the bloody sodding diary and the list I wanted you to compile when all I really wanted to do was this.'

And with that he kissed her, hard.

CHAPTER 12

Oh god, the taste of him as his lips burned into hers; his scent was all over her, his hard body against hers. His lips were so soft and she moaned when his tongue slid into her mouth. She ran her hands round the back of his neck, fingering his soft curls at the nape of his neck. He let out a soft moan of need and slid his hands down to her bum, lifting her. Instinctively she wrapped her legs round his hips and a second later he had her pinned against the wall with his glorious weight.

Desire and passion and need erupted in her, a longing so fierce that it was almost painful. If he started to make love to her against the wall of her office there was not a single bone in her body that would have stopped him. She clung to him tight and as the kiss continued she could feel how much he wanted this too.

The kiss suddenly slowed, becoming tender and softer than the fierce passion that had consumed them both. He pulled away slightly, placing a gentle kiss on her forehead, then he leaned his head against hers as he steadied his breathing.

'Crap. That wasn't supposed to happen,' Isaac whispered, kissing her on the forehead again before he lowered her legs to the floor. 'I lose all sense of control when I'm around you.'

'I'm really glad it did happen,' Bella said, leaning her head against his chest. She was gratified to hear his heart pounding against his chest as hard as hers was.

He pulled back slightly, holding her around the waist to make sure she could stand on her own.

'I'm your boss Bella, this can't happen between us.'

She reached up to stroke his face. 'I understand.'

'You do?'

'I'm disappointed but I do get it. I was once involved in a work romance myself and it all went wrong. And you're the boss; it's so much more difficult for you.'

He stared at her in confusion. 'I just pinned you to the wall of your office and kissed you on your first day of work. Then told you that it can't happen again. I feel you're letting me off very lightly.'

She smiled. 'I'm not going to slap a sexual harassment suit on you, if that's what you're worried about. Look, this thing between us is obviously just passion and lust. It's not love.'

He frowned slightly. 'No, I don't suppose it is.'

'Of course it isn't, we barely know each other. Besides, if it was, you wouldn't be willing to walk away from it so easily. If it was love you wouldn't let something as small as us being work colleagues get in the way. You'd grab onto it with both hands and never let it go. But it's not. It's chemistry, nothing more. There's no point letting it get all weird between us at work just for the sake of a quick roll in the sack. So let's just leave it as it is. We can be friends and we'll both agree that it doesn't go any further than this amazing kiss.'

He nodded, though as he took a step back, she couldn't help notice how disappointed he looked.

He took another step away. 'Just so you know, if we did, there'd be nothing quick about it.'

She laughed. 'Don't worry, in my fantasies, I won't sell you short.'

He groaned and walked to the door. 'Get on with your work, Miss Roussel. I'm not paying you to stand around enjoying yourself all day.'

'I promise, I won't enjoy myself for the rest of the day.'

He smiled and walked out, closing the door behind him.

Bella stayed leaning against the wall for a few seconds, her heart still banging against her chest. That kiss had been incredible and she couldn't help wonder if he kissed like that, what it would be like to make love to him. But at least now she understood how he felt. It was the right thing really because if they did end up having a whirlwind passionate affair, when it inevitably ended it would leave them with a whole load of awkwardness to deal with. This was for the best. She would just ignore the niggling doubt in her head that said she shouldn't walk away from this kind of connection so easily.

She sat down at her desk and stared at her screen. A few minutes later, there was a soft knock on the door and Elsie poked her head inside.

'Are you OK? Mr Scott seemed really angry when he walked in here?'

Bella smiled. 'I'm fine. But let's just say I won't be stepping out of line with him in future. Not if I want to keep my job.'

There was more truth to that than she could say.

Elsie nodded, sympathetically. 'He can come across a bit bullish sometimes but he's a very fair man.'

Bella nodded.

'I'll make us some tea, it'll make you feel better,' Elsie said, ducking back out of the office.

Bella turned her attention back to the computer though she knew she wasn't really seeing it. It was going to take a bit more than a cup of tea to make her feel better because after that wonderful kiss all she was left feeling was incredibly frustrated.

※ ☆ ☆

Isaac left his house and let Rocket run on ahead up the little path that led to the fields and meadow behind his house. Dark damson rain clouds were rolling in over the hills but the sun was still shining over his little cottage as he looked back at it. The place had been a complete state when he had bought it a few months before but slowly it was becoming more homely. The outside walls had been repaired and repainted and the only thing that needed doing to the outside was having a new thatched roof fitted. The garden had all been landscaped and there was a proper driveway round the front too.

Inside was almost completely done as well. He had slowly made his way through each room, plastered, painted, new carpets, new ceiling in some cases. The kitchen and bathroom had been gutted and renovated and he couldn't be prouder of how it had turned out.

His favourite part of the new development was the summerhouse, which had large windows overlooking the bay, comfy sofas and a fire pit outside. It was the perfect place to spend the long summer evenings and it would be even better if he had that perfect someone to share those evenings with.

He left the house behind and walked up the hill, his thoughts immediately going to Bella.

Life in London had felt claustrophobic and the people that flocked round him, especially the women, did so because of his money. He couldn't move on the streets, or attend a party or an event, without someone coming up to him because of what he could offer them. They all wanted something. His life had taken him in a direction he hadn't wanted to go and he wanted to reclaim some of that. His other companies were now in a position where they mostly ran themselves. As Bella said, he had good people that he could trust in charge up in London and he was increasingly taking more and more steps back.

When the charity had started to take off, he had deliberately decided to open the head office on Hope Island instead of London with smaller offices in a few other major cities. He'd wanted a new start and returning to the place where he had grown up had seemed like a good place to do it. He had such fond memories of the island and it would be the perfect place to settle down and maybe one day start a family. He knew part of that was to find someone to share that life with. And although he had been back and forth to London a lot over the last few months during the transition, which meant that he hadn't yet met a lot of people on the island, among those he had met there was no one he'd felt such an affinity for as he had for Bella.

Would it be really wrong to start something with her?

Rocket ran full pelt back towards him and turned and dashed off to the top of the hill, her little black curly ears bouncing as she ran.

He shoved his hands in his pockets and followed her up the hill.

Carter, his ex-partner at BlazeStar, had had an affair with his assistant and everyone in the company had known about it. Jennie had been young and naïve and she'd bought everything that Carter fed her about him and his wife agreeing to split, that they lived apart during the week and that he only went home at weekends just to see the kids. None of which was true. The staff there had not been kind about Jennie, laying the blame for the affair entirely at her feet. Thankfully most of the comments about her had been made behind her back and she'd been spared their animosity, but when, inevitably, the affair was discovered by the wife, life had not been easy for Jennie and she had eventually left the company. And although both he and Bella were single, Isaac knew that office gossips would still have plenty to say on the matter and he wanted to protect Bella from that.

There was such a vulnerability to her. He'd seen that today when she'd been so hurt over his blasé comment about the kiss. And when he'd found her crying in her office, he'd had such an overwhelming urge to bundle her into his arms and hold her there forever.

No, he couldn't let anything happen between them. They would be friends and he would be absolutely fine seeing her at work every day knowing that he couldn't touch her or be with her. Absolutely fine.

He heard yapping up ahead and quickened his step. Rocket suddenly dashed past him followed by a bigger dog he instantly recognised as Alfie. Rocket turned and leapt up at Alfie, tugging on his ears before dashing back up the hill and nearly knocking Bella over as she emerged at the top of the hill. Alfie gave chase, his tongue lolling from his mouth.

Despite his resolve, Isaac couldn't help the huge smile from spreading across his face when he saw her.

She stood there, her wild tangle of red hair blowing in the wind, a big smile on her own face as she waved at him.

After that incredible kiss in her office, he had managed to successfully avoid her for the rest of the day. He had actually started working on her Easter egg hunt game, telling himself he was doing it because he wanted to, and it was nothing to do with her. Throughout the day, he had noticed that his diary had been updated with several events over the course of the year, and he had to smile when he saw that one of them was indeed a zombie run in London later on in the summer. There was also going to be a funfair on Hope Island and he loved that she was bringing that back to the island again. He hadn't commented though and his message inbox had stayed resolutely empty of messages from her. He had waited until he knew she had left before he went home himself just so he wouldn't accidentally see her in the lift again.

Yes, he was coping absolutely fine with working alongside her. And here she was now. He was never going to be able to avoid seeing her on an island the size of Hope Island. Even if he could actively avoid her at work, he would always see her around.

He took the last few steps so he was standing in front of her; because of the hill she momentarily had the height advantage.

'Your dog is out of control, Miss Roussel.'

She laughed and on this chilly, grey evening, she was like a ray of sunshine.

'I think it's your dog that's out of control. Alfie was walking quite respectably by my side until your dog came up and tormented him.'

'That's quite ironic when I was quite happy in my little life until you came along to torture me.'

To his surprise she fell in at his side and slipped her hand into his. 'I think you're torturing yourself.'

He stared down at their entwined fingers. How could something so wrong feel so completely utterly right? But as she continued to walk up the hill by his side, he made no attempt to remove his hand from hers.

'So tell me, how come you were homeless when you were younger?'

It was not something he ever really discussed with anyone but for some reason he had no issue telling Bella.

'As I told you, my dad died when I was seven and for a long while it was just me and my mum. We moved to St Mary's and then, when I was fifteen, we moved to Twickenham in London. Mum started dating this absolute asshole. He was lovely to me in front of my mum but an absolute git to me when she wasn't around. So I ran away. I'm not sure where I thought I would go or what I would do for money and food. I ended up in the centre of London and as I was fifteen I found it impossible to get work. I ended up sleeping rough for four weeks before I was found by the police. It wasn't like I was properly homeless, I had somewhere to go back to, but my pride stopped me from going back to my mum. And the weather at that time was unseasonably hot, so I never froze on the streets. But I was sort of adopted by a small group of homeless people who looked after me and I've never forgotten that.'

'I can't even imagine what that must have been like, living on the streets and not feeling like you had any other place to turn to. Did you go back to live with your mum after the police found you?'

'Yes, she was absolutely distraught that I'd run away. She guessed it was something to do with Colin, her boyfriend, and she finished with him before I'd even been found. I felt like an ass for putting her through that.'

'And you lived there in London ever since?'

'Yes, well Mum moved to Australia with her new husband around five years ago, but until recently London was my home.'

'Why did you come back here?'

He swept his arm out to encompass the sea that surrounded them on all sides, the curves of the emerald hills, the harbour with the little boats that looked like nothing more than toys from up here. Even with the darkening clouds it was an impressive sight.

Bella laughed. 'It is pretty spectacular. I don't think I could ever leave but I do sometimes wonder what it would be like to live in a big city. I've been to London a few times to see a show or to do the touristy stuff and the place scares me a little if I'm honest. Well actually a lot. People move so fast, heads down; no one talks to each other. They're crammed into the underground trains like sardines in a can, there's a constant stream of traffic, the buildings are so tall and it all just feels so—'

'Claustrophobic. Yes, for me too. I yearned for the bright lights of a big city when I was growing up here and on St Mary's but when I was there I couldn't wait to get back. I missed the sea and I never realised how much until it was gone. But London does have its good side.'

Bella smiled as she looked up at him. 'I bet it does, although I've never really appreciated it. What do you miss about London now you're here?'

'The food. You can get any food you want, Indian, Portuguese, Lebanese, Iranian, Italian, Australian, you name it, you can get it in London somewhere. I miss the entertainment, how you'd be walking down by the Thames and you'd see jugglers, fire breathers, a street artist drawing incredible landscapes on the floor with chalk. Everything is there, every culture, every walk of life, it's a melting pot of every country in the world and I love that about London.'

'I think I would love it too, but maybe just for a week or two.'

He laughed.

Thunder suddenly rumbled off out over the sea.

'We're going to get wet,' he said.

'Most of the storms don't blow inland, they stay out there. And they take ages to build. I think we'll be home by the time the rain starts.'

'Your home or mine?'

She grinned. 'I'll be in mine, you'll be in yours. We certainly don't want a repeat of what happened the other night.'

He smiled. 'No, we certainly don't want that.'

'So you live over there?' Bella asked, pointing back in the direction they'd just come.

He pointed. 'The little yellow house with the large chimney.'

'That's not where I pictured you living at all.'

'Where did you picture me living?'

'In one of those swanky penthouse suites in the apartments overlooking the harbour.'

'Nice, but not really me.'

'And a cute little farmhouse is?'

He shrugged. 'It feels like home.'

'So… just you and the crazy dog live there?'

He smiled at her not-so subtle digging. 'Rocket,' he gestured at the dog that was still chasing Alfie around the hills. 'Yes, just me and her. I have a dog sitter who looks after Rocket for me if I'm out at meetings all day or sleeping on the sofa of a beautiful red-head but no wife, girlfriend, significant other, no children, no lodgers, if that's what you're asking.'

'I kind of assumed there wasn't anyone after the way you kissed me.'

He laughed in confusion. 'I kissed you like I don't have a wife?'

'You kissed me like someone who hasn't had sex in a while. Believe me, I should know.'

He smiled. She was so honest. And he loved that about her. 'So the last guy you dated, was he the one that broke your heart at work?'

'Ha. No. And Andrew never broke my heart, not even close. He did humiliate me at work. Told everyone what I was like in bed. But I wasn't in love with him. At least I don't think I was. I don't think I've ever been in love actually.'

'If you'd been in love, then you would know.'

'Well in that case I've never been in love.'

Isaac thought about this for a moment. She was twenty-seven years old and she'd never been in love. That was slightly strange.

'No teenage crushes, no childhood sweethearts, no crushes on sexy film stars that have bordered on the obsessive?'

Bella laughed. 'Not really. I thought Orlando Bloom was pretty cute in *Pirates of the Caribbean*, but I can't say I was ever in love with him. What about you? Ever been in love?'

'Verity Forbes was my first.'

'Your first? How many have there been?'

'Five. Well, six technically if you count the twins.'

'You were in love with twins?'

'I couldn't choose between them. Gaby used to let me catch her in every game of kiss chase. Grace never did but I loved her for that.'

Bella laughed. 'Kiss chase? How old were you?'

'Nine.'

'And how old were you when you fell in love with Verity Forbes?'

'Five. We were both fish monitors and we had to go and feed the fish outside the headteacher's office every day. On the way back, we'd sneak into the cloakroom and kiss each other.'

'At five?' Her voice was high-pitched and incredulous.

'Just a little peck on the lips.'

'No wonder you're so good at kissing, you've been practising for a lot longer than me.'

'I thought she was marvellous. I gave her a chocolate heart on Valentine's Day and she gave it to Billy Walker. She broke my heart.'

'Oh you poor thing,' Bella said, not sounding sympathetic at all. 'Let me rephrase the question. Have you ever been in love since you turned eighteen?'

Isaac thought about this. There had been several women he had dated over the last fifteen years, some of them he had even dated for a few months. But there was not one that stood out in his mind, not one he had ever considered forever with, not one that had made him feel what he'd felt when he was kissing Bella.

Crap. That was a dangerous road to go down.

'I don't think so.'

'A wise man once said to me: "If you'd been in love, then you would know."'

He laughed. 'Then no. Well maybe. Carly Beckett was pretty special. I dated her when I was at university. She was American so of course was super exotic for a small-town boy like myself. When she went back home, I was gutted.'

Light spots of rain splatted against their skin and he looked up at the slate grey clouds above them that were threatening to unleash their load.

'What was special about her?'

He laughed awkwardly. 'She was my first. You never forget your first.'

'Oh.'

Bella was quiet for a moment and he wondered what was going on inside that head of hers.

'I was pretty late on that side of things. All the other boys in my dorm had lost their virginity years before, or so they said. We all sat around one night and swapped stories of our first time. At that point I'd not even met Carly. I was mortified that I was the only virgin. I ended up making up some story about some beautiful red-head that was several years older than me and had taught me everything I needed to know. Looking back now, I imagine a lot of those boys made up their first-time stories too.'

'A red-head?'

He eyed her wonderful red hair. 'Yeah, it seemed like the kind of person I wanted my first time to be with. Wild, beautiful, rare.'

'So Carly, she was a red-head?'

'No, she was blonde.'

'And she taught you everything you needed to know.'

She sounded jealous and he couldn't help but smile. 'I was her first too actually, so there wasn't a lot of teaching.'

'I bet you loved that. Isn't that every man's dream to sleep with a virgin?'

'God no, I was terrified. You can never have a do-over on your first time and I wanted her to treasure it, to look back on it fondly. I knew she was going back to America and things would end between us but I didn't want her to regret it. I didn't want it to be a drunken shag in someone else's bedroom at a party or a quick shag in the back of the car. She deserved more than that. I tried to make it special for her, even though I had no idea what I was doing myself. I lit candles, I brought her flowers, took her for dinner.'

She looked up at him and smiled. 'You're quite the gentleman really, aren't you?'

'Don't tell anyone, you'll ruin my reputation. So what about your first time? Was it memorable?'

She pulled a face. 'Sadly memorable for all the wrong reasons. I was the drunken shag in someone else's bedroom at a party cliché. I can't even remember his last name. I was twenty-one so even later to that side of things than you were. I never wanted to let anyone get close to me so I pushed people away. Everyone at university was going out, getting drunk, sleeping with a different person each night, and there was me always going back to my room alone. I never really drank, didn't like clubbing. I started to think there was something wrong with me. The other girls in the dorm began taking the piss so I started going out on dates when I'd have been much happier staying in my room reading a book. I'd been going out with Steve for a few weeks when we were invited to a party. He got raging drunk, took me upstairs and started kissing me and I thought let's see what all the fuss was about. Sadly, he didn't sell it for me. A few thrusts and then he fell asleep on top of me.'

His heart sank. 'Oh Bella. That's not how it should have been for you. I wish I had been your first time.'

She smiled up at him. 'I wish you had too. In another life you could have been; had you stayed on the island, we'd have probably met, mixed in the same social circles, felt the same connection we do now. We'd probably have married, be living in your little yellow cottage by the sea and there would have been four screaming kids ruining your life round about now. Maybe it's for the best that we didn't.'

He looked out at the dark clouds churning and swirling over the sea. He could suddenly picture that life so vividly. Bella in his home. Bella in his bed. Bella pregnant with his child as she made cookies with the other children in his kitchen. He suddenly wanted that more than anything. He shook his head, pushing those random thoughts away. He'd clearly been watching too many cheesy Hallmark movies. He'd never really thought of his future like that. He'd thought that one day he would get married and have a child but he'd never imagined it in such a rose-tinted way before.

He turned back to her. Her hair was misted with the light rain in the air, tiny water droplets clinging to her long eyelashes and dusting her cheeks. He swallowed down the huge lump of emotion in his throat.

He quickly changed the subject from the scene of domestic bliss that was still playing in his head. 'So please tell me that you've had better sexual experiences since then?'

Bella laughed. 'Yes, not many, but a few lovely men who did indeed show me what I had been missing.'

Isaac pushed away the jealous thoughts of her being with other men.

Suddenly, the rain got harder.

Bella laughed, raising her face to the rain, but that laugh turned to a squeal as the rain began to come down with even more force, hammering down on top of them.

Still with his hand in hers, he ran towards the nearest tree, a towering oak that had probably been here before anyone else. He called for the dogs and they came running as he tugged Bella under the limited protection of the great boughs and pulled her in front of him.

Her little t-shirt was soaked through and she shivered against him, still giggling at getting caught in the rain.

'Did your mum never teach you not to leave home without a jacket?' Isaac said, shrugging out of his own. As soon as he said the words, he felt horribly guilty. Her mum had abandoned her when she was little. She had probably missed out on so much love and care from her life. 'Sorry, that was insensitive.'

She smiled, reaching up to stroke his face. 'Don't be sorry. I have a brilliant mum who raised me and loved me even if she wasn't my real mum. My aunt Lucy is a wonderful woman and, yes, she taught me the important life lesson of wearing a jacket which I obviously chose to ignore.'

He wrapped his jacket round her and she slipped her arms into the sleeves. It swamped her, her wet red curls cascading in waves down the front. He had never seen anyone look as beautiful as she did right then, cloaked in his jacket and looking up at him with her clover green eyes and wide smile.

He tugged the collar of the jacket closer together, pulling her into him at the same time.

The rain lashed down around them but there under the tree they were cocooned from the world. They were so close, her sweet coconut scent surrounding them both. The atmosphere changed between them, the world beyond the tree fading away.

Her eyes cast down to his lips for a second before she looked back up into his eyes. He ran his hands down her shoulders to her waist. They both knew what was going to happen next.

He bent his head down to hers, her eyes darkening with lust the only encouragement he needed.

'I thought you said this wouldn't happen again,' Bella said, against his lips.

'This doesn't count, we're not at work,' he whispered as he kissed her.

CHAPTER 13

The storm was the only sound that Bella could hear, the rain splashing on the ground, thunder roaring off the coast and off in the distance lightning lit up the sky, echoing the feeling that was ripping through her body at Isaac's kiss.

The chemistry between them was something almost tangible. This man could kiss, there was no doubt about that. But underneath this sexual attraction was something much deeper, something neither of them could deny. She couldn't stay away from him and it seemed the feeling was completely mutual. She had no idea why she had held hands with him as they had walked, only that it had felt the most natural thing in the world, as if they were supposed to be connected in some way.

His hands wandered up underneath his jacket she was wearing, caressing her back and holding her close. This kiss was slower, gentler, more considered, and it was hot as hell.

They both knew where these kisses were going to lead. He could deny it all he wanted but it was only a matter of time before they ended up in bed together. And this delicious anticipation, this build-up was just going to make the main event even better.

Long after the rain had stopped, long after the dogs had curled up at their feet and gone to sleep, the kiss continued. It was only when the sun came out, dazzling them as it reflected off the sea, that they pulled apart.

He smiled down at her. There were no regrets in his eyes this time.

'I think our first time would have been amazing,' Isaac said, not releasing his hold on her.

'I'm looking forward to it,' Bella said, grinning mischievously.

'Bella—'

She ran her hand down his cheek. 'As long as we don't do it at work then it doesn't count. I have to go, *Mr Scott*, I'm having dinner with Eden and Rome tonight in Rosa's. It's my turn to pay so I'm sure if I'm late they'll be hunting me down. I'll see you tomorrow.'

'Goodnight Bella.'

She leaned up again and kissed him briefly on the lips, gratified that he held her tighter and kissed her back before she stepped away. She whistled for Alfie and walked off down the hill and as she looked back she smiled when she saw that Isaac was watching her go.

❦❧

Eden and Freya were already sitting in the restaurant when Bella arrived. Freya always came to their siblings dinner. Over the years they'd all had many boyfriends and girlfriends but by some unspoken rule none of them came to dinner with them at Rosa's. But Freya was different. Somehow she had wheedled her way into all of their hearts. Bella looked at her like a sister but frustratingly so did Rome. The man himself clearly hadn't arrived yet which meant she'd be able to talk freely about Isaac without the overprotective glare from her big brother.

'Hey,' Eden grinned as she saw Bella approach. She got up from the table and embraced Bella in a big hug.

Freya stood up and hugged Bella too.

They all sat back down, and Bella helped herself to a piece of garlic bread oozing with melted cheese.

'Sorry I'm late, I got caught in the rain and I had to go home and get changed.'

'Urgh, I hate the rain,' Freya said.

Bella looked out on the rain-soaked street as it gleamed in the sun and she couldn't help but smile. 'I love it.'

Eden's phone flashed up with a text on the table and she quickly read it and smiled. Bella knew instinctively who had made her react like that.

'Dougie texted me while I was on my way over here,' Bella said. 'He said he's looking forward to catching up with us.' She watched Eden smile as she shoved her phone away.

'I know, he's been texting me lots too.'

Bella smiled. She'd had only one text from him so it was quite clear to see where his priorities lay.

'He arrives Thursday, how are you feeling about seeing him again?'

Eden sighed though she was still smiling. 'Same as always, excited, elated, terrified, annoyed that he makes me feel this way, angry, happy. I told him I might not have time to see him but I know I will. He knows it too. He even suggested that he stay with me but I was firm about that. He can stay in a hotel. I don't need to be tortured any more.'

'Why don't you want him to stay with you?' Freya asked.

'Because then he'll be walking around naked like last time, driving me insane. I'm sure he does it deliberately to wind me up.'

'You've seen him naked?' Freya said with wide eyes. 'Is he hot? Who am I kidding, of course he is.'

'Yes he's hot but I'm not sure why he does it. He's not remotely interested in me.'

'How do you know?' Bella said. From what she could see, Dougie only really came over to Hope Island so often to see Eden.

'Because I'm like a sister to him,' Eden said.

Bella pulled a face. 'He said that?'

Eden nodded, the smile fading from her face.

'Urgh, I hate it when a guy says that,' Freya said. 'When they look at you as a sister, you've got no hope. No one fancies their own sister. It's so unsexy. It's even worse than being relegated to the friendzone.'

'Being friends isn't bad,' Bella protested. 'At least when you're friends there's a chance that the friendship could develop into something more.'

Freya sighed. 'Sometimes you can be the best of friends and still there's no chance of anything happening.'

Bella smiled, sadly. 'Rome adores you.'

'He's never gotten over Paige's death,' Freya said, quietly.

'Well it's about time he did,' Eden said. 'He'd only known her a month when he proposed, and then she was working in London for the next eighteen months and they'd only get to see each other at weekends when they'd spend most of their time in the bedroom. They never had time to have a proper relationship before she died in that awful rollercoaster accident. It was horrific and it messed him up spectacularly but it's been six years. She's been dead longer than he knew her. I really liked Paige but I have no idea if they would have lasted if they had been in a proper relationship and not one built on great weekend sex. He's closer to you than he ever was to her. But he's afraid of getting hurt again. Just be patient with him.'

'He said the other day that he thinks he's ready for love again. That he wants the companionship and intimacy of a proper relationship. If he's not thinking about that with you then the boy's an idiot,' Bella said.

Freya sighed. 'Between me and Eden we're both lost causes. Oh, let's change the subject. How was your first day at work?'

Bella's smile grew. 'Today was pretty special.'

Freya stared at her for a moment. 'You've kissed him again, haven't you?'

'Well he kissed me, but yes.'

'You kissed the boss?' Eden squealed and Bella and Freya shushed her.

'Yes, I really like him. And I think he really likes me. At the moment he keeps insisting nothing can happen because he's my boss and work politics but I met him while I was walking Alfie tonight and we got caught in the rain and we kissed again.'

'Awwww. A kiss in the rain. How sweet,' Eden said, smiling happily. 'I've got a good feeling about Isaac. I think he might be the one.'

Bella laughed. 'You say that about every one of my boyfriends. There is no "one". Isaac is sweet and funny and attentive. We have off-the-chart chemistry. He is, by a mile, the best kiss I've ever had. And I'm sure when we eventually end up in bed together, it will be phenomenal but he doesn't love me. I don't think this is anything serious for him.'

'Maybe it isn't serious now, but it could be something serious later. It'll probably never be love straight away with anyone; that takes time to build. Just don't dismiss it just because he hasn't whipped out an engagement ring just yet. Enjoy it, see what happens. Don't push him away when he gets close.'

Freya nodded. 'It might not be love yet but he seems pretty keen. Did you happen to mention that you were coming here tonight?'

'Yes, I did.' Bella turned round to see what Freya was looking at and felt her smile spread across her face when she saw Isaac at the counter buying something.

Obviously feeling her eyes on him, he turned and waved when he saw her. While Rosa got his order ready he wandered over.

'I'd say him turning up here is a bit more than a coincidence,' Freya said, under her breath.

'Hi,' Isaac said.

'Hi.'

There was an uncomfortable silence for a moment or two while they grinned sheepishly at each other.

'What are you doing here?'

'I'm just getting a lasagne for dinner. Rosa's are the best I've ever had. I promise I'm not stalking you or anything. I was, erm… out a little longer than I thought I would be while I was walking Rocket and when I got back the dinner I had left in the oven had gone a bit black so this sounded like a good alternative.'

'Bella was just telling us about her first day at work,' Freya said, a big cheeky smile on her face. Eden nudged her but she was undeterred.

Bella blushed. 'Yes, I was telling them about the plans for the spring fair, we're all excited about having it here on the island again.'

'You're bringing the fair back to Hope Island?' Eden said, her eyes wide and excited. 'That's so wonderful.'

Bella stared at her pointedly and Eden blushed. 'Sorry, I, erm… must have been in the toilet when you discussed the fair.'

Isaac laughed. 'I'm excited to see the fair again too. I'm very much looking forward to working with Bella on all future projects.' His eyes found hers and she swallowed. She didn't think they were talking about work any more.

Rosa called across to him and he looked over to see that his lasagne was ready for collection.

Isaac looked back at Bella, touching her arm briefly. 'I'll see you tomorrow.'

'You can count on it.'

He grinned and walked off just as Rome came towards the table. He glared at Isaac as he walked out the shop before he sat down next to Bella.

'Stop glaring at him, he hasn't done anything wrong,' Bella said.

'Apart from lie, seduce you under false pretences and—'

'OK, OK, apart from that,' Bella said, feeling deflated all of a sudden.

'I take it something is going on between you two,' Rome said.

'What makes you think that?'

'The way you two were looking at each other with all soppy eyes when I walked in. Have you slept with him?'

'Rome! You have no right to ask her that!' Eden said.

Rome shrugged as he helped himself to a piece of garlic bread. 'Just looking out for my little sister.'

'I really like him,' Bella said. 'And maybe something will happen and maybe it won't but he makes me happy and it's been a long time since anyone made me feel like that, so don't ruin it by going all overprotective big brother on me. If we start seeing each other I want you to trust in my judgement and be nice to him.'

'I do trust you, and I'm always nice.'

Eden and Freya made various noises of objection.

'What? I am nice.'

'If grumpy is a kind of nice, sure,' Eden said.

'I'm not grumpy,' Rome protested.

Freya reached across to pat his arm consolingly. 'You're not exactly sunshine and roses.'

Rome considered this for a moment and shrugged. He turned his attention back to Bella. 'If he makes you happy then I'm happy. I'll be nice to him and I might even give him a smile occasionally. Just be careful, OK? I don't want you to get hurt.'

Bella nodded.

'You should have invited him to have dinner with us,' Eden said. 'Then we could have vetted him for you.'

Rome shook his head. 'Dinner at Rosa's is family only.'

'Oh, maybe I should go then,' Freya said.

'Don't be daft. You are family. You're like a sister to me,' Rome said, completely missing how gutted Freya suddenly looked at that comment.

'Not a sister,' Bella said, kindly, catching Freya's eye. 'A really good friend who is like family because of how important she is to us. Dougie is like family too. But neither Eden nor I look at him like a brother.'

Rome frowned in confusion. 'OK, not a sister, my best friend, which makes you like family. Whatever the distinction is, Freya belongs here with us. Isaac would be an interloper.'

'That interloper might be your brother-in-law one day,' Eden said.

Bella rolled her eyes. 'I don't think that will ever happen.'

Eden reached for Bella's hand. 'Look, Rome is always going to play the overprotective big brother and tell you to be careful and I will always tell you to take a chance at love and not throw it away or dismiss it because you're scared. Be brave and be open to love. Because if it does come your way and it is reciprocated it will be the best thing that ever happens to you.'

Bella nodded. She had never been in love and never really wanted to be. Loving someone meant you could get hurt, rejected and let down and she'd already had her fill of that. But she had promised Eden and Rome that she would take a chance on love if it came her way and, although she didn't think this thing with Isaac would turn into love, if it did she was willing to see what all the fuss was about.

❦

Isaac walked into the Umbrella Foundation the next day with a smile on his face. He had no idea what was going to happen with Bella but it was going to be a lot of fun finding out. He had tried to keep away from her, he had tried to be firm with her about nothing happening between them, but their resolve around each other was non-existent. He was finding it hard to find reasons not to be with her any more.

He walked into the lift and when the doors pinged open on the first floor, he couldn't help but smile when Bella and a few other people walked in. She was wearing a beautiful bronze dress that came down to the knee and had a high collar that was embellished with gold jewels, making her look like some kind of Egyptian queen.

'Good morning, Mr Scott,' Bella said, smiling sweetly at him before moving to stand to the side of him. As the other people got on behind her, she shifted to make room for them and ended up, either deliberately or innocently, standing in front of him with her back towards him.

His heart leapt because the bronze dress slashed down in a narrow V-shape from the shoulders, leaving a small sliver of her bare back completely exposed. He couldn't take his eyes off it.

At the very bottom of the V, which finished halfway down her back, was a tiny glimpse of her turquoise bra strap.

Little conversations continued in the lift but Bella wasn't talking to anyone and no one was paying either of them any attention. He reached out and ever so gently stroked his thumb across the indent of her spine.

She let out a soft gasp and one of the men at the front of the lift looked over at her. Isaac busied himself with his phone. When the man looked away, Bella deliberately shuffled back a few inches.

The lift pinged open on her floor and a few people got out. She made a move to leave too but as he grazed her back for a second time she stayed where she was.

There was now only one other person in the lift with them so they still couldn't talk and Isaac didn't dare do anything else because it would be much more noticeable. What was he doing? If he was caught touching Bella like this, everyone in the building would know by the end of the day and he would be tarred as some kind of pervert.

The lift pinged open on the next floor and the man got out. The doors closed behind him.

'It seems you missed your floor, Miss Roussel,' Isaac said.

'I was distracted.'

He moved to her side and looked down at her to see her cheeks were flushed, her eyes sparkling. 'Well, I'll see you in the meeting in half an hour. Try to keep your mind on the job.'

She rolled her eyes and shook her head at him, smiling fondly as he left her alone in the lift.

He had no idea what he was doing but he was enjoying every second.

Bella's nerves were shot to pieces, her heart was racing, her breathing was accelerated as if she'd just run a mile and all he had done was touch her back.

She pressed the button in the lift to take her back down to her floor. As much as she was loving this build-up, what if he had no intention of taking this any further? What if he was just teasing her and that was it? She had never wanted anyone as badly as she wanted him right now and if it didn't culminate in something more than kisses and comments soon she was going to spontaneously combust. The tension was unbearable and he was just making it worse.

The doors pinged open on her floor and she stayed in the lift for a second, her heart suddenly thundering like rain as she made a decision. She jabbed the button that would take her back to his floor.

A few seconds later she had arrived. Claudia wasn't at her desk so she strolled past and knocked on his door.

'Come in.'

She opened the door and saw Isaac was alone sitting at his desk. He grinned when he saw her. She shut the door behind her.

'I think we should sleep together.'

The smile fell from his face.

'You've already said you don't want a relationship because it could get in the way of work but this thing between us is not just going to go away and you're not exactly being restrained about not letting anything happen. I want you, you want me, so let's just get this out of the way and then we can get on with just being friends or colleagues again.'

There was a silence for a few seconds before a woman's voice filled the room.

'Oh my god Isaac, is that her, is that the girl you've been telling me about? I like her. Let me talk to her.'

Isaac leaned over to his phone. 'Mum, I'll call you back.'

'No, wait. If you don't marry this girl—'

Isaac slammed his hand down on a button and the voice was disconnected.

Bella flushed. 'That was your mum?'

Isaac nodded, a smile playing on his lips.

'And I just told you I want to sleep with you and she heard every word.'

'Yes, she'll dine out on this for weeks.' He got out of his chair and walked towards her.

Her heart was hammering; she knew her cheeks were burning red. She wanted to turn and run and hide under her desk at least for the rest of the week. He was her boss. She had just made things a hundred times worse. What was she thinking? She had never done something like that before, walking up to someone and demanding they sleep with her was way out of her comfort zone. She'd never even asked a guy out before. What was it about Isaac that made her do things she had never done before?

'Well you got the mum seal of approval,' Isaac said as he approached her.

She swallowed. 'You talked about me with her?'

'Yes, I told her there was this thorn in my side that wouldn't go away,' Isaac said, before he captured her mouth with his own.

All other words dried in her throat and she found her hands in his hair as he pinned her back against the door. There was something truly wonderful about being pinned to any surface by Isaac Scott. He was so big that he surrounded her and that was such a turn-on. His hard, muscular body against hers, his hot lips against her own. She could kiss this man forever and never get tired of it.

No not forever. Love never lasted forever so there was no point in even thinking about going down that road. She would live for now, enjoy the moment, and at this very moment there was a gorgeous, sweet, sexy hunk of a man kissing her like his life depended on it.

His hands swept up from her waist, cupping her head. It was so gentle and so sweet and so completely opposite to the way he was kissing her with a fierce need. She hooked her leg round him, pulling him closer, and he ran his hand up her thigh, sliding her dress up to her hip. For one wonderful and terrifying moment she thought he was going to make her wish come true right here against the door but then he pulled away slightly.

'So you want me to make love to you?'

Her cheeks flamed red again. How could she have asked him that? Normally she would date a man, dinner, the cinema, maybe a few drinks in a bar. They'd go for walks on the beach and it would be several weeks or sometimes even months before she would go to bed with them. But Isaac had made it very clear they couldn't do that so where did that leave them other than lots of frustrating kisses that were never going to lead anywhere?

'I think we should. Then maybe once it's out of the way we can get on with our day at work without the need to maul each other.'

'I don't know, this mauling is fast becoming my favourite part of my day. Meetings, emails, reports, and then there's you.' He sighed, leaning his forehead against hers for a moment. 'Come to my house for dinner tonight. I'll cook for you, something that won't go black and hard because I'm too busy kissing you.'

She nodded. 'And then after dinner?

He kissed her briefly. 'I'll take you home. No sex. If we're going to do this, we'll do this properly.'

Her heart leapt and soared. 'That's beginning to sound a bit like a date, Mr Scott.'

'Oh it's definitely a date. But it's a first date, so we'll eat and we'll talk and we'll probably kiss a lot. And I'll have you home and tucked up in your bed by ten o'clock.'

She laughed. 'Will you be joining me in that bed?'

'Don't tempt me. Now go. I need to ring my mum back and reassure her that I haven't just slept with one of my staff across my desk and I have to prepare for a meeting where I'll be sitting next to this beautiful, wonderful woman and trying very hard not to grab her and *maul* her, as you so eloquently put it, in front of all my staff.'

'Shit, the meeting. I was going to prepare some notes for you. And I have a PowerPoint half-finished on my computer downstairs.'

'I'm sure whatever you bring to the table will be amazing, even if it's just you.' His eyes glanced down to where his hand was resting on the waistband of her knickers. 'Dinner at my place at seven, wear this beautiful dress, and I'm going to spend the rest of the day trying not to think about the possibility of seeing your matching turquoise underwear later this evening.'

Bella laughed.

He stepped back and straightened her dress for her, then his hands moved to her hair and gently stroked that back into place too.

She leaned up and kissed him on the cheek and left the office. Claudia was back at her desk and she looked over at Bella in confusion as she walked to the lift. Did Claudia have any idea that Bella had just been kissing her boss on the other side of that door? In a small office like this, it wouldn't take long for people to know or at least to guess. But with the prospect of a hot date with this incredible man tonight, Bella was finding it hard to care.

CHAPTER 14

Isaac flicked through some reports in the boardroom as he waited for the other staff to arrive. Claudia was at the back of the room, sorting out the teas, coffees and pastries. Brian and Tina from the finance team were looking through a report and talking quietly to each other at the far end of the table and Madge was sitting halfway down the table, busily writing notes. He was still waiting on several people to arrive, including the woman he had just agreed to have a date with that night.

He should be nervous and worried about this. This broke every rule he had ever made. Don't mix business and pleasure was one of the most important rules in all walks of life and he had done that several times since meeting Bella at the weekend. If things ended between them, it could be really difficult at work, and he certainly didn't want anyone there to find out but as the woman herself came strolling in, he couldn't find it in himself to care.

She was the most incredible woman he'd ever met and instead of thinking about what would happen if things ended between them, all he could think about was how he could make things last. He wanted to spend every day kissing her, talking to her, spending time with her and instead of being scared about that prospect, he was loving every minute.

'Miss Roussel, I just wanted to talk to you about something before the meeting starts,' Isaac said, indicating the seat next to him.

Bella walked round the table hugging her clipboard to her chest and trying to look as if him asking her to sit next to him was the most normal, professional request in the world. She sat down and looked at him.

He drew her attention to the minutes in front of him. As a few more people walked into the room laughing and talking and drew everyone's attention on them, he shuffled closer to her so their knees were barely touching.

'Are you OK to present a few minutes about forthcoming fundraising events?' Isaac asked, quietly, knowing that she was fully prepared to do just that. He looked down at the minutes and wrote a brief note to her.

You look so beautiful today in that dress.

He watched her read the note and her pale cheeks flushed pink.

'That's fine, Mr Scott, I have a few notes prepared just in case,' Bella said as she wrote her own reply.

If you like the dress so much, I'll let you take it off later.

He grinned. As much as he was really tempted to do that, he didn't want to rush things with her. If he had any chance of this working between them, he knew he had to take his time, build her trust. It had been a long time since he had properly dated someone but this time round he was going to do this right.

Dinner only. And maybe a nice long goodnight kiss.

She smiled at his note just as the last few people arrived. Thankfully there were quite a few people around the table now, which necessitated everyone sitting quite close to each other. So when Bella shuffled closer to him to make room for someone to sit next to her, it was quite innocent that she brushed arms with him.

As everyone got themselves comfortable, concentrating on the drinks and pastries that were being passed around, he slipped his hand under the table and very briefly, very gently, stroked the inside of her knee before returning his hand back to the table top again.

This was a dangerous game but he was loving it.

He stood up and everyone went quiet.

'Thanks for coming; we have quite a few reports to get through so I'll keep this brief. We've had a good few months since the start of the year. Some of the reports will go into that in a bit more detail. We've continued to help several hundred homeless people in towns and cities across the UK but a lot of the funding for the projects has come from BlazeStar. This year I want to concentrate on creating our own funding with the goal of being a self-sufficient charity by the end of next year. And that's where our new fundraising events manager comes in. This is Bella Roussel who brings with her a wealth of experience, knowledge and a load of enthusiasm for the role.'

To his surprise and annoyance, there were a few whispers around the room, some of them were not good. Clearly people knew about the embezzlement at Magic Wishes and were surprised by her appointment.

He glanced down at Bella and the bold confident person he had seen a few moments before had dimmed somewhat. Bella smiled and gave a little wave but it was quite obvious she didn't like being the centre of attention or appreciate the judgement from some of the people in the room. He was going to ask her to talk a little about herself and her experience but, considering the company she had worked in before, perhaps he had better skip past that part.

'Bella has a lot of passion for this role. She only started in the job yesterday so we haven't created a lot of events just yet, but Bella, why don't you give us a brief summary of some of the events that we are to look forward to in the coming months.'

He sat down and Bella took a sip of water from the glass in front of her and stood up. She glanced at him and he gave her an encouraging smile.

She looked down at her clipboard and back at the room.

'Firstly, we are launching a nationwide Easter egg hunt but with a difference. This is going to be a game-based app very similar to *Pokémon Go*. For those of you who don't know, people would have to travel around real-world locations to collect virtual eggs on their phone. The eggs will add up to points and the points can be swapped for real chocolate eggs. There will be in-app purchases as well, which is how we will raise money.

'A week on Saturday, the start of the Easter school holidays, there will be a funfair right here on the island. As many of you know, we used to have a big funfair with rides and food and fireworks every year on the island until they stopped when the Harrison family moved away and this year we're going to bring it back. We have already booked the fair but there are several other things we need to organise for the event to run smoothly, one of the main things being transporting the lorries onto the island.'

Elsie put her hand up, unsure whether to interrupt Bella or not. Bella nodded encouragingly. 'When the fair used to be held on the island, the Harrisons would organise landing crafts to bring the lorries over and the lorries would just drive straight onto Buttercup Beach and then into the park.'

'Great idea. I'll look into that. Thank you. In June we have a zombie run booked for Hyde Park in London…'

Isaac sat watching her, absolutely mesmerised. This was where she was in control, this was what she was good at. She didn't like standing up and talking in front of people, making speeches, but events management was her thing and the fact that she could talk so confidently when she didn't like this kind of thing showed how brave she was.

Bella talked about several other events that she had either booked already or was going to book and he was stunned with what she had achieved in just one day.

He glanced around the room to see what other people's reactions were. Eric still obviously wasn't happy about her appointment to the position but a lot of the others seemed to be impressed by her. Maybe she could win them all over with her charm, dedication and passion for the role.

He suddenly caught Claudia's eye. She wasn't watching Bella, she was watching him.

Crap.

Claudia knew him so well. She had been his PA for so many years now that he'd lost count. Thanks to a hefty bonus, she had moved down to Hope Island when he had made the move here, which he was glad for. She was so efficient, so organised and she knew him better than he knew himself.

Had he been staring at Bella with adoration? Had Claudia seen him touch Bella or the way they had almost flirted when she'd first walked into the meeting room? He thought he was being subtle but the way Claudia was staring at him now, he knew something was up.

He returned his attention to Bella and ensured that for the rest of her short speech his facial features were arranged in a much more professional expression. He even pretended to take some notes at one stage so he wasn't staring at her the whole time she was speaking.

Bella finally finished and sat down and Isaac passed the meeting over to the different departments for them to give their reports.

Nicely done, Isaac wrote on the corner of his minutes.

She smiled briefly and then turned her attention to the rest of the staff and, although she didn't look at him again, her knee was pressed up against his throughout the whole meeting.

Tonight couldn't come soon enough.

❦

The meeting finally came to an end and everyone got up and left, some of them taking the remaining pastries with them. Bella hung back for a little while on the pretext of gathering her notes and the handouts together. It was quite clear she wanted to speak to him but Claudia wasn't moving so Bella eventually took the hint and left.

He stood up to leave himself but Claudia got up and closed the door and then rounded on him.

'What's going on with you and her?'

'Nothing,' Isaac said, way too quickly.

'Don't give me that, you were staring at her like a puppy would stare at a piece of chocolate cake. Don't think that I didn't see you touching her either. Do you want her to slap some kind of sexual harassment charge on you?'

He sighed and sat back down

'Bella wouldn't do that.'

'No, I don't suppose she would. I saw the way she was looking at you too. Have you slept with her?'

'That's absolutely none of your business.'

'I'll take that as a yes.'

'No, I haven't actually.' Though it had come close too many times so he could hardly take the moral high ground, especially as he had kissed Bella on her first day at work.

'After the horrible mess that Carter left behind with his affair, I wouldn't think you would risk an office romance yourself. You know so many people thought that you starting this charity was a big mistake, everyone said that you moving to the Scilly Isles when your head office for BlazeStar was in London was a big mistake. Everyone is going to be watching us, waiting for us to drop the ball, you don't need any scandal. Why risk it just for a bit of fun?'

Isaac stared down at the notes that he and Bella had written to each other throughout the course of the meeting. 'She's not just a bit of fun. I went to her house in disguise and she invited me in to stay the night. She had no idea who I was and she was prepared to share her last bowl of porridge with me. We chatted for hours. I've never had that with a woman before. And I left there Sunday morning knowing that I had just spent the night with this really remarkable, special person. I ended up going back there on Sunday night and we talked again and we ended up kissing. Well, she kissed me, but I damned well kissed her back.'

Claudia stared at him in shock. 'I've never seen you like this before. Not once in all the years I've known you have you ever looked at a woman from work. You've always kept that part of your life separate.'

'I know. Believe me I did consider not employing her so I could date her without any conflict of interest but you've seen her. She's been here one day and she's organised all that already. She's brilliant.'

'She is,' Claudia said softly, sitting down. 'You really like her, don't you? She isn't just some random woman that you'll date a few times and never see again, is she? This is something serious.'

'It is serious. At least it is for me,' he sighed. 'I don't know what this is, this feeling I have for her, it's not like anything I've ever felt before. It's not love, it can't be. I've only known her for a few days but this feeling is so strong she is all I can think about. And not just in a sexual way, but in a way that I just want to spend every single second of my time with her.'

Claudia half smiled. 'That sounds like love to me. Love doesn't work on a schedule. You can't say because you've known her three months or a year then it qualifies as love.'

'But love at first sight is a myth. No one really falls in love after knowing someone for a few minutes. Lust at first sight maybe, but not love.'

'I think thousands of people out there would disagree with you. Personally I think love at first sight is impossible – as you say, you're judging that person on looks and a sexual attraction alone – but that's not to say you can't fall in love with that person after half an hour of talking to them. You spent two nights talking to her; I'd say you know her well enough to know whether she's important to you. Whether it could be love one day.'

Isaac looked out the window at the tiny glimpse of the sea. 'So what do I do, Claudia? If people here find out then the gossip and the comments won't be kind to her. If we do go for it anyway and it ends a few weeks or months down the line then it will be beyond awkward having to work together every day.'

'I don't think you really have a choice.'

Isaac looked back at her. 'You think it's too risky.'

'Of course it's risky. Love is always a risk. But if there is a chance that this could be love for you, if there's a chance that Bella is the one that you're going to settle down with and marry one day then you grab hold of this chance with both hands. Forget the gossips or the comments, forget the what ifs, because if this is really love then all of that will be worth it.'

Isaac grinned. 'I could kiss you right now.'

Claudia gathered all her stuff up. 'Save that for Bella. She will probably appreciate it more than me. And don't worry about what people will say. There will always be gossip and it will only last until the next piece comes along.'

'I want to protect her from all that though. You know what people will say, that she slept with the boss to get the job, or that I only gave her the job because we were sleeping together. I don't want her exposed to that kind of crap.'

'So keep it a secret. Keep it professional at work, no more looking at her with puppy-dog eyes, no more kisses in your office,' she said, pointedly.

'How did you know?'

'Because she walked out of your office this morning with her hair looking like it had been dragged through a bush and the biggest grin on her face. It wasn't hard to put two and two together. Keep your hands off each other and there's a chance we can keep it out of the rumour mill for a while.'

Isaac nodded. He could do that.

Claudia moved to the door. 'I'm happy for you.'

He laughed. 'Steady there, we've not even had our first date yet. I wouldn't go buying a big hat for our wedding day just yet.'

'I wouldn't do that.'

'No?'

'I'm much more of a fascinator type girl.'

He laughed and she left him alone.

He knew marriage was a very long way away but Claudia was right, he wasn't going to pass up this chance. Bella was way too important for that.

❦

Bella had spent the rest of the day working with Elsie and Roger organising the fair. With a little over one week until the fair kicked off the start of the school holidays there was a lot to do. She had organised fairs in the past but she had never organised one in such a short amount of time. She had a great list of reliable contacts and she knew several people on the island who would help her dot the i's and cross the t's in terms of the permissions needed to hold such an event. A large part of the organisation now was advertising it, getting the word out so people knew it was happening. And not just the people on Hope Island too, they needed to spread the word to all of the Scilly Isles and maybe as far as Cornwall as well.

She got in the lift with Elsie and Roger, thinking about what kind of radio advertising she could do.

'Any plans for the evening, dear?' Roger asked as Bella scribbled some notes on her pad.

Bella stuffed her notepad in her bag to hide the smile that had suddenly erupted on her face.

She shrugged. 'Just dinner. I'll probably be tucked up in bed by ten o'clock.' She smiled to herself at the thought of who was going to be doing the tucking up. 'What about you two?'

'I'm having çoffee and cake with the WI,' Elsie said.

'Oh be sure to tell them about the fair,' Bella said.

'Of course. I bet some of them would like to hold a cake stand there, would that be OK?'

Bella smiled. They really couldn't get away from the cake sale but as it was going to be part of a much bigger event she didn't think Isaac would mind. 'I think that's a great idea, just as long as there's some chocolate cake, I'll be happy.'

Elsie smiled. 'My chocolate cake is one of the best on the island, even if I do say so myself.'

'I'm sure it is,' Bella said, knowing that no one on the island would be brave enough to dispute it.

The lift doors pinged open and she walked out into the foyer with them. Isaac was there talking to Mary, the receptionist. He had his suit jacket on and was clearly getting ready to leave for the day too.

As she walked past, he flashed her a brief smile which she returned but a second or two later he caught up with her as she walked out the front door.

'Miss Roussel, I just wanted to catch up with you about the fair, do you have a second?' Isaac drew her to one side and Bella smiled and waved at Roger and Elsie as they walked off together in the direction of the town. No one else was around but when Isaac spoke again it was very quietly. 'I forgot to say that I have an outdoor hot tub at my house, so you might want to bring your swimming costume for later.'

Bella laughed. 'You have a hot tub? That's not at all pretentious.'

He grinned. 'I know. When I bought my house in London, it already had one which I vowed I would get rid of as soon as I moved in. But after spending one night in it, staring at the stars, I loved it and knew I had to install one here too. I promise everything else in the house is quite tasteful.'

'No animal-print bedspreads or disco balls, no mirrors on the ceiling?'

He laughed. 'No, I promise.'

'Well I have just the thing to wear in your hot tub tonight,' Bella said and enjoyed the darkening of his eyes as he looked at her.

'I'll look forward to seeing it later. Seven o'clock and don't be late.'

Ever so briefly, he touched the back of her hand and then turned and walked away.

Butterflies erupted in her stomach. She couldn't wait to spend another night with this man and even if they weren't going to make love to each other she knew there would be a lot more talking and kissing. And although spending the night in a hot tub was a little cliché and like something from an eighties porn film, she couldn't think of anything more romantic.

※彩C@⁀

Isaac looked around the kitchen. The red wine was open, the steaks were out and marinated, the crumble was slowly cooking in the oven, everything was ready.

He was so nervous about tonight; he needed this to go well. He felt like he had something to prove to Bella as the last time they had sat down to dinner he had been someone else entirely. Although to a large extent a lot of what he had told Bella was true, he wanted her to get to know the real him.

He walked into the lounge and Rocket, obviously sensing that he was nervous or excited, leapt off her dog bed and jumped up at him.

Isaac stroked her velvety head before he moved over to the mantelpiece and lit a few candles. He stood back to see the effect the golden light had on the room and then moved a couple of candles to the coffee table too. The log fire was burning merrily in the grate; even though it was probably a bit too mild to warrant it, it added a warm cosy ambience to the room.

Rocket leapt up at him again, wagging her tail, clearly as excited about the evening as Isaac was.

'Stop jumping, you daft beast. After your behaviour the other night, I think you need to prove to Bella that you have manners and are perfectly respectable.'

Rocket took no notice and went to grab one of her toys from her bed and brought it back to Isaac to play with her.

'In a minute, let me just go and get the summerhouse ready and I'll come back and play with you for a while before she comes.'

Isaac walked out the back door fully expecting Rocket to follow him but he was alone when he walked up to the doors of the summerhouse; the silly dog had probably gone back to sleep.

He opened the doors to the summerhouse and set about lighting candles in there too. He plumped up a few of the cushions, shook out the blankets and spread them over the sofas and turned the heaters on to take the chill off the place. He switched on the fairy lights that were hung around the outside of the summerhouse, found the right music on the stereo and turned the volume down low and then stepped outside onto the decking at the back of the summerhouse. This was where the hot tub was with views over the whole bay. He had envisaged they might come and sit in the summerhouse and watch the sun set before dinner and then they could come back out here later and enjoy the hot tub and the view of the moon and the stars over the sea.

He lifted the lid of the hot tub and checked the temperature. It was warm but not hot yet. It would be another few hours before it reached its hottest but they had plenty of time and even if they used it now it would still be comfortable. He fished out a few leaves that had fallen in from the tree that hung over the top of the hot tub and then pulled the lid back into place. He walked back into the summerhouse, lit a few of the larger candles that were in jars and carried them out onto the deck.

He looked out over the bay again. The sky was that gorgeous pale gold as the sun made its way into the sea.

The smell of burning drifted past, maybe someone was making the most of the lovely weather and having a barbeque nearby.

He walked back off the deck and round the summerhouse and looked up at the sky behind his home which was painted with a flickering orange glow, almost as if the sky was on fire.

His heart dropped into his stomach, a horrible sick feeling twisting his gut as he realised that it wasn't the sky that was on fire at all.

It was his house.

Great orange flames danced across the roof, burning through the windows, consuming the walls.

He ran forward, his blood freezing to ice in his veins. His house was on fire and it was spreading so quickly there was nothing he could do to stop it.

CHAPTER 15

Bella walked over the hill towards Isaac's house with a big smile on her face about what the night would hold. Dinner, kissing in the hot tub under the stars. It was going to be magical.

Up ahead a steady plume of black smoke rose in the air; someone was obviously having some kind of fire in their back garden, probably burning some rubbish or waste from the garden.

As she reached the top of the hill that led down to Isaac's house she stopped, frozen to the spot at what she could see. The little yellow cottage that was Isaac's home was completely ablaze.

She was running down the hill as fast as she could before she knew what she was doing. The thatch on top of the roof was burning so hard and fast that the whole house would soon only be ashes.

She screamed for Isaac but there was no sign of him. What if he was trapped somewhere inside? What if he was hurt? The front door was closed and she tried the handle but it was obviously locked or at least secured somehow from the other side. She slammed her shoulder against the door but it didn't give. She took a few steps back and threw herself against the door again. It shifted a bit but still didn't open. She took a few steps back, ran to the door and slammed her whole body against the wood again. This time the door flew open, banging against the wall in the hallway.

'Isaac!'

Flames licked the hall walls as she stepped inside, holding her arm across her face to protect her from the smoke. Where was he? The thought that he was lying somewhere inside hurt or even worse filled her with a sick dread. She inched her way down the hall shouting for him as she coughed and spluttered through the thick smoke.

Suddenly a hand grabbed her around her arm and she whirled round to see Isaac. He looked furious.

'What the hell are you doing?' he shouted over the roar of the fire.

Bella launched herself at him, wrapping her arms around him and holding him tight.

He scooped her up in his arms and carried her back outside. He sat down on the low garden wall with her on his lap. It was only when he wiped the tears off her cheeks that she realised that she'd been crying.

'I need to call the fire brigade,' Isaac said. 'My phone is still inside.'

Bella stood up and grabbed her bag from where she had dumped it when she was trying to break in. She returned to Isaac's lap and he wrapped his arms tightly around her again. She fumbled around inside her bag and grabbed her phone, quickly dialling the emergency services. She explained the situation then hung up and threw the phone back into her bag.

'I'm so sorry,' Bella said, staring at the house. 'What happened?'

Isaac shook his head as he stared at his house burning. 'I have no idea. I wasn't in there at the time. I was down in the summerhouse. I can only presume Rocket knocked over a candle and it hit the rug and…' he gestured with his hand.

Bella sat up and looked around. 'Where is she?'

Isaac swallowed, tears filling his eyes. 'I don't know. I tried to get back in to get to her but the flames were too high. The back door was open so I only hope the stupid dog got out before she got herself trapped. I was looking around the house to see if I could see her when I saw you bursting in there like a little ninja. What on earth were you thinking?'

'I was trying to find you.'

Isaac sighed and kissed her on the head.

'God, what if Rocket didn't get out? I was supposed to look after her and I didn't even think about leaving her alone with candles, what kind of idiot am I?'

Bella's heart broke for him. She stroked his face. 'It was an accident, you can't blame yourself.'

He kissed her hand and then pulled her to him tighter as if he was scared to let her go. And that was how the fire brigade found them when they arrived a few minutes later, clinging to each other like their lives depended on it.

❦

Isaac watched as the fire brigade started to pack away their hose pipes. It had taken them about an hour to put out the fire, which considering the fire had taken hold in a matter of minutes, that hour had felt like a lifetime. The roof was gone completely and all that was left was a blackened shell and a pile of smoking rubble. There was nothing they could do to save the house, but Isaac had seen how bad the fire was even before Bella had arrived.

One of the crew had even gone into the house to look for Rocket but there was no sign of her anywhere, not even a body, which Isaac was thankful for. He didn't think he could cope with seeing his dead dog.

He hadn't been back on the island long enough to make friends so he was surprised by the number of people who had turned up to see if they could help. Some of them offering their houses for him to stay, others offering food, or passing him details of builders who would be able to help him rebuild his home; other people turned up just to offer their sympathies and to see if he was OK. He didn't even know most of their names and here they were offering to help. He hadn't been able to speak to most of them. There were no words in his head at all.

Bella had dealt with them all, thanking them for their kindness and reassuring them all that he would be in touch if he needed any help. She had asked them all to keep an eye out for Rocket just in case she had made it out alive. It was all the things he should have said. As CEO of three companies, he had dealt with his fair share of disasters over the years and he had dealt with them calmly and efficiently but this had hit him hard.

Bella hadn't left his side throughout, though his arms were wrapped around her so tightly she had little chance of getting away even if she'd wanted to leave. As first dates went this had to be the worst. His home, everything he owned was up in smoke, the upheaval this would cause in his life would be immense. Who in their right minds would want to stick around to deal with all that? Maybe it was for the best. Maybe it was foolish to try to start something with Bella when they worked together. Maybe this was fate intervening to make sure it stopped before it even got started. He wondered at what point she would make her excuses and leave.

The fireman who was clearly in charge came over to talk to them.

'You'll get a report in a few days. Shall we send it to your office, Mr Scott?'

Isaac nodded, unable to talk.

'You'll need to get in contact with your insurance company as soon as you can.'

He nodded again.

'Obviously the house is not safe to go in. Do you have some-where you can stay tonight?'

He would have to stay in a hotel but how could he do that when he didn't even have a bank card to pay for the room?

'Yes he does,' Bella said.

Isaac tore his eyes away from the smouldering remains of his life to look at her.

'You can stay with me.'

The fireman nodded and left them to it.

Bella dug her phone out of her bag again and he heard her calling a taxi. He knew it was probably only a twenty-minute walk to get back to her house from here, but he also knew he would be unlikely to be able to walk anywhere. He turned his attention back to his house. It was a surreal experience to be conscious and aware of what was happening around him, but also so completely detached, as if it was happening to someone else or he was watching it on TV. He felt numb. That was the only way to describe it. Time seemed to move slowly and then so fast all at once. He felt exhausted and buzzing all at the same time.

Bella disentangled herself from his arms and went down to the summerhouse, presumably to blow out the candles and turn off the hot tub. A few minutes later she was back, just as a car pulled up in his driveway.

She offered him her hand. 'Let's go home.'

He took her hand and followed her back to the car. He got in and was aware of her talking to the taxi driver before she got in next to him. He stared out the window as the car moved along the roads, passing people and houses that were obviously completely unaffected by the fire. Life carried on as normal for everyone else, completely unaware that his life had just come crashing down around him.

Bella lifted his arm and snuggled into his side and he turned his attention away from the window to focus on the woman in his arms.

'I'm sorry about tonight. This is not what I had planned at all,' he said, finding his voice for the first time in over an hour.

She kissed him on the cheek and rested her head on his shoulder and her hand over his heart. 'Tell me what you had planned?'

He knew she was trying to distract him but he was glad of it. 'I had steak with this amazing garlic and brandy marinade.'

'Did you make it yourself?'

'Yes, it's something I've perfected over the years. I can cook fairly well but my steak is my one meal that would blow your socks off.'

'You were trying to impress me.'

'Of course, I wanted you to go away from tonight wanting a repeat performance. I think I failed on that score.'

'There was never any fear of me not wanting to do this again. You have me under your spell, Isaac Scott. I want to spend every single second with you… in a non-obsessive kind of way obviously.'

He laughed softly. 'I said exactly the same thing about you.'

She smiled. 'What else would we have done once we had eaten the steak?'

He ran his hand through her hair, which was dark with smoke and ash. 'We could have drunk a few glasses of wine as we sat on the decking around the summerhouse, maybe taken a dip in the hot tub as we sat under the stars.'

'I like the sound of this date very much. We will have to recreate it one day.'

The taxi stopped outside her house and Bella leaned forward to pay the driver. It only occurred to him then that they had hardly been subtle talking in front of him. Knowing island gossip as he did, the fact that they were quite clearly together and were going back to spend the night at her house would probably be around the whole island by the next day.

She got out and, without taking her hand from his, she led him up the garden path and let them back into her house.

It felt odd to be back there again after leaving in such weird circumstances on Sunday night. He had left wanting to make love to her so much and now he was back and that feeling hadn't changed. But this was different. This was a need to feel alive when he had felt so numb for the past hour. A need to feel his heart pounding and to bury himself in her so passionately that for a brief time he could forget everything except her, except being with her. But even in the back of his confused and fractious mind he knew that wouldn't be a good idea. When sex was propelled by need it was never going to be the sweet, gentle lovemaking that he wanted for their first time together.

He took a step back away from her, though she didn't relinquish her hold on his hand.

'I should go. I don't think I should stay here tonight.'

She closed the front door and looked at him. 'You're filthy. Let's take a shower.'

She was a state as well, smoke coated her skin and hair in a thin film, and he knew he probably looked the same. A hot shower sounded really good, a hot shower with Bella would be heaven.

But still he held back. 'This isn't a good idea. I feel like I'm holding on by my fingernails and that I'm going to lose it at any second. And I don't even know what me losing it is going to look like, whether I'm going to shout and scream, whether I'm going to fall to my knees and cry or whether I'm just going to end up pinning you to the nearest flat surface and making love to you until you're screaming out my name. In fact all of those options are looking pretty good right now and I really don't want to scare you off—' He stopped when she stepped forward and placed a finger over his lips.

'You don't scare me, Isaac. This horrible situation with your house doesn't scare me. If you want to scream and shout and cry then you go ahead. If you want to hit something then I have some lovely pillows upstairs that you can pummel. If you want to make love to me for the rest of the evening to try to forget what a devastating night it's been for you then go right ahead. Believe me it will be no hardship for me. If you want to climb into my bed and pull the duvet over your head and go to sleep for the next twenty hours then that's fine too. But I'm not leaving you alone tonight. You need someone with you when the meltdown appears. And you know what, I really need you with me too.'

To his surprise tears filled her eyes.

'When I saw your house on fire I have never felt fear like it. When I thought about losing you it tore me apart.'

'I felt the same when I saw you run into my house. I had lost my house, my dog, but I couldn't cope with losing you too.'

'Stay with me tonight. Even if we just go straight upstairs and go to sleep, please just stay with me,' Bella said.

He stared at her for a moment and then took her face in his hands and kissed her. The moment her lips touched his, he felt some of the stress and tension seep out of him, like she was a cure taking away his pain. As devastating as it was to lose his home, they were both alive and unharmed. Property could be replaced but lives couldn't.

She pulled back slightly.

'Let's go take a shower,' Bella said. 'And we'll deal with whatever happens next together.'

Still holding his hand, she led him upstairs and into the bathroom. She turned the water on and stepped under the spray without taking off her clothes. She pulled him into the shower with her and as they stood underneath the water she wrapped her arms round him and held him tight with her head against his chest.

They stood there for the longest time, not moving, and it was enough. The feel of the hot water against his skin, her heart pounding against his. This was all he needed right now and somehow she knew that.

Eventually she stepped back slightly and started to unbutton his shirt but it wasn't sexual. She was taking care of him. Getting him out of his smoke-filled clothes so he could start to feel more human again. She slipped the shirt off his shoulders and let it drop onto the floor. She ran her hands over his chest and down his arms, trying to soothe him with her touch.

He kicked his shoes off and pulled off his jeans and socks so he was completely naked and then he turned his attention to Bella, wanting to take care of her too. He released the clasp at the back of the collar of her dress and it pooled to her feet, leaving her in that beautiful turquoise underwear that he had caught a glimpse of earlier.

The atmosphere in the room changed immediately and one look at her eyes told him she felt the same.

They came together so hard, their mouths clashing, their bodies meshed together in a passionate, needful kiss.

He eased her back against the wall, the water still pounding over them as the kiss continued. He quickly removed her bra, filling his hands with her breasts and she groaned against his mouth.

But before he could take it any further he felt like his legs gave way beneath him and he stumbled backwards and hit the wall behind him hard.

'God, are you OK?' Bella moved towards him, holding him up with her tiny frame.

'Yes, sorry. I just need to sit down for a moment.'

She switched the water off and helped him out the shower and into her bedroom where he sat down on the bed, his legs feeling so shaky all of a sudden. She went back to the bathroom and brought back a glass of water and a towel. While he took a cooling sip, she gently towelled him dry.

She was standing there in only her turquoise knickers and with her wet red curls tumbling down her shoulders looking every inch like the goddess Venus and he had no energy to even kiss her. He felt as weak as a kitten all of a sudden, like he had been hit by a wrecking ball.

'Get into bed,' Bella urged and he lay down watching her as she quickly towelled herself dry, peeled off her wet underwear and then slipped into the bed with him.

He immediately pulled her into his arms. She was warm and soft pressed against him and he felt instantly calmer having her close. He closed his eyes, breathing her in and drifted off to sleep.

❦

Bella held Isaac to her, stroking the back of his neck. He had fallen asleep about an hour or two before but she sensed he was awake now, or at least not sleeping as heavily as he was before: his breathing was lighter and, while his hold on her had lessened as soon as he had passed out, his grip had tightened again now, clearly aware she was there.

She could not even begin to imagine how devastating it was for him to lose his home, especially after all the time and money he had spent doing the place up, but the worst thing must be losing Rocket. She'd only had Alfie for a few days and she already loved him completely. Her only hope was that Rocket had managed to get out and if she was scared of the flames she might have run off. Luckily the island wasn't that big so if that was the case they would find her eventually.

She just wanted to take away Isaac's pain and she had no idea how to do that.

He shifted slightly, his eyes fluttering open, and he lifted his head from where it was buried against the side of her neck to look at her. He looked confused for a moment before awareness clouded his eyes.

He groaned and she ran her hands down his back.

'Please tell me none of that really happened, that it was all part of some horrible dream?'

He was clearly feeling calmer and more accepting of what had happened. Whereas before he'd been teetering on the brink, his eyes wild and manic, he was back to the Isaac she knew now. Still sad but more resigned to it. She wanted to distract him, even if it was only for a short while, in the hope that he wouldn't slip back into the darkness again.

'Which bit? The part where I missed out on the best steak marinade in the world? Or the part where we were just about to have sex and you clearly didn't have the stamina for it?'

He chuckled softly. 'As first dates go, it has to be one of the worst.'

She stroked her hand through his hair. 'I don't know about that. We had a shower together, we slept and cuddled in the same bed together. It's rating pretty high on my list.'

He kissed her neck. 'You must have had rubbish first dates.'

'No, I'm quite an affectionate person. Cuddling is probably my favourite part of being in a relationship. Sadly most men I know are not big on cuddling.'

He pulled back slightly to look at her. 'Cuddling is your favourite part of being in a relationship?'

'I know. Every time I tell a man that he laughs. Most men's favourite part of a relationship is regular sex.'

'And you don't like sex?'

'Sex is great. I've had some pretty amazing sex over the years but sex isn't affectionate, is it?'

He frowned. 'It isn't?'

'It's just a physical need, just like satisfying a deep hunger or quenching a thirst. When you haven't eaten for a long time and you take a bite of a sandwich, it tastes pretty bloody amazing. But I never feel adored by my sandwich. Sex is the same. It just fulfils a need. A cuddle or a hug is something different; it comes from genuinely caring about the other person.'

'Is that what this is?' He gestured to how their arms were wrapped around each other. 'You genuinely caring about me?'

'Yes.' She didn't hesitate. 'It's OK though, don't get freaked out. I'm not under any illusions that this is what it is for you. I know that tonight you just needed some comfort. But it was nice for me too, so you don't need to worry about me enjoying myself. I know it was a horrible night for you but it did end for me in one of the nicest ways.'

He leaned forward and kissed her briefly and that wonderful need for him erupted in her again. 'You continue to surprise me. Sometimes you come across as so bold and confident. That first time we kissed, it was you that initiated it. You wanted to kiss me so you just grabbed me and kissed me while I was too afraid to even make that move.'

'That's not like me at all. I always hold back in a relationship, I always wait for the man to make the first move, well, any move. There's something about you that brings out this confidence in me.'

'And yesterday in my office, walking in and demanding that we have sex.'

Bella groaned and covered her face with her hands. 'I can't believe I did that.'

'Hey, I'm not complaining. I don't think I've ever been so turnèd on in my life as I was in that moment. But then you tell me that you love being cuddled and I just find that so sweet and endearing.'

He removed her hands from her face and kissed her so softly, she ran her hands behind his neck and he slid his hand down to her waist. There was something so wonderful about lying together when they were both naked, their bodies touching in every way. Almost every way.

Leaning on his side, he pulled back to look at her, brushing the hair from her face.

'You're wrong about sex though.'

'About what?'

'About it not being affectionate. How many men have you been with?'

Bella flushed. 'Four. Well, if you count the thirty-second fumble that was my first time, then five but I try not to count him.'

'And not one of them has ever made love to you?'

Bella didn't know how to answer that question.

'Sex and making love are two very different things. People use the words interchangeably but in reality they are different. Sex is a physical need, you're right about that. But making love is something you do with someone you love or adore.'

He kissed her again and this time he rolled her back onto the bed so he was on top of her.

'I absolutely adore you Bella, let me make love to you.'

CHAPTER 16

Bella wanted to whoop for joy. This tension, this spark, the looks, kisses and touches were finally going to amount to something.

She leaned over and grabbed a condom from her bedside drawer and passed it to him.

He looked at it. 'I'm glad you came prepared. Were you hoping for a bit more than a bedtime story when I offered to tuck you up in bed by ten o'clock?'

She laughed. 'I was hoping you might join me.'

He placed the condom next to her on the bed. 'I won't be needing that just yet. But the speed at which you grabbed that does tell me a lot about the men you've dated in the past.'

'Hey. There's been nothing wrong with the men I've dated in the past. As I've said, I've had some pretty amazing sex.'

'Amazing sex that didn't involve any kind of foreplay?'

'Foreplay is overrated.'

'Not the way I do it,' Isaac said, before kissing her again.

God, he was so deliciously good at kissing, the taste of him was so divine. But instead of the passion she'd experienced with him before this was so much slower, taking his time. The kiss seemed to go on for a while; he clearly wasn't in any rush to take things any further. He kissed her until her body, which was coiled like a spring, desperate for that release, started to relax and melt around his, until all she could think about was this kiss, his mouth against hers, and the rest of the world just faded away. Whereas before she'd been desperate to sleep with him, right then she was content to kiss him for the rest of the night.

That was until he touched her, his hand snaking between them and stroking at the very top of her thighs. He wasn't lying about his skill with foreplay, he knew exactly where to touch her to elicit a reaction, his fingers sliding over her most sensitive area and then dipping inside her. She groaned against his mouth, the kiss continuing slowly and steadily, mirroring what he was doing with his hand.

Her orgasm, when it came, crashed through her so hard and fast that it took her by surprise and she writhed underneath him, crying out against his mouth.

As her body came down from her high, the shock waves subsiding, she was aware of him stroking her, soothing her as she clung to him even though she could feel that he was as turned on as she was.

She reached for the condom again but he caught her hand, linking his fingers with hers as he continued to kiss her and stroke her shoulder and arm tenderly with his other hand.

Finally he broke the kiss, kissing her nose, her chin and then layering kisses on her throat.

'I love the way you smell,' Isaac whispered. 'So sweet like coconut.' He pressed a kiss directly over her pulse point. 'I love that when I kiss you here, I can feel your pulse hammering against my lips.' He kissed the hollow at the base of her neck and then peppered kisses along her collarbone towards her shoulder. 'I love that dress you wore today that showed these beautiful shoulders off and I love that V at the back especially.' He stroked a finger down her spine and she shuddered against his touch.

'Isaac,' Bella said, reaching for him but he captured her hand again, pinning it up above her head as he continued to pepper kisses down her shoulder, down her arm and then moved over to her breast, capturing it in his mouth.

She cried out and strained against his hand, desperate to touch him. He released one of them and she ran her hand through his hair as he continued his thorough attention of her breast. She was already humming with need again, which seemed impossible when she was still coming down from the previous time. He turned his attention to the other breast and she arched against him and his wicked mouth. He finally pulled away, throwing the duvet off them as he feathered tiny kisses over her belly, her hips. She had never felt so exposed before and she didn't care. She had never been a big fan of her own body – she wasn't overweight but she wasn't exactly thin and toned either – but with the way he was adorning her with kisses and the way he was clearly turned on by her, she felt suddenly beautiful. When he dipped his tongue inside her belly button she moaned. His mouth went lower and lower and she arched up to meet him but when he got to the apex of her thighs he just placed the tiniest of kisses there before he continued his onward journey down the inside of her thigh.

She had never been with a man like this before. The most foreplay she'd ever had was a quick fumble, maybe a quick grope of the breasts. This was why she always looked forward to the main event so much because all the men she had been with really had no clue which buttons to press to turn her on. But Isaac knew. Every place he kissed her was sensitive and achingly sweet. He was adoring her and she was loving every second. Everything was about her pleasure not his and she'd never been with any man who put her needs before his own. It was almost as if he was getting as much pleasure kissing her and stroking her as he would from having sex with her.

His mouth travelled lower, kissing the inside of her knee and then travelling onwards towards her ankles.

She had never really thought about her feet as being places that would turn her on before but one feather-light kiss just behind her ankle had her writhing on the bed.

He layered kisses up the arch of her feet and then each toe and then he repeated the process on the other foot before slowly, achingly, kissing back up her leg, kissing her knee and then slowly up her inner thigh.

This time when he got to the top, he paused, shifting her legs apart with his shoulders as he kissed her right there, lavishing her most sensitive area with an inordinate amount of attention, and in a matter of seconds she was coming again, screaming out his name.

He moved back up her body, kissing her belly, her breasts, before kissing her on the mouth again as she was still trying to catch her breath.

He pulled back slightly to look at her as he settled himself between her legs and moved his hips against hers.

'I think I can be persuaded to come round to your way of thinking when it comes to sex,' Bella said. 'You clearly know what you're doing when it comes to making love.'

He kissed her briefly then reached over to grab the condom. He tore it open and slid it on. 'Not really. You're the only woman I've ever made love to,' Isaac said.

And while she was pondering that statement, he slid carefully inside her. She closed her eyes and arched against him, taking him all in, and he let out an animalistic groan of pleasure and relief.

'Open your eyes Bella,' he whispered before claiming her lips with his own in a needful kiss. He was shaking and she wrapped her arms and legs around him, holding him close.

He pulled back slightly to look at her, his breath coming out in shaky puffs.

'I had no idea how much I needed this tonight,' he said, as he gathered her close against him.

'Sex?'

'No, you. Being with you like this. After my whole world crashed down around my ears a few hours ago, there's you, my burning light in the darkness.'

She leaned up to kiss him, holding him as close as she could and slowly, ever so slowly and gently, he started to move against her. It was so unhurried, so soft and languid, she'd never had sex like it. There was no rush to get to the end goal for him. This was the end goal, lying here wrapped in each other's arms, joined in every way possible. And for the first time she truly understood what it meant to make love to someone. He pulled back to stare into her eyes and she saw nothing but tenderness and complete adoration and it was that look that sent her tumbling over the edge again and this time he quickly followed, kissing her hard. She held him close as his body shook against hers and then he collapsed with his face buried in the side of her neck.

'I think I could really fall in love with you, Bella Roussel,' he whispered in her ear.

She stroked his hair and didn't say anything because she knew she could easily feel the same. For the first time in her life there was a feeling inside her chest that she had never felt before. It erupted from her heart and spread out across her body in this glorious warmth. If this was love then it scared her to death.

※⁓⊙⌇

It was the early hours of the morning, the sun just peeping up above the waves and painting the sky with a rosy gold.

Isaac hadn't been asleep but he didn't think that Bella had either.

He'd scared her off with that comment, he knew that. She was still cuddled up against him, still holding onto him as much as he was holding onto her, but he had sensed her closing up. Everything had been going great; he had made love to her and showed her what it was like to be part of a proper relationship, not one that was born simply out of desire and sex. He had taken care of her, showed her how important she was to him and, just when she was relaxing into this new relationship, he had to go and throw the love word into the mix.

He shifted her against him so she was on top and stroked her hair down her back.

'Fancy round two?' Isaac said, his hand drifting down to her bum.

Bella giggled against his chest. 'I was just thinking the same thing.'

She propped her head up on her hands as she looked at him from her position on his chest. Affection shone from her eyes but he could see there was a wariness there too.

He stroked her hair. 'Don't pay any attention to what I said after we made love. It was just the emotions of the moment. I certainly don't want to do anything to scare you off.'

She smiled at him.

'I told you last night, you don't scare me. Love doesn't scare me.' She said it in such a way that he knew immediately she was lying. For someone who was so completely honest, lying didn't come easily for her.

'It doesn't?'

'It's not something I really believe in.'

Isaac had no words.

He cleared his throat. 'Yet again you continue to surprise me. You are so warm-hearted, generous, sweet and kind. You never struck me as someone who was jaded, cynical and bitter about love.'

'I'm not bitter. People bandy the "love" word about so much it becomes meaningless, I love Disney films, I love pizza, I love my Levi jeans, I love Chris Pratt. I hear these words of love every day and the word becomes as common as autumn leaves. And what does it really mean? I just think the concept of love is a false one. Love is supposed to be everlasting but it never works out like that.'

'Which asshole do I need to punch that made you feel like that?'

She shrugged. 'There's probably two assholes actually.'

'Two?'

'Yeah, my mum and my dad both taught me that love is disposable, love is nothing more than getting excited over a shiny new toy and when the shine wears off you can just cast the toy aside and pick up a new one.'

He groaned inwardly. She always seemed so happy and although he knew a bit about her past he hadn't realised that it had left her with such a huge emotional scar. But of course it would. Her parents abandoning her would obviously have an impact.

'My dad married my mum, stood at the altar of the church and promised to love her forever, through good times and the bad and until death do us part. I came along, this little girl that was half him and half her, and my dad left. He didn't love my mum enough to want to stay. He didn't love me enough to want to stay. What does that tell you about love?'

He thought carefully how to answer. The man was clearly a dick but he could hardly say that. 'Well, that tells me that your dad never really loved your mum in the first place if he could walk away from her so easily. Maybe he liked the idea of love and marriage and thought he was in love with her but he wasn't.'

'It tells me that love fades fast, if it ever was there in the first place. And what about the unconditional love of a parent? They are supposed to be the one person that will love you no matter what. But my dad left me when I was five years old and for the next year, right up to my sixth birthday, my mum told me she hated me. It wasn't every day but it was fairly often. Every day she would sit and cry over my dad leaving and she blamed me entirely for it. He broke her heart and she hated him for it even though she never stopped loving him. What kind of messed-up love is that?'

'She actually told you she hated you?'

'Yes, frequently.'

Isaac swallowed down the pain that clawed at his throat. Bella had been through hell and there was nothing he could do to take that pain away.

'I spent a lot of time with my aunt and uncle and the time I spent there grew longer and the time I spent with my mum grew shorter until one weekend she dropped me there and never bothered to pick me up again. That was the last time I ever saw her. She never wrote, never sent me a card or a present, she just vanished and wiped me from her world altogether. There was definitely no unconditional love there. I just think love is a farce. It's a word people use to describe a deep feeling of affection but it's not as infallible and everlasting as the movies and books will have you believe.'

He stroked her hair and ran his hands down her back, holding her to him. He understood now why the most important thing in a relationship for Bella was affection. Words were meaningless; sex had always been physical for her, until last night. But gestures like cuddling and hugging, holding hands like she had held his the other night when they had met on the walk, those gestures showed love and care and she needed that in a relationship. He would just have to show her what a loving relationship really looked like.

'Bella, you had a really crappy start to life and I totally get why your opinion of love has been tainted. No one should have to go through what you went through and I understand that you would be scared of falling in love knowing that it could just get thrown back in your face. But just because you've never experienced love, it doesn't mean that it isn't real. There are thousands or millions of people out there that are in loving relationships, couples that live very long and happy lives together, parents that absolutely adore their children. You must have seen it yourself. You can't tell me that love is a farce for them.'

She nodded to concede this. 'I think some people are lucky enough to experience real love, though the high divorce rate in this country tells you that it fails for a lot of people. I think some people are definitely more suited to love than others. Maybe it's an inherent thing, like playing a musical instrument or being good at art. Maybe some people are born capable of love and some aren't. I think that as my parents were completely incapable of it, then I doubt that loving gene was passed down to me.'

'Being able to play a musical instrument or paint a picture is something that can be taught. Maybe you can be taught to believe in love again.'

'Maybe,' Bella said, though she didn't sound convinced.

'So you don't love Rome and Eden? You don't love your aunt and uncle?'

'No, I do love them. Very much. But that's a very different kind of love. I'm not sure I could trust anyone else with my heart.'

He frowned. 'So what are we doing here? Was this always just about sex with you?'

But as soon as he asked that question, he knew that it wasn't. Last night she had taken care of him after the fire. This was a lot more to her than just sex and desire, whether she wanted to admit it or not.

'I really like you Isaac, we get on well. I like to talk to you and spend time with you. I really do care about you. And the sex is… well, honestly the best sex I've ever had. It doesn't need to be more than that, does it? We can just enjoy this until such a time that you're done with me.'

And right there was the crux of it. She was waiting for him to finish with her. Her parents had rejected her and so she would never let herself fall in love again because she would inevitably be rejected again.

But this was something he could work on. He just had to prove to her that she could trust him. He had to show her what love really felt like, how wonderful it was. Because after last night, he had no intention of ever letting her go.

'We can enjoy it. I've got something very enjoyable planned for the next few hours before we have to get up for work.'

She smiled, catching onto his mood. She kissed his chest, right above his heart, and then sat up straddling him. God, she was a glorious sight.

'What is it you have in mind?'

He ran his hands down to her hips, running his thumbs over the apex of her thighs and she shuddered against him. 'Let me show you.'

She reached over to grab a condom from the drawer and he caught her hand again, cupping her face in his hands as he kissed her.

'There's no rush, Bella,' he whispered against her lips, then wrapped his arms around her, hugging her to him. 'In fact, I could stay here forever.'

He caught the wariness in her eyes but he didn't care. She was just going to have to get used to him saying it.

❦

Bella ran back up the stairs and into the bedroom just as Isaac walked out the bathroom, dripping wet and gloriously naked. He was using the towel to dry his hair but he had no reason to be hiding his nudity; she had spent the last few hours becoming very accustomed to every hard inch of his wonderful body.

'See something you like?' he said, clearly amused by her staring.

'Just some guy I fancy.'

'Fancy? I don't think anyone has told me they fancy me since I've been at school. Next thing you'll be telling me you have a crush on me too.'

'Isaac Scott, I have a crazy crush on you. I bet all the girls do. But I'm the only one that gets to squeeze this gorgeous piece of ass.'

'And I'm glad of that. I'm a "one-ass-squeezing girl" kind of guy.'

Bella laughed. 'I got you some clothes. I asked Kevin next door. He's very tall so I thought something of his might fit.'

She didn't tell Isaac that Kevin's wife had been asking about the two of them, had heard that they were dating and knew he had spent the night. He didn't need to know anything that might scare him off.

'Thank you, that's very sweet. I have a spare suit in the office, so I just need something to wear so I can get there. I need to go in early as I have a Skype call from Japan at eight and then I need to get some new clothes delivered. I need to sort out a hotel or somewhere to stay until I can get my house rebuilt.'

'But you can stay here, you know that.'

'That's very kind but this is so new between us and I think it's best if we don't leap straight into living with each other within days of knowing each other. We probably need a bit of space.'

'You can't live in a hotel for the next few months.'

'I can't live here either.' He grabbed a shirt from the bed and pulled it on. It was tight across his arms but it mostly fitted everywhere else. 'I'll rent somewhere, I just need somewhere to stay until I can find somewhere to rent.'

'Look, stay here for the next few days.' She rooted in her drawer and found her spare key. 'You're in London all of next week anyway. Then you can find somewhere to stay when you come back.'

He thought about this for a moment then nodded, taking the key from her.

'What's your schedule like today? Maybe we could do lunch?' Bella said, then felt her heart crash into her stomach when he hesitated. What did she expect, they'd been on one date and it technically wasn't even that. Now she was inviting him to come and live with her and wanting to see him all the time. Could she be any more needy? 'Actually I'll probably work through lunch, there's loads to organise ready for the fair next weekend.'

'I have a ton of stuff to sort out with the house and there's a few meetings too,' Isaac said. 'So probably best if we don't.'

Bella nodded. 'Right well, I'll, erm… see you tonight. I better go, I've got to take Alfie for a walk before work.'

She stared at him for a moment, wondering if she should give him a kiss goodbye or just a wave.

Was this actually it? Was this thing over between them before it had even really begun? She had bared her soul to him the night before and now was he running for the hills, too scared to get involved with the emotionally stunted crazy lady from work? She didn't really blame him if he was.

He must have seen all these doubts running across her face as if she had shouted them out loud because he quickly moved across the room and took her face in his hands, kissing her softly. 'You don't scare me, Bella.'

She smiled against his lips.

He pulled back slightly. 'I would like to keep it a secret at work though. I'm sure half the island must know we are together by now after all those people who offered to help saw us and the fire brigade, and we weren't exactly subtle in the taxi, but I don't need to hear the comments from people at work and I would prefer you not to have to put up with that crap either. If we are seen together having lunch every day or walking in and out of each other's offices all the time, people will start to twig and I'd like to keep this just between us for as long as possible.'

She nodded with understanding, though she couldn't help but feel a little bit disappointed with that.

'I better go.' He kissed her on the nose. 'Message me on the internal message system when you get in.'

'OK.'

He kissed her sweetly on the forehead and then left the room. A few seconds later she heard the front door close.

She ran to the window and watched him leave. She noticed the curtains of Indigo Cottage were twitching as he walked down the road. Dorothy would be delighted at this turn of events. But if Isaac thought he could keep this thing between them a secret, he had forgotten what island life was like.

CHAPTER 17

Bella was walking Alfie over the hills a while later and she pulled her phone out of her pocket and gave Eden a call.

She answered on the first ring. 'Well, tell me all about your hot date?'

Clearly the town grapevine had not reached Eden's ears yet. But then she probably wasn't at work yet. Lots of people popped into Eden's pottery café in the mornings to grab a coffee and one of Eden's homemade pastries. The pastries were apparently the best on the island so she always had a steady stream of customers buying them before their day at work and quite often bringing all the latest gossip with them.

'It was very hot.'

Eden squealed.

'Isaac's house burnt down.'

'No! Oh my god, that was his house? I saw the smoke and heard the fire brigade rushing to the scene, I didn't realise it was Isaac's house on fire. Is he OK?'

'He lost his dog.' Bella swallowed down the pain she felt at Isaac's loss. The dog wasn't even hers but she knew how much that would have destroyed him and she hated for him to go through that. 'Isaac was pretty cut up about it, as you would expect. He lost everything, the house was completely destroyed, but I think more than anything it was losing his dog that destroyed him.'

'Oh no, how horribly upsetting for him. I take it the date was well and truly over after that.'

Bella bit her lip. It was awful that they had ended up making love mainly because Isaac needed the comfort of it after the fire, but she couldn't stop smiling about the incredible night they had spent together. It would have happened anyway, the chemistry that had been sparking between them since they'd met was a clear indication of that, but the fire had probably brought it forward by a few days.

'Well he stayed at mine and we took a shower together and then we—'

Alfie barking up ahead distracted her, especially as there was a familiar yapping joining in with the barking.

'Eden, I'll call you back.'

'What? You can't leave it there. That's the worst cliff-hanger ever.'

Bella laughed. 'I have to go.'

She hung up as Eden squawked her protest and ran into the little copse of trees up ahead.

There was Rocket, jumping up and down all over Alfie, gleefully greeting him as if she hadn't seen him for days. The dog was covered in mud but looked completely unharmed and unfazed by her brush with death. Bella's heart soared at having found her. It would be so much easier for Isaac to cope with the loss of his house knowing that Rocket had made it out alive.

'Rocket, here girl.' Bella sank to her knees and Rocket leapt up to lick her face. She threw her arms round her, tears spilling over onto her cheeks. She was alive and she couldn't wait to tell Isaac.

Bella ran into the office with Rocket bouncing on the end of Alfie's lead as if the last twenty-four hours hadn't been horrible and terrifying. She had given her a bath and checked her all over and she seemed fine, but now she was a few minutes late for work which didn't look good on her third day at work. Though she had a sneaky suspicion the boss wouldn't be firing her for it.

She had thought about just telling Isaac that Rocket was OK, but she knew that he would want to see the dog.

She rushed into the lift, ignoring the curious looks from people at her bringing a dog into the building. She pressed the button to take her to the top floor, suddenly having doubts that she was doing the right thing. Isaac had specifically said not to come to his office in case people started to get suspicious. But as the doors pinged open on his floor, Bella knew it was too late to back out now.

As she walked out, she noticed a blonde woman she hadn't seen at the Umbrella Foundation before sitting where Claudia normally sat. She looked up at Bella as she exited the lift and Bella immediately recognised her. Melissa Bridge had been in her year at school but like everyone else in her class had moved away from Hope Island and not come back. Well, she was back now. Bella sighed. Unless Melissa had changed significantly over the years, she was going to make it difficult for her.

Melissa arched an eyebrow at her as she approached and it was clear she remembered Bella too.

'Hello, Bella.'

Just in those two words, there was so much contempt.

'Hello Melissa. I need to see Isaac,' Bella said.

'All meetings and appointments have been cancelled today. Claudia will be in touch later to reschedule.'

She tried her best smile. 'I don't have an appointment, I just need to see him. It's important.'

'Mr Scott has left specific instructions that he is not to be disturbed by anyone. I don't think you're important enough for me to break that rule.'

Bella swallowed down her impatience. 'Look, if you can just call through to his office and tell him I'm here. I'm sure he would be able to accommodate me for a few minutes.'

'I'm not allowed to do that. Claudia said no calls through to the office.'

Rocket gave a bark of frustration, pulling at her lead, and Melissa looked down at her. 'I don't think you're allowed to bring dogs in here.'

'I don't think there is any rule about dogs,' Bella said, contemplating storming past Melissa and just letting herself into the office.

'Bella?'

Bella turned round to see Claudia, who had evidently just walked out of Isaac's office. Clearly the whole 'not to be disturbed by anyone' rule didn't apply to her.

'Are you OK?' Claudia asked.

'I just really need to see Isaac.'

'Sure, go on in.'

Bella was surprised at how easily Claudia had caved when Melissa was clinging onto the rules so tightly. She glanced over at Melissa who also looked surprised.

Not wanting to waste any more time, she hurried over to the door but Claudia stopped her with a hand on her arm. She spoke quietly so that Melissa couldn't hear.

'He's exhausted; he said he didn't get any sleep last night.'

Bella didn't want to say that the main reason that neither of them had got any sleep was that they had made love three times and spent most of the night talking.

'I've cancelled all his meetings for the rest of the week so he can sort out the issues with the house. He has a telephone call at half eleven that he has to take but after that I've booked him into a hotel and I think he's going to go straight there after the call.

I think it all hit him this morning when he realised how much stress is going to be involved in getting the house sorted. Thank goodness you were there for him last night, I hate to think of him dealing with this alone.'

That surprised Bella. Claudia knew about them? Isaac had specifically said not to tell anyone but he'd told his PA?

'Go on in, I'm sure he'll be glad to see you…' Claudia noticed Rocket for the first time. 'Is that… his dog?'

'Yes, I found her, that's why I'm here.'

'Well I think that's just what he needs this morning.' Claudia gestured for her to go in and then walked back over to the desk.

'I thought you said no one was allowed in to see Mr Scott?' Melissa said, grumpily.

'Bella's a friend,' Claudia explained.

Bella slipped inside the office, still confused that Claudia seemed to know all about them. As she shut the door she saw Isaac lying on the sofa with his eyes closed. She wasn't sure if he was asleep but if he was Rocket soon took care of that as she let out a yelp of excitement at seeing Isaac again.

Isaac immediately sat up and Bella was gratified to see first his smile at seeing her and then that smile growing with relief as he saw Rocket.

'Rocket!' Isaac called her and Bella let go of the lead and Rocket ran over to the sofa and leapt up on Isaac's lap, yelping and jumping all over Isaac with excitement. Isaac hugged her tight, burying his face in the top of Rocket's head. 'God, you stupid daft dog, you have no idea how happy I am to see you.'

Bella smiled at them, knowing instantly she'd done the right thing in bringing Rocket here, even if it did put their relationship at risk of being found out.

'I've given her a bath and I've checked her over and she doesn't seem hurt in any way but I can always take her to the vets tonight for you.'

Isaac looked up at her, and as Rocket leapt off to explore and sniff around the office, clearly done with the reunion, he got up and walked over to her.

'I can't believe you found her,' he said, kissing her head fondly before gathering her into his arms.

'I wish I could take the credit but it was Alfie that found her, not me.'

'Then I'll give Alfie a kiss later,' Isaac said before kissing her sweetly on the lips. 'Thank you for bringing her to me.' He held her close again. 'I've had a crap morning and it's only nine o'clock. The call from Japan was cancelled and so I made a list of everything that I needed to do with regards to the house and, after three pages of notes, I honestly wanted to curl up in a ball and cry. I've lost everything. And then you walk in here with your big beautiful smile and I suddenly feel I'm the luckiest man alive.'

Bella smiled at the compliment, that warmth of affection for this man growing in her chest. 'I wish I could do something to help you with all of this.'

'You are, believe me you are. Claudia is going to take care of a lot of it for me. That's why she's borrowed Melissa from the admin team to help deal with any of my calls and emails for me, while Claudia is going to try to find me somewhere to live and sort out what happens next with the insurance.' He sighed. 'Come and lie with me for a little while.'

Bella laughed. 'I have to go to work. I have a fair to organise and only just over a week to do it in.'

'Just a little while. I promise you won't get into trouble with your boss.'

'I don't know, I've heard he can be quite strict.'

'I'll handle him.'

Rocket was already curled up on the rug in front of the sofa, snoring loudly. Isaac tugged Bella back over to the sofa and lay down and then shuffled over to make room for her. She lay down next to him and he wrapped his arms around her and held her close. She snuggled against him with her head on his chest and her arm across his stomach.

His breathing became heavy and a few minutes later it was quite evident that he was fast asleep. She closed her eyes and snuggled closer.

The next thing Bella was aware of was Claudia standing over them. Crap. If there was any doubt at all in Claudia's mind that they were together, that doubt had certainly been dispelled now.

Claudia smiled at Bella and gently shook Isaac awake. 'Isaac, Mr Tyler is on the phone for you, I know you need to take this call.'

Isaac stretched and groaned. Bella tried to remove herself from his arms but he instinctively held her tighter against him, seemingly not at all bothered by Claudia seeing them. 'What time is it?'

'Half eleven exactly. You know Mr Tyler is never late.'

'Crap. Half eleven? I need to go,' Bella said. How had she fallen asleep for over two hours?

Isaac sat up and Bella did too. 'Thanks Claudia, can you just stall him for thirty seconds? Tell him I'm just finishing up on another call or something.'

Claudia nodded with understanding and left them alone.

'I have to go,' Bella said, straightening her hair and standing up.

Isaac stood up too, cupped her face in his hands and kissed her sweetly. God this man. She could easily stay there all day and kiss him.

She pulled back slightly. 'You're a bad influence on me, Mr Scott.'

He grinned. 'You're the best influence on me.'

She smiled. 'Take your call. I'll see you later.'

'You can count on it.'

She scurried out the office, ignoring the glare from Melissa. Bella was quite sure Melissa would have made her own mind up about what Bella had been doing in the office with Isaac for the last two hours. She waved at Claudia and hurried into the lift.

꧁✿꧂

Bella was sitting in her office later putting together a press release for the spring fair. Everything was slowly coming together.

She hated that she'd been late this morning and although she was going to stop a few hours later tonight to make up for lost time, she felt guilty that she had left Roger and Elsie to get on with the job on their own while she had been upstairs asleep with Isaac. She had told them that she'd had a meeting with Isaac – knowing that several people had seen her entering the building earlier with Rocket, she could hardly lie and say that she was at the dentists. But lots of people had already heard about Isaac's house and that he had cancelled all meetings. The fact that he had made time for her and a supposed two-hour meeting was clearly a bit suspicious. She was sure Melissa would have told everyone she could by now about the inordinate amount of time Bella had spent in Isaac's office. Coupled with the gossip that had no doubt spread around the island from the fire brigade and the taxi driver about the two of them being together, the chances of them keeping it quiet for much longer were looking slim.

Isaac had messaged her earlier to say that he was leaving, shortly after she had left him in his office to take the phone call. A few minutes later, Bella had seen him and Claudia getting into a taxi and disappearing towards the main part of the town. Claudia seemed really nice but Bella wasn't sure if she could trust her. Now she knew about them, how many people would she tell?

She picked up the phone and made a call through to a local radio station. She was just running through what was going to happen at the fair when Claudia walked in and closed the door behind her.

Claudia gestured for Bella to carry on talking on the phone as she placed a hotel key card for the Royal Oak hotel on her desk. Claudia grabbed a piece of paper and wrote on it a room number. Bella couldn't help but blush. It suddenly felt a bit seedy.

She gestured for Claudia to hang on and she quickly wrapped up the phone call and hung up.

She picked up the key, not knowing what to say. 'Is he OK?'

'He's fine. He just needs some rest. He said to come round whenever you want and to bring Alfie too as the hotel allows dogs.'

It was quite obvious Isaac intended for her to spend the night with him and that Claudia knew this too.

'Claudia, this thing between me and Isaac…' She trailed off. How could she even begin to categorise it? She couldn't say it wasn't serious because it was. It was something incredible but she could hardly tell Claudia that either. 'We're trying to keep it secret.'

'I know, that was my idea. Though to be honest, I don't think we'll be able to keep it quiet for much longer. But Isaac wants to protect you. I'm sure everyone will have an opinion about the two of you once they find out and I imagine most of it will involve you sleeping with the boss to get the job or him giving you the job because you were dating.'

Bella gasped. 'That's not how it is at all.'

'I know, I understand. I've known him for many years, too many to count and—'

'Let me guess, you've seen many women come and go.'

'No. I mean, sure there have been quite a few women that he has gone out on a few dates with and never seen again, but there's never been anyone serious for him. I guess you can say he has trust issues. He made his money very quickly and everyone wanted a piece of him after that. It's hard for him to find someone who genuinely wants to get to know him for him, not for how much money he has in his pocket. It's not just the women who hang around him like bees around a honeypot.

All the men want to be his best friend too. I think in part that was why he wanted to come back here; everyone knows who he is in London. No one cares who he is here. You took him in and befriended him when you thought he had nothing, that's a huge novelty for him. I've honestly never seen him like this about a woman before. I think he's falling in love with you. And judging by when I came into the office shortly after you'd arrived and found you both fast asleep, you curled around him with the biggest smile on your face, I'm guessing you're falling in love with him too.'

'I'm not in love with him,' Bella said, surprised by how easily the denial slipped from her lips when just the thought of him made her smile so much. The feelings she had for Isaac were not like anything she had ever experienced before but she was scared to label it as love. Love came with so many expectations and ultimately so much disappointment. 'I care about him. A lot. He makes me ridiculously happy. But it's too early for love.'

Claudia smiled as if she thought differently. 'He said the same thing, but as I told him, love doesn't work to a schedule. Just enjoy it, Bella. It's rare that something as special as this comes along for us. Don't let fear of what might happen ruin it for you.'

Bella nodded and Claudia left her alone in the office. She looked at the key and smiled. She would just enjoy each moment as it came and she was definitely going to enjoy that evening.

❦❧☙

Bella walked into the hotel that night with Alfie. She had stayed a little later at the office and then gone home and walked Alfie before getting changed and coming over to the hotel.

She wondered what the hotel staff thought of her staying in Isaac's room for the night. Everything had happened so fast between them, and island gossip with its own embellishments and opinions travelled equally as fast, so she was sure half the island knew about them by now and, as Claudia had said, many of them would think the worst.

She walked into the lift and smiled at the porter she recognised as one of her uncle Finn's friends, Abe.

'Good evening, Miss Roussel,' Abe said, pressing the button for the top floor without even asking where Bella was going. Evidently Isaac had made it clear to the hotel staff that he was expecting her. The doors closed and her cheeks flushed that one of her uncle's friends knew she was spending a night of passion in the hotel. Would Abe tell her uncle, would Finn be disappointed? Abe turned to her. 'And who is this handsome chap?'

Bella smiled. 'This is Alfie.'

Alfie wagged his tail furiously as Abe bent down to stroke him. 'I had the pleasure of meeting Rocket earlier today, adorable little thing. I think Rocket and Alfie would make a good partnership. Mr Scott was telling me about her and how she spooks easily and it took her a long while for her to learn to trust him. He thinks she had a rough few years and was treated badly but he thinks she knows now that he's never going to let her down. It fills my heart to see that Rocket now has this chance at happiness. I think Alfie will be good for her. He has that calm, loyal quality I admire in a… dog.'

Bella stared at him and then the doors pinged open.

'Have a good evening, Miss Roussel.'

'Thank you,' Bella said quietly as she walked out, knowing that Abe had certainly not been talking about Rocket.

Were a lot of people looking at her and Isaac and thinking, like Abe and Claudia, that it was love and that they were happy for Bella after her awful childhood? Is that what people thought, that Bella just needed a nice man to look after her? She didn't need anyone to look after her. Relying on someone else for her own happiness was a mistake because then they were also responsible for her sadness too.

She let herself into Isaac's room and Rocket came running to greet them, well specifically Alfie. She called out to Isaac but there was no answer. She looked around the room as the two dogs chased each other around.

The room was huge, with a large U-shaped grey velvet sofa sitting opposite a TV that took up most of the wall. The bedroom, which had the biggest bed she had ever seen, was to the right of the lounge, but it was the view that captured her attention, the moon glowing over the silver sea. Blueberry Bay was immediately in front of the hotel, one of her favourite places on the island because it was so secluded. Beyond that, on the edge of the headland was Mistletoe Cove surrounded by the hawthorn trees that were just starting to bloom. Later in the year the trees would be covered in the white berries of mistletoe that gave the cove its name.

She turned her attention back to the dogs and saw that Alfie had settled himself down on the large dog bed that Isaac had bought for Rocket and Rocket was leaping over him, but eventually his stillness calmed her down and she snuggled into his side. Alfie licked the top of her head a few times and then rested his head on top of hers and closed his eyes. Abe was right, Alfie was good for Rocket, and in her heart she knew that Isaac was good for her too.

Suddenly she didn't care what people thought, whether they judged her for sleeping with the boss, whether they thought she had got the job by jumping into bed with him. She knew the truth and she knew they were doing nothing wrong. She didn't care if people were looking at her thinking she had found love and were happy for her. It was no one's business but hers and Isaac's. He made her happy, it was as simple as that. And Claudia was right, there was no point in letting fear of the future ruin what they had now.

Thinking about the welcome she could give Isaac when he finally returned from wherever he was, she slipped out of her dress and underwear, dimmed the lights and arranged herself naked on the sofa in prime view of the door when he walked in.

Minutes ticked by and there was still no sign of him. She couldn't even call him as he had lost his phone in the fire and she wasn't sure if he had a replacement yet.

Eventually, just as she was starting to get cold, she heard the key in the lock and Rocket shot to the door to greet Isaac.

She quickly arranged herself in what she hoped was a sexy pose and the door opened.

'That's brilliant,' Isaac laughed. Clearly he'd had a new phone delivered to him and he was talking to someone on it.

Isaac hit the lights, turning them on full, and as his eyes became accustomed to the brightness he saw her and the smile fell from his face. That wasn't the look she was hoping for.

'I know, that's what I thought,' came a familiar male voice, right behind Isaac.

Bella's heart leapt as she saw Dougie Harrison step into the room and bend down to stroke Rocket.

She let out a little yelp, desperately looked around to try to find something to cover her nudity, realised there was nothing, and as Dougie started to straighten back up, she did a little ninja roll over the back of the sofa and hit the floor by the window hard.

CHAPTER 18

There was silence for a moment. Had Dougie seen her?

'Wow. That view is incredible,' Dougie said and to her horror she heard footsteps walking over towards the window.

'Erm. What do you want to drink? Come over to the mini bar and you can help yourself,' Isaac tried but the footsteps kept coming.

Scrabbling up onto all fours, Bella crawled round the back of the sofa and round to the other side of the U-shape, where Isaac was still standing helplessly by the door. He let out a snort of laughter when he saw her. She leaned against the back of the sofa as Dougie admired the view out the window.

'God, I've missed that view,' Dougie said and then to her horror she heard the footsteps walking back over towards the door and the mini bar again. 'I think I'll just have a beer.'

He clearly intended to stay for a while. Bella quickly crawled back towards the window again. At least now he'd seen the view he wouldn't be coming back to the window. He would just have his drink and go and she would have to trust Isaac to get rid of him as soon as he could.

She heard the hiss of a can of beer opening and, just as she made herself comfortable leaning her back against the sofa, she heard footsteps coming back to the window.

She scrabbled up and crawled back round to the front of the sofa again, where Isaac was clearly finding it hard not to laugh.

'I do love that view. I think if I ever came back to this island, I'd need to get a place with that view.'

'Most places on this island have a view of the sea,' Isaac said, trying to keep the laughter out of his voice.

'Yes but Mistletoe Cove is one of the most beautiful places on the island. It was there that I kissed the only woman I've ever loved.'

Bella pondered that statement. Who had he kissed in Mistletoe Cove?

'I might get a glass actually,' Dougie said as he walked back towards the mini bar.

'That's a bit posh for you, isn't it?' Isaac said as Bella quickly crawled back towards the window again. She wouldn't be entirely surprised if Dougie was doing this deliberately, it was just the sort of thing he would do. But she also knew him well enough to know that if he had seen her, he would have made some comment straight away. He certainly wasn't restrained enough to hold it in.

She heard the sound of the beer being poured into the glass and then footsteps. She made to crawl back to the front again when the sofa shifted with the weight of someone sitting down, right next to where she was. If Dougie looked over the back of the sofa now, he would see her. But now she didn't dare move in case she caught his attention.

'Well, as your beautiful girlfriend hasn't turned up, why don't me and you make a night of it? We could play a few games on that games console over there, order a pizza, sink a few more beers.'

Girlfriend? Is that how Isaac had referred to her? She couldn't help smiling about that.

'I'm a bit tired actually. It's been a long day,' Isaac said.

'Ah come on mate, it's been too long since we hung out,' Dougie said, taking a sip of beer.

'We can hang out tomorrow, mate. I'll be much more awake then. But tonight I'm just ready to crash.'

'Anyone would think you just want to get rid of me.' Dougie took another sip of beer. 'Or would that have anything to do with Bella Roussel sitting naked behind this sofa?'

Bella knelt up, concealing her nudity with the sofa, and flicked Dougie's ear. 'I knew you were doing it on purpose, you ass.'

He yelped as he stood up, laughing. 'I'm sorry, I couldn't help it.'

'I forgot that you two know each other,' Isaac said.

'Me and Bella go way back. I couldn't resist winding her up. Good to see you again, cuz, though I have to say I didn't expect to see quite so much of you.'

'Cuz?' Isaac looked between them in confusion.

Dougie gestured to his red curly hair and Bella's red hair. 'As we used to hang out together as kids, everyone thought we were related. We told everyone we were cousins. Bella, how about a hug for your cousin?'

Bella laughed. 'Not right now. Why don't you sod off so I can seduce my hot boyfriend as I'd planned?'

Dougie laughed and put the beer bottle down on the table. 'Fair enough. I'll let myself out.' He turned his attention back to Isaac. 'Let's hang out tomorrow.'

Isaac nodded.

'And as her cousin, I feel it's my duty to say, if you hurt her, I'll have to beat you up for it.'

Bella laughed. 'Get out.'

Dougie gave her a wave and left and Bella sank back down to the floor with a groan. The lights were suddenly turned off, plunging the whole room into darkness, lit only by the great moon, casting its silvery blanket over the sea below them.

She heard footsteps walk round the sofa towards her but this time she didn't run away. Isaac came and sat next to her. He leaned against the sofa and swung his arm round her shoulders, kissing her head fondly.

'How embarrassing. I just wanted to give you a nice welcome.'

'It was the best welcome I've ever had. So how were you planning to seduce me?' Isaac asked.

Bella laughed. 'I have no idea. I'd got as far as stripping naked and waiting for you. You know I'm no good at this kind of stuff. You'd be better off with someone who has a bit more sex appeal than me. I bet you've dated women that could turn you on with a single look, who could bring you to your knees with a simple touch and know their way around the bedroom a lot better than I do.'

'I've been with a few women, probably not as many as you think, but not one of them turned me on as much as you do. I have never kissed a woman from work, never even been tempted. I've known you less than a week and kissed you when I was undercover, kissed you in your office on your first day, kissed you in my office, stroked your back in the lift in front of several other people and made love to you three glorious times. Believe me when I say you bring me to my knees in every single way.'

She grinned as she leaned her head against his shoulder, the warmth in her chest spreading throughout her body making her fingers and toes tingle with what felt like excitement and something much more.

'I didn't know you and Dougie knew each other,' Bella said, not wanting to focus on the incredible feeling that was surging inside of her.

'We go way back too. We used to be in a video game club here after school. When I left to go to St Mary's, he had cousins on the island so, whenever he'd visit them, he'd visit me too. When we both went to university, we were both doing really similar courses, even though he was in America and I was in London, and we stayed in touch about the different assignments, helped each other out with coursework on more than one occasion. We've stayed in touch ever since. When you mentioned Dougie the other night, I wondered if it was the same Dougie but I was undercover then and I didn't want to ask too many questions about him in case I was found out. I have to say I forgot all about it after that. You stayed in touch with him too?'

'Yeah, on Facebook mainly and we always meet up whenever he comes over.'

'He comes over to see you quite a lot?'

She smiled, noticing the hint of jealousy in his voice. She looked up at him, running her fingers through his glorious stubble. 'He comes over to see Eden quite a lot although he'd never admit it, and me and Rome catch up with him too. You have nothing to worry about there.'

'I'm not worried.'

'Jealous then.'

'I'm jealous that another man got to see my beautiful girlfriend naked.'

The smile grew on her face. 'Girlfriend, eh?'

He frowned slightly. 'I'm not sure what else I can call you. You're a lot more than just some girl I'm shagging. Is it OK that I call you my girlfriend?'

'As your girlfriend do I get special privileges?'

'What kind of privileges do you want?'

'Sex whenever I want?'

'Of course.'

'Massages?'

'I can't say I've ever given one before but I'm sure I could give it my best shot.'

'And lots of cuddles?'

Isaac pulled her tighter against him, wrapping both arms around her. 'Always.'

She closed her eyes and smiled against him, every doubt, every worry about what people might think or say just fading away. None of that mattered.

She opened her eyes and gasped as a sudden arc of white appeared over Blueberry Bay. She quickly scrabbled up and moved to the window.

'Oh my god, is that a moonbow?'

'Wow. Yes, lunar rainbows are very rare.'

The moonbow glinted like silver in the moonlight and, reflecting off the calm water beneath it, it created a perfect circle with the moon as the centrepiece. 'It looks like a pearl ring. If you were going to propose to me, now would be a perfect time to do it,' Bella teased, though of course Isaac did no such thing. 'It's wonderful.'

'I've never seen anything so beautiful in my entire life,' Isaac said from behind her.

She turned back to look at him and realised he was staring straight at her and not at the moonbow at all. She felt the smile fade from her face as the chemistry sparked in the air between them.

'You say you have no idea how to seduce me but you standing there completely naked, bathed in the light of the silvery moon, is the sexiest thing I've ever seen.'

She moved towards him and sat down on his lap. He wrapped his arms round her and she kissed him deeply. He held one hand around the back of her neck as he kissed her too.

'Make love to me,' Bella whispered against his lips.

Isaac eased her back against the floor, moving on top of her. 'How about I make love to you here in front of this *incredible* view.'

Bella giggled as she removed his shirt. 'He really did like the view.'

Isaac let out a little growl. 'I think he was trying to catch a view of another beautiful sight.'

He kissed her shoulder and then kissed her breast, swirling his tongue over her nipple before sucking it into his mouth. She arched against him, pleasure spiralling through her stomach already. When he slid his hand between her legs it was only a few seconds later when she went tumbling over the edge.

He fished a condom from his pocket and passed it to her before kicking off his trousers. He braced himself over her and she quickly tore open the foil packet and slid the condom on, relishing in the feel of him beneath her fingers.

He settled himself between her legs and she wrapped her legs round his hips, holding him close as he slid carefully inside her. He looked so beautiful washed in the glow of the silvery moonlight. She felt so complete, so utterly at peace right then that she felt almost overwhelmed by it.

'As your boyfriend, do I get special privileges too?' he said, moving slowly against her.

'Right now, I'd give you the world,' Bella said, feeling the pleasure growing again, tightening through her body, on the verge of her release.

'I want this, always.'

He lowered himself down on top of her, so she could feel his velvety hardness from her toes up to her lips as he kissed her. And the thought of having this wonderful man in her life forever was the thing that sent her rushing over the edge, her orgasm ripping through her like a dam bursting its banks.

He held her close, whispering sweet words of affection in her ear, not taking what he needed until she had stopped shaking beneath him. When he finally let go, he did so staring into her eyes and for the first time in her life she wanted forever too.

❦

Bella was dozing in the massive bed, though she couldn't really sleep as Isaac was sitting next to her working on his tablet, the blue glow from the screen lighting up the room. She opened one eye and watched him as his fingers sped across the screen. It was the first time she'd seen him like this; in all the time they'd spent together, he was simply not one of those people that was always checking his phone, which surprised her given how busy he always was.

She shifted closer to him, pressing a kiss on his bicep, in the hope of tempting him to go to sleep with her. They had a few hours yet before they needed to be up for work and after spending several hours making love the night of the fire and that night, she really needed the sleep.

He kissed her fondly on the head and then returned his attention to the screen.

'What are you doing?' Bella said, snaking her hand across his stomach as she curled into his side.

'I'm working on *The Great British Egg Chase*.'

Clarity pierced the fog of sleep in her mind and she sat up. 'You're making the game?'

He nodded. 'Every spare second I've had, I've been doing it. As I wasn't at work yesterday afternoon, I spent the whole time working on this.'

'But you said you didn't have time, and that you were going to ask your colleagues at SparkStar to do it for you.'

'I don't have time, but I wanted to do this for you.'

Bella smiled, the warmth in her chest growing so much that it felt like it would burst from her. Tears pricked her eyes as she bent forward and kissed him. 'Thank you.'

'I've really enjoyed making it. I love doing this stuff and I've forgotten how much. It's made me think about doing more in the future with it.'

'Can I see?'

He lifted his arm up and she moved to sit between his legs with her back leaning against his chest.

'It's very crude at the moment and there are a few technical glitches but it works. Given the time constraints we have on this, and that Easter weekend is just over two weeks away, I'm going to probably have to give it to SparkStar to finish it off and make it look all pretty. The eggs are just flat red eggs at the moment, but SparkStar will make it look 3D and give the eggs a bit of a makeover to make them look more interesting. They can also make the things the kids can find in the eggs look like actual objects, magnifying glasses, hammers, things like that, where at the moment all I have are stars. But the basic concept is here.'

He pressed play and a small map with a little flag over the Royal Oak Hotel to show their current location suddenly appeared on the screen. Bella used her fingers on the screen to zoom out and saw there were several eggs all over the island.

'Oh my god, we can play this now; it's ready?'

'Well like I said, it's not pretty but it works.'

'How many eggs are there on the island?'

'Six at the moment.'

Bella scrabbled out of bed. 'Let's go find them.'

'Now? It's four in the morning.'

'Come on, I want to see how it works.'

Isaac sighed and got out of bed and started getting dressed. 'Remind me again why I'm with you.'

Bella laughed as she found her clothes and got dressed, impressed by how quickly Isaac had caved. 'Because you have a thing for red-heads.'

Isaac threw on a shirt. 'Never been with a red-head before.'

'Well probably, as Claudia said, I'm a novelty to you; I was never after you for your money. I liked you way before I knew you had any. I'm sure the novelty will wear off soon, especially when I keep making you leave the comfort of your bed at four in the morning.'

Isaac walked over to her, doing the buttons up on his shirt, his eyes furrowed with concern. 'Is that what Claudia said?'

Bella stopped dressing for a moment, standing in her underwear and a t-shirt. 'She didn't mean it in a horrible way, just that it's something different for you, which is what attracted you to me.'

'You're definitely not a novelty to me; you're not something that I'm just trying on for size to see if you fit. I was attracted to your kindness, your brilliant smile, but it was the easy way that we could talk for hours that I fell for, that you made me laugh a lot, the fact that I just really enjoyed spending time with you. Those were the things that made me come back on the Sunday.'

She leaned up and kissed him on the mouth and he gathered her to him. As the kiss continued, his fingers snaked underneath her t-shirt and she pulled away laughing.

'I know your game, ply me with compliments, kiss me until I can't even remember my own name and then tempt me back to bed so we don't have to go traipsing over the island at four o'clock in the morning. I'm not falling for it.'

He groaned. 'You can't blame me for trying.'

He grabbed a jumper and turned round and pulled it over her head. 'You'll get cold out there.'

She looked at it; it hung halfway down her thighs like a woollen dress. She looked up to see that Isaac was staring at her hungrily. 'Does this turn you on, me wearing your clothes?'

'You have no idea.'

Bella laughed and pulled her skirt on, shoving her feet into her red Converse.

'Are you ready?' she asked as she watched Isaac shove his feet into trainers too.

'I'll make you a deal. We find the three nearest ones and then we come back to bed for a few hours.'

'Sounds like a good deal on the proviso that we find the other three tomorrow.'

'That's fine with me.'

Bella looked over at Alfie and Rocket who were curled up together in the dog bed. 'Shall we take the dogs?'

'Let's not torture them with a four am walk. They haven't done anything to deserve that. I, however, must have been very wicked in a former life.'

'Or very blessed, depends how you want to look at it,' Bella said, taking his hand.

They walked out the hotel and only the night porter was there to notice their departure.

Isaac passed her phone to her.

'You've downloaded it to this?'

He nodded. 'The tablet needs Wi-Fi to access GPS, the phone should be able to use its network provider to access the internet.'

Bella glanced down at the map and saw there was an egg down by the harbour. She grabbed his hand and started walking in that direction. They walked along the deserted streets, the orbs of the streetlights sending puddles of gold across the wet roads. There was not a soul to be seen and there was something magical about that. It was chilly without the warmth of the sunlight yet, but it wasn't too cold.

'Hurry,' Bella said when Isaac seemed to be dawdling.

'Five minutes ago, I was sitting in a comfy bed, with the most beautiful woman in the world curled up by my side. I thought to myself, I'll just finish this one thing and then I'm going to wake my girlfriend up with gentle kisses and persuade her to let me make love to her. Then she wakes up before I get that far and my cosy night is gone forever.'

Bella laughed. 'I do feel sorry for you.'

'Besides, that egg isn't going anywhere. There's no rush.'

'The quicker we find these eggs, the quicker we can get back to the hotel where you can make love to me again.'

Isaac started running towards the harbour, dragging her behind him, and she laughed again.

There were a few more people down by the harbour, fishermen coming back from a night's fishing. A few of them stared at Isaac and Bella as they walked past – it must be fairly unusual to see anyone other than fishermen at this time of the day – but most didn't give them a second glance.

'It's just up ahead,' Bella said and Isaac leaned over and pressed the button which changed the game to the augmented reality. Now, using the camera on her phone, she could see the egg sitting on one of the docks just a bit ahead. She ran towards it until, according to the phone, it was sitting right in front of her.

'Now what?'

'You smash it,' Isaac said, leaning over the phone. 'I've given you a full complement of tools to use, whereas the children will have to earn points to buy these tools. Choose whichever one you want. This egg is wooden, so you'll need something that will break apart wood.'

'An axe?' Bella said, looking down the choice of tools.

'Sure, that will do it.'

She selected the axe and tapped the screen several times over the egg and watched the axe chop against the wood. Finally the egg smashed open and a gold star popped out.

Bella laughed. 'I love this game so much. Will this egg still be here for other people to find though once I've smashed it?'

'Yes, your game isn't linked to other people's so it will always be here, but once you've smashed it, you can't come back at a later stage and find it and smash it again.'

'Let's find another one.'

Isaac smiled. 'Let's go to the one at Rosa's. If she's open we can get a coffee and a pastry.'

'Sounds like a good plan.'

They walked through the streets and there were a couple more people around now, many of them heading towards the ferry terminal to make the early ferry over to St Mary's. There were a few others that worked in some of the shops, clearly going in early to get ready for the day even if the shops wouldn't be open for hours yet.

Rosa's was open. It didn't seem to matter what time of day it was, it was always open. Rosa and her two daughters worked shifts to cover all times of the day and there were several other people that worked a few hours here and there. There were quite a few people sitting inside at tables when they arrived outside.

Bella switched on the camera screen and saw the egg, sitting right outside the door.

'This one is a chocolate egg so how would you like to break it?' Isaac asked.

'Umm.' Bella scrolled through the tools; everything seemed a bit too savage to destroy a chocolate egg with. 'I normally just use my hand to smash my Easter eggs.'

Isaac scrolled to the bottom of the list of tools and pointed at the hand. Bella laughed and used the hand tool to smash the egg and out popped another star. 'I really love this game.'

'Let's have a pit stop before we find the last one,' Isaac said, pushing open the door to Rosa's.

The warmth of the shop leaned out and pulled them in with its delicious smells drifting around them. A few people looked their way; it was obvious the shop had regulars even at that time in the morning and they weren't among them. Bella was gratified that Isaac didn't relinquish her hand though. Maybe he had come to the conclusion that there was no point hiding it too.

'Crap, I didn't bring my purse.'

'It's OK, I got this. I don't think you'll be earning a gold-digger reputation from letting me buy you a coffee and a croissant.'

Bella grinned. 'Maybe not, but what about a hot chocolate with whipped cream and marshmallows? That's a whole extra fifty pence more than a coffee.'

'I think my budget will stretch to it,' Isaac said, dropping a kiss on her forehead, making her smile.

Rosa was serving behind the counter and she couldn't disguise her pleasure at seeing them together.

'You're up early this morning, Bella. Are you both catching the early ferry somewhere?'

'No, just out for a walk,' Bella said and she couldn't help grinning at Isaac. The Easter egg hunt was their little secret for now. Rosa didn't need to know that there'd be people coming from all over the island to smash a virtual egg outside her shop door.

'What can I get you two?'

'Hot chocolate with all the trimmings for Bella and I'll just take a latte,' Isaac said. 'Would you like something to eat?'

Despite the fact that Bella was never up at this time, her stomach gurgled appreciatively at all the wonderful smells. 'Can I have a pain au raisin please?'

'I'll have a chocolate one,' Isaac said.

Rosa left them alone for a few minutes while the hiss of the coffee machine and billows of steam indicated their drinks were being made.

'I feel a bit disloyal to Eden coming here, she makes wonderful breakfast pastries,' Bella murmured as her thoughts strayed to her sister. She wondered if she knew that Dougie was back.

'We can go and get some later for breakfast if you want, then she need never know.'

'OK, but I'm treating you to that.'

Isaac smiled. 'I'm just going to pop to the bathroom.'

Bella released his hand and he disappeared into the back of the shop.

Rosa returned with their pastries in a bag and their steaming drinks. 'I heard the two of you were seeing each other, I think it's wonderful.'

Bella blinked. She knew they had hardly been discreet and the islanders loved a good bit of gossip, but was it really that interesting that she was dating Isaac Scott?

Rosa registered her surprise. 'Well Cynthia from Blossom Grove said he stayed the night on Saturday night and Sally's husband is in the fire brigade and he was there when that awful business happened at Isaac's house – he saw the two of you together. And I've heard a few people talk about it in here.'

Bella frowned, remembering what Claudia had said about what people would think about them dating.

'And what have they said?'

'Oh nothing bad,' Rosa reassured her so quickly it made Bella think that there had been a few things that had been bad. Rosa obviously saw her sceptical face. 'Well, obviously a few people think that's how you got the job. You know a few people are still bitter about this whole embezzlement farce and they didn't think that the Umbrella Foundation would hire you based on your past so some think that you got round that by…' she gestured with her hand to imply all that was left unsaid. 'But anyone who has seen you together knows it's the real thing and I told them that you're not the type to do that sort of thing, although a few people have said how desperate you were for a job so maybe you were willing to do anything to get it.'

Bella was stunned. This was why she mostly kept to herself. Although most people on the island were lovely and looked out for one another, there were some that could be very unkind.

Rosa clearly realised that she had said something to upset Bella so she quickly changed the subject. 'I hear you're bringing the fair back to the island,' Rosa said. 'Everyone is so excited for it.'

'I just hope people come,' Bella said.

Rosa looked confused. 'Why wouldn't they?'

Bella shrugged. 'Well if they know I'm organising it, they might boycott it.' That thought hadn't really occurred to her before, that Isaac's charity might suffer because of her involvement, but now the fair was booked she couldn't help but worry that it was going to be a big disaster because of her. This was her first event for him and she wanted to get it right.

'Everyone knows you're organising it,' Rosa said, still confused.

Bella sighed. She had hoped that people would know it was for the Umbrella Foundation and not associate that with her. But of course the islanders knew everything. Rosa's face cleared with sudden recognition. 'Almost everyone on this island knows you had nothing to do with the embezzlement saga at Magic Wishes. We all felt so sorry for you when all that nonsense was going on. And you don't need to worry about those that do, they will find fault with everything no matter what you do. If they want to live their life being bitter and angry, let them get on with it. Everyone will be there, I can promise you that,' Rosa said with such determination that Bella wouldn't be surprised if she intended to go round to every single house on the island and force everyone to attend.

Isaac came back to Bella's side then and she offered him his drink. Bella smiled and waved goodbye to Rosa and they left the shop.

'Where to now?' Bella said, taking a big bite of her pastry and consulting the app again. She wanted to distract herself from the thought that everyone on the island was talking about her. 'There's two we could go for, there's one in Blueberry Bay or there's one in the park.'

'Let's go to Blueberry Bay, it's closer to the hotel and I'm still holding you to your promise.'

Bella laughed and they took off in the direction of the sea. She slipped the phone into her pocket and finished her pastry so she could hold Isaac's hand again. It felt so natural, so right, as if they had been together for years, not just a few days.

Blueberry Bay wasn't a formal public beach like the nearby Buttercup Beach. There were no steps or proper paths and it lacked any kind of facilities, which meant that it was largely deserted most times of the year, but there was a path of sorts that wound down through the trees and out on to the beach. It was very small, only twenty metres wide, but with the rosy glow of pre-dawn lighting up the waves over the sea, it was beautiful.

The phone vibrated in her pocket to let her know she was near to the egg and she pulled it out to see that the egg was resting on a rock just in front of them.

'This one is made from sand so...'

'A sandcastle egg?'

Isaac laughed. 'Yes, exactly.'

Bella quickly scrolled through the tools, looking for anything that could be water, but there didn't appear to be anything.

'How do you normally get water when you're on a beach?'

'A bucket,' Bella said, scrolling back up the list of tools and finding what looked like a child's bucket and spade set. She clicked on it and watched as water splashed on the egg and dissolved it. A gold star appeared on the screen.

She slipped the phone back into her pocket and slung her arms round Isaac's neck.

'Thank you for this. It's so brilliant. The children are going to get such a kick out of it. I can't wait to see it when it's all finished.'

He slipped his hands around her waist. 'You're very welcome. I really did enjoy doing it so I have you to thank for that.'

He kissed her sweetly and then she leaned her head against his heart as he wrapped his arms tightly around her, making her feel safe and adored all at once.

The waves were lapping gently onto the shore and out over the horizon the first slash of gold appeared over the sea. Bella had never felt so utterly contented before.

'You make me so happy,' Bella whispered.

Isaac tipped her chin up to face him and kissed her, slowly. He pulled back slightly. 'I could make you happier.'

She caught the dark look of intent in his eyes and laughed. 'Here?'

He shrugged. 'There's nobody here, it's just you and me.'

She looked around and it was very clear they were secluded from anyone unless they were on a boat and the sea was completely empty.

Before she could voice any further objections Isaac shuffled her back against the rocks, and a few minutes later he proved just how very happy he could make her.

CHAPTER 19

Isaac watched Bella sleeping in the bed next to him. After they had made love on the beach as the sun rose above the waves, they'd come back to the hotel where they'd made love again before Bella fell asleep. He simply could not get enough of her.

The sun had well and truly risen in the sky now, a burning ball of gold in a cloudless blanket of periwinkle blue. He would have to wake Bella up soon but right now he was content to watch her.

He was in trouble.

He was in love with her, he knew that. He wasn't sure at what point it had turned into love for him or if he really had been in love from the very beginning. It filled every inch of him, his heart felt too big for his chest. He had never felt like this before and he wanted to shout it from the rooftops. But he couldn't. She would run a mile if he suddenly declared his feelings for her after a week. She would probably still run a mile if he told her he loved her after a year. She was scared of love and for good reason. Although her aunt, uncle and Rome and Eden had showed her love, she had also had really bad examples of love too. For both her parents to abandon her, it showed her how fickle love could be, how ultimately the people that were supposed to love you more than anything in the world could let you down.

The frustrating thing was that he was pretty sure she had the same feelings for him. He could see it in her eyes, especially when they made love. But she was trying to deny it to herself too.

By labelling it love there was so much more to lose.

So what could he do?

It was too early. Maybe a few months down the line, when she was more settled with their relationship, he could tell her then. And in the meantime he would just continue to show her with his actions. Why risk ruining something that was perfect with one little word?

He glanced across at the clock and groaned. As much as he wanted to lie here next to her all day, he knew she would be mad at him if he didn't wake her.

He trailed a gentle finger down her cheek and her eyes fluttered open and she looked at him before breaking into a huge beautiful smile.

'You'll be late for work if you don't get up soon and I know your boss will get mad if you are.'

She giggled and rolled on top of him. 'He's a bit of a pushover actually. Let's just say I have him exactly where I want him.'

He held her against him. 'Is that right? I might have to tell him he needs to be a lot stricter.'

'I don't think he has it in him.'

She glanced at the clock and groaned. 'I really do need to go. I have to walk Alfie before work.'

'I'll walk him for you, I have to walk Rocket anyway. Alfie can keep her out of mischief.'

'He'll be good at that; he has a calming influence over her. Come and have a shower with me.'

'If I have a shower with you, you're never getting out of here on time.'

She nodded. 'That's true. You are a bad influence on me.'

She climbed out of bed and he watched the wonderful sight of her wandering naked across the bedroom and into the bathroom. He heard the shower starting and resisted the overwhelming temptation to join her. A few minutes later she returned, drying herself down.

'Are you not going to work today?' she said as she got dressed.

'I have some deliveries being made here, clothes and other things I need, and there's a man from the insurance company coming over later this morning. So I'll be in later. I'll probably work some more on your egg hunt game. What are your plans for tonight?'

'I'm having dinner with my aunt and uncle actually, every Friday night we always have dinner together.'

'Whereabouts do they live?'

'Up on Baker's Rise.'

She hesitated for a moment and he wondered whether she was going to invite him but she didn't say anything else. It was too soon for meeting families, he knew that. Well, it was too soon for her. He could be patient.

'I thought I would meet up with Dougie actually. I have a proposition for him and it's been too long since we hung out properly. But you could come by after.'

'I'd like that and I'll keep my clothes on this time.'

He laughed. 'Only while Dougie is here, after that you can wander round naked for the rest of the night.'

'Ha. OK, I'll look forward to that.'

She leaned over to kiss him and he held her to him, lingering over it that moment too long.

She pulled back. 'Behave Mr Scott, save it for tonight.'

He nodded and watched her walk out. The door closed behind her.

'I love you, Bella Roussel.'

He smiled to himself at his little secret, hoping it could stay secret for a while yet.

❦

Bella had just got off the phone to a local radio station when Elsie knocked on the open door and walked in, looking very worried.

'What's wrong?'

'It's Mr Scott. I was down in reception talking to Mary and he walked in and I could just tell he was furious. I've never seen him like that before and then I heard him shouting at someone. He never shouts. He likes things done and he expects efficiency but he never shouts at anyone. Poor love is obviously still stressed out about the fire at his house. I thought perhaps you might want to know that he was upset.'

Bella was already on her feet. She didn't stop to find out why Elsie thought it was appropriate that she was told or hang around to explain to her why she was going to see him. Elsie clearly already knew that something was going on between them.

'Thanks, Elsie.'

Bella left the office and quickly caught the lift up to his office. He'd arrived but he hadn't told her he was here. Did he not want to see her?

The doors pinged open and she walked straight past Melissa who was still sitting at Claudia's desk without even stopping to explain.

'He's in a bad mood,' Melissa called after her. 'He said he didn't want to be disturbed by anyone. Not even Claudia.'

Bella ignored her and let herself into his office.

He was standing at the window looking out at the sea when she walked in and whirled around furiously at being disturbed. He stalled when he saw it was her and then looked back out the window again.

'Bella, I'd really like to be alone right now.'

She could tell he was trying to keep calm with her but his tone suggested he was livid. She hesitated for a moment and then walked up to him, wrapping her arms around him and leaning her head on his back. She placed a kiss between his shoulders.

'Are you OK?'

She could feel how tense he was. This was a man that was a million miles from being OK.

'No, I'm not. Not at all.' Isaac disentangled himself from her arms and she got the sense he wanted to be away from her. He went to sit on the sofa with his head in his hands.

'What's happened?'

'The insurance company have said it's very unlikely they'll be paying out for the fire. They want to do a proper investigation but they seem to think it was started deliberately.'

'That's ridiculous.' She sat down next to him, sliding her arm round his shoulders.

'I've lost everything. I poured so much money into that house and now I have no way of getting any of it back.'

'How can they even think you would set fire to your own house? There has to be something we can do.'

'I don't know. They are still looking into it but the insurance man wasn't hopeful. Christ. One candle, that's all it took. One stupid candle I lit to impress you and because of it I've lost everything.'

Bella let her arm slide from his shoulders. Was it her imagination or was there a note of accusation in his voice? Did he blame her?

'I'm sorry,' she said, quietly.

He stared at her in confusion. 'Why are you sorry?'

'You think it was my fault.'

His eyes widened and then he stood up. 'Of course I don't bloody think it's your fault. How could it possibly be your fault?'

Bella stood up too. 'Well if I wasn't coming round to your house for dinner then none of this would have happened. If I hadn't marched into your office demanding that you sleep with me then you'd still have your home.'

He groaned in frustration and stormed away from her.

She stared at him, feeling a void between them for the first time. 'Maybe I should go.'

'Maybe you should. All I want to do is scream and shout right now and I certainly don't want to do that with you.'

'I'm sorry, I'm not making you feel any better, am I?'

He sighed.

'I'll make it up to you tonight.'

He shook his head. 'Let's leave tonight. In fact, maybe we can try this again in a few weeks' time. When things have calmed down a bit for me. You have the fair to organise and I'm away in London all of next week. This is just a bad time to start something.'

She felt like he'd just slapped her. He was breaking up with her. She felt sick. But then she'd never expected this to last forever. He'd made it very clear he didn't want a relationship and now he'd slept with her why would he stick around?

'OK,' she said, ensuring the pain she felt didn't come across in her voice. 'I understand if you don't want this any more.'

Bella walked to the door, willing herself not to cry. She opened the door hoping he would call her back but he didn't and she closed the door behind her.

She ignored Melissa's smug face as she jabbed the button for the lift. It felt so wrong to leave it like this after the connection they had shared. But if he didn't want her around then what could she do? She paused. But they had shared an incredible connection. It wasn't just sex, she knew that. The lift doors opened and she cursed her own tenacity as she stormed back towards his office. Before she could even open the door, it was flung open and Isaac stopped in his hasty exit when he saw her just outside. He grabbed her hand and pulled her in, closing the door hard behind her.

'OK?' he said. 'After what we shared, you just want to walk away like that?'

'Look, if you want to end things between us because this was just sex and lust and chemistry for you and now you've had your fill you want to walk away, if you want to end things because you have no interest in having a relationship, then fine. I'm certainly not going to beg you to stay. But if you are ending it because you're worried you're going to hurt me, because you need to scream and shout and you don't want to scare me away then it's absolutely not OK. I'm here for the good times and the bad. And I know there isn't anything I can do to help you with the house, but I'm here to hold your hand or to hold you if that's what you need. If you need space then I can give you that too, but I'm not walking away from you just because you're going through a really crap time right now.'

He gave a small smile before kissing her on the forehead, then dipped his head to look into her eyes.

'I wasn't breaking up with you. I just didn't want to upset you or hurt you because I'm so stressed out.'

She reached up to stroke his face. 'I can't imagine what you're going through and now this rubbish from the insurance company on top of losing your home. I wish I could take your pain away.'

He touched his lips against hers, kissing her so softly and gently that it completely disarmed her. She slid her arms round his neck as he gathered her against him. He pulled back slightly, leaning his forehead against hers. 'You already are.'

He stepped away but still held her in his hands. 'I think I'm going to go back to the hotel – I'm no good to anyone here and at least I can distract myself with your game for a few hours. Will you come round after you've had dinner with your family tonight?'

'Are you sure?'

'Yes, of course.'

She smiled. 'OK.'

He grinned. 'OK?'

And she knew that he was asking if they were OK. She nodded and he kissed her on the forehead again.

'Now get back to work.'

She laughed and moved back towards the door, but he stopped her. 'Unless you want a quickie on the sofa.'

She laughed again. 'Tonight, I promise.'

He let her go with a smile and she walked out of the office.

Bella stood up and stretched. It had been a long day but Elsie and Roger had proved their weight in gold as they busily helped to organise the fair for the following weekend. And now that Bella knew *The Great British Egg Chase* was underway, they had to prepare the press releases and promotion for that too so it would be ready before Easter weekend in two weeks. There was no point creating a brilliant game if no one knew about it. She had got in contact with Cadbury's who had agreed to donate real chocolate eggs as prizes and she had started running Facebook ads to tell people the game was coming. That was always fun, creating a visual that would appeal to lots of different people. She had never run a national event before so she had a much wider audience to reach in a much shorter amount of time. Local radio stations were proving beyond helpful too, but she always found it easier and more productive if she actually spoke to someone – emails could get lost or forgotten but phone calls had to be dealt with there and then. But this task was a bit beyond calling the three or four stations in the immediate area of the event, she had to contact them all, and there were many many local radio stations. Thankfully Roger's gentle nature and Elsie's no-nonsense attitude were a good mix for getting it done, but even with their help she had been on the phone all day.

But without Isaac being there she had no distractions, though just thinking about him was enough to make her mind wander. She was completely smitten by him and she had been unable to stop smiling all day.

The sun was on its downward journey across the sky and although it wouldn't set for hours yet, the sky was already turning a candyfloss pink over the sea.

'We're off now, dear,' Roger said from the doorway of her office.

Bella turned away from the view to see Elsie hovering near him too.

'Thanks for your help today, I really couldn't do this without you both,' Bella said as she leaned over and turned her computer off.

'No problem,' Elsie said as she was doing up the buttons on her red coat but Bella got the feeling that she wanted to say something else. 'Do you have any nice plans for the weekend?'

Bella smiled at the way she asked. Elsie was clearly hoping that Bella would confirm that something was going on between her and Isaac, though Bella running to help Isaac earlier had probably been confirmation enough.

'I'm having dinner with my aunt and uncle tonight; I'm not sure what else I'll be doing.'

Bella guessed that her weekend would actually involve lots of sex, as she and Isaac could barely keep their hands off each other, but although Elsie probably knew about her and Isaac, Bella certainly wasn't going to share those details.

'We just want to say… we're happy for you,' Roger blurted out, clearly not striving for the discreetness that Elsie was going for.

Bella considered denying it but there was no point in lying. Everyone would know soon enough; they had hardly been discreet outside of work. They had hardly been discreet at work either.

She nodded and smiled. 'Thank you. Do you two have any nice plans?'

'I'm taking Elsie to that posh restaurant overlooking the harbour,' Roger said.

Bella couldn't help the smile from erupting on her face. They were dating. They were so mismatched and not at all two people Bella could ever see together but maybe those differences would be the thing that would make them work. She certainly could never see Elsie going geocaching with Roger but she couldn't exactly see him making cakes for the WI either so maybe it didn't matter.

Roger nodded at her as if he could see what she was thinking. 'I've been asking her to go courting for a while now but she has always refused. She didn't want people to talk at work but life's too short to worry about what people will think, isn't it dear?'

Bella smiled. 'Yes, it really is.'

She watched them go and smiled when she saw Roger take Elsie's hand as they got to the lift.

She grabbed her jacket and with a last wistful glance down the coast at Blueberry Bay, remembering the events of the night before, she walked out. Without Alfie to consider, she decided to make her way straight round to Lucy and Finn's. Rome and Eden probably wouldn't be there yet but it would be nice to catch up with her aunt and uncle.

She walked down the main street, past the little chocolate shops and gorgeous little craft shops, waving and saying hello to people as she went. She walked up the hill where the shops disappeared and the little white cottages started to appear.

She turned into Baker's Rise and her phone suddenly vibrated in her bag. She pulled it out and was surprised to see another egg had been added up by the post-box ahead of her.

When she had seen the map of the eggs the previous night, there definitely hadn't been one in Baker's Rise then. She smiled as she remembered telling Isaac earlier that day that's where her aunt and uncle lived. He must have added an egg just for her.

This one was made from ice so she scrolled through the tools looking for an ice pick or something similar, but then she saw the box of matches. She selected that and when she clicked on the ice she was able to light a small fire underneath the egg but instead of a star popping out, a little scroll came out the top. She clicked on that and was surprised to see a message.

Have a good night. I'll miss you.

Her heart exploded with joy. This man was going to ruin her but she couldn't help the smile from spreading on her face.

She slipped the phone back in her bag and walked up the path to her aunt's house.

Lucy answered the door and immediately enveloped Bella in a big hug. Bella smiled with love for her aunt.

'Come on in, I want to hear all about your first week in your new job and this nice boy Isaac that I hear you're seeing.'

Bella laughed. Nothing got past her aunt. She knew Rome and Eden would be loyal enough to her not to mention that she was seeing Isaac so Lucy must have found out some other way but Hope Island being so small, nothing stayed secret for long.

A few minutes later Bella was sitting at the kitchen table with a slice of chocolate cake in front of her and a huge mug of tea. She waved at Finn as he emerged from his greenhouse with a tray of little flower pots. He smiled at her and placed them down on the ground and started removing the little seedlings from inside and planting them in the soil.

Lucy sat down opposite her, clearly waiting to hear all the details.

'Work has been fun, very busy but a lot of fun. I'm sure you've heard we're bringing the fair back to the island which is taking quite a lot of work to organise in such a short amount of time. I just hope people will come; it's been a long time since we had the fair, people might not care about it any more. They might care even less once they know I'm involved.'

'People will come. I've heard many people talking about how excited they are about the fair. Even if they weren't excited they would still come. Don't underestimate the loyalty of the islanders or how much everyone here loves you. No one here thinks you had anything to do with the embezzlement and they'll do anything they can to help you. You know that.'

Bella wasn't so sure. People didn't forgive and forget easily and although she hadn't been snubbed in restaurants or shops as she had been on St Mary's, she still felt that some people were giving her the side eye when she was walking down the streets.

She took a bite of her cake. 'We are also bringing a new game out which people will play on their phones. They can search for Easter eggs and win prizes.' Bella skated over the specifics of the game as she knew the technology would be lost on her aunt. She'd only just got a smartphone and had no idea how to use it. Her uncle Finn would have more of a clue about the game and how it utilised the GPS and maps inbuilt into the phone but there was no point in blinding her aunt Lucy with how it worked. She also hoped that talking about work would be enough to distract Lucy from talking about Isaac.

'That sounds great, Bella, you are so creative when it comes to fundraising ideas. And I understand you're dating the boss.'

Bella focussed on the cake, though she couldn't help smiling at the thought of Isaac. 'Umm. Yes, we've just started seeing each other.'

What would Lucy think about that? It wasn't a good idea to mix business and pleasure, anyone would tell you that. It'd be bad enough if they were colleagues but him being her boss could make things difficult if it ended between them. That thought was like a punch to the gut; it had only been a few days and she couldn't imagine not being with him any more.

'I think it's lovely. You know, me and Finn met in the same way.'

Bella looked up. 'He was your boss?'

'No, I was his. We both worked at the bank down the road.'

'And how was that, was it weird working with each other and dating at the same time? Did people make comments about the two of you dating?'

'Of course there were comments, but they soon got used to it. But working with him and dating him was wonderful,' Lucy said, dreamily. 'When we first started dating, I used to engineer a meeting with him in my office now and again and he would come in and ravish me across my desk. It was so exciting that I ended up making the meeting a daily thing. No one knew. My office was above the main branch and no one came up there. Everyone just took it as the norm that Finn had these daily meetings with me. He was chief cashier, I was branch manager, it was expected that we would have stuff to take care of. No one knew that, every day for ten years, Finn was taking care of much more personal needs.'

Bella stared at her. They'd always had a very open relationship and Bella had talked to her about sex before, but it was hard to imagine her aunt having sex with her uncle across her desk. In fact it was something she didn't want to imagine.

'He was new to the island,' Lucy went on, clearly reminiscing very happily now. 'One of the branches in St Mary's closed and if he hadn't moved to Hope Island he would have been out of a job. He moved here temporarily over forty years ago and never left. He came in all angry about having to move here and… well, it was love at first sight.'

'Do you really believe in love at first sight, Lucy? Surely you can't fall in love with someone when you've only just met?'

'His first day, I bought him a cake at lunch time to cheer him up because he looked so fed up about having to move here. He flashed me this wonderful smile and I knew right there and then that I was going to marry that boy. We were engaged after a month and married the following year. When you meet the one, you just know.'

Bella smiled at the simplicity of it. Lucy and Finn were testament that love did work for some people. They had found their forever and never looked back.

'I see the way you smile about Isaac; you really like him, don't you?'

Bella nodded. 'I really do.'

'Do you think this could be love for you?'

Bella shook her head automatically. 'I'm not interested in love.'

Lucy looked horrified. 'Why are you not interested in love?'

'Because it's terrifying and scary and horrible.'

Lucy frowned. 'I try not to think badly of my sister – she gave us you and I'll always be grateful for that – but what she taught you about love and relationships makes me so angry. Love is not something to be feared. Just because you had a bad experience of it doesn't mean you should run away from it in the future. Love is wonderful. It's the best thing that can ever happen to you.'

'It just lays you open to a whole heap of hurt. If you love someone then you're just handing them your heart on a plate for them to destroy whenever they want.'

'Or they could treasure it, look after it, adore it, keep it next to theirs for the rest of their life. What could be better than that? Love is scary, I'll grant you that. It doesn't always work out the way we would hope for, but I promise you it's worth the risk. When you find the one, and they love you back, it's the best feeling in the world.'

Bella shook her head.

Lucy took her hand. 'You can't stop yourself from falling in love. It just happens no matter how inconvenient. It's how *you* deal with it that will determine your happiness. How would you feel if things ended with you and Isaac now?'

'I'd be gutted,' Bella said, honestly, and immediately knew that was an understatement.

'And the other boys you dated, Andrew, Daniel, Jeremy and Kane. Did you care when it ended with them?'

Bella shrugged. 'Probably my pride was hurt more than anything but no, I didn't care. Doesn't mean that this thing with Isaac is love. I just care about him more than the others.'

'Denying that it's love is not going to stop it hurting if it comes to an end.'

Bella took a big bite of her cake. Lucy didn't understand. She had never been rejected so spectacularly that her heart was damaged beyond repair. Bella had to protect herself from love because the pain of her parents rejecting her had never gone away. She couldn't go through that again. She would just enjoy what she had with Isaac now and she wouldn't let herself fall in love with him, knowing it would eventually come to an end. And it would come to an end. There was something about her that meant she was unlovable. Her parents didn't love her, none of the men she had dated in the past had ever uttered that word, and Isaac would be no different. Isaac would walk away from her just like everyone else and it would hurt like hell when it happened but if she could keep her heart under lock and key, then maybe she could just about survive it.

'Oh Finn shouldn't be planting those white flowers there, they need to be on the other side of the garden, excuse me a moment,' Lucy said, flying out the door.

She watched Lucy as her arms flew around dramatically and Finn stood up and watched her with a smile of adoration. He leaned forward and kissed her on the forehead and picked up the tray and walked to the other side of the garden.

She would never have what they had. She was broken, damaged goods and no one could fix her.

There was a knock on the door and, as Lucy was still directing proceedings outside, Bella went to answer it.

Eden was standing on the doorstep looking very sorry for herself. Bella gave her a big hug and led her back to the kitchen.

'I'm presuming the long face is to do with Dougie being back on the island,' Bella said, cutting a slice of cake for her sister.

'He popped in to see me this morning, big grin on his face, giving me a big hug as if we're best friends.'

'You are best friends, just because you're thousands of miles apart doesn't change that,' Bella said, glad that Eden was here so Bella could focus on someone else's problems rather than her own.

'I know,' Eden said. 'I just… Do you have any idea how it feels to like someone and love them and hate them all at the same time?'

Bella stared at Eden. 'I have no idea what that's like.'

Eden sighed. 'He makes me laugh so much and we get on so well and every time he comes over I fall in love with him all over again and every time he goes back I hate him for leaving, because in another life we should have been happily married with fifteen kids by now.'

'I don't think anyone can be happily married with fifteen kids.'

'I would have been,' Eden said. 'And when he's gone I convince myself that I don't love him, that next time he comes over, we'll just be friends and I won't keep looking at him like a lovesick puppy. And I try dating other people, I really have tried but nothing works because, no matter what I do, no matter how long it goes by without me seeing him, I can't seem to fall out of love with him. It's been twelve years and he walks into my café and the feelings for him are as strong now as they were when he left.'

Bella reached out and pulled Eden into a hug. She knew Eden had feelings for Dougie but she hadn't realised that she was so tortured like this every time Dougie came over from the States.

'I still maintain he has feelings for you too,' Bella said.

'If he does, he's gotten very good at hiding it,' Eden sniffled. 'Why else would he keep coming back all the time?'

'If he had feelings for me he would have moved back here a long time ago.'

'Just like you could have moved to America to be with him,' Bella said, diplomatically.

'And do what, watch him sleep with an endless parade of women? He has given me no indication at all that he has feelings for me. Why would I move away from here without any kind of sign that he feels the same way?'

'Just like you've given him no indications at all that you have feelings for him; why would he move away from the bright lights of New York and come back here unless he knew for sure that you felt the same way?'

Eden stared at her. 'Whose side are you on?'

'Yours, always yours. I'm just saying that if you really want to move on, maybe it's time you tell him how you feel. If he doesn't feel the same way then at least you'll know and it might help you move on instead of always wishing and hoping for some kind of lovers' reunion every time he comes back. And if he knows how much it upsets you every time he comes over, maybe he'll stop. Something has to give here.'

Eden nodded though Bella knew it would take more than a few words from her to make Eden want to bare all her feelings to Dougie.

Lucy came back through the door and took one look at Eden and then pulled her into a hug.

'I saw him in town today,' Lucy said, instinctively knowing why Eden was so sad. 'I never know whether to hug him or be angry at him.'

'Always hug him,' Eden said. 'I'm angry enough for all of us and he doesn't deserve that.'

'I always do,' Lucy said. 'And I always tell him it's time he moved home for good. This time he said that he might be doing just that.'

Eden pulled back from her mum. 'He said that?'

Lucy nodded.

Eden sat down with a sigh. 'I have no idea whether to be overjoyed at that prospect or fed up. At least when he's gone I get some peace from this heartache. The thought of seeing him every day and knowing he'll never be mine is a truly depressing thought.'

Finn chose that moment to come barrelling through the back door, adorning Eden and Bella with hugs and kisses and breaking the emotional despair with his usual jovial manner.

'Bella, I want to hear all about your new job,' Finn said as he sat down and cut himself a huge slice of cake. 'And this Isaac chap I hear you're dating.'

Eden brightened at the mention of Isaac. 'I want to hear all about him too.'

Bella smiled with love for her family. It was going to be a long night.

CHAPTER 20

Isaac watched Dougie sink yet another ball into the pocket of the pool table and glared at him, hoping that would be enough to stop Dougie's marvellous winning streak.

Dougie just laughed off the scowl and lined up another shot. Isaac groaned as the yellow ball disappeared inside the pocket.

'What's wrong with you tonight? You normally play bad, but this is a new level of bad for you,' Dougie said, as he lined up another shot. Thankfully the ball glanced off the edge of the pocket and he sat down next to Isaac and took a sip of beer.

'Nothing's wrong, just thinking about the future. I think things need to change. I want something different than what I have now.'

'Does this new bright future include Bella?' Dougie teased as Isaac got up and walked around the table.

'I really hope so, but that's not what I meant.'

'Wait.' The smile fell off Dougie's face. 'You're really serious about Bella? I figured this was just a bit of fun for you.'

Isaac glanced up from his cue to look at Dougie. 'Am I treading on some toes here, is there something between the two of you?'

'No. Absolutely not. She's family. Nothing has ever happened between us. I assure you there are no toes being trod on here. But I've never known you be serious about anyone before.'

'Bella's different.'

'You've got that right.'

Isaac stood up, his arms folded across his chest. 'What does that mean?'

Dougie was his friend, probably his only one, but if he said one bad word about Bella this would not end well for Dougie.

'Whoa.' Dougie obviously saw the look and understood what it meant. 'I adore Bella, she's one of my oldest friends. But she's fragile. And I know that doesn't come across with her – she's feisty and has a hell of a temper on her when she gets mad – but underneath that prickly armour is this layer of finely spun glass. That glass was shattered a long time ago and I don't think it will ever be fixed.'

'I know all about her parents.'

'Then you'll know how badly that affected her. The kids round here were so cruel about it, mocking her for being so unlovable that even her parents dumped her. I know that had a massive impact on her too. Rome and I were like her bodyguards when we were growing up, surrounding her wherever we went, beating up anyone that dared to say anything, but she became so withdrawn. She pushed everyone away apart from us and Eden. I don't think she ever really got over that. I stayed in contact with quite a few people here after I left. I know some of the guys she's dated in the past. She never let them in. They said she was great fun but she was emotionally closed off. She pushes them away. She's scared of love and I really don't think this is going to end in the way you think it will.'

Isaac sighed. He knew how bruised Bella's heart was but he had hoped he might be the one to be able to fix it. What if she never felt the same way he did? What if she always held him at arm's length? Would it be enough for him to just have what they had now? But then he thought about it and he knew this was something different for her too.

'What we have is special,' Isaac said. 'I think she's falling for me too.'

Dougie looked even more horrified at this prospect. 'If you are the lucky one to break down her barriers and she really does fall in love for the first time in her life, she will be devastated if it ends. Just be careful with her. I'd hate to have to beat the crap out of you for breaking her heart.'

Isaac laughed. 'I promise that won't be necessary.'

'Phew. I don't fancy my chances against you.'

Isaac resumed lining up his shot and watched with some satisfaction when his red ball disappeared into the pocket. 'I wanted to talk to you actually about your new business. How's it going?'

'Good. Well I have more business than I can handle actually; I took a lot of clients with me when I left Poseidon Games. I thought it would be easy working for myself but now it looks like I might have to employ a team or at least take on a partner. Do you fancy it, Isaac? You were always a big gamer.'

Isaac took a shot at another ball but it bounced off the back cushion. 'Actually, yes.'

Dougie stared at him. 'I was kidding. Being a CEO of three companies not enough for you?'

'It's never been enough for me. I've never enjoyed my work for BlazeStar, or even SparkStar. My work for the Umbrella Foundation is at least more rewarding but I can't say it's enjoyable. I've been working on a game for Bella the last few days, a location-based augmented-reality game similar to *Pokémon Go* and I have loved it. I've forgotten how much I enjoy making games. You went on to live my dream, working for big gaming companies and now setting up your own gaming business. I went on to develop computer programs for big companies which made me a ton of money and made me bored as hell. Being with Bella has made me look at my life and what I want from it. I want to do more games. I'm already taking a giant step back from BlazeStar and SparkStar so I can focus on the Umbrella Foundation but I'm thinking I want to come away from the computer programming side altogether. Dawn and Matthew are doing a great job of managing the companies for me while I'm down here but I'm thinking of making them company directors. I'd still be a shareholder but the companies would be under their control. I want a new challenge and if you're looking for a partner then I'd be very interested.'

Dougie stared at him for a moment. 'I would love to work with you. It would be great to have someone with your skills and knowledge working on some of the projects. And if I did make the move back here, which is looking more and more likely, it would be great to work alongside you.'

'But?' Isaac could tell there was definitely a 'but' coming.

Dougie grinned at how easily Isaac had read him. He stood up and potted another ball without any kind of effort.

'*But*, it has been my dream as far back as I can remember to own my own gaming company and now I'm finally doing it and I love it, but I'm just starting out and I want to see if I can make a success of it. I'm not ready to relinquish fifty percent of my company just yet.'

Isaac nodded. He could respect that. 'How about twenty-five percent? It will take a while to completely hand over control of both Spark and Blaze and I'm committed to ensuring the Umbrella Foundation is funded from them for at least the next two years or until it is completely self-sufficient. I'm working hard to get them sponsorship and Bella is doing a great job with the fundraising so that might be sooner than two years but I certainly want to help them for as long as they need me. I wouldn't be able to commit to working for you full time for a while yet. But once the handover of Blaze and Spark is taken care of, I could certainly commit to you for two days a week. You said you needed the help and I'd be happy to give it.'

'Can your ego handle working for someone else?'

'My ego can handle it fine,' Isaac said.

Dougie grabbed his beer bottle and offered it up against Isaac's. 'Welcome aboard.'

Isaac grinned and chinked his bottle against Dougie's. His working life was finally slotting together. He just needed his love life to work out now.

✻✺ЄѺ⌇

When Bella let herself in to Isaac's hotel room later that night, Alfie and Rocket came over to greet her and she gave them fuss and attention before standing back up and looking around for Isaac. When she saw him she burst out laughing. He was lying on his side in the exact same position that she had laid in the night before, stark naked, clearly trying to be seductive. He had even gone so far as to have a rose between his teeth.

She wiped the tears of laughter from her eyes. 'You look ridiculous.'

'Does this not turn you on, baby?' Isaac said, clearly trying not to laugh himself.

'You look like something from an eighties porn film. Did I look that silly last night?'

'You looked amazing. I'm quite affronted that this doesn't do it for you.'

'Ah, don't be disappointed, I'll still do you.'

'I think that's the most romantic thing anyone has ever said to me,' Isaac said, sitting up and wrapping a blanket round himself. 'I'm glad you're home actually, it was getting a bit chilly lying there naked.'

'I've got the perfect thing to warm you up,' Bella said, as she stripped off her own clothes.

When she was naked she sauntered over to him. He opened the blanket and she straddled him, before he enclosed her in the blanket again and hugged her close, kissing her forehead sweetly. She leaned her head against his shoulder and wrapped her arms around him.

They had progressed so quickly to this sweet, intimate stage in their relationship. She loved hugging him, holding him close. She'd never had this before with a man. He ran his fingers down her back but it wasn't sexual at all. It was sweet and loving and he didn't seem to want anything more than that.

She pulled back slightly to look at him. 'Do you like hugging me, or do you do it because you know I like it?'

'I love it. I can't say I've ever been a big hugger, but since I've met you I have to say I can see the merits of it. It's probably up there in my top five favourite things.'

She smiled. 'Really?'

He nodded, brushing the hair back from her shoulders. 'I mean making love to you is pretty high up there in that list too but hugging you is pretty special.'

She laughed; he was teasing her. 'So if I was to say that tonight I didn't want to make love, I just wanted to spend the night hugging, you'd be OK with that?'

'Sure I would.' His eyes shone with a mixture of amusement and sincerity. He cupped his hands round her neck, stroking her cheeks with his thumbs. 'Just as long as I could hug you while I was buried inside you.'

Bella laughed. 'That's some kind of compromise.'

He ran his hands down her shoulders, skimming his thumbs over her breasts. She let out a little gasp. 'And maybe I could hug you and touch you a little,' Isaac said, his hands moving lower.

'I think I'd be OK with that.'

He kissed her shoulder and then her breast, sliding his tongue across her nipple.

'I'd definitely be OK with this,' Bella said, her voice high with sudden need.

He grabbed a condom from the nearby table and slid it on. He lifted her hips slightly and slid carefully inside her.

'Let's see what else you'd be OK with,' Isaac said.

As he layered gentle hot kisses down her throat to her collarbone, she thought she'd be OK with pretty much anything Isaac did to her.

❦

Isaac woke the next day with Bella wrapped tightly in his arms, her head on his chest. It was Saturday so neither of them needed to work though he knew he would work on the egg hunt game before he handed it over to the team at SparkStar on Monday.

He glanced down and realised Bella was awake, staring out over the sea, her beautiful green eyes seemed very far away from here.

He was still half asleep but given the choice of going back to sleep and spending time with Bella, he knew which he wanted to do more.

He ran his hand through her hair and she blinked and looked up at him, flashing him that wonderful smile when she saw he was awake.

'I need to go home today. I only brought a change of clothes for yesterday,' Bella said.

Isaac nodded. 'I need to pack ready for my trip to London tomorrow. And I need to find somewhere to store all this stuff I seemed to have accrued over the last few days. Claudia has been super-efficient making sure I have everything I might need delivered here but, without a home yet, I have nowhere to put all this stuff when I leave tomorrow.'

'Have you not found anywhere to live yet?'

'Claudia has found me this lovely little house down by the sea, but it won't be ready until next week.'

'Why don't you stay at mine tonight, bring all this stuff with you and I'll keep it there until you come back.'

'If you're sure? I probably won't be back for two weeks.'

Bella's face fell. 'Wait, two weeks? I thought it was only a week?'

'I have some stuff I need to take care of.'

'But you'll miss the funfair next weekend.'

'I know, but as you quite rightly pointed out, I hired you to organise the fundraising events. I don't need to be at every event when you are more than capable of representing the charity for me.'

He watched the disappointment wash across her face.

'If you want help I can make sure there are other people from the charity there to help you.'

'No, it's not that. I can take care of it and Roger and Elsie have said they'll come down and help too. The funfair will pretty much take care of itself; the company have done this many times before. I just thought it would be fun if we could go together. It's OK, I understand. You have more important things to do.'

He frowned. 'You're important to me. I'm just trying to finish up my life in London properly so I can start my life here with you.'

That hadn't come out right. If he had been more awake he would have said that differently.

Bella picked up on it straight away, panic flaring in her eyes. 'What do you mean?'

'I'm resigning as CEO of my technology companies. I'll still be a shareholder but I have a brother and sister team that will take over as company directors. It'll mean that my involvement with those companies will be reduced to next to nothing and I can stop travelling backwards and forwards to London all the time. Which will mean I have more time to spend with you.'

'You're doing all that for me?'

He recognised fear in her voice. What was the right answer here? 'No, well, partly for you, mostly for me.'

'We've known each other a week, you can't start giving up everything for me. You love London.'

'I love this place more. That part of my life is over now. I've worked at a job which I've hated for the last ten years and the worst thing was it was my company. I couldn't just leave. But being with you over the last few days has made me reassess what I want in my life.'

Bella sat up, her eyes wide, and shook her head. 'This thing between us, it's been fun and I love spending time with you but you're suddenly making it sound a lot more serious than it is. You can't change your whole future, your whole life, because of one incredible week together. What happens when it ends?'

When? Not *if* but *when* it ends. That was a worrying distinction. In her mind she was expecting it to end. She didn't see a future for them. It was too soon to start thinking about marriage and children, he knew that. It was way too soon to even think about living together, even though he had no home and they had spent every spare second in each other's company since they'd met. But he did see a future with her and she was panicking because he was talking about that.

He sat up determined to diffuse the situation. There was no way he wanted to scare her off when she was only just getting used to the idea of being with him.

He rested his hands on her shoulders, sensing she was in flight mode. 'Bella, I'm not doing this for you. I'm not changing my whole life because of you. This has been on the cards for a very long time. I started to plan my move to Hope Island many months ago before I'd even met you. I've been taking more and more steps back from Blaze and Spark partly because I wanted to focus on the charity for a while and partly because I wanted to do something else but I still held back from leaving them completely. They're my companies, I built them from the ground up, and I'm proud of what I've achieved even if I don't particularly enjoy it. It was what you said the other day that made me think that things in my life needed to change. You said that I'm doing something wrong if I haven't got time to have fun. And that stuck with me. What's the point of having all this money if I never have time to enjoy it? Do I really want to get to the end of my life and look back on it and say, "Yes I earned a hundred million pounds but I was bored out of my head my entire working life"? You said I need to delegate more. That I need to have people to take charge so I can do more things I enjoy, like making your game. And I do have excellent people in charge of my companies while I'm here and while I'm working with the charity, so why not let them take charge all the time? I have loved making your game over the last few days and I'd forgotten how much. I want to do more of that.'

He tucked a curl of red hair behind her ear. 'When I said that being with you has made me reassess what I want in my life, I meant that what you said hit home for me. You inspire me to want more. I am doing this for me and if this thing between us ends tomorrow I would still be resigning as CEO of Blaze and Spark. I would still be moving here for good. This is not me proposing to you or buying a seven-bedroom house for you and our six kids. I am simply trying to build a better life for myself and I hope, in time, that you will want to be a part of that life, but if not, then that doesn't change any of my plans.'

He could see his words had calmed her down. 'OK.'

'OK?'

'Yes, sorry. I just didn't want you to regret being with me.'

'I could never regret that. If this ends between us, I would never regret this wonderful time we've spent together.'

'I'd never regret it too.'

'Good. Now let's stop talking about the end of our relation-ship. I'm having way too much fun with you to even think about letting you go.'

She smiled and he leaned forward and kissed her. She hesitated for a moment then wrapped her hands round the back of his neck and kissed him back.

He wasn't going to push any more now but it worried him that she didn't see a future for them. Was this really just a bit of fun for her? Because if it was, then he needed to get out soon before he fell further in love with her.

CHAPTER 21

Bella woke to an empty bed on Sunday morning and when she snaked her hand across the sheets and felt how cold they were, it was evident the bed had been empty for some time. Had he left without saying goodbye? That hurt more than it should for two people who were just having a bit of fun. She tried to ignore the voice in the back of her head that told her this was a hell of a lot more than that.

They had spent the whole day together the day before, walking their dogs over the hills, having lunch in town, making love and talking, and it was wonderful and lovely. She couldn't remember ever being with a man who made her so ridiculously happy. But why did she feel like she had to hold back? Why did she hold her breath in fear every time he looked at her fondly just in case he decided to tell her he loved her? In truth, she wasn't that scared about Isaac loving her. She had been let down in the past by people who loved her. Isaac would walk away just like everyone else and she was prepared for that. What scared her was falling in love with him. She had never felt this way about anyone before and she knew if she fell in love with him, and it ended, it would break her heart all over again. She didn't think she could go through that pain again.

These two weeks away from him would help put things into perspective. A break would be a good thing. Life would return to normal, as it had been before she met him instead of spending every spare second with him. And she would see that she didn't need him to make her happy.

Isaac suddenly walked into the room and her body betrayed her when a huge smile spread across her face when she saw he was still here. He was dressed in trousers and shirt and a wonderful waft of his spicy clean aftershave reached her nose.

He was carrying a mug of tea and he placed it down on the drawers next to her bed.

'I need to go soon,' Isaac said.

Bella lifted the duvet for him and, without hesitation, he climbed into bed with her fully clothed and pulled her into his arms, kissing her head as he held her.

'Don't go. Stay here in bed with me. We can call in sick at work and spend the whole week having mad passionate sex.'

'Seriously tempting but I can't,' Isaac said.

She ran her hand down his chest. 'Can I tempt you to stay for a quickie?'

'You say the most romantic things to me. But sadly not. The taxi will be here in a minute. I need to take my boat to St Mary's, fly from there to Exeter and then catch another plane to London and there's only one plane a day. So I can't miss it.'

'I can't believe you're going to be gone for two weeks. I'm going to miss you,' Bella said then suddenly reprimanded herself. What was wrong with her? She wasn't going to miss him. She was perfectly fine on her own. She would miss the sex. That was all. So why did her chest hurt at the thought of not seeing him?

'I'm going to miss you too. But we can call each other and text and Skype. Plus there's always phone sex.'

She looked up at him and laughed. 'I've never done that before.'

'I can't say I have either.'

'What will it involve?'

'I don't know but from the films I've watched, you'll tell me what you're wearing—'

'Mickey Mouse pyjamas?'

'Yes, that will work.'

'That will turn you on?'

'You turn me on, it doesn't matter what you wear.'

She grinned. 'Good answer.'

'It's the truth.'

'OK, so we'll try phone sex and I'll marvel you with how good I am at seducing you over the phone.'

Isaac laughed. 'Yes, as the last time you tried to seduce me ended *so* well.'

'Hey. It ended with us having sex so I can't have done too badly.'

'Pretty much any time you're naked is going to end with us making love.'

'I'm naked now,' Bella said, stretching herself against him.

'I know and if the taxi wasn't going to be here in thirty seconds, I would be happy to oblige.'

'The taxis are always late round here.'

A horn beeped outside.

'Damn it.'

Isaac rolled her over, pinning her to the mattress under his glorious weight. He kissed her deeply.

He pulled back slightly to stare into her eyes. 'I promise when I come back, I'll more than make it up to you.'

'You better.'

'And I'm going to continue in my mission to get you to fall in love with me.' He winked so she knew he was teasing but there was something in his eyes that hinted he was being serious.

Bella decided to play along. 'Bring me back those chocolate-covered strawberries from Godiva and I think that might just seal the deal.'

He smiled. 'I'll see what I can do.'

He dropped a lingering kiss on her forehead and with a groan he climbed out of bed. As the horn sounded again, he quickly pulled his shoes on. 'Are you sure you're OK to have Rocket for me?'

'Of course. She'd only be sitting in your hotel room getting bored if you took her to London. At least Alfie can keep her company while I'm at work.'

'Thank you.'

He leaned over, gave her another peck on the cheek as if he couldn't tear himself away and then he left the room.

Bella quickly got up, grabbed a robe and rushed to the window. A few moments later she saw Isaac leave dragging a suitcase behind him. He instinctively looked up and gave her a wave and she watched him get in the taxi and disappear down the hill.

God she really was going to miss him and that worried her.

❦

Monday morning, Bella was already sitting at her desk by half past eight. There was so much to do and so little time to do it in. She took a sip of her coffee that Elsie had made her and looked down the list of people she needed to call that day. The funfair was going to start arriving this week and she knew that she would have to spend most of the day down there on Thursday to make sure everything was set up for the grand opening on Saturday. Although the fair would be there for a little under a week, she knew the biggest day would be Saturday and she wanted everything to run smoothly. She also hoped to be able to launch the egg game by the start of the next week in the lead-up to Easter the following weekend.

Her computer beeped with an internal message and she looked up and saw it was from Isaac.

Her heart leapt. He had texted her from his hotel when he'd got there on Sunday afternoon and he had texted her to wish her goodnight, but she hadn't heard from him today.

She quickly opened the message, her workload forgotten.

Morning Beautiful.

She couldn't help the huge smile that erupted on her face. She quickly typed back.

Hey Sexy.

You're in work early.

Lots to do and without the boss here to maul me I might actually be able to get most of it done today.

Your boss sounds like a pervert, sexually harassing his staff.

He is a pervert. All he thinks about is sex. He can't keep his hands off me. If I didn't love it so much, I'd have to make a complaint.

The phone suddenly rang on her desk. She picked it up.

'Bella.' Isaac's voice sounded so deep and masculine and indescribably sexy over the phone.

'Isaac.'

'What are you wearing?'

Bella looked down, what a weird question. 'Umm, black trousers, pale blue shirt, blue ballet pumps.'

She heard him laugh a little. 'You really are good at this seduction malarkey.'

Bella laughed. 'Oh. Sorry. I forgot we were going to have phone sex. Ask me again.'

'What are you wearing?'

'I'm naked, Isaac. I'm sitting at my desk stark naked.'

'No clothes at all?'

'No, I got some really funny looks when I walked into work today. It was quite chilly too. I even walked the dogs while I was naked this morning. Though I had to wear my wellies obviously, but they don't count.'

It was so easy talking to him, flirting with him. It was as if they had been doing this for years not just a few days.

'Are you still wearing the wellies now?'

'Do wellies do it for you?'

'I'm still hung up on the thought of you sitting at your desk naked, I'm not really focussing on your shoes right now.'

'I'm wearing black high-heeled shoes and nothing else.'

'I take it back; I'm very interested in your shoes.'

'Well maybe, when you come back, I'll greet you at the door wearing nothing but black high-heel shoes.'

'Now that's an image that will keep me smiling for the rest of the day.'

'Well now I'm naked, what would you like me to do next?' Bella said in her best seductive voice.

'I'd like you—'

He was suddenly interrupted by a woman's voice in the background and Bella recognised that it was Claudia that spoke.

'Isaac, we need to go downstairs to the meeting in five minutes.'

'Thanks Claudia, I'll be out in a second.' There was a pause, presumably while he waited for Claudia to leave the room, and then Isaac spoke again, his voice returning to his sexy purr. 'Bella, I have to go, but when I next call you, I want you to think about where you want me to touch you.'

Just the thought of that sent shivers down her spine.

'OK.'

He said his goodbyes and then rang off. Immediately the phone rang again.

'Bella, I got so distracted with your wellies and high-heel shoes that I forgot the main reason I called.'

'Having phone sex with me was not the main reason? I'm offended,' she teased.

'Of course that was the main reason,' Isaac laughed. 'But I did have a smaller reason. I'm talking to Oak and Acorn this afternoon.'

'The bank?'

'Yes and I'm trying to persuade them to come in as permanent sponsors for the Umbrella Foundation. Would you be happy to do a telephone conference at four this afternoon and just talk through with them some of the ways their logo will be used at our events?'

'Oh sure, I can do that. I can send through a quick PowerPoint as well if you want.'

'That would be great. And I'll phone you at two for our phone sex session.'

Bella laughed. 'Will you be naked too?'

'Of course.'

'Then I look forward to it.'

She put the phone down and a few moments later her diary was updated with two events. One was the telephone conference at four with Oak and Acorn and the other at two o'clock was simply titled, 'Phone call with Isaac.' A thrill ran through her at the thought of that phone call.

If him being away was supposed to make her realise that she didn't need him or miss him, it was having the completely opposite effect. She was falling for him and it scared her to death.

❧❧❧

Bella found herself so busy for the next few hours, eating at her desk over lunch as she created the PowerPoint, that she barely noticed that two o'clock came and went without the promised phone call. She didn't mind. She was sure she would catch up with Isaac after work that night and then she might be able to enjoy the phone sex a bit more in the privacy of her own home. Something had clearly come up for Isaac which meant he couldn't call her.

When two thirty came and there was still no phone call, she ran down to the marketing department to talk through the

Facebook adverts and the other promotions they were going to run for the egg game. She came back to her office around three just as the phone was ringing.

She quickly snatched up the phone and grabbed an orange from her desk.

'Hello?'

'Bella.' Isaac's quiet authoritative voice was enough to make her knees turn to jelly.

Determined to do better at her seduction than she had in the previous conversation, she decided to start the ball rolling straight away.

'Isaac, I'm so glad you called,' she purred. 'I've been sitting here naked waiting for you to call. I'm touching my breasts and thinking of you.' Bella quickly checked her emails to see she'd had a reply from the council in London about the zombie run she had planned in Hyde Park in the summer. She popped a chunk of orange in her mouth and scanned through the email to see if it was anything important.

There was a sudden clatter on the other end of the phone as Isaac's voice suddenly became louder and clearer.

'Um, Bella, I'm sitting in the conference room with the representatives from Oak and Acorn. The meeting was brought forward. I did update your diary accordingly.'

She quickly swallowed the orange segment and nearly choked on it. 'Oh my god. Please tell me I'm not on speakerphone.'

'You're not at the moment but you were. That's sort of the whole point of a telephone conference call.'

CHAPTER 22

Bella's cheeks flamed red and hot, sweat prickling down the back of her neck. 'Oh god no, did they hear me say I was touching my breasts?'

'Yes, I think everyone in the conference room heard you.'

'Everyone?' she squeaked. 'How many is everyone?'

'Er, I think there's twenty of us in here.'

'No! Oh god no, I'm so sorry. I'm not even touching my breasts, I'm sitting here reading my emails and eating an orange. I can't believe I told a room full of twenty people that I was touching my breasts.'

She wanted to curl up and die. She wanted a great big volcano to suddenly erupt off the coast of Hope Island and completely obliterate her from the surface of the earth. She was going to get the sack for this. It was all well and good that people knew she and Isaac were dating at work as long as it didn't interfere with their jobs or they weren't rubbing it in people's faces. Telling a conference room of twenty people that she was sitting naked at her desk, touching her breasts as she thought of her boss, was about as in your face as it could possibly get.

She felt sick.

How was she supposed to come back from this?

'Tell them I'm your wife,' Bella blurted out. 'It looks better if I'm your wife rather than just some random woman you're shagging at work.'

There was silence from Isaac. Was he angry? Of course he was. This was a huge sponsorship opportunity for him and she had just ruined that.

In the background, she could suddenly hear laughter. It was a man but other people were laughing too.

'Bella, I'm going to put you back on speakerphone,' Isaac said.

She quickly took a drink of water, trying to get moisture back into her mouth. What was she going to say?

Should she just launch straight into her spiel and ignore the huge elephant in the room, just pretend that she hadn't been talking about touching her breasts a few minutes before? Or should she make some reference to it, try to explain it away?

'Well,' the man said, laughing. 'I've been to many of these sponsorship meetings and I've never had a company go to these lengths to get us on board.'

They found it funny. It was going to be OK. She should make some joke about it and clear the air.

'Well we're committed to getting your name out there at every event in any way we can,' Bella said. 'Even if that means tattooing your logo on my breasts.'

There was silence. Idiot. She'd made the situation ten times worse. She should have just apologised and skated over it.

But then laughter erupted in the room again and it went on for some time. Finally it quietened down.

'Let me introduce Bella properly,' Isaac said, and it was evident he was laughing too. 'Bella is our fundraising events manager at the Umbrella Foundation and she is also my fiancée. We always joke with each other like this whenever I'm away from home. I can assure you that Bella is not naked and is currently sitting in a communal office with around thirty other people nearby so definitely not touching her breasts.'

'It's true,' Bella said. 'I've just eaten an egg and cress sandwich. There's nothing sexy about that. I'm so sorry. I was expecting a call from my fiancé at two and I wasn't expecting to talk to you guys until four and when I heard Isaac's voice, I thought I would tease him as I always do. This is not standard practice for our charity, I can assure you.'

'It's OK, Bella,' the man said. 'Best laugh I've had in a long time.'

'Bella, this is Graham Miller, he's in charge of sponsorship at Oak and Acorn,' Isaac explained. 'Why don't you tell him how his sponsorship would be integrated into our events?'

She could do this. They'd just explained it away, cleared the air. Now it was time to be professional. She could curl up with embarrassment later.

'Do you have the PowerPoint to hand, Isaac?'

'Yes it's up on the whiteboard as we speak. Can you talk us through the slides?'

Bella quickly loaded the PowerPoint on her own computer. She started to launch into her presentation and knew that she would never ever live this down.

❦

Isaac got in the back of his car and Marcus, his driver, pulled out into the traffic to take Isaac back to the hotel. It had been a busy day with several meetings but lots of good things had come out of it. Graham from Oak and Acorn had been very impressed with what Bella had come up with despite the fact that the meeting had started in such a strange way. Bella was charming and proficient and she had soon smoothed out the mistake. It had all but been forgotten by the time they got to the end of the meeting, though he knew it would be a long time before Bella forgot it.

He took his phone from his jacket and called her. She should have left work by now, though he wasn't sure if she'd be at home.

It rang once before she answered.

'I hate you, Isaac Scott,' Bella answered.

He burst out laughing. 'It's not my fault.'

'It so is your fault. You said you'd ring at two and you wanted me to think about how I wanted you to touch me.'

'Bella, you're on speakerphone,' Isaac teased.

'WHAT?!' Bella squealed.

'I'm kidding, I promise, I'm kidding. I'm sitting in the back of the car alone and no one can hear you but me.'

'I hate you.'

He laughed. 'No, you don't, you love me really.'

'We're never having phone sex again.'

'Why? You were so good at it.'

'Shut up. I was not. I couldn't be sexy if I tried.'

He smiled. 'Believe me, you don't have to try.'

'Still never going to happen. While we're at it, we're never having proper sex again. That's your punishment for getting me into trouble like that.'

'I think that's called cutting your nose off to spite your face.'

Bella laughed. 'What? I won't miss the sex. Not at all. Whereas you'll be begging me for it as soon as you come back.'

'I bet you'll instigate sex before I do. You're insatiable,' Isaac said.

'How much do you want to bet?'

Isaac looked out the window as they drove past a chocolate shop. 'An Easter egg.'

'OK.'

'If you instigate sex first, you have to buy me a giant Yorkie egg.'

Bella laughed. 'OK and if you instigate sex first you have to buy me a giant Crunchie one.'

'I'll agree to those terms. And remind me, where do the Godiva chocolate-covered strawberries come in?'

'Those are separate. You have to buy me those to win my love, but the price has just gone up to two boxes because of today.'

'That seems fair.'

The noise on the other end of the line changed and he got the sense that she had just gone indoors.

'Where are you, Bella?'

'Just got in from walking the dogs. I'm going to have dinner then probably go straight to bed. Being humiliated has taken its toll on me. What do you have planned for tonight?'

'Dinner and bed too. Nothing exciting.'

'Alone?'

He frowned. 'Bella, I'm not going to bed with anyone else. What kind of asshole do you think I am? I know this is only a bit of fun for you, but regardless how you want to categorise it, I'm not going to be sleeping with anyone else behind your back. And I hope you won't too.'

There was a silence from Bella. 'I meant, are you having dinner alone, or would you be having dinner with people from work or Claudia? I didn't think for one minute that you are up in London screwing around behind my back. I trust you.'

Isaac cringed. 'Sorry.'

'It's OK. And… I don't think this is just a bit of fun.'

He swallowed. 'You don't?'

'No. It's something more, we both know that.'

The car pulled up outside his hotel but he didn't get out.

'How much more?'

Bella didn't answer.

'How much more, Bella?' he asked softly.

'I like you.'

He smiled, this was like trying to get blood from a stone. 'OK.'

'I like you a bit more than like.'

'I'll take that,' Isaac said.

'It doesn't mean I love you,' Bella said, backtracking.

'I know.'

'Just that I care about you, I'm fond of you. That's it.'

'I adore you, Bella.'

'Despite the fact that I completely embarrassed you today at work.'

'Because of it. Because every single thing about you makes me adore you even more.'

'I adore you too,' Bella said, so quietly he barely heard it.

'I so wish I was there to kiss you right now.'

'Me too. If I wasn't working at the funfair this weekend, I'd come up to London to see you.'

'You don't like London, it scares you.'

'I know, but I'd brave it to see you.'

Isaac glanced out of the window and could see the doorman was getting irate about having their car parked outside when other cars were trying to unload their guests too. The doorman was gesturing to Marcus to move on. Marcus was unmoved by the angry glares.

'Bella, I'd better go, but I'll call you later. And I need to go shopping tomorrow to see if I can find a giant Crunchie egg.'

Bella laughed loudly. 'You're caving already.'

'You bet I am.'

He said his goodbyes and hung up. Well that was definitely progress. He wouldn't push for anything more from her and he certainly wouldn't tell her he'd already fallen in love with her. She wasn't ready to hear it yet. But this conversation had given him hope that she would get there eventually.

※ ❧ ☙

Bella plonked herself in the booth at Rosa's the following night, sitting down opposite Rome and Dougie.

It had been another full-on day at work and she was exhausted. She would have quite liked to have gone home and gone to bed, but it was Eden's birthday and she wouldn't miss that for the world. She had spoken to Isaac several times that day, some of it about the egg hunt game, but most of it was just lovely little chats in between his meetings. No more phone sex though, she was not risking that again.

'You look happy,' Rome noted as he popped an olive in his mouth.

'I am happy,' Bella said. 'Things are going well at work, people seem nice, I love my job, the plans for the upcoming funfair are all going smoothly. Life is good.'

'And the fact that you're shagging the boss might have something to do with that huge smile you were wearing when you came in here,' Dougie said and she playfully smacked his hand away from the last slice of cheesy garlic bread.

Rome choked on his drink. 'Do you mind, that's my sister you're talking about. I don't need those images in my head.'

'That might be a big reason why I'm smiling, yes,' Bella said.

'So it's true?' Rome's eyebrows knitted together.

'Yes, and you were going to trust my judgement on this, remember.'

Rome visibly tried to force his frown away and failed. 'I'm just not sure it's a good idea.'

'It's OK, I already gave him the big brother warning,' Dougie said. 'Told him if he hurts her, I'll have to beat him up.'

'Good, well at least he knows where he stands,' Rome said, seriously.

Bella stared at them. 'Are you kidding? We're not in school any more. You don't get to beat up people that are mean to me.'

'Don't see why not,' Rome said.

'Look, this is the last time we're going to speak about this, whether it's the right thing to do or not is down to me to decide, not anyone else. I am happier right now than I have ever been in my entire life and that's all down to Isaac. If it ends, then it ends. Yes, I'll be gutted but I would never regret this time with him. I adore him and, quite frankly, he's the best thing that has ever happened to me. I'd really like it if you were happy for me instead of threatening to beat him up if he puts a foot wrong.'

Rome stared at her. 'This is something serious for you, isn't it?'

'Yes I think it is.'

'He said the same about you,' Dougie said, softly. 'He's a good man, Rome. I mean sure he's had his fair share of girlfriends, haven't we all. But you know I'd never let some asshole go out with her.'

Rome nodded. 'I am happy for you, Bella. If he makes you this happy then I promise I'll say no more about it.'

Bella was saved from any more overprotective words of wisdom by the arrival of Eden and Freya.

Dougie immediately got up and hugged Eden, his arms wrapped tightly around her. Eden clearly couldn't decide on an appropriate place to put her hands, so she opted for a quick pat on the back.

'Happy birthday, buddy,' Dougie said and then held her at arm's length. 'You look amazing.'

She did too, she was wearing a beautiful deep blue dress, which had tiny flowers and beads sewed around the top.

'This is Freya's present for me. She always has wonderful taste in clothes,' Eden said.

Dougie tugged her down next to him in the booth before she had any ideas about sitting somewhere else. It was the strangest thing to watch her sister be equally elated at being in such close contact with Dougie and utterly miserable at the same time.

Wanting to distract her from her torment, Bella slid Eden's present across the table. 'Happy birthday.'

Eden smiled gratefully. 'Thank you.'

She tore open the wrapping paper to reveal a thick book, an illustrated collection of fairy tales. Bella had seen it in a second-hand book store and fallen in love with the beautiful pictures and gold-edged pages. Eden was a massive fan of fairy tales and Bella knew she would appreciate it.

'Oh wow, this is beautiful, thank you so much,' Eden gushed, carefully flicking through the pages. 'I love it.'

'Open mine next,' Dougie said, sliding her a tiny square present.

Eden ripped open the paper and stared at the little black velvet box before steeling herself to open it. They all knew it wasn't a diamond ring, but Bella knew there was a tiny part of Eden that kind of hoped it would be.

Inside, nestled against the velvet, was a crystal star necklace.

'Oh it's lovely, thank you,' Eden said, touching the sparkly surface.

'It's for all those wishes you used to make as a child. You'd wish on the first star you'd see each night, you'd wish on a falling star, you'd throw pennies into a well and make a wish, and I thought that perhaps this would give you one place to store all your wishes, until they came true. Instead of waiting for the stars to shine, you can wish on this at any time.'

'This is very sweet,' Eden said, sadly.

Dougie looked at her in confusion.

'I just… don't believe in wishes any more.'

'Why not?'

Eden shrugged. 'I learned a long time ago that wishes don't come true.'

'Some wishes take a little longer than others to come true,' Dougie said.

'I had one wish growing up; every time I wished upon a star or on the candles on my cake, it was always the same wish. It wasn't even something ridiculous either, I never wished for a pony or a castle in the sky or a vault full of gold coins and fancy jewels. It was quite a simple wish really and it never came true. Made me realise that no matter how much you want something, doesn't mean you'll get it.'

Dougie stared at her and no one said anything for a moment.

'It's a beautiful necklace though.' Eden forced a smile on her face as she clipped the star round her neck. 'Thank you.'

Rome leaned round Dougie, trying to diffuse the tension. 'Did Dougie tell you that he's moving back to Hope Island?'

Eden looked at Dougie. 'Are you?'

'For a year or two. See how it works out. I love New York, but I've always considered this place my home. Now I own my own company I can work anywhere in the world. I have a lot of clients in America and I'm not sure how it will work out because of the time zones but Isaac is going to come and work with me too, so it kind of makes sense to move here. I thought I'd give it a try.'

Eden smiled. 'It'll be good to have you home.'

Rome raised his bottle of beer. 'Maybe this really will be the year of new beginnings for all of us.' He looked at Bella and smiled.

They all grabbed their glasses and raised them in the air. 'To new beginnings.'

❦

Bella collapsed into bed on Friday night, barely able to keep her eyes open. It had been non-stop all week and especially over the last few days as the funfair had arrived and started setting up for the grand opening tomorrow. Local radio stations on Hope Island and the other Scilly Isles had been advertising it all week. There were posters in every shop in town and everywhere she went people were talking about it. She only hoped that people would come.

She looked down at Isaac's t-shirt she was wearing. She hadn't spoken to Isaac since lunch, which was a bit strange. Normally he would call her as he left the office and then call her again to say goodnight. It was weird how quickly they had fallen into this routine, and how much she missed it when he didn't call.

Bella switched off her lamp and closed her eyes, her mind drifted, and she soon fell asleep.

A noise stirred her from her sleep a few hours later and she opened one eye, not sure if the noise had come from outside the house or if the noise was Alfie or Rocket outside her bedroom door.

She heard a shuffling again and this time she knew it was inside her bedroom. She sat bolt upright in bed and saw a shadow move at the side of her bed.

She leapt out of bed the other side from the shadow, grabbed the nearest thing to hand, which happened to be an iron, and slammed the bedroom light on.

Isaac was standing there, his shirt undone, looking tired and deliciously sexy.

Her heart soared. He was here in her bedroom. He had come home. But he'd never said he was coming, she wasn't expecting him until the end of the following week.

Suddenly it didn't matter. She dropped the iron and leapt up onto the bed and threw herself into his open arms, wrapping her arms and legs around him and kissing him hard. He kissed her back, holding her tight against him, his tongue inside her mouth as he tasted her, devoured her as if he hadn't eaten for a month. His hands were everywhere, trying to touch her in every place at once. She was wide awake now, suddenly wanting his body against hers. The kiss was so urgent, so needful that it quickly escalated into something more.

He tore his mouth from hers. 'Wall or bed?'

'Wall.'

He turned and pinned her against the wall with his weight. 'Good choice.'

He kissed her again as she wrestled his shirt off his shoulders.

'Nice t-shirt,' he said, as he pulled it over her head then kissed her neck, his mouth travelling down to her breasts where his tongue licked against her flesh.

He yanked a condom from his jeans pocket, and then kicked his jeans off and a frustrating few seconds later he was buried deep inside her. He let out a groan that was pure relief. She clung to him, feeling the strength in the muscles across his back. His hands held her tight in the exact position that ensured that every thrust hit that sweet spot inside her. His mouth was on hers kissing her so hard she could barely breathe. He layered kisses across her shoulders and curved himself round her as his mouth travelled south. She arched against him and he placed a lingering kiss exactly where her heart was pounding furiously against her chest. It was this sweet gesture in the midst of all this urgent need that sent her tumbling over the edge, crying out his name as he quickly followed.

They clung to each other for a few minutes after, neither of them able to speak or move. Her heart was thundering against her chest and she could feel that Isaac's was doing the same.

Eventually he moved, with her still wrapped round him, and carried her back to the bed, laying her down on the cool sheets. He quickly dealt with the condom and then climbed into bed next to her. Immediately he started kissing her again, but it was much slower this time, the urgency was over, his hands wandering over her body in a tender caress. She stroked her hands round the back of his neck, stroking down his arms and shoulders. He kissed her until every bone in her body had melted into his and only then did he stop, but only long enough to grab another condom from her drawer. He slid it on and captured her mouth with his as he moved carefully inside her. She wrapped her arms and legs around him and finally he drew breath to look at her.

'Hi.'

She stroked a damp curl from his forehead. 'Hello.'

'I take it you're pleased to see me,' he said.

'I could say the same about you.'

'I bought you a Crunchie egg. I admit defeat.'

She giggled, which did wonderful things to her body in the place they were connected. 'I bought you a Yorkie egg too. So let's call this one a draw.'

He grinned and kissed her softly and briefly, moving slowly against her.

'I even bought you Godiva chocolate-covered strawberries.'

She smiled, feeling her heart swell inside her chest for him. 'You know what that means?'

'I'm hoping it'll mean that you'll declare your undying love for me.'

'It means, I'll take you to the fair tomorrow and win you a giant teddy at the coconut shy.'

He laughed. 'I only came back for that. Well that and your amazing hugs.'

He gathered her against him, one arm round her back and one hand round her bum, bringing him deeper inside her.

'You're pretty good at this hugging malarkey yourself,' Bella said, her voice high with need as her climax started building inside her with every gentle thrust.

'I'll hug you forever if you let me, Bella Roussel.'

She looked up into his loving eyes and almost every fear slipped away.

'I might just let you do that, Isaac Scott,' Bella said and he smiled and kissed her.

CHAPTER 23

Bella ran into the kitchen, hopping on one foot as she pulled on her red Converse. Isaac stood watching her in amusement as he sipped his coffee.

'Stop smirking Mr Scott; I wouldn't be running late if you hadn't insisted on having a shower with me and then took advantage of me.'

He shrugged. 'I have no regrets. Look, I'll walk Alfie and Rocket, so that's one less thing for you to worry about and I'll see you down the fair soon and I'll help you with whatever you need to do then.'

'That would be amazing, thank you.' She leaned up and kissed him briefly on the lips.

He hugged her to him and then whistled for the dogs. They both came running, leaping up at him in excitement. He grabbed the leads and, with another quick kiss on the cheek, he left.

Bella grabbed her bag and threw in some water and her purse and was just looking around for her phone when there was a knock on the door.

She quickly ran to answer it and found Eden standing on the doorstep, looking decidedly worried.

'What's wrong, are you OK?'

'Can we talk?' Eden said.

Whatever had put that fear on Eden's face meant that the fair could wait. Something was clearly very wrong.

'Of course, come in.'

Eden followed her into the lounge and sat down, playing nervously with the beads on her bracelet.

'I didn't know whether to tell you, Rome said I shouldn't but I didn't want it to be a shock for you,' Eden said.

Bella sat next to her and took her hand. 'Tell me what?'

'I was just over on St Mary's, Rome took me to buy me a pair of boots I wanted for my birthday and… we ran into your mum.'

Bella took a breath in. 'I thought she was living in Scotland somewhere.'

'I thought so too.'

Panic slammed into her. 'Is she coming here?'

'I don't know. Bella, it gets worse. She's with your dad.'

Bella stared at her. 'What do you mean with? They split up. He walked out on her when I was five years old and never came back. They got a divorce.'

'Bella, they got married again.'

A lump of emotion lodged in her throat. 'When?'

'Twenty years ago.'

'Just after she left me with you.'

'They came over to talk to us; apparently they are in St Mary's to visit your dad's mum.'

Another person who wanted nothing to do with her. She hadn't missed her grandmother's presence though as she had no recollection of ever meeting her, but she remembered asking Lucy about her when she was a bit older and felt sad that her grandmother didn't care enough about her to want to be a part of her life, even if her son didn't.

'Did they ask about me at all?'

Eden hesitated and then shook her head. 'They said they had heard about the fair and thought they might pop over to see it.'

Bella stood up. She didn't want to see them. She didn't want anything to do with them.

'Bella, I don't think they'll come. Rome exploded at them when they said they might come over.'

Bella smiled, slightly. 'He did? What did he say?'

'He told them that it wouldn't be good for you to see them, that life was good for you and you were happier now than you'd ever been. And seeing them now would drag it all up again. He really laid into them and said that them dumping you and you growing up knowing that your parents didn't want you had ruined your life. He told them that he was disgusted by them, that as your parents they were the two people who should never have let you down and they walked away from you and you never forgave them for that.'

'Sounds like he said all the things I would have liked to say to them if I ever saw them again.'

'They seemed really surprised and hurried off after that, but not before Rome told them that no one from the island would welcome them back with open arms after what they did and it would be best if they stayed away. Rome told me not to tell you about it, but I worried about them coming over anyway and I didn't want it to be a shock for you seeing them after all this time and especially together. Now at least you can prepare for it just in case they do come.'

Bella felt numb. 'No, you did the right thing. I had no idea they got back together after they left me.'

Eden stood up and hugged her. 'Are you OK?'

Bella nodded against her. 'I'm fine.'

'Look, I know that being left with us was the worst thing that happened to you, but it was the best thing that happened to me. I got a sister out of it and I love you so much.'

Bella pulled back slightly out of the hug to look at Eden. 'It wasn't the worst thing that ever happened to me. I love you and Rome and Lucy and Finn. I grew up with a wonderful family and I'll always be grateful for you guys. I feel so incredibly lucky to have you all in my life. But it doesn't stop it hurting that I wasn't enough for my parents. They didn't even care enough to ask how I was.'

'Maybe they would have done if Rome hadn't exploded at them and scared them off. You know how he can get.'

Bella nodded. 'Thank you for coming to tell me; it's good to be prepared.'

Eden smiled, sadly.

'I'd better get to the fair, I'm sure there's lots to do before it opens this afternoon.'

'I'll see you down there later.'

Eden left Bella alone with her thoughts as she stared out the window at the gold-encrusted sea.

Bella had always thought that although she must have played a part in her dad leaving, that also it must have been her mum that he fell out of love with too. That maybe she wasn't entirely to blame but that maybe her mum had pushed him away as well. But now to hear that her mum and dad had got back together after she had been left with Lucy and Finn and had been married for twenty years, it showed that the only reason he left was because of Bella. He clearly loved her mum, but he never loved Bella. There really was something wrong with her. She had been a child, what could she possibly have done to push him away, to make him hate her so much he wanted no part in her life? Then, a year later, her mum had walked out on her as well.

She remembered as a child, knowing that her dad had left her and that her mum hated her for it. Bella had showered her mum with love and affection in a desperate attempt to make her mum love her too. She had made cards at school, picked flowers for her, made her little gifts, hugged her and kissed her and it was never enough. She remembered the last time she had seen her mum when she had driven her round to Lucy and Finn's. She remembered that her mum had told her she was going to live with Lucy and Finn and when Bella asked how long for, her mum had snapped, 'Forever.' Bella couldn't escape that feeling she had been left with that day, that her parents simply didn't love her at all. That no matter how much Bella had loved her mum, that love had never been returned and how devastating she had found that.

She felt tears prick her eyes and she angrily wiped them away. She was happy now and she wasn't going to let her parents ruin this for her.

She grabbed her bag and walked out the house. She had to get to the fair; she could fall apart later.

❦

Isaac walked into the park and looked around at all the rides. Everything seemed to be perfect, awaiting all the people that would arrive later. Although the fair wasn't due to open for another hour or two, there were still a large number of islanders milling about and looking at the different rides, and a few of the stall holders were already selling their goods and encouraging some of the children to have a go at winning teddies, goldfish and sweets. Food stands were starting to cook their foods and wonderful savoury smells of meat and onions lingered in the air. Up on the hill the firework crew were putting the last-minute touches to the firework display that was going to happen later. Everything was ready.

He spotted Bella standing in the middle of it all, wearing a green beach dress and her beloved red Converse, her gorgeous red hair tumbling down her back in curls. She looked beautiful. And after having visited his house, or the remains of it, while he had been walking the dogs, she was just what he needed right now.

He went over to her, placing a hand on her back to let her know he was there. She jumped and whirled round and then sighed in relief when she saw it was him.

'You OK?'

She seemed jittery.

'I'm OK, slowly losing my mind but I'm OK,' Bella said.

'Can I do anything to help?'

She wrapped her arms around him and leant her head on his chest. He hugged her back, holding her tight. 'Just this,' Bella said.

He realised she was trembling slightly and he held her tighter. 'Hey, are you OK? Did something happen?'

'Yes, but I'll tell you later. I think I'll end up being a blubbering mess if I tell you now and I need to hold it all together for the fair.'

He pulled back from her slightly to look at her face. Her eyes were wet with tears.

'Forget the fair. Everything is perfect and as you said, these guys have done it a hundred times before. Let's go home and we can talk.'

She hugged him again, burying her face in his chest. 'I'm fine, really. This is more than enough right now. I'll talk to you later, I promise.'

He held her tight, placing a kiss on top of her head. 'Whatever it is, I'm here for you. Always.'

She held him tighter. 'Don't make promises you can't keep.'

He pulled back slightly to look at her. 'I don't intend to.'

She smiled up at him then frowned. 'Are *you* OK?'

He smiled that she could read him so easily. 'I went by my house this morning, it was just a little upsetting to go back and see it for the first time since the fire.'

'Oh no, Isaac, you shouldn't have gone back there alone. I would have come with you.'

'I didn't even think about it really. I wanted to switch the hot tub on so we could relax in it tonight after the fair; it was only when I walked up to the cottage that it hit me again that I've lost everything.' He held her hand over his heart. 'Well almost everything. I'm fine, really. We're alive, Rocket is alive. Things can be replaced.'

Bella nodded. 'Things can be replaced, people can't.'

Isaac frowned slightly; it felt like she wasn't talking about the fire.

A man suddenly walked up to them. 'Sorry to interrupt but Bella, I just wanted to check something with you before the fair opens.'

Bella smiled at him. 'Of course, I'll be with you in just a second.'

She turned back to Isaac and reached up and kissed him briefly, then pulled away. 'I need to go and check everything is ready, the fair starts in one hour. Can you go and see all the food stalls and make sure they are OK and duck into the WI cake tent and check they have everything they need too?'

He studied her, sensing her need to move on from whatever had upset her for now. 'Yes, of course. Then I believe you owe me a giant teddy which you're going to win for me at the coconut shy.'

Bella laughed and he was relieved to see the smile back on her face. 'Definitely. My coconut shy skills are good. One giant teddy coming right up. I'll catch up with you later.'

He watched her go. He was determined he was going to get her to talk to him later but for now he would do everything he could to make sure the fair ran smoothly.

※ॐぞの

The fair couldn't have gone better. Bella strolled through all the stalls as the skies darkened above them and the lights of the rides lit up the park. Squeals of delight and laughter echoed around the park, the smells of candyfloss, chocolates and sweets wafted around them. The weather had been glorious and it promised to be a warm dry evening for the fireworks later. Best of all it seemed that every single person who lived on the island had turned up either to support her or just to enjoy the festivities. In fact, quite a few of the people who had passed her evil looks or snide comments over the last few weeks since the embezzlement scandal, had come up to her to say what a great job she'd done with the fair. Maybe this would be a way that she could move on from those rumours and the doubt that shadowed her once and for all.

Isaac was walking next to her, his hand in hers, not caring who saw them together. He was carrying a large cuddly hippo in one arm that she had won him on the coconut shy and seemed utterly content to be walking around the fair with her.

She should be blissfully happy and there was a huge part of her that was, but despite everything going well in her personal and working life, she couldn't escape the feeling that her life was about to unravel and she couldn't do a thing about it.

There had been no sign of her parents all day, something she was beyond relieved about, but she knew she would have to deal with these feelings they had stirred up with their visit to St Mary's.

At the moment, though, she just wanted to enjoy the fair.

'Let's go on the ghost train,' Isaac said, tugging her towards it. She smiled and let herself be led onto the ride.

'Don't worry, I'll protect you,' he said as he paid the ride operator and sat down on the train. He put the hippo next to him and slung an arm round her shoulders.

The train took off, juddering down the tracks, and she snuggled in closer to him. As they rounded the corner and they were plunged into the darkness, Isaac kissed her on the head.

'Don't be scared,' he whispered. 'Sometimes facing your fears is not as scary as you think it will be. And when you come out the other side you feel better and stronger because of it.'

She looked up at his silhouette in the darkness, knowing he wasn't talking about the ghost train.

'And I'm here to hold your hand,' he said.

Suddenly, with a hiss and a cackle, a skeleton leapt out of a coffin inches from Isaac's face. He jumped at the sudden movement and Bella laughed, papering over the cracks. 'Maybe I'm the one who'll be holding your hand.'

He laughed too. 'We can hold each other's hands; it's a lot easier that way. That's what being in a relationship is all about, supporting each other.'

Bella stared up at him as they zoomed around the corner. She reached up and kissed him and all the spiders, bats, vampires and ghosts couldn't tear her away from him.

As the train emerged into the noise and lights of the fair, Isaac took her hand and led her off the train. Bella spotted Lucy and Finn over by the 'Hook a Duck' stand.

'There's my aunt and uncle, would you like to meet them?' Bella said, before realising that Isaac probably had no intention of meeting her family this early into their relationship. 'You don't have to if you don't want to, we can quickly hide before they see us.'

'I'd love to,' Isaac said, without any kind of hesitation. 'Are these the ones that raised you?'

'Yes, my real parents,' Bella said. And before she could change her mind, Lucy spotted them and waved, grabbing Finn's arm and dragging him over to see her.

'Hello, my lovely.' Lucy enveloped her into a giant hug and Bella smiled with love for her. 'This fair is simply wonderful. You've done such a fantastic job. Dare I say it but I think this fair is miles better than the ones that Mr and Mrs Harrison used to organise.'

'Thank you; don't let Dougie hear you say that though. Lucy, Finn, this is my boyfriend, Isaac.'

Isaac stuck out his hand for Lucy to shake and Lucy ignored it and pulled him into a big hug too. Bella giggled as Isaac hugged Lucy back.

'So good to finally meet the person who has put such a big smile on our Bella's face.'

Lucy finally released him and he stuck out his hand to greet Finn. But if Isaac was hoping for a more reserved greeting from Finn, he would have been disappointed as Finn pulled him into a big hug too.

'Good to meet you, son,' Finn said and Bella stifled another giggle at the word *son*, as if they were married off already.

'It's good to meet you both, I've heard such wonderful things about you,' Isaac said, ever the charmer.

'You'll have to come round for dinner one night, Finn here does a little fishing on the other side of the island and if he catches something, he makes a wonderful fish pie.'

'I'd really like that,' Isaac said.

'How does next week sound?' Lucy said, clearly not one for offering a vague invitation.

'Sadly, I'm back up in London again next week. I've been there this past week and I have more meetings to attend next week but I would love to come to dinner with you the week after.'

'That would be great, let's say Wednesday at seven?'

'Perfect,' Isaac said. 'I'll look forward to it.'

Lucy nodded, unable to disguise her grin at meeting Isaac, and then she waved at someone else. 'Oh look Finn, there's your cousin Bob, let's go and say hello. Lovely to meet you, Isaac.'

Lucy and Finn waved goodbye and left them alone.

'You've been accepted into the family now,' Bella giggled and looked around to make sure that everything was still running smoothly.

Isaac pulled her into his arms and kissed her head. 'Let's get out of here.'

'I can't, the fireworks are coming up soon.'

'Which you've checked on three times, everything is running smoothly, everyone is happy, you've done a fantastic job. And I have a hot tub that's heating up nicely and a bottle of wine chilling in the fridge in my summerhouse. Let's go and we can watch the fireworks while relaxing in the hot tub.'

Bella looked around – Isaac was right, nothing else needed doing. And she really wanted to make love to him now and just forget about the world, especially the unwelcome news that she had heard this morning.

She turned back to him. 'I haven't got my swimsuit.'

He arched an eyebrow at her. 'I don't think you'll need one.'

Bella smiled and took his hand. 'Let's go.'

Isaac lifted the lid from the hot tub and steam billowed in the air. They were sheltered here, the summerhouse protecting them from the view of anyone walking over the hills and the trees below them sheltering them from being seen from the town. But with beautiful views over the sea, it was a perfect place to celebrate a bit of romance.

It had been hard coming back here that morning to turn the hot tub on, the first time he had been back since the fire. To see the whole place gutted and destroyed in that way was heartbreaking after all the work he had put into decorating the place. But coming back here with Bella made him feel happier. Maybe when he rebuilt the house, it would be their home together. He knew he was getting ahead of himself, it had only been a few weeks, but Bella finally seemed to be coming round to the idea of a future with him too.

He ditched his robe and climbed into the hot water, sinking down in his seat and stretching his arms out over the top of the tub so he had prime position to watch Bella come out of the summerhouse.

She came out dressed in his spare robe, carrying two champagne glasses. She walked round to the front of the hot tub and he moved so he could watch her. She placed the glasses down on the side of the hot tub and slid the robe off. His eyes feasted on her body as she climbed into the hot tub with him.

'See something you like?' Bella said, as she sank into the water.

'Very much.' He pulled her onto his lap and wrapped his arms around her.

She kissed him deeply, then pulled back and swivelled round on his lap, leaning her back on his chest as she looked out over the sea. He kissed the back of her neck and her shoulder, giving her time to talk if she wanted to.

'It's so beautiful here,' she sighed as she looked out over the sea.

'It is. I finally feel like I'm home after all these years away,' Isaac said. 'The fair was a huge success tonight. People love you here.'

'I wouldn't say that.'

'I would, the amount of people that came up to you tonight and said what a great job you've done with the fair, there was no animosity there. They all love you, you can see that.'

'Maybe I do have some redeeming features after all,' Bella said, quietly, leaning her head on his shoulder and closing her eyes.

He got the sense that this was at the crux of what had upset her earlier.

'Do you want to talk to me about what happened today?'

She didn't say anything and she was saved from talking to him when a riot of colour exploded over the bay. Great blazes of green, silver, gold and red filled the inky sky above them and shimmered over the water. It was an incredible sight.

She turned round in his arms, straddling him, and suddenly he didn't care about the fireworks in the sky, all of his attention was on the woman in front of him.

She cupped his face in her hands and kissed him.

'Why did you come back this weekend when you have to be back in London again next week?'

'Because when I spoke to you yesterday lunch time you said you wished I was coming to the fair with you.'

A huge smile lit her face. 'That's why you came back?'

'I knew it was important to you. I wanted to see you anyway so it wasn't completely altruistic.'

'But it hardly seems worth it when you have to leave again tomorrow.'

He stroked her cheek with his thumb. 'Believe me, it was worth it.'

She smiled. 'God, I love you.'

CHAPTER 24

His heart stilled then thundered in his chest. She loved him. God those three little words had never meant so much in his life before.

Her face fell as she registered the words that had fallen from her lips. She suddenly scrabbled off him, backing up to the far side of the hot tub.

'I didn't mean that. Ignore it. It's not true, I don't love you.'

Isaac moved towards her. 'Bella, it's OK, don't look so scared. I—'

'I'm not scared. I don't love you. I told you I don't believe in love. Being in love just means leaving yourself open for a whole load of hurt and ultimately rejection. Being in love means handing someone your heart and letting them stamp all over it.'

'Wait, Bella, that's not what love is.'

'And you'd know, would you? Someone who has never been in love in his life. Someone who drifts from woman to woman and never commits to anyone. You're a great advocate for love.'

Bella scrambled out of the hot tub and pulled on his robe and then ran off in the direction of the summerhouse.

Isaac stared after her for a moment as the finale of the fireworks exploded in the night sky. What the hell had just happened? It wasn't supposed to go down like that. He had been so careful not to tell her he loved her so as not to scare her away that when she had taken him by surprise and told him she loved him, he hadn't even said it back. He should have said it back. He would tell her. He would march into the summerhouse and tell her that he loved her, that he had never felt this way about anyone before.

He quickly climbed out the hot tub and grabbed his robe. He walked into the summerhouse but the doors that led up to the hills were flung open and there was no sign of Bella anywhere. Her clothes were still in a neat pile on the bench, her bag with all her things in was there too, but there was no sign of her. He moved to the door and looked out. She was gone, seemingly wearing only a dressing gown.

Isaac pulled up outside Bella's house a while later to find her sitting on the doorstep, wrapped in his robe, sobbing into her hands. Her feet were bare and covered in mud from her run across the hills and it was utterly devastating to see her this way. She was always so happy and full of life, but this was what defeat looked like.

He got out the car, and using the key she had given him, he unlocked the door to her house, then knelt down and scooped her up and carried her inside. She wrapped her arms round his neck but she didn't look up or say anything.

Alfie came wandering out to see who was disturbing his sleep, but when he saw that it was Isaac and Bella he returned to his basket with Rocket.

Isaac kicked the door closed behind him and carried her through to the sofa. He laid her down and then lay next to her, holding her to him.

She didn't say anything but her crying seemed to have subsided a bit now.

'Bella, I love you. I think I have been in love with you since that first weekend we spent together. I want to spend the rest of my life showing you how much I love you and what that really means, not this tainted image that your parents left you with.'

Her eyes flicked up to his and they had real fear in them.

She suddenly sat up and clambered over him.

'This isn't going to work between us.'

He sat up, feeling like he had just been punched in the gut. 'What?'

'This. It wasn't supposed to happen,' Bella cried. 'I never wanted this. I was perfectly happy until you came into my life.'

'I thought I made you happy.'

'You do, but it'll never last, will it. I need to stop this now before I fall any further in love with you.'

'Wait a minute. I love you, you love me and you want to break up with me because of it?'

She started pacing. 'I thought I could make it work, I thought about what you said about my dad never really loving my mum and that was the problem, not me, and I thought maybe you were right, maybe it had nothing to do with me. But I found out today that they got married again shortly after my mum dumped me with my aunt and uncle. They've been married for twenty years. It was always me that was the problem. I'm unlovable. There's something wrong with me if my own parents didn't want me and you'll soon realise it too. Every other man I've dated has dumped me a few months after dating me and I'm sure you will too. I need to get out now. You're the only one I care about and it will break me when it comes to an end if I let myself fall any further in love with you.'

Isaac stood up. How could this perfect night have gone so badly wrong? 'So you'll end it now and hurt us both?' The only woman he had ever loved was standing in front of him telling him she was walking away. He moved towards her, stopping her pacing with his hands on her shoulders. 'I love you; I have never felt this way about anyone before. We have something special here and I can't believe you would walk away from that.'

'I don't want to hurt you; that's the last thing I want.'

'Yet you're doing just that.' Emotion clawed at his throat. He was losing her and there was nothing he could do about it. 'This is killing me and you don't care enough to stop it. Clearly you don't love me after all. This was always just a bit of fun for you.'

'No it wasn't. I know I said that but I never meant it. This was something wonderful and it will destroy me if you finish with me,' she sobbed.

'So you'll finish it and destroy yourself. You're not making any sense,' Isaac yelled.

She flinched away from him and he knew he had to calm himself down.

'Bella, I know you're scared. You've been hurt horribly in the past. And you're trying to protect yourself from it happening again. But love, real love is worth the risk. What if we carry on exactly how we are, spending time with each other, enjoying each other's company and one day, when you're ready, we get married to each other? What if this never ends?'

'What if it does?'

He groaned in frustration and walked away from her. Anger, hurt and betrayal burning in his veins. There was nothing he could say to change her mind. She had been hurt earlier, he'd seen it at the fair, and he should have talked it through with her then. Instead he'd let it build in her mind; escalate into something so much more than it was. Maybe she just needed some time. He needed to walk away from her before he said something he couldn't take back.

'I think you should go,' Bella said, quietly.

'Maybe I should.' He whistled for Rocket and the little dog looked up from where she was cuddled around Alfie. And reluctantly, after a few moments, she climbed out of the dog bed and walked over to him. Even Rocket didn't want to be with him.

He grabbed Rocket's lead from the hook where it was hanging on the wall and walked towards the door. He turned back to Bella, hoping she would say something to call him back.

'I have no home here, I can run my companies much easier in London than I can here. I'm going back to London tomorrow. Give me one reason to come back here at the end of the week. At the moment, you're the only reason to come back. Give me that reason, Bella.'

She looked absolutely devastated at the prospect of him leaving but she didn't seem to realise that she was the only one who could take that pain away.

She took a step forward but still said nothing, tears running down her face.

He turned and walked out, closing the door behind him.

❦

Bella watched the door close and then burst into tears. What had she done? She had overreacted in the worst possible way. This had been eating away at her all day and instead of talking about it rationally she had buried it inside until it came out in a big mess of emotions. And now Isaac had seen the crazy irrational side of her that came out every time she thought of her parents, he wouldn't want anything to do with her even if she apologised. She couldn't blame him. And the worst thing was her parents had won again. Her whole life had been blighted by their rejection and she had just let them ruin the best thing that had ever happened to her.

She quickly ran outside to stop Isaac, but his car was gone. But what would she have said to him if he had been there? She still believed that he would walk away from her. She was unlovable. It was better to get out now before she fell even further in love with him. But as she walked back into the house, she knew it couldn't possibly hurt more than it hurt right now.

❦

Isaac threw his bag on his boat the next morning and then lifted Rocket aboard. It was still early and the sun was only just above the horizon, so he didn't really expect to see anyone, least of all Rome running towards him. Although as he watched him, he realised that he was in his running gear so probably not deliberately running towards him at all. Rome's face cleared with recognition as he drew close and he pulled his headphones out of his ears and stopped.

'Isaac, we've not properly met. I'm Rome, Bella's brother.'

He offered out his hand and Isaac shook it.

'You've made Bella happier than I've ever seen her, so thank you for that. I have to say, I wasn't too impressed when I heard how you lied to Bella at the beginning, but I was clearly mistaken about you and I'll be the first to admit that. You're good for her. It's good to see her smiling again.'

Clearly Rome didn't know what had happened the night before.

'Well, you won't need to worry about me being bad for her. We broke up last night,' Isaac said, hurt and anger still boiling through him.

Rome looked aghast. 'What? Why?'

Isaac shrugged and turned back to the boat, but Rome caught his arm. 'Wait. This is to do with her parents, isn't it? We saw them yesterday and I know Eden told her even though I told her not to. I knew it would ruin her to find out that her parents were happily married, that they carried on with their lives after they abandoned her.'

'I know about her parents and I know how devastating that must be for her, but if she won't trust me there's nothing I can do.'

'Don't give up on her, please,' Rome said urgently. 'Her parents rejecting her messed her up spectacularly; she built these walls around her so she couldn't get hurt again. You're the only one who she has let in. I've never seen her as happy as she is with you. If you care about her at all, don't walk away from her.'

'This is up to her,' Isaac said. 'I can't force her to stay with me. She kicked me out last night – what would you have me do, refuse to leave? Nothing I said had any effect. I begged her not to finish it. I told her I loved her and she still showed me the door. I have to go to London and at the moment I have nothing to come back for. If she changes her mind, she can call me but right now I can't see any way back from this.'

He climbed in the boat.

'She loves you,' Rome said. 'She might not know it but she does.'

'If she does she has to be willing to take a risk. Love is about trusting someone and I'm not sure Bella is capable of that.' He started the engine. 'Take care of her, Rome.'

With that he manoeuvred the boat out of the harbour.

❦

Bella knocked on Lucy's door on Sunday afternoon. She had spent the morning feeling sorry for herself and she knew she needed to talk to someone who would be sympathetic and shower her with love regardless of her stupidity.

Lucy answered the door and smiled when she saw Bella, but that smile immediately fell from her face when she saw that Bella had clearly been crying.

'Oh my darling, what's happened?' Lucy said, swooping around her and pulling her into a big hug.

'Me and Isaac broke up, well, more specifically, I broke up with him.'

Bella allowed herself to be led inside but stopped when she saw Dougie sitting at the kitchen table. He grinned hugely when he saw her though that smile quickly faded away when he saw how upset she was.

'Bella, are you OK?'

She nodded, feeling foolish for crying in front of him, and quickly wiped the tears away. 'Just stupid matters of the heart.'

Dougie stood up and pulled her into a big hug. 'Do you want me to beat him up for you?'

Bella smiled, sadly. 'No, that's OK. It wasn't his fault, it's mine.'

'Dougie, be a dear and go and help Finn in the greenhouse for a while,' Lucy said.

Dougie took a step back to look at Bella and then nodded and left them to it, disappearing out the back door.

Lucy pushed her down into Dougie's seat at the kitchen table and sat down opposite her.

'Tell me what happened,' Lucy said, gently. 'You seemed so happy with him.'

'I am. I was…' she trailed off, not having any kind of decent explanation for what she had done.

'Eden told me she saw your mum and dad yesterday morning, is this to do with that?'

Bella nodded. 'I thought my dad left because he had fallen out of love with my mum but clearly the problem wasn't with each other, it was solely to do with me. There must be something wrong with me if my own parents didn't love me. It's only a matter of time before Isaac realises it and he leaves me too. I needed to get out now before I fall even further in love with him.'

'Oh my darling, your parents leaving you wasn't anything to do with you at all. Is that what you thought all this time, that you were to blame?'

Bella nodded, wiping the tears from her eyes.

Lucy sighed and shook her head. 'I've tried to talk about this with you many times while you were growing up but when you were small talking about them used to upset you so much, and when you were a teenager it used to make you so angry. We should have talked about it properly before, but we didn't want to confuse things and upset you even more. We messed everything up for you and we blame ourselves entirely for how you grew up with this shadow over your shoulder. We thought it was best if we just put the past behind us and moved on but I didn't realise how deeply it had damaged you or that you blamed yourself for this. Bella, your dad, Alistair, the man you knew as your dad, isn't your biological father.'

Bella stared at Lucy in shock. 'What?'

'Alistair and your mum married very young, probably too young. They enjoyed the party lifestyle and never wanted kids. Your mum was the least broody person I know; when I had Rome and Eden, she didn't even want to hold them or come anywhere near them. Alistair was so adamant that he never wanted children that he had a vasectomy. There's no nice way to put this but Alistair was a complete dick. He slept with so many people while he was going out with your mum and I have no idea why she stayed with him. I think we all hoped that that would stop once they were married but it never did. In retaliation your mum had an affair too and she got pregnant with you. Of course, there were many people on the island who knew that Alistair couldn't possibly be the father and Alistair hated that. Your mum told everyone that Alistair was the dad, she even put him on the birth certificate, but a lot of us knew the truth.'

Bella stared at her, trying to take it all in.

'Alistair hated that your mum was carrying another man's child. He begged her to give you up. I persuaded her not to, I told her she would always regret it if she did. I will always be grateful that she listened to her big sister with regards to that and not him, even though she worshipped the ground he walked on. Alistair carried on sleeping with lots of different women all the way through her pregnancy and that caused your mum to go into a deep depression which I don't think she ever really recovered from.'

Bella stared at her. It was like a lightbulb going off in her head. 'They hated me even before I was born? It was nothing to do with who I turned out to be at all?'

'No, they didn't hate you. No one could look at you and hate you. You were the most beautiful baby. You had this thick mop of red curls and those beautiful big green eyes. You were adorable.

They just didn't want a child. Well, Alistair more than your mum. Your mum became quite protective of you, especially when you were born. I can't say she ever settled into the mother role, but I think she wanted the best for you. For the next two or three years, Alistair barely came home, he was always out with some other woman. Your mum spent the first two years of your life crying constantly. I felt so sorry for her but there was nothing we could do. Finn spoke to Alistair about his behaviour and how he needed to face up to his responsibilities as a husband and a father but Alistair was adamant he didn't want anything to do with you. We started taking you more and more, you'd stay with us for weeks before your mum would feel guilty and come and take you back. It must have been so unsettling for you. But myself and Finn had completely fallen in love with you. We adored you and it always broke our hearts to have to give you back. When you were three years old we approached your mum and asked if we could formally adopt you.'

Bella swallowed down the huge lump of emotion in her throat. 'You chose to adopt me? You wanted me? Not just because I was dumped on you?'

Lucy frowned. 'You were never dumped on us. We loved you and we wanted to give you a proper loving home. Your mum agreed. She wasn't coping with being practically a single parent and Alistair didn't care. You came to live with us permanently and we started the very, very long road of adopting you formally. But without you there Alistair started spending more and more time at home and your mum started to come out of the depression. Things were clearly on the up for her, she was back to her normal self. She had counselling, something we had being trying to persuade her to have for years. She started visiting you more and more and just before the adoption became official your mum changed her mind. We were heartbroken. At that stage we already considered you our daughter and we weren't allowed to keep you.

It was such a mess. I have never been so devastated in my whole life having to hand you back. You were four and a half when you went back to live with your mum and Alistair after you had lived with us for over a year. Alistair was clearly not happy about this but in his weird, twisted way, I think he loved your mum and he wanted to make it work for her.'

'But he hated me,' Bella said.

'He hated everyone knowing you weren't his, but that was never your fault. You were a constant reminder of your mum's infidelity. It lasted six months before Alistair gave your mum an ultimatum. Him or you. Your mum chose you.'

Bella gasped. 'She did?'

'Your mum was never going to win any mum of the year awards, she was pretty lousy at it and she knew that, but I think she did love you. Alistair left and your mum just fell straight back into a deep depression again. We hoped she would come out of it, that she would realise that she was better off without him, but she never did. She started being really horrible to you and that was something we couldn't allow. Every time you came round to my house, you used to beg me to let you come back to stay, as if we had given you back to your mum because we had grown tired of you. It broke my heart. We told her that we were taking you back and that if she allowed us to adopt you formally without any further interruptions or objections we wouldn't press charges against her for abuse or neglect. I don't think what she was doing to you would count as abuse in the eyes of the law but telling you she hated you was so damaging for you.'

'I don't remember any of this. I just remember staying with you a lot and then going back to my mum and not wanting to live with her because she was so mean.'

'It must have been so confusing for you. When she brought you round that day you came to live with us permanently, Finn made it very clear that she wouldn't be welcome there again and if she cared about you at all, she was to stay away from you and never make contact with you again. We just thought it would be too upsetting for you. We thought it was for the best. We never realised that in doing that it would cause so much upset for you over the years, that her lack of contact reinforced her lack of love for you. We thought our love for you would be enough,' Lucy said, tears filling her own eyes.

'Oh god, Lucy. It was enough, I had a wonderful childhood because of you. I felt loved for the first time in my life when I came to live with you. I never realised that you had tried to adopt me formally years before. I remember staying with you a lot but I didn't realise that was because you wanted to adopt me.' Bella couldn't stop the tears from falling down her cheeks. She hadn't been dumped with her aunt and uncle at all, they had wanted her to live with them. They had loved her as soon as she was born. They had fought with her mum for custody of her. She always thought that love from her aunt and uncle was born out of loyalty and family ties but that hadn't been the case. And her dad wasn't even her dad. She had seen the anger from him as she had grown up and she'd never known why, but now it all made sense. This wasn't her fault at all. She put her head in her hands and couldn't help sobbing into them. It was like a weight had been lifted off her shoulders. It wasn't that she was unlovable at all. Lucy held her tight until all her tears had dried up.

She lifted her head. 'Who is my real dad?'

Lucy hesitated and glanced over Bella's shoulder. Bella turned round to see Dougie had come through the back door and he was frowning. Bella looked back to Lucy and then back at Dougie in confusion. They clearly both knew who her dad was but didn't want to say. Eventually Dougie shrugged and sat down at the table next to her.

'My uncle Tom. He died not long after you were born.'

Bella stared at him in shock. 'Your uncle was my dad?'

Dougie nodded.

'We're cousins. We always joked about being related and now you're telling me we actually are. Why didn't you tell me?'

'It wasn't my place to say. My uncle Tom had an affair with your mum. He was married too and had children of his own. His wife never knew. Tom would come over here on the pretext of seeing my dad but really he was seeing your mum. From what I can gather it was never anything serious between them, it was a summer fling that resulted in you.'

'And I guess he wasn't exactly delighted about my arrival either,' Bella said.

'Quite the opposite,' Lucy said. 'I think he was a little scared initially that his wife would find out, but your mum was never going to tell her; she wanted everyone to believe that Alistair was your father. She didn't want money or anything from Tom. But he came over to see you after you were born. He was so happy about becoming a father again, he always wanted a big family and he had two sons so he was delighted about having a daughter. I don't know how he imagined it working out because he didn't want his wife to find out but he wanted to be a part of your life somehow. He said he wanted to visit you regularly even if he was only ever introduced as a family friend. Alistair didn't want him anywhere near you. As it happened, Tom died a few weeks later so we never found out how that would have played out.'

'I have two half-brothers,' Bella said, quietly.

'My parents decided to keep it quiet for their sake and for his wife,' Dougie said. 'I think a lot of people on Hope Island knew but Sarah lived on St Mary's so she was spared a lot of the gossip.'

'That's why your parents always invited me round for dinner when we were kids,' Bella said.

'They adored you. My dad felt responsible for you in some way. Tom wasn't there so my dad wanted to help. I know he gave your mum quite a bit of money in the beginning,' he glanced at

Lucy. 'He was quite instrumental in persuading your mum to let Lucy adopt you.'

Bella couldn't believe it. Dougie was always so protective of her and now she knew why.

'You knew we were cousins, even when we were kids?'

Dougie nodded. 'My mum told me when I was very young that I needed to look after you because you were family. I didn't really appreciate how true that was until I was a bit older. They always referred to you as my cousin. I guess that's why I started calling you it too.'

Bella couldn't help smiling. Not only had Lucy and Finn adopted her because they loved her and wanted her but she suddenly had an extended family that cared about her too. She had another cousin, another aunt and uncle who had cared about her. She was loved. She wasn't unlovable at all.

Immediately her thoughts turned to Isaac. She had been scared by her feelings and tried to protect herself.

'Oh god, Lucy, what have I done? Isaac told me he loved me and I told him I wanted to break up with him. He's going to hate me for this.'

'He'll be hurt and angry, of course he will, but love is not something you can switch off. Go to him; explain why you felt this way. Don't be afraid of love Bella; love brought us you and it was the most wonderful thing in the world.'

She looked at Dougie and he nodded. 'I was in love with the most wonderful woman, still am if truth be told, and I never told her, life got in the way and I could never see a way that we could make it work. I fear now it's too late but once I move back over here, I'm going to give it a go. Go and see Isaac. Tell him you love him too. Don't waste time regretting what you should have said or done.'

'I need to talk to him.' Bella stood up decisively. 'I need to go to London and tell him I love him. If nothing else he needs to know that.'

'I'll look after Alfie for you while you're away,' Lucy said. 'Take as long as you need.'

She gave her aunt a hug. 'When I get back, I'm going to change my last name to Lancaster. I'm not going to carry the name of a man that never wanted me. He doesn't deserve that.'

Lucy smiled. 'I would love it if you would take our name. But it makes no difference what you're called, you'll always be our daughter.'

Bella kissed her on the cheek and gave Dougie a hug then turned to run out of the house. Before she got to the front door, she turned back. 'Oh cuz, I doubt very much that you're too late.'

He grinned. 'I really hope not.'

She ran out the house and down the street. She knew she had to talk to Isaac and, as daunting as it was, it looked like a trip to London was in order. She'd never been on her own before, but how scary could it be?

❦

Bella wanted to cry.

It had taken over twelve hours for her to arrive in London. Once she had arrived in St Mary's she realised she had missed the last plane out of the Scilly Isles and had been forced to take a three-hour ferry ride to Penzance where she found she had missed the last train and had to wait for the sleeper train, which finally got her into London just after five in the morning. To her surprise she had still found it a bustle of people and cars. Not knowing where Isaac was staying and, knowing his office wouldn't be open for several hours, Bella had sought refuge in a café for a while. It had felt so different to the warmth and friendliness of Rosa's. People avoided eye contact with everyone else here, staring into their breakfasts and coffees.

She had already phoned Elsie to explain she wouldn't be in today. She felt awful but now the fair was out the way and the launch of the egg hunt app was happening tomorrow and all the marketing for that had been taken care of, there wasn't a lot left to do that couldn't wait a while.

After nine Bella had set out to find Isaac's office, using an address she had found online. She had caught the wrong train on the underground and when she had tried to rectify the situation by taking a different train she had made the situation worse and ended up in completely the wrong part of London. People were not friendly here – she had tried to stop several people to ask for directions and they had all side-stepped her and hurried on to wherever they needed to be without even a look back. The place was frenetic, filled with people in suits travelling to important meetings, tourists, people clearly going on holiday with their oversized suitcases.

She had finally found Isaac's office only to be told that she was at the wrong office and she needed to head over to the other side of London again. Now she was standing in front of what she hoped was the right place, a towering glass building that reached right up into the sky.

It was late afternoon and she had been awake for over twenty-four hours. She was still in the clothes she had worn to visit her aunt the day before, it was raining and she was decidedly damp all over.

She caught sight of herself in the mirrored glass doors: with her blue dress and red Converse, she looked like Dorothy in the *Wizard of Oz*, whisked away from the small-town life she loved to a magical land – only London didn't feel that magical right now. Her hair was a frizzy tangle of curls, the bottom of the dress was torn slightly from getting it caught in the train doors and she was pretty sure she didn't smell that good. Isaac was going to take one look at her and run for the hills.

Bella had called Isaac several times throughout the night and that day but he hadn't answered, which was not helping her to keep hope either.

She took a deep breath and stepped forward towards the revolving doors, just as a man barged past her with a large suitcase, knocking out her knees. She toppled over the suitcase and landed face down on the pavement. In a puddle.

'Oh my god, I'm so sorry,' the man said. 'Are you OK?'

Bella sat up and stared down at her dress, which was now covered in a muddy wet stain. 'I'm fine,' Bella lied, trying to keep the wobble out of her voice.

The man offered his hand to help her up and she took it and he pulled her to her feet.

'Are you hurt?'

Bella touched her cheek which felt sore and looked down at her knees to see one of them was bleeding. She wasn't going to cry. She just needed to get to Isaac and put right what she had done. 'No, I'm OK.'

'I'm so sorry, I just have a flight to catch and I'm running late and—'

'It's fine,' Bella smiled to reassure him. She just needed to get away from him now, because with him fussing all over her, she was going to lose it any second.

She moved off towards the door before the man could apologise or ask her if she was OK again. She pushed her way through the revolving door and went up to the main reception desk, well aware that lots of people in suits were staring at her like something the cat had dragged in.

The pretty receptionist looked up as she approached; she was obviously very professional because her smile didn't falter at all when she saw the state Bella was in.

'I'm here to see Isaac Scott,' Bella said.

The girl nodded. 'Do you have an appointment?'

'No, I—'

'I can't let you up unless you're on the appointment list.'

'I have a meeting with him, I'm very late,' Bella lied, hoping the girl would be sympathetic to her.

The girl looked down her clipboard again. 'Are you part of the Oak and Acorn meeting?'

That was the bank she had spoken to while trying to have phone sex with Isaac. She grabbed the opportunity with both hands. 'Yes, I'm Graham Miller's assistant. I'm new and this is my first day in the job. I'm supposed to take minutes in this meeting but I went to the wrong office on the other side of town.'

'OK, what's the name?'

Bella hesitated but if they asked for ID she would only have something with her name on. 'Bella Roussel.'

The girl consulted her list again. 'I have an Isabella, is that you?'

Bella nodded, cringing inside. She never lied and now the lies were falling out of her mouth one after the other.

'Isabella Taylor?'

'Oh yes, that's my maiden name. I'm just married,' Bella added another lie to the list.

The girl didn't look too sure. 'I'll just ring up and check.'

'Please,' Bella said. 'This is my first day and I really need to make a good impression or I'll lose this job and I really need it. Graham is expecting me and I'm already late. My name is down on your list even if it's my maiden name. I really need to get to this meeting.'

The girl eventually nodded. 'The meeting has already started, so you'll need to check in with the reception at BlazeStar to see if you can be admitted. Take the lift to the twenty-fourth floor.'

Bella nodded and walked to the row of lifts, where several other people in smart suits were waiting. The doors pinged open and everyone poured in, pressing several different buttons. Bella followed them in, knowing she stood out like a sore thumb in her pretty summer dress. She looked down at herself; well it had been pretty at one point.

How was she going to play this? She could hardly walk straight into the meeting and declare her love for Isaac. But at least if she was up there she could wait for him to come out.

The doors pinged open on several floors where people got on or got off. Her heart was racing. Would he forgive her? Would he kiss her as soon as he saw her? Would he just throw her out back onto the street?

The doors pinged open on the twenty-fourth floor and she quickly hurried out.

There was another receptionist sitting behind a silvery desk emblazoned with the BlazeStar logo and Bella had no idea how to play this. She couldn't give the same excuse she had given to the girl downstairs because she certainly couldn't just waltz into that meeting like she belonged there, especially not dressed as she was. That wouldn't look good for Isaac and the Umbrella Foundation, not after the phone sex scandal. She walked up to the desk.

'I'm here to see Isaac Scott,' Bella said.

The receptionist looked her up and down. 'Do you have an appointment?'

'No, but—'

'Mr Scott won't see you unless you have an appointment.'

'He asked me to come in and see him today. I work for the Umbrella Foundation.' Bella was relieved that was one thing that wasn't a lie, though she wasn't sure how much longer she would be working there when she had taken a day off. 'He told me to just pop in whenever I could and he would see me.'

'What's your name?'

'Bella Roussel.'

'I don't have any record of that name here.'

Bella swallowed down the tears that were threatening to come. She was so tired, her knee was still bleeding and all she wanted was to see Isaac and feel his arms around her.

'As I said, it was a casual arrangement.'

'Well he's in a meeting at the moment so—'

'Bella?'

She whirled round at the sound of Claudia's voice but she didn't seem as happy to see her as the last time she had turned up outside Isaac's office with Rocket. Clearly Claudia knew that she and Isaac had broken up.

'What are you doing here?'

'I really need to see Isaac.'

Claudia stared at her for a moment or two then gestured for her to follow her.

'Let me see if I can get him out of this meeting for a few minutes,' Claudia said.

Bella didn't argue, even though she was sure Isaac wouldn't appreciate being interrupted in the middle of a meeting.

She followed Claudia down a corridor and then she opened a door and walked in. Bella held back when she could see that it was a meeting room and Isaac was sitting with his back to the door listening to someone talk. Her heart soared. Finally, almost twenty-four hours after leaving Hope Island, she had found him.

Claudia bent to whisper in his ear and immediately he turned in his chair and his eyes found hers. He was on his feet a second later and in two big strides he was out of the meeting room, closing the door behind him.

It was just the two of them in the corridor now and he seemed frozen to the spot, not moving towards her, not saying anything either.

She didn't know what to say but her body took care of that when she suddenly and inexplicably burst into tears.

CHAPTER 25

Isaac took her by the arm and guided her into the room next door, a little canteen with soft chairs and tea and coffee making facilities. He encouraged her to sit down then he grabbed some kitchen towel from the roll, wet it and knelt down to dab at her cut while she sobbed so hard she could barely breathe.

'What happened Bella; are you hurt?'

'I needed to see you and I took the ferry to St Mary's yesterday and I'd missed the last flight out and had to take the boat to the mainland and the sea was really rough and then I had to take the sleeper train to London and I ended up sharing a cabin with some lady called Brenda who glared at me the whole time and I was too scared to fall asleep. I got into London at five and I sat in a café where no one spoke to me and then I tried to find your office and I got lost and then ended up at the wrong office and then came here and got mowed down by some idiot with a giant suitcase and landed in a puddle. Then the lady at reception wouldn't let me up here to see you and I had to lie and say I was Graham Miller's assistant and I never lie and I called you several times and you never answered and…' she trailed off, knowing she sounded like a blubbering idiot. Isaac was staring at her in shock but he still hadn't done or said anything that gave her any hope and the big romantic reunion Bella had had in her mind had clearly fallen by the wayside.

Isaac grabbed the small first aid kit off the wall and pulled out a plaster which he placed with great care over the cut on her knee. 'I think my phone is still at your house, it must have fallen out when I was there.' He looked up at her. 'What are you doing here, Bella?'

Just then Claudia walked into the room. 'Sorry to interrupt but they need you back in the meeting, Isaac.'

Isaac stood up and pushed his hand through his hair, clearly torn. Was this it? She'd had her one minute of time with him and instead of grabbing him and telling him she loved him she had spent the time crying and blathering on about her ridiculous journey. Clearly the tiredness was getting the better of her.

'Claudia, can you ask Marcus to take Bella back to my hotel.' He fished his wallet out of his pocket and handed Bella a black key card. 'I'm in the Lunar Suite. Order room service, have a shower, I'll be back as soon as I can.'

Bella nodded numbly and Isaac moved to walk out the room.

'Wait.' She quickly stood up, grabbed a fistful of his shirt and kissed him. He didn't kiss her back and tears welled up in her eyes again. She pulled back slightly. 'I love you; I came to tell you that I love you.'

He nodded. 'I'll see you soon; we can talk about it then.'

With that he walked out of the room and Claudia went with him.

This wasn't what was supposed to happen at all.

A few minutes later Claudia reappeared. 'I've just called Marcus, Isaac's driver. He's waiting for you outside. I'll escort you down.'

She numbly followed Claudia back to the lifts and Claudia walked in with her. They were alone so as soon as the doors closed, Bella turned to her.

'Did Isaac tell you what happened?'

Claudia nodded. 'He was heartbroken. I told you before that he has problems with trust. He trusted you with his heart and I don't know if there's any way back from this.'

Bella had no words. Had she really ruined everything between them?

The lift doors pinged open and Claudia escorted her out. She walked up to a large black car that was waiting outside and a man got out and opened the back door.

'Good luck, Bella,' Claudia said, softly.

Bella nodded her thanks, feeling empty inside. She climbed in and the man shut the door. She saw him talking to Claudia for a moment before Claudia walked away and Marcus climbed into the driver's seat.

He didn't say a word as he drove through the busy city streets to a tall building next to the Thames. Once at the hotel, he opened the door for her and escorted her inside. One of the porters came rushing over and Marcus spoke to him.

'This is Bella Roussel, a good friend of Mr Scott's. Can you escort her up to the Lunar Suite? She already has a key.'

'Of course, Miss, if you'd like to come this way,' the porter said.

Bella turned to Marcus. 'Thank you.'

He nodded and flashed her a brief smile before walking away.

The porter escorted her into a lift and up to the top floor where there were only four doors. He directed her to the one in the corner clearly labelled the Lunar Suite and then left her alone.

She used the key and let herself in and immediately Rocket came tearing across the room to greet her, leaping up and barking excitedly. At least someone was pleased to see her. The room had a large seating area and even a large kitchen off to one side. There was a bedroom leading off the lounge and a wonderful view of the Thames and the city beyond which dominated the room. She scooped Rocket up in her arms and sank down onto the sofa, staring out on the view. Claudia's words echoed in her head. *I don't know if there's any way back from this.*

She hugged Rocket to her chest and closed her eyes. What was she going to do now?

꧁❦꧂

Isaac pressed the button on the lift to take him up to his suite and as the doors closed he leaned back against the wall and sighed.

Bella was here.

There was a huge part of him that wanted to cheer and shout with joy that she had come back to him when all hope seemed lost, but the cautious part of him that was protective over his heart was saying he shouldn't just welcome her back with open arms. It was that cautious part that had him frozen to the ground when she turned up in his office; that had him standing in shock when she kissed him when all he'd really wanted to do was grab her, pin her to the wall and kiss her back.

He needed some answers from her and most of all he needed some reassurance that this wouldn't happen again. It was OK if she got upset about her parents, it was OK if her worry of rejection caused her to get scared, but it was not OK if that fear meant she would finish with him every few weeks. If this was to work she needed to trust him and he knew he needed to trust her too. He had been through hell in the last forty-eight hours and he couldn't take her back only for it to happen all over again in a few weeks' time.

The doors pinged open and he took a deep breath and walked out. He opened the door to his suite and Rocket came tearing across the room to greet him. He scooped up the dog and looked around for Bella and his heart dropped when there was no sign of her anywhere. Had she left? Had his lack of reaction at the office caused her to run away again? He had rejected her, which was what she feared the most.

He moved quickly into the bedroom and stopped when he saw her lying on his bed, fast asleep. She was dressed in his t-shirt and, judging by the amount of leg that was peeping out from under the covers, not a lot else. Her hair was slightly damp, splayed out in gorgeous glossy red curls across the pillow.

Every bone in his body was screaming at him to climb into bed with her and just forget about everything. But he couldn't.

He threw his jacket over the chair, loosened his tie and sat down, unable to take his eyes off her. She didn't stir and he didn't know whether to wake her or not, because he still had no idea what to say to her.

For want of something to do, he clicked open his briefcase and pulled out a new blurb they were working on for the Umbrella Foundation. It needed a lot of work but he wanted to get the basic message right before he passed it on to a professional team.

He read it through but his eyes caught on one paragraph in particular.

We know it was scary for you to come to us, your fear of people judging you was a big one to overcome. But we don't care about the mistakes you've made in the past. We care about the person you are now. You've come to us because you want a second chance and we want to help you take it.

He read it again and then looked over at Bella. His heart filled with love for her. She had travelled all this way into London, which he knew she hated, to tell him she loved him. She must have been scared of him rejecting her and she came anyway. She wanted a second chance with him and he knew he had to give it to her. He loved her and she loved him, it really was as simple as that. All the rest they could figure out later but as long as they were together that was all that mattered.

He noticed her breathing was getting heavy and accelerated as if she was running and in her dreams she frantically called out his name.

He moved quickly to the bed, kneeling beside her and stroking her arm. 'Bella, I'm here.'

She gave a little sob, obviously she was still dreaming. And he knew he had to show her that real love meant not running away when things got tough. He had to show her that one silly row was not going to break them. Love meant sticking by her always. Rocket had taken a long time to trust him and he'd never given up on her; he wasn't about to give up on Bella either. And while he knew he still needed to talk to her to get some reassurance that this wouldn't happen again, he knew her travelling across the country to a place she hated and was scared of just to fight for him told him more than words ever could. She wanted forever with him too.

He rolled her onto her back and stroked her hair, trying to stir her from her dreams. 'Bella, I'm here, I'm not going anywhere.'

Bella blinked a few times and realised she was in Isaac's hotel room and he was kneeling next to her on the bed. Outside the sun was just setting, casting a scarlet blanket across the clouds and painting the room with a rosy glow.

When Isaac saw she was awake he lay down next to her. While her mind cleared itself of sleep, the nightmares drifting away, he gathered her to him, pulling her onto his chest.

He was here. And he was holding her as if everything was OK between them. Her heart soared with complete joy.

Maybe they would be OK after all.

'I need to talk to you. I need to explain,' Bella said.

'The fact that you're here says everything I need to know.'

'I love you, you need to know that.'

'I love you too. There will be bad times and you will get scared but we will get through it because we love each other.'

Her heart roared in her chest. He didn't hate her. She hadn't pushed him away. Regardless of all her craziness and insecurities he still loved her.

She leaned up to kiss him and when he didn't hesitate to kiss her back this time she nearly cried with relief. They really were going to be OK.

'I'm not scared any more. I was scared that I wasn't enough for you—'

'You are always enough. Don't ever doubt that.'

She ran her hand through his stubble and, safe in his arms, she explained everything about her childhood, her aunt and uncle trying to adopt her when she was only three and the fact that the man she thought was her dad actually wasn't related to her at all and hated her because of it.

Isaac didn't speak for the longest time, obviously trying to take it all in but eventually he spoke.

'How do you feel finding out that your dad wasn't actually your dad? That must have been such a shock.'

'It was but to be honest it was such a relief. I understand now why he hated me so much. It wasn't anything to do with me at all; it was all down to the very messed-up relationship my parents had and the fact that I wasn't his. I never grew up with him around anyway so it's not like I've suddenly lost this great father of the year. Finn was my dad in every way that mattered. But all this time I lived with this fear that I was unlovable, that there was something wrong with me. I was scared of love, of falling in love and being rejected all over again. I built these walls around me and you came along and knocked them all down. I fell so hard and so fast for you and it terrified me. I kept thinking if I denied that I was in love, then I'd be safe, I could protect my heart, but denying it didn't mean that I didn't feel for you what I have never felt for anyone before.'

She held him tighter. 'I was so stupid pushing you away so I wouldn't get hurt in the future because watching you walk out the door was more painful than I could possibly imagine. And the worst thing was knowing how much I had hurt you too. I saw how heartbroken you were when I was pushing you away and that tore me up inside. But I couldn't stop it. I was losing the only man I've ever loved and I was so paralysed by fear that I couldn't do anything to stop it. I'm so sorry. When I came here, I didn't know if you'd forgive me but I still needed to tell you that I loved you – even if it all ended between us, you deserved to know what this was for me. It was never just a bit of fun.'

Isaac nodded. 'I knew that – despite your denials I could see that it meant as much to you as it did for me. I knew I was in love with you the first time we made love, although if I'm honest I think those feelings were there even before that. I strongly suspected you felt the same. I was prepared to wait until you realised it too.'

'You've been so endlessly patient with me. Why do you put up with me?'

He grinned, kissing her forehead. 'Because I love you and I'm not going to walk away from you just because you have a few insecurity issues. We all have baggage.'

She looked up at him. 'What's yours?'

'I never trust anyone. I've been burned a few times by so-called friends trying to get close to me only to find out that it was because of money or wanting a job. I can count on one hand the people I truly trust: Dougie, Claudia, there's not many others I could name. I keep people at arm's length; it's really hard to spot if people genuinely want to get to know me because of me or because of how much money I have.'

'But you trusted me straight away.'

'I did. I guess it was the circumstances under which we met. You kissed me when you thought I had nothing. I was homeless and you didn't care. I never had any doubts about your intentions. You gave me this feeling of being home which I haven't had since I left Hope Island all those years ago.'

'I feel the same too. I'm not running away any more. This is where I belong.'

He kissed her sweetly.

'This is forever for me, Bella.'

Tears filled her eyes. 'Me too. I promise, no more rows.'

'Don't make promises you can't keep. We will fight and argue and then we will have amazing make-up sex,' Isaac said, rolling on top of her.

She giggled. 'I love the idea of make-up sex.'

'Me too.'

She stared up into his eyes filled with absolute love and knew, even though she was miles from Hope Island, right here in his arms, she had found home.

EPILOGUE

Bella looked at her watch again, Isaac definitely said to meet him by the fountain in the park at seven that night. They were supposed to be going somewhere to celebrate their six-month anniversary but he was already fifteen minutes late.

She tightened her scarf around her. They were experiencing a pretty mild October but once the sun went down it got quite chilly in the evenings.

Her phone buzzed in her pocket and she quickly retrieved it, wondering if it was Isaac telling her he was late.

To her surprise it was the Easter egg hunt app, updated with a new egg. Bella frowned in confusion. *The Great British Egg Chase* had launched to massive success, with children and families all over the country enjoying searching for virtual eggs hidden in the real world. It had raised over twenty thousand pounds for the Umbrella Foundation and they were going to launch another one in the lead-up to Christmas, searching for Santa and his many elves and reindeer. Although the egg hunt game was still live, the interest had dropped off significantly once the Easter holidays were out the way and the prizes of real chocolate had come to an end. Though many people had still been playing it for a few months after Easter, the fad had faded and the last time the app had been downloaded had been two or three months before. Why then had a new egg been added?

She looked around for Isaac and then, seeing that she was still alone, she walked a little way towards the new egg. The phone turned to the augmented-reality screen as she approached and she could see the egg sitting on a park bench.

This egg was made from autumn leaves so Bella selected the rake from the tool box and raked the leaves apart. Out popped a scroll which unravelled and she read the message.

Eggciting new eggs have been added. Find the next egg, follow the trail. Isaac x

She smiled. This was just for her. What was he up to?

She checked the big map and saw there was another egg at the stile which marked the start of the footpath over the hills.

She hurried ahead and waited for the augmented reality to kick in so she could see the egg. An egg appeared on the screen, sitting next to the stile. The egg was wrapped in a holey blanket with a woolly hat on, much as Isaac had been dressed the first time she had met him. She laughed but she wasn't sure how to break open an egg that was wrapped in a blanket.

She scanned through the tools and found a new one that had been added that merely said 'kindness'.

She selected the tool and then clicked on the egg. The blanket and hat disappeared and the egg was left with only a towel around its lower half. Isaac had given the top half washboard abs.

Bella laughed loudly.

The egg popped open and another scroll appeared.

It has been an eggceptional six months.

Bella giggled at another bad egg pun.

She looked back at the map and saw there was another one halfway along the path up over the hills. She wouldn't ordinarily walk over the hills in the dark, mostly because she wouldn't be able to see where she was going and would most likely fall down a rabbit hole, but the path was lit up with lanterns guiding the way with little pools of gold. Isaac had put a lot of thought into this.

She walked up and over the hills, following the lanterns, and she realised that the egg was sitting under the tree where they had shared that incredible kiss in the rain. The egg was made from fire and she quickly selected water from the tool box and poured water over the egg, dousing the flames. She swallowed as she realised these eggs were representative of their relationship and this was to represent the fire where Isaac had lost his home, but also the night they had made love for the first time.

Inside was another scroll.

You make me so eggceedingly happy.

She smiled again. When she clicked on the map she saw the next egg was in Blueberry Bay. Lanterns lit the way as she followed the path down the hill towards the sea.

She walked past the area where Isaac's old house had been. The insurance company had finally paid out but Isaac had decided that he didn't want his house rebuilt on the same land as his old house, saying it felt tainted somehow, so he'd sold the land and bought a lovely big house overlooking Blueberry Bay. Surprisingly, after three months she had moved in with him. More surprisingly was that it didn't feel quick or scary. It felt right and as she was spending practically every night at his house anyway it made sense.

She walked through the trees and on to the beach in Blueberry Bay and smiled at the moon glinting over the sea. It was so beautiful here that she barely noticed when the app shifted into the augmented-reality screen. She tore her eyes from the view to look at the egg. It glowed silvery white like the moon and great arcs of silver were coming from it. Just like the moonbow they had seen that night. It reflected onto the water, creating a perfect circle which looked like a pearl ring.

How could she crack open an egg that was made from the moon?

'You won't be able to open that egg,' Isaac said from behind her. She whirled round to look at him as he emerged from the shadows, dressed in jeans, a long charcoal woollen coat and the beanie hat he had been wearing the first night they'd met. 'Why don't you open this one instead?' He handed her a silvery egg that was hinged in the middle.

Bella laughed. 'You said no presents, that we were just going to go out somewhere for a meal.'

'I lied.'

'Some things never change.'

Isaac laughed. 'Just open it.'

Bella giggled and then cracked open the silvery egg. Nestled against the black velvet inside was a platinum pearl ring, the pearl held in place by tiny diamond leaves that curled around it. Her heart stopped beating and then started pounding furiously when Isaac sank to one knee in front of her.

He took her hand. 'Bella, my life changed six months ago when I camped outside your house. I never thought I could trust anyone enough to let them in, but you have turned my world upside down in the best possible way. I love you so much, more than I ever imagined possible, and you would make me the happiest man alive if you would marry me and be my wife.'

Bella had no words at all. Tears filled her eyes.

Isaac's hand tightened around hers, clearly scared she was going to run away.

'I know this seems fast but I know what is in my heart. I know this wonderful thing between us is forever. We don't even have to get married straight away, we can wait as long as you want, but just say yes and I will spend the rest of my life trying to make you as completely and utterly happy as you make me.'

Bella sank to her knees in front of him and reached up and kissed him. He wrapped his coat around her and pulled her tight against him. The thought of forever with this man was not scary in the slightest. She pulled back to look at him.

'How about we get married at Christmas?'

He broke into a big smile. 'Is that a yes?'

Bella laughed and took the beautiful ring out of the box. Isaac took it from her and slid it onto her finger. Excitement bubbled through her. 'I love you, Isaac Scott. You broke down my walls and you showed me what love really is. I have never felt so safe, so adored as I am when I'm with you. So yes, I will marry you and as soon as possible. I cannot wait to start my life as your wife.'

Isaac kissed her again and she had never felt so complete before. She pulled back, running her hands behind his neck.

'I might have a present for you too,' Bella said.

'You do?'

'Why don't we skip dinner, go home and I'll let you unwrap it.'

He grinned. 'That sounds like a perfect plan.'

A LETTER FROM HOLLY

Thank you so much for reading *Spring at Blueberry Bay*, I had so much fun creating this story and I hope you enjoyed reading it as much as I enjoyed writing it.

One of the best parts of writing comes from seeing the reaction from readers. Did it make you smile or laugh; did it make you cry, hopefully happy tears? Did you fall in love with Bella and Isaac? Did you like the beautiful Hope Island? If you enjoyed the story, I would absolutely love it if you could leave a short review. Getting feedback from readers is amazing and it also helps to persuade other readers to pick up one of my books for the first time.

To keep up to date with the latest news on my new releases, just click on the link below to sign up for a newsletter. I promise to only contact you when I have a new book out and I'll never share your email with anyone else.

The second book in the Hope Island series will be out this summer, so keep your eyes peeled as more information will be revealed soon.

Thank you for reading.

Love
Holly x

www.bookouture.com/holly-martin

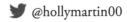 HollyMartinAuthor

🐦 @hollymartin00

hollymartinwriter.wordpress.com/

ACKNOWLEDGMENTS

To my family, my mom, my biggest fan, who reads every word I have written a hundred times over and loves it every single time, my dad, my brother Lee and my sister-in-law Julie, for your support, love, encouragement and endless excitement for my stories.

For my twinnie, the gorgeous Aven Ellis for just being my wonderful friend, for your endless support, for cheering me on, for reading my stories and telling me what works and what doesn't and for keeping me entertained with wonderful stories and pictures of hot men. I love you dearly.

To my friends Gareth, Mandie, Angie, Jac, Verity and Jodie who listen to me talk about my books endlessly and get excited about them every single time.

For Sharon Sant for just being there always and your wonderful friendship.

To my wonderful agent Madeleine Milburn and her assistant Hayley Steed for just being amazing and fighting my corner and for your unending patience with my constant questions.

To my wonderful editor Claire, for putting up with all my crazy throughout the whole process, for replying to every single email and for listening to me freak out with complete and utter patience. My editor Celine Kelly for helping to make this book so much better, my copy editor Rhian for doing such a good job at spotting any issues or typos. Thank you to Kim Nash for the tireless promoting, tweeting and general cheerleading. Thank you to all the other wonderful people at Bookouture; Oliver Rhodes, the editing team and the wonderful designers who created this absolutely gorgeous cover.

To the CASG, the best writing group in the world, you wonderful talented supportive bunch of authors, I feel very blessed to know you all, you guys are the very best.

To the wonderful Bookouture authors for all your encouragement and support.

To Tracey Gatland who patiently answered all my questions about life in the Scilly Isles and helped me round a problem in my story that wouldn't quite work in the Scilly Isles but we found a way.

To anyone who has read my book and taken the time to tell me you've enjoyed it or wrote a review, thank you so much.

Thank you, I love you all.

Lightning Source UK Ltd.
Milton Keynes UK
UKHW02f0000231217
314874UK00010B/309/P